HOT PURSUIT:
UNDERCOVER
DETAIL

HOT PURSUIT: UNDERCOVER DETAIL © 2024 by Harlequin Books S.A.

The publisher acknowledges the copyright holders of the individual works as follows:
CRIMINAL ALLIANCE
© 2020 by Angela Platt
Philippine Copyright 2020
Australian Copyright 2020
New Zealand Copyright 2020

First Published 2020
Second Australian Paperback Edition 2024
ISBN 978 1 038 90125 5

SECRET AGENT SURRENDER
© 2017 by Elizabeth Heiter
Philippine Copyright 2017
Australian Copyright 2017
New Zealand Copyright 2017

First Published 2017
Second Australian Paperback Edition 2024
ISBN 978 1 038 90125 5

ALPHA ONE
© 2013 by Cynthia Roussos
Philippine Copyright 2013
Australian Copyright 2013
New Zealand Copyright 2013

First Published 2013
Third Australian Paperback Edition 2024
ISBN 978 1 038 90125 5

MIX
Paper | Supporting
responsible forestry
FSC® C001695

Published by
Harlequin Mills & Boon
An imprint of Harlequin Enterprises (Australia) Pty Limited
(ABN 47 001 180 918), a subsidiary of HarperCollins
Publishers Australia Pty Limited
(ABN 36 009 913 517)
Level 19, 201 Elizabeth Street
SYDNEY NSW 2000 AUSTRALIA

Printed and bound in Australia by McPherson's Printing Group

HOT PURSUIT:
UNDERCOVER
DETAIL

ANGI
MORGAN

ELIZABETH
HEITER

CYNTHIA
EDEN

MILLS & BOON

CONTENTS

CRIMINAL ALLIANCE   7
Angi Morgan

SECRET AGENT SURRENDER   257
Elizabeth Heiter

ALPHA ONE   507
Cynthia Eden

Criminal Alliance
Angi Morgan

MILLS & BOON

Angi Morgan writes about Texans in Texas. A *USA TODAY* and *Publishers Weekly* bestselling author, her books have been finalists for several awards, including the Booksellers' Best Award, *RT Book Reviews* Best Intrigue Series and the Daphne du Maurier Award. Angi and her husband live in North Texas. They foster Labradors and love to travel, snap pics and fix up their house. Hang out with her on Facebook at Angi Morgan Books. She loves to hear from fans at angimorganauthor.com.

Books by Angi Morgan

Harlequin Intrigue

Texas Brothers of Company B

Ranger Protector
Ranger Defender
Ranger Guardian
Criminal Alliance

Texas Rangers: Elite Troop

Bulletproof Badge
Shotgun Justice
Gunslinger
Hard Core Law

West Texas Watchmen

The Sheriff
The Cattleman
The Ranger

Texas Family Reckoning

Navy SEAL Surrender
The Renegade Rancher

Hill Country Holdup
.38 Caliber Cover-Up
Dangerous Memories
Protecting Their Child
The Marine's Last Defense

Visit the Author Profile page
at millsandboon.com.au.

DEDICATION

Thanks for the years of encouraging words and support, Therese!
You deserve a great, capable heroine named after you.
Lori, Amanda and Robin…couldn't have done it without you.

CAST OF CHARACTERS

Wade Hamilton—Lieutenant in the Texas Rangers, Company B. He trusts his gut and has a habit of acting before he thinks things through.

Therese Ortis—An undercover FBI agent working hand in hand with Homeland Security. Wade owes her a favor after saving his life, and it's time to collect.

Company B—Jack McKinnon, Heath Murray and Slate Thompson. Wade helped with their love lives; now they intend to return the favor.

Rushdan Rival—A billionaire who tried to kill Wade. He has a finger in almost every illegal pie in Dallas.

Public Exposure—A group actively promoting to use less social media. Are they real or a cover for a domestic terrorist group?

Prologue

"Dammit, Hamilton. It doesn't matter if you were right. You broke every rule we have. If it were up to me, I'd kick you to the curb like you deserve." Major Clements slapped his hand against his thigh as he paced in front of the door.

Wade Hamilton stood at attention, something he'd rarely done since becoming a Texas Ranger. Eyes straight ahead, he couldn't see his commander walking behind him. But hey, even if he stood directly in front, Wade couldn't focus on the major's expressions. His left eye was still swollen from the beating he'd taken a week ago and everything was blurry. He couldn't judge if this was the end…or just a very long reprimand.

Wade could feel Major Clements just over his right shoulder. Out of his peripheral vision, he saw the major's hand clenched in a fist, the knuckles white from the tight grip. His supervisor had been angry before.

Yeah, several times before.

But hopefully, he could remember that Wade had saved lives. Didn't that count for something? His partner had reminded him often enough that Wade trusted his gut too much. But this time Jack was grateful for it.

"It seems that I don't have a final say," the major continued. "Seems that someone at headquarters put in a good word. Who knows, maybe the woman you helped save talked with someone. Or maybe the top brass doesn't want to have to explain why a Texas Ranger from Company B was fired after saving someone from the state fire marshal's office. Hell, I have no idea."

Major Clements's boots struck the floor, paused and pivoted again.

It wasn't the first time the major had given him a lecture. It *was* the first time he hadn't been looking at Wade when he delivered it. No matter the words about how lucky he was and unknown friends at headquarters, Wade still wasn't too sure about job security.

"I drew the line at the suggestion you be given a commendation. Rule breakers should not be rewarded. The example you've set is not a good one. I'm very disappointed in you, Lieutenant." The major's voice was tempered with sadness instead of anger.

"I understand, sir."

"Good." He walked back to his desk, putting both fists knuckle down on the polished wood and leaning toward Wade. "And yet, I don't hear an apology or simple words like *it won't happen again*."

"That goes without saying, sir."

"Do you really believe that, Wade? I hope you'll at least try not to play the hero. You barely survived this time. But since I can't fire you, in order to rein you in a bit…" He sat. A good sign that Wade hadn't lost his job. "You're benched."

"Excuse me, sir?" Wade's eyes moved to make contact with the major. One stern look was enough to have him back at attention. "I'm not sure I understand."

"Desk duty, Lieutenant. You'll report here every day. And every day there will be files for you to work on. You are not to leave this office from the hours of nine to five. I don't want to hear about you even going for lunch. You got me?"

"Loud and clear, sir."

"Dismissed."

"But what about the case, sir?" Wade looked just above the major's head, concentrating on keeping his eyes from pleading with the man in charge of his fate. "We only touched the surface of what crimes Rushdan Reval is behind. This is our way into that scumbag's organization."

"We've been ordered to stand down, Lieutenant. I said dismissed."

Wade left the office barely able to swallow, feeling grateful that he had a job, wondering how he'd survive sifting through files—especially paperwork that wasn't even his—and disappointed in himself that he'd been close to accessing Reval's group and had messed up...bad.

His partner, Jack MacKinnon, gave him a "what's up" look from across the room. Slate Thompson and Heath Murray, along with the other Company B Rangers, gave him a wide berth and no eye contact. They all probably thought he was heading to his desk to clean it out. No one really expected him to keep his job, his rank or his anything.

He made it to his desk, still using the crutch the hospital had forced on him. Honestly, he could barely see his chair since his left eye was killing him. It was the roll-y thing behind the big block of wood. Yeah, he could joke but not laugh—the cracked ribs were too painful.

The doctors had been straight about the headaches that wouldn't go away for a while. Even straighter about the possibility his sight might not ever be 100 percent again. Rest—sitting-down-and-not-moving kind of rest, to be more specific—was what they demanded.

They hadn't cleared him for anything. But after two days of sitting inside his house, he'd finagled his recovering body behind the wheel of his truck and driven the fifteen minutes to headquarters. It had been more painful sliding out and hitting the ground with both feet.

He sat, putting the crutch on the floor next to the wall his desk was pushed against. He heard himself suck air through his teeth as he rolled into place.

"You okay?" Jack patted him lightly on the back. "Looks like you're still employed."

Dammit, he hadn't seen Jack come up behind him. He jumped, then hissed again in pain.

"For the moment. And only at this wonderful desk." He petted it like a dog.

"Always the cutup. How long?" his partner asked before sitting on the corner of his desk.

"You got me." It hurt too much to shrug. And it hurt too much to focus across the aisle. Everything really was mostly a blur.

"Man, I'm not sure how long it'll take for him to trust you again." Jack rubbed his chin, then the back of his neck—or at least that was what it looked like through the fog. "I'm sort of surprised I'm not stuck here, too. On second thought, it was entirely your fault I was involved in the first place."

"Don't go there, man. Not only did you get to make a serious arrest because I asked for a favor, but you also got a girlfriend out of it. Who I should probably thank for saving my job with a word from her state-level boss. You can say that I'm responsible for setting you two lovebirds up."

"You could say that." Jack stood, removing his gun from his desk drawer and placing it in its holster. "But if you do, I might just have to kick your butt." He laughed. "Your desk duty explains why I'm on loan to Dallas PD for a while."

"They're still shorthanded after the loss of their officers. You'd think the major would want me out there with you."

His partner raised his eyebrows almost into his hairline. "Get real. You know I trust you with my life. But man, you got to learn to play the game. Rangers have a specific duty and—"

"And are restricted to following the law. Yeah, I know. I heard that lecture for the past hour while standing at attention. I thought the major would go harder on me if I reminded him I'm having problems standing."

Jack clapped him on the shoulder. Wade tried not to wince. He was determined to force his body to at least stay upright.

"I was going to say," Jack continued, "that we have a proud tradition. Our motto might be 'One Riot, One Ranger,' but that doesn't mean it has to be us doing things alone. I'm here for you. Always will be. No matter what."

"Thanks, Jack. It's appreciated."

"Keep your head down and fly under the radar. Don't go looking for trouble."

"I never look, man. It just always seems to find me. Watch your back since I won't be there to protect you."

"Like you did by getting beat up so bad you can't stand?"

"Three cracked ribs isn't too bad." He squinted through his good eye. "Besides, they took me by surprise."

"Right."

Wade watched his partner leave the office without

him, passing one of the clerks on his way. A clerk with a box, heading straight toward his desk.

"Major Clements said you should go through these, Wade." She dropped the box on the floor next to his chair. "You need to verify that all the appropriate reports are in order and scanned or the data inputted. Basically, that everything's ready for trial or to turn over to headquarters. When you're done, I have the rest of the alphabet waiting." She turned to leave but pivoted back to his desk. "Remember that these files need to be locked up each night."

Wade lifted the lid and pulled the folder at the end… Carla Byrnhearst. "That's just great." One box got him through two letters. He shoved the file back inside and pulled the Ader file from the other end.

Keep his head down.

Do the time at his desk.

Accept the punishment.

Keep his job.

He could do this. He'd wanted to be a Texas Ranger for too long. One man had put everything on the line to keep him from a life of crime. After that, all his focus had been toward obtaining that goal. College, Texas DPS, the highway patrol, three long years near the border and finally an opening and assignment to Company B.

These men were his brothers now. His desk phone rang and he answered.

"Hey, sexy. Just checking up on you."

Therese. Trouble did have a habit of finding him. God, just the woman's voice sent electricity shooting through his veins. Where had she been? Where was she now? Last week in the hospital, he'd forced another ranger to run Therese Ortis's name. She should have been awaiting trial for her involvement with Rushdan Reval, the Dallas crime syndicate leader who had just tried to kill him. But there had been nothing.

"I guess I owe you something—at least dinner— for saving my life." His mind was already following the steps to have the call traced.

He'd seen her once. Spoken to her fewer than half a dozen times. And he was caught, dangling at the end of her string. In fact, he'd swallowed her enticing voice and innuendos hook, line and sinker.

"Even though I'd enjoy that very much, I don't think it would help you get off desk duty," she purred.

"You're the one who kept me my job?"

"Ladies never kiss and tell, Wade." She paused long enough to let the words have their desired effect. "Gotta run, Ranger Big Man. Till next time."

"Wait…"

Too late. The line disconnected. He didn't have to inquire about the number—he knew it would be a dead end. Just like each time before. His mystery woman had a habit of swooping in for the save and disappearing until she needed him again.

He opened the file and started. With any luck, he could get through a letter each day. Twenty-six days stuck in a chair. Behind a desk. Watching his fellow rangers do the heavy lifting.

No playing hero.

Most investigating happened from a chair any-way. Sitting here would give him plenty of time to discover just what the mystery surrounding his lady was all about. Yeah, he could do this. Especially now that he was properly motivated.

And man oh man…he was definitely motivated to find Therese Ortis.

Chapter One

Present day

Just another two-for-one longneck Friday special. Wade sat on the same barstool he'd ended his nights on and had claimed for years. This particular stool was the last one next to the wall, located where no one could catch him by surprise. Only his right side was open to patrons. Better for his vision, especially now that it got fuzzy from time to time.

He should be somewhere else.

Maybe somewhere more respectable for a Texas Ranger. That wasn't here. Someplace he could share that he was a ranger. Or maybe be with his friends. But they all had girlfriends. Heath was back home with his wife. Slate might as well be married. And Jack—his so-called partner—was engaged.

He should find some other friends. Maybe some who liked to…to what? Watch a game? Play trivia over some chicken wings? It didn't matter where he went or what barstool he ended up on. He'd still be looking at every dark-haired woman who walked in the door to see if it was her.

Dammit. He couldn't keep this up. Six weeks was long enough visiting bars on lower Greenville Avenue. His search for Agent Therese Ortis needed to end.

Soon. No. Tonight. He'd shown his face once too often in other dives. Earlier the barkeeps had waved him past their place, in a hurry to get the discouraged ranger on his way. His badge was far from good for their business.

So here he sat. His go-to joint that knew him from way back. The one place where they gave him a pass for having a badge.

Twisting the rest of his lime slice into his Mexican beer, he studied the peel—more interested in the citrus than in anyone around him. He needed to take Jack's advice. If Therese wanted to get in touch… Well, she knew how. She'd done it before to save Megan and a second time to save his hide before Rushdan Reval blew him up inside a building.

Across the room, the door banged open. Heads—including his—turned toward the noise.

What the hell?

"Wade!" The woman who had haunted his dreams crossed the sixty feet, dodging drunks and other happy-hour patrons who had quickly returned to their conversations.

"You have got…" she began, too loudly, before nervously looking around and landing next to him at the bar. "You've got to stop your…your inquiries. Are you listening to me? I'm furious."

No, he hadn't been listening. Dressed in the smallest bright yellow dress—more like a piece of a dress that could still be respectful—he barely noticed anything else. The color set off her dark brown hair.

The bling around her neck drew his eyes straight to the diving-low plunge between her breasts. How the hell was she walking in those heels?

Shoot. How did the dress stay in place?

The woman who'd actually 100 percent saved his life licked her lips and drew a deep breath. Trying to ignore her, he looked down at the bar, stabbing the three lime slices with a plastic sword.

"Hey, Wade, hon?" Her erotic voice whispered close to his ear while her feathery touch on his hand shot all sorts of feelings through him.

Six weeks without a word.

And she was mad. *At him?*

Even though she'd been caught working with crooks last year, he'd never believed she was on the wrong side of the law. Something in their sparse conversations had forbidden him from thinking badly of her. Then six weeks ago he'd found out—like a kick to the head—she was working with the FBI or something. Nobody talked. Lots of secrets. Had he forgiven her for taking away a major case?

Probably not.

There was no mistake who she spoke to. She'd stopped so close her breath of air brushed his bare neck, encouraging him to act. But he wouldn't. He didn't have the right. Even if she had called him *hon*.

"I like you in a T-shirt. It shows off these strong arms. But this button-up looks great on you, too. It brings out the steel blue in your eyes."

He could tell her he liked her dress. Or not.

Yeah, she squeezed his biceps. Yeah, she puckered her lips together like she waited for a kiss.

"No."

"Are you sure?" She eased onto the stool next to him, her long legs reaching sideways under his. Damn, that yellow silky thing climbed up to her hip. "I haven't even asked anything."

Wait. Were they talking about a kiss or the favor he thought she was about to ask? He should consider himself lucky that the stools weren't close enough for him to pull her onto his lap to find out. *Lucky?*

Therese twisted away from him to face the opening door and back again with a blank look. A big fella walked inside, propping the door open with his foot and calling to a buddy on the sidewalk. They both entered, finally shutting the door to keep the cooler air in and the blistering summer heat outside.

Everything about her demeanor changed. Where she'd been full of anger she was now soft. She closed her eyes, drawing a deep breath through her nose and making her breasts swell in the tight dress. Then she wet her lip gloss with the tip of her tongue. To stop his drool, he tipped the beer to his mouth, drinking her in with his eyes.

The fresh burst of lime made him lick his lips, or

was he mirroring the seductress beside him? Then her dark red lips parted ever so slowly. Slower than necessary and very practiced. Hell, he could give in right then, doing whatever she asked, having no idea what it might be.

Instead he broke off his stare and looked around the intimate, off-the-beaten-path bar. Mostly regulars with the exception of the last two men. Every corner was shadowed and filled with secrets, but he didn't butt his nose in. He knew the ins and outs. Knew what to expect. He'd been coming here since college and it didn't hurt that no one broadcast that he was a Texas Ranger. He'd never had a need to show his badge. Not here.

"I know it's been a while since I've called. Please don't be annoyed with me." She swiveled on the stool, reaching for his limes, daring him not to look down the low-cut dress she flashed under his chin.

"I'd have to care to be angry. Or annoyed," he lied. He didn't know the reason for her personality switch, but he'd play along.

"There's just been a lot going on, hon—" She pouted.

Pouted? Therese Ortis didn't seem the pouting kind.

What the hell was going on? She knew he'd been looking for her and seemed pretty doggone upset about it less than five minutes ago.

"So you aren't angry, annoyed or even a little hurt, baby?" she smiled with a knowing smile, circling a deep red nail around the back of his hand.

Hon? Baby? What was she trying to pull? She reached out, taking his extra lime and swiping her tongue across it. She knew exactly how to make *him* nervous. But she was the one shaking like a leaf in a windstorm—the only thing that kept him from showing her just how angry he wasn't.

Yeah, he was succumbing to the seductress line. What man wouldn't? But it was the trembling that got him.

Her eyes darted in every direction, checking for trouble. The bartender walked to the other end of the room and she leaned in close.

"I need a big favor. I can explain everything if you give me a chance."

Even though the intensity changed from flirtatious to urgent, he still answered, "I'm all out."

Explain? Nice fantasy. Therese never explained. He poured more than a sip of beer down his throat. He tipped the bottle toward her, politely asking if she wanted something. She shook her head while he caught the bartender's eye and ordered two more.

"I promise not to land you on desk duty again. What do you say?" she asked in a low, sensual voice he had fallen prey to a few times already.

Wade had wanted to connect with her for over a year. Why the hesitation? *Desk duty. Uncertainty. Tired of being used. Downright irritation at being ignored.*

"I say—" he grinned way too big "—that you haven't mentioned anything I haven't heard before."

"I'm sure that can't be true," she still whispered.

"Considering I can recall all seven conversations we've ever had… Yeah, I'm pretty sure I can clearly remember every word that you've said." *And exactly what you haven't.*

"I really, really think you're going to be interested in my favor, hon."

"Nope." He kept his voice low, matching hers.

He was done. Had nothing left. Finished. Kaput. Refused to get involved. *Remember?* And yet, completely curious.

"Is there anything I could do or say to change your mind?" She drew circles on his shoulder, dragging her long fingernail down his arm until she got to his hand.

She looked innocent. If he knew her better he might think she seemed desperate. But he didn't know her better. She came to him when she needed something. Case or no case, he didn't like being used.

And he hated giving in to her, to anybody.

Therese's eyes darted to the mirror.

The two large men moved away from the opposite end of the bar and Therese stiffened. Obvious to him since she held his hand. Probably not obvious to the men who had eyes for no one else in the room. They looked like typical guys, with the exception of the bulges under their jackets. Jackets worn for the simple reason of hiding the weapons.

They were there for her—obviously.

"Wade," she said way too loudly. "I'm so hungry."

"What?"

She dropped a finger across his lips to stop his

next question. Her eyes moved to the mirror. His hand gently tugged hers from his face back to the bar and slid a longneck bottle into it.

"I guess I need to hear about that favor after all." He squeezed a lime slice and pushed it through the neck of the sweating bottle.

Chapter Two

Normally, Therese wouldn't have paid any attention to someone as good-looking as Texas Ranger Wade Hamilton. He was almost too good-looking.

Dark brown hair swooped back off his forehead. Dark blue eyes framed by masculine-shaped brows. And a sprinkle of chest hair. Just visible tonight with the open collar in his Texas-blue dress shirt. She'd seen the outline of that chest in a T-shirt a couple of times, too. Just like she'd admitted a few minutes ago.

Oh, yeah, she'd kept up with him. Back when she was in control. Right up to coming face-to-face with him at a crime scene six weeks ago.

She should have gone to him covertly and explained what she was doing. Wade would have left things alone then. When she'd told her handler her plan, he'd laughed and ordered her to stay clear of the ranger. Everyone had seen what they called "smoldering looks" from Wade. And they'd made it known they'd seen right through her attempt to act immune.

So she'd avoided the tall, handsome ranger and paid off the bars where he kept asking after her. But the damage was done. Wade had shown his badge one too many times. Rushdan was convinced she'd sold him out to the cops.

Of course she had. But he'd had no clue before Wade Hamilton kept asking everywhere for her.

The moment she'd seen Wade sitting on that very barstool last year she'd lost her breath. When he hadn't recognized her cowering in the corner, she'd just watched. She hadn't stopped thinking about him since that Friday night.

The very first time they'd met, he'd literally swept her off her feet while rescuing her teenage version. When he hadn't recognized her as an adult, it had stung a little, but it was totally understandable. A lot had gone down that night. And wouldn't you know it, now he was the only man she could trust to keep her alive.

Being alone would get her killed. Period.

If only she could wait or fill him in on why she needed him. Crossing her fingers that he'd be sitting on his barstool, she'd come here looking for him. Unlike how she'd avoided it every Friday night since she'd returned to Dallas. She'd been ordered not to speak to him or meet him under any circumstances.

Her last conversation with Rushdan had left her uncomfortable. He did the hinting thing, talking around her to only the men, asking why a certain Texas Ranger was asking all over Dallas for her.

When she'd left the offices, the two thugs behind her had followed.

Okay, she felt desperate and her brain began to panic a little. Pretty sure those men had been sent to take her out. Three years of undercover work shot because she'd been ordered not to talk to the man beside her. Yeah, panic closed in, making the bar feel even smaller.

With one eye on the bar mirror, she watched Rushdan's men loitering just inside the bar's door. She pushed her nerves aside and daringly placed her palm on Wade's thick-muscled thigh. He actually jumped a little. How sweet.

"This seat taken?" Rushdan's head hit man knew it wasn't. He knew she'd come in alone. And knew she didn't carry a weapon. Or at least thought he knew.

Leaning away from Wade, she tried to give the man following her a brilliant, reassuring smile. "We're on a date, sugar. Please don't try to pick me up."

Please go with it, Wade. Don't yell at me for acting like we're lovers. It is all your fault.

"As a matter of fact…we were about to leave." Wade tipped the remains of his beer between perfectly handsome lips. "We're meeting friends for dinner."

"Then you're not drinking that longneck?" Rushdan's guy slanted his body, blocking her view of the entrance. He moved so close to her as he reached for the beer she hadn't touched that she was afraid she'd slide off the stool trying to avoid him. Wade's legs connected with her body, effectively catching her. Too bad there wasn't more time to flirt. As nervous as he seemed, she could have had some fun.

"Go for it. The little lady's afraid she'll spoil her appetite." Wade stood, dropping money on the bar before sliding his hands back onto her shoulders, his body next to her back, steadying her. "You can have our stools just as soon as we go."

His gentle twang could melt her heart under different circumstances.

"We'll never make our reservation, hon. Not if you do anything…to slow us down." She licked her lips and knew they appeared sexy. She had much too much practice at flirting and yet it still made her uncomfortable.

Give her a 9mm and a target at fifty yards and she'd be completely at ease. She mentally demanded her nerves to settle. Otherwise she'd need a bucket to catch the sweat from her palms.

The dumb blonde routine—even if she was a brunette—had never been her dream assignment for undercover work. But she was stuck with it. Her carefully constructed identity called on her to be soft, vulnerable and not too smart. At least Rushdan Reval considered her soft.

Leaving the stool, she deliberately fell into the side of Reval's man, letting her hands play across his flabby chest and lifting his weapon from his holster.

Rushdan's second goon took a quick step toward them. She backed up quickly, passing the gun to Wade, who aimed straight at their assailants. The bartender jerked to a halt along with the rest of those in the bar.

"Uh-uh-uh." She waved a finger at Rushdan's hired help. "What will your friends say if they knew you lost your weapon? I won't tell if you don't."

Wade jerked her back to his side.

Damn, he's a rock. She dropped the thoughts about Wade's body and planned their walk past Rushdan's men. Wade acted like she'd been his for a decade—not two minutes. Maybe he was used to women throwing themselves at his feet, but she wasn't used to being held.

She might play the part of easy…but she hadn't had a real relationship since college. Undercover work had major pitfalls.

Her stomach did a double backflip when Wade's hands darted a little lower on her waist than she'd intended. She didn't change their direction. She needed to leave this bar and take him with her. How else could she explain her presence on lower Greenville and try to salvage three years of undercover work?

Lying to Rushdan about why Wade had been looking for her bought her time this afternoon. Time to find him. Granted, it had been spur of the moment and she'd been unable to contact her team for backup. But something—or someone—had made

Rushdan suspicious. When the crime boss sent these guys to follow her, it was for one reason…elimination.

She began the longest walk of her career. Wade's long fingers slid over her hip and back up around her waist, distracting her with their heat. Her hands flew to fan her face—half acting and half needing to cool her hot cheeks.

Wade pulled the door open, waiting for her to go through. She wanted one last look at the men chasing her and turned. The movement brought them closer, making her aware of Wade's body, the complete maleness of him.

A sparkle in his eye caught her attention. *The jerk. He's laughing at me.* Maybe she'd been flirting a little too much and couldn't stop herself. It was as if the sensual woman in her—although scarcely unleashed—chose that very moment to take control.

She turned completely into Wade and the slinky thing the salesgirl called a dress rose higher along her thigh. His fingertips brushed the bare skin just below the hem. She froze.

Something happened.

The look in his eyes turned volcanic.

Somewhere in the back of her mind she was aware they stood just inside the doorway of a semi-crowded bar. Somewhere in her nonfunctioning gray matter she knew she'd only spoken a handful of sentences to this man. But somewhere in a part of her soul that had never been touched, a magnet flipped on and pulled her to this unselfish ranger.

When their lips connected, she forgot everything. She forgot the reason she was on lower Greenville. The reason she needed to leave. The reason she shouldn't be standing there kissing her escape plan.

Soft, firm lips grabbed hers, gently sucking and pulling. She parted her own. What should have been a strange invasion felt…perfect. His wonderfully strong arms reached around her body, pulling her into his hard angles. This wasn't kissing. It was more than fabulous. A simple lip-lock shouldn't make her weak in the knees.

"Get a room," someone in the bar shouted, followed by erupting laughter.

Wade's dark blue eyes watched her face as he pulled slightly away, his breathing just as rapid as hers. "Yours or mine?" he whispered, but the entire room listened.

Then she remembered the necessity to leave. Could the kiss have convinced Rushdan's men she'd really met her lover? Would sticking with him for a while save her life?

"Yours. Mine's too far," she heard herself say.

He didn't let her pull away. He kept her safely tucked into his side as they let the door close and headed toward a parking lot. That in itself was unusual… She wasn't used to someone else keeping *her* safe.

It had been a long time since she'd been nervous. What if they jumped them? Her Beretta was hidden in her car. The car several miles away. And now she'd involved an innocent man who had no idea what he'd just agreed to.

A slight laugh escaped. *Innocent?* The hunger in his eyes made her doubt her strong hero had ever been innocent.

Either way, she shouldn't involve him. It was against orders. She'd get to his truck and find another way out of this mess. But as they got outside, she looked up just as he glanced down. If she'd wanted to be heroic, she'd made a fatal mistake.

It happened again.

Raw energy pulled her to his mouth for a second time. He plunged between her lips, molded his hands to her butt and brought her into his instant hardness.

Someone cleared their throat. The sound jerked Wade away from her mouth, but not from her body. He kept her close, whispering what he wanted...what they'd eventually do. Small tremors shook from her into him. He skimmed her ear with his teeth.

There wasn't any doubt what would ultimately happen.

What they both needed.

Wade dug in his front pocket and shoved bills into the parking lot attendant's extended hand. Keeping his arm around her waist, he brought them both at a fast walk to his truck, forcing her to stay in step with him. Then he opened the driver's door and lifted her inside. She began slipping across the front seat, but spying Rushdan's men rounding the corner stopped her.

Before Wade could get the key in the ignition, she

pulled his face to hers, kissing him again but keeping her eyes on the men. Just like him.

Her rescuer pulled away, leaving both of them breathing hard. "I swear…if you keep kissing me like that, it won't matter what kind of favor you need me to do. We really will be heading straight for my place."

Chapter Three

Hell's bells, what was all that about? Wade couldn't wait for answers. The men following Therese were outside. Probably the reason Therese had kissed him again. And again.

She began to slide to the passenger side, but he stopped her, tugging her back to his hip. "Nope. You're staying right here. You aren't going anywhere without me. No disappearing acts."

"I was only getting a seat belt. We can't afford to be stopped by the police."

He reached to the far side of her, remembering the silky feel of her thigh. He took pleasure in skimming her hip while he dug between the seats for the middle belt, then fastened it, pulling it tight across her lap.

He put the truck in gear and pulled past the men she obviously knew. "So what's the problem? Or should I refer to it as a favor?"

"Oh, I think you noticed." She waved to the men. "I hate it when they think I need protection."

"Hold on a minute," he interrupted while pulling from the parking lot. "You might as well come clean,

Therese. You chose to bring me into this. Now give it to me straight. No sidestepping the truth. Those guys were not a protection detail."

"I understood when you indicated that you didn't want to get involved. You can't have it both ways. I respect that. If you drop me at a corner, I'll call a rideshare to get back to my apartment." She tried to put space between them. It didn't work.

"You aren't going anywhere. And I *am* involved. They just took pictures of me and my truck." He pointed to the last man to head to their vehicle. "It won't be long before they know who I am, where I live and what I do."

"Oh, God. I forgot you'd be in your truck instead of a government vehicle. I can fix this before anything happens. I promise."

"No fixes. I need the truth for once, without any stalls." They were still near the bar as he watched the men get into a car double-parked on the street.

They crept along at a snail's pace. If you were driving to a bar on Greenville, you couldn't get upset about not getting anywhere fast. It was just part of coming to this part of town on a Friday night. Everyone expected to be stuck and frustrated in happy-hour traffic. But it guaranteed that the two cars would be sticking close to his tail. Something he didn't mind for the moment.

Not if it finally got him information about Therese.

"Turn on a side street, speed up and lose them," she said, stretching a little closer so she could see out of the rearview mirror.

But he'd made up his mind. He deserved answers. He made a couple of turns and headed into downtown.

"Where are you going? Wade? Are you... Are you trying to keep them in sight?"

"I thought you said you were hungry." It was a stall, pure and simple. Not fooling her a lick, judging by the roll of her eyes.

"Right. So now you're interested?"

He couldn't see her face. She sat next to him, one arm around her waist and leaning into the other—fingers against her forehead. He had no gauge—no history—to know if she was serious or not.

"About what? Being hungry? I happen to eat regularly."

She turned to look behind her. "They're not even bothering to hide that they're following." She tugged her cell phone from a small pocket he hadn't noticed before.

Feeling like a kid on his first real date, he dropped his arm around Therese's shoulders at the next stoplight. He looked back and counted how many cars behind him the two threats were.

"Where did you want to go?"

"A fancy hotel?" She rubbed his knee, causing his mind to detour.

He kept driving. Proud that he didn't run off the road with all the distracting images he had running though his head. A protection detail or hit men? Could he keep her safe if they went to a... He swallowed hard and replayed her words.

Dammit—too much sarcasm.

"Okay. Enough games and put away that phone." He pulled through the light, slowing enough to make certain he was still followed until he had answers. "Maybe you should just tell me what's going on? And I mean everything, Therese. Don't leave out anything. You should consider me part of whatever operation you're running."

"I can tell you part of the story." She turned slightly, scraping her fingernails across his after-hours scruff.

"First." He squeezed her shoulder, tugging her slightly back to him. "You should probably know that if you invite me to a hotel again, I'm heading straight there. And don't plan on me sleeping any-where except next to you."

She smiled. It might have even been genuine in-stead of completely calculated to capture his atten-tion.

"And second?" she asked, outlining his ear with the tip of her finger.

He pulled to a stop at a red light. Her *friends* had moved closer—as in the car was now beside the truck. She looked at him and he prepared. The sul-try lips were in front of his face, and her lips con-nected to his in slow motion. She kissed him deeply, deliberately and for longer than it took the light to turn green.

Horns honked. Both cars blocked a full one-way downtown street in Friday night traffic. Horns honked more. It registered in his mind, but he didn't want to let her go.

She slipped from his arms with a very satisfied grin. "They blinked."

"What?" He pulled forward on autopilot after the cars behind him veered around his truck.

"Drive slow and they'll have to pull through the next light. Then we're in the clear."

Oh, yeah, the men following her—them. Dammit, he'd completely lost focus. He couldn't blame anything except holding her—the only woman he'd thought about more than twice since meeting her.

"I think all the kissing fooled them," she said. "Oh great. They're pulling over to wait on us."

"We should use their following to our advantage," he threw out. How? He wasn't sure.

"What do you mean?"

"Tell me what's going on, beginning with the thugs behind us." He kept heading west on Commerce, past downtown, past the county jail. They stayed close on his tail, not trying to hide. "Are you in danger?"

"Short version?"

"We'll start with a simple yes or no."

"How about an *I think so*?"

"You've got to be kidding me. I need some answers, Therese. Or I'm making a U-turn back to County and a hundred police officers. You can try explaining to one of them. What will your friends do then?"

"No. Good grief, you don't have any right to make demands." She unfastened her seat belt, turned and brought a bare leg up next to his, dropping a hand in her lap and using the other to twirl her hair. "You know this is all your fault."

"My fault?" He couldn't let all that bare skin get under his. But it was definitely getting harder to concentrate. He should make her turn back around and refasten the belt.

"Asking around town for me actually got these guys all in my face. I wasn't prepared with answers and had to come up with some type of excuse."

"What the hell are you sidestepping, Therese?" Maybe his words could have been a little less confrontational, a little less loud. *Not really.* "Dammit, I need some answers."

"The truth is I've been on this case for over three years."

Case? Three years on a *case*? "I knew it." He slowed to a stop, wanting to caress all that silkiness. "You're undercover FBI. That's why you were with Steve Woods that day."

Her hands waved him to silence even as her lips puckered sexily again. "Shh. Don't say it aloud even if we're alone. When you started asking around town for me, I shrugged it off. But then you kept asking and it's made my 'boss'—" she shrugged, using air quotes to stress the word "—a little angsty."

"Angsty enough to send your um…protection detail?" Hit men, more like it. God, he wanted to pull her to him and kiss her. He shook it off. Men. Guns. Undercover. Favor. Focus.

"Last chance, Therese. Who is your boss?"

"What I'm working on isn't important."

"It is to me. I can keep my mouth shut. Secrets are easy."

"You can't mess this up, Wade. It took me over a year to work my way into Rushdan Reval's confidence. I just need you to stop asking—"

"You're working with Reval's group? So that's what you were doing when we arrested him last year? Have you been in Dallas this whole time without contacting me?"

"No…not…really." She stared him down like he was insane if he thought she'd hide from him.

"Don't try that look on me again, Therese. You have a successful disappearing act."

"I wanted to reach out, but I was given a direct order to avoid contact. It might have ruined my cover. After he was arrested, Rushdan pushed me off on one of his side gigs in San Antonio. I've been waiting for him to clear the charges you brought before I could continue here." She waved him forward with a finger. "You should probably keep driving even if we don't know where."

He'd sat through the light twice. Reval's men were hanging farther back, and as he moved forward through the yellow glow, they raced to catch him but got stuck instead.

"I know where I'm going. We need backup."

"No. Believe me. If they were going to attack, they would have by now," she said, looking back over his hand, still around her shoulder.

He retrieved his phone from his back pocket, reluctantly losing contact with Therese. "I need to take care of some cover issues before we go forward." He dialed Company B headquarters.

"Wade, seriously. I've been at this a long time. You've helped enough. I can't put you in danger again. Reval's going to recognize you as the Texas Ranger from last year." She sat straight on the seat, scooting toward the passenger door.

No!

"Dammit, Therese, there's no reason for you to jump out in the middle of nowhere. I can hide us for a few days until we sort out what to do."

He reached out to grab her arm and missed before she opened the door. Therese could probably jump—he'd slowed for a curve—but he slammed on the brakes so she wouldn't have to.

"Just keep driving, Wade. They won't bother you if I'm not here."

Out in a flash, she passed the truck and ran for a path between the trees. He couldn't follow her before he parked. And as soon as he did, they'd know they were out of the truck. Speeding up, he was far enough ahead of the men following that he could whip into a warehouse lot and cut his engine before he was seen.

"Dammit. Razor wire." He couldn't go over and had to go out through the same gate he'd come in. They'd probably see him if he did. *You are not disappearing on me again, Therese Ortis.* "Not this time."

He couldn't make his customized truck disappear or blend in with the others taking up the spaces. The built-in compartments made it impossible to mistake. And Therese was right, several of Reval's men would recognize it as belonging to the ranger they'd captured last year after he'd taken out one of their men.

There was an upside to him being in his truck—the built-in gun safe holding his weapon. But if he pursued Therese on foot without notifying headquarters... If things went haywire... If he messed up an FBI undercover operation...

No more being a Texas Ranger. He was done.

Was she worth it? He didn't need a thoughtful reflection. There wasn't a choice. He needed her safe.

"If I didn't owe her my life, I could drive away and do nothing." He eased from the truck. "Hell."

The longer he took to make a decision, the farther Therese got ahead of him.

So be it. There were a lot of *ifs* in his life. *If* he hadn't made a couple of scenes looking for her during the past six weeks...she would have blown him off forever. And *if* Therese hadn't come to his rescue by contacting Jack last year... Well, he wouldn't be here now, needing to make a decision.

Keeping his head down, he retrieved his weapon. He couldn't go over the eight-foot fence, or around it. Not with the thug car just outside the gate—not without the thugs seeing and following. Okay. Then he'd just have to go through the building and find a rear exit. He could make it to the open loading dock door.

That was all. Cross an open parking lot directly in front of the two cars and jump onto the four-foot loading dock without being seen. He didn't trust Therese's opinion about being safe. He couldn't get

caught. Once these yahoos realized who he was…
he'd be dead. Therese, too. When they caught her.

One step at a time. A honk from a big rig made
the car that had followed them pull to the side of the
road closest to the lot.

But the eighteen-wheeler pulled inside the gate,
effectively allowing him to cross the lot without the
thugs seeing him. He kept running until he passed
two building doors. The third had the street view
blocked by a box truck. Once he made it there, it was
easy to enter the loading bay. He casually walked
through the manufacturing company's warehouse.
Few people were around as he made his way to the
west side of the building, which backed up to the
railroad.

He needed wire cutters or something to get
through the fence. Nothing. Noticing a man taking
his cigarettes from his pocket and heading to an outside door, Wade followed and took a look.

There was a gate. So instead of sulking around
kicking himself, he made his job work for him. He
headed straight to the office.

"Man, am I glad you're open twenty-four hours,"
he entered. "Texas Rangers, ma'am." He flipped open
his creds. "Would you happen to have a key to your
back gate?"

Chapter Four

The evening hour had made it easy for Therese to hide. Unfortunately, it made it terribly difficult to move through the brush. The heels didn't help, either. She pulled them off, looping a finger in each strap to carry them. They were too expensive to leave behind and a pair of her favorites. Slowly picking her way from one oak to the next, she carefully walked through the dirt and debris, hoping for a path.

Far from a Dallas city park, the two ruts were about the same distance apart as a four-wheeler. Nothing was around. Even the ambient light from the city was getting scarce. As scarce as her dress that snagged on every tree she passed.

Another rip and she groaned. "Shoot. What a night to wear the sexiest thing I own."

"It is really sexy."

Her heart leaped into her throat. She totally understood what that meant now as her pulse beat at an insane pace. "Oh my God, Wade. You scared me. What are you doing here?"

"Right. I scared you." Wade grabbed her hand.

"What the hell, Therese? You jumped out of my truck."

"If you get involved with this—"

"I already am."

"I admit that it was stupid to march into that bar and ask you for anything. Whatever you're thinking, you don't owe me. You have no obligation. Nothing. Do you hear me?"

"Everybody will hear you if you don't keep your voice down. Your friends found my truck and caught on that we're out here in the trees."

"And if you'd kept driving like I meant for you to…they would have followed you until it was too late to realize I was no longer there."

"Pardon me, but you didn't ask me to keep driving. What you did was apologize."

"I don't apologize."

"Well, you did to me." His voice was louder.

"Shh." She couldn't kiss him into silence this time.

It didn't matter. He took her hand, leading her away from the sounds of men tromping through the brush somewhere behind her. They ran and the sounds of the men searching for them grew fainter, but Wade kept pushing forward.

"How did you find me?" she whispered. "Ow. Hey, slow down."

"What's wrong?"

She pushed her high heels into his chest. He pushed them right back, then bent in half. Oh, Lord. He stifled her gasp when his hands touched her backside as he lifted her, with the pressure of his shoulder cutting off a lot of her air.

Hearing above the truck traffic on the nearby road grew more difficult, but voices seemed to carry. She had an unusual view behind them to see if they were being followed. No one seemed to be around.

"Um… Wade, honey?" she chastised as his fingers slid under her dress to stabilize her on his shoulder.

"Oh, pardon me." He laughed.

The thong only covered so much. Embarrassingly, he'd found a whole lot of nothing. He continued to carry her toward the open railroad tracks. No cover put them at a greater risk.

She tapped on his back. "Come on, put me down. No one's following."

"Are you sure you can walk?"

He did a deep knee bend, pulling her dress down, then smoothing it over both hips as her feet hit the ground. After all the kisses she'd laid on him, she deserved whatever teasing he dished out. The playfulness between them had been there since the very first phone call.

This was all her fault. She couldn't stop encouraging him. She slipped her shoes back on her feet, admitting two things. No matter how expensive the shoes were, they could never be worn in public again. And she didn't want to stop whatever attraction she had for this man.

"I really shouldn't have involved you in this."

"Better than paperwork." He shrugged. "No need

to beat a dead horse, Therese. I'm here. I'm involved. Let's deal with it and get out of here."

They'd both been talking in a loud whisper, but noises from the trees had them shutting their mouths and running—even in heels along the train tracks. Hitting the old wood slats was much faster than trudging through the washed-out gravel, and they could avoid the risk of stepping in a hole and turning an ankle.

"We're almost at Westmoreland Road," she told him over her shoulder.

"Your friends are catching up. Will they shoot?" Wade's question was answered with a couple of rounds from a handgun.

"Head for the far trees," Wade yelled.

To hell with the shoes. She kicked them off, leaving them as they ran full out for the trees to their right. She couldn't be bothered with how much the gravel hurt her feet. If she stopped, Rushdan's men would capture her. She might survive to be taken back to the slimy pig, but Wade probably wouldn't. He'd die before he let those men take her.

That was the kind of guy he was. Honorable. Trustworthy.

"Stop whatever you're thinking and head down the tracks. We'll never make those trees," he said. "I've got this."

"How?"

"I came prepared. Just run to the right once you hit the street." He pulled his phone from his back pocket.

More shots.

The industrial area allowed them only one direction left to run. They were boxed in by the grove of trees behind and on either side businesses with eight-foot fences and razor wire on top.

Rushdan's men were too close behind them. The only direction left was the open area along the railroad tracks until they crossed Westmoreland Street. Then where?

She hit the sidewalk and turned right as Wade instructed. He stopped at the fence pole—as if that would stop a bullet—and fiddled with his phone.

"Keep moving to the intersection!" he told her.

The men following shot again. "Come on." She tugged on his elbow.

"Get going. I'm right behind you." He waved his hand holding the cell and leaned around the poll.

She was out of breath and her feet were hurting enough to make her scream, but she ran the long block to the intersection. Still half a block behind her, Wade waved her forward.

"Go on! Cross!"

The light was in her favor, so she ran…again. And kept running to the brick wall of the small convenience store. Wade received honks from the cars he darted in front of. Rushdan's men didn't follow him.

"Where to now?" She gulped air into her lungs. "Were you calling for backup or 911? Do you think anyone else did?"

"Our ride's here." He waved his phone at a sedan pulling into a parking space.

"This is a bad idea. We can't involve a ride-for-hire driver."

"It's only a short distance. Or would you rather run? Your *friends* are probably getting into their cars now."

"This is really dangerous."

He blocked her from view and tilted her face to look at him. "Do we blow your cover?" he asked in a whisper.

"Over three years of undercover work…" She hesitated.

"I don't think anyone has seen us, but we've got to go. Now." He drew her to him and gave her lips a quick kiss as if they'd known each other for years.

"Take the car and get as far away from me as possible. Leave town. Go on vacation. Let me talk my way out of this with Rushdan."

"Isn't he the one who sent these guys to take you out? You gotta let me help with this, Therese." He laced his fingers through hers and opened the car door, helping her inside.

"Evenin'," the driver said. "You going to the Westin at the Galleria mall?"

"That's right," Wade answered.

"Wait a minute. Isn't that a hotel?" She remembered his promise. And by the twinkle in his eye, so did he.

"Funny you should mention that." Wade winked.

"They're going to find out where we've gone," she told him.

"I'm counting on it. But to give us a little time…"

He tapped the front seat to get the driver's attention, then showed him his credentials. "This is going to sound weird. I need you to take the long way through downtown."

"Whatever you want, but it'll cost more."

"If someone asks where you dropped us, just tell them. There's no reason to be a hero. Okay?"

"You got it. But how long of a ride are you talking?"

Wade tugged her securely into his arms and tilted her lips to his. "As long as it takes."

"Sure, man. Anything for law enforcement."

"This is insane," she whispered against his lips. "Are you seriously going to neck with me in the back seat of a rideshare car while Rushdan's men try to find us?"

"As soon as I use the credit card in my wallet, they'll know where we are. Besides…when's the last time you had some fun in the back seat?" He pulled her onto his lap and devoured her mouth until she gently pushed against his chest.

"You know we'll most likely be dead tomorrow. Since this is the last bit of pleasure either of us will ever enjoy…I'm in."

Chapter Five

"This won't work," Jack MacKinnon yelled through the phone.

"Sure it will. You're mainly angry because you'll have to work all night to make it happen. Give me some bad debt, add a couple of reprimands to my file— Okay, a couple more reprimands. It'll give me a reason to need money. I've got the setup from last year when that stuff with Megan went down."

"I think they hit you one too many times on your head. That *stuff* is when they tried to kill you. Remember how these same people were going to drop a building on top of you as your tomb?"

He rubbed his ribs. "It's hard to forget."

"This is a bad idea."

"I keep telling him that," Therese said from beside him.

"You're on speaker. She insisted on listening in," he told his partner. "I've got a hunch that you're giving in, Jack. You know it's a good idea. It's logical and if you get the finances falsified, Rushdan Reval will be completely suckered in."

"Your hunches have been close to getting us both killed, pal."

"You'll do it?"

"You two can't be serious. You're both crazy." Therese walked away from the phone, throwing up her hands and heading to the bath. "You *are* crazy, Wade. Major Clements will never go for this," Jack said.

"He will if you plead the case. What can I do? She's the woman who saved your girlfriend and me. Remember? Don't you think you owe her?"

A long, indecisive sigh from his partner filled the dead air. "You know that favor you owe me, Wade?"

"What favor?" Yeah, he knew full well what Jack meant.

"Remember when you asked me to pick a woman up from the airport. No big deal, you said. Keep her out of trouble, you said. Out of sight until I hear from you again. No big deal."

Wade took him off speaker. He knew exactly what Jack was recounting. Therese did, too, since she was the person who'd asked him to protect her friend.

Out of the blue, Therese had asked for a strange favor. After all was said and done, the Company B Rangers had discovered that Megan Harper's life had been in danger. Jack had saved her. Sure that Therese had been in trouble, Wade had searched for her, gotten caught and been beaten within an inch of his life.

"Look how good that turned out for you, Jack. You met your future wife."

Wade's occasional banter and favors for Therese

had become an obsession to find her. But she'd really disappeared.

"Ha. I think it's time for me to redeem a favor from you."

"Yeah, I remember owing you a favor. But I thought you'd ask me to pay for the limo at your wedding or something." He had to dig deep in order to convince Jack to help. Time to make the big man feel indebted. "Okay, I sort of promised I'd never mention this again. But Therese is the one who saved you from MS-13 when your dad blew your cover."

"How? I thought you said... Dammit, Wade. You never mentioned where that helicopter came from. Therese was the one who arranged it?"

"I didn't ask who it belonged to. She didn't say. I just found out she has access to privileged information. That's when I knew. Now you do, too."

"She saved my hide and then Megan's." Jack sighed again. "And yours."

Wade looked around at the closed bathroom door. "She won't admit it, but I think she's in trouble. Big trouble. She's afraid to go to the FBI or any other backup she has."

"Is she afraid of a breach?"

"Jack, why else would she have come to me?"

"Right. She trusts you. I get it. I'll get Heath onto your finances. He's going to love working all night. What kind of problem do you want? Gambling would be the easiest."

Gambling. It hit a nerve he'd kept buried for a decade. He didn't want to slip back into the familiar world. But he could to save their lives.

On their way to the hotel they'd shared a lot of kisses and a few whispers of how to convince Reval not to kill them. It was up to him—and a fake financial background—to prove he was dirty. A dirty Texas Ranger who needed quick cash and was willing to do anything for anybody. Including the man who'd ordered his death last year.

It turned his stomach, but it would work.

"Sure. Just as long as Heath can—and will—make it all go away. I'm going silent. I'm locking my stuff in the safe. Send someone to pick it up."

"Watch your back."

Wade turned his phone off. It was the best he could do.

"About that explanation…" He poked his head between the bathroom door and the frame.

Therese was under the streaming water, naked like she should be for a shower, her long hair flowing down her back. Her arms were raised to her face just enough for him to see the curve of her breast and lots of smooth skin.

"Sorry." He averted his eyes to the bottom of the towel hanging on the wall rack. "I heard the water running and expected the shower curtain. Not clear doors."

"No need to be embarrassed. I think our relationship is far beyond professional. Don't you?" She turned the interesting parts of her body toward the back wall.

He could see the outline of her legs and her beautifully shaped derriere. Had he just thought all the interesting parts were facing the other way?

"You know that I didn't mean that stuff about the hotel. Right? I'm fine sleeping in the chair." He stepped backward to give her privacy and to stop acting like an ogling lecher.

"Maybe we should talk about this in a minute? You're letting in a cold draft." She laughed at him.

"Got it. I'll order us some food."

"Or you could join me," she teased.

Against every desire he had, he managed to close the door. The first time he made love to Therese, it wouldn't be while they waited on Reval's men to take them to the second-rate crime boss. He ordered two steaks and the works, hoping that the woman he'd been kissing for the past hour wasn't a vegetarian. He didn't know a thing about her.

"Oh, man, I feel better." She was wrapped in a towel, her wet hair slicked back, and her bare arms raised to pat the long strands dry with a second towel. "I am so starved. I had to skip lunch today."

She looked at the dress, now with several tears on the sides. The towel slipped. He lost his concentration as she caught it, tugging the end back into place.

"What food did you order?" she asked, laughing as she sat on the edge of the bed next to him.

He jumped up. "We should probably keep some distance between us." He pulled his dress shirt from his shoulders and handed it to her.

How did she stay cool about being naked under

that towel? A little towel that would drop from her body with a gentle tug.

"Such unusual modesty as he takes his shirt off. This coming from the guy who just necked with me for the half-hour drive." She bent her arm and hooked her long hair that was beginning to curl behind her ear.

Did she have curly hair?

"This is different," he finally got out.

"You could have fooled me. Our rideshare driver had a lot of fun watching."

God, he loved her laugh. She didn't do that enough. He turned his back, shutting his eyes tight while she put his shirt on.

"Maybe you should tell me about Reval and how he fits in with Public Exposure? Yeah, I connected those dots. Last time I saw you we just took down part of that domestic terrorism group. Is Reval working for them or vice versa?"

"You're right. We've had credible intel for quite a while—"

"The beginning, remember?" he interrupted. He wanted every piece of information she had. "Who's 'we'? And how long have you been under, working with that scumbag?"

"I'll save the real beginning for another time. Sharing this amount of the intel will probably get me fired."

"Hey, it won't matter if we're dead like you keep telling me." He wished room service would knock on the door. He wanted a beer in his hand.

"That's true. But since you've put yourself in the middle of everything, you probably should know what's going on." She covered her face with her hands, then crossed her fingers on both sides of her face with a very fake smile. "I sure hope you're a good liar, Wade Hamilton."

"I can fake it when necessary."

"Great. If you can't, we really don't stand a chance." She stood. "Turn around."

He obliged but saw an arm extend through a blue sleeve.

"All done." She wandered around the room examining fliers and hotel info, straightened the lamp and discovered robes in the closet. A robe she didn't put on until room service arrived.

When the robe was safely around her body, relief washed over him along with the smell of food. His stomach growled as he signed for the feast. They settled on either side of the bed with two trays set between them.

"Back to our story," he urged. "From the beginning."

"I was at the police academy in San Antonio. I guess I fit the profile of someone the FBI needed. Honestly, I don't know why they chose me over anyone else," Therese said between bites.

"Is that where you met Jack's girlfriend, Megan?"

"Yes. Everyone was told that I was forced to drop out after cheating or something. The Bureau used that when Rushdan—or anyone else—checked out my background."

He knew that partly from Megan, partly because it was so prominent in any report on her that he'd initiated. "So you went to work for the FBI?"

"They wanted to discover where Rushdan's money came from and who his contacts were."

"Let me guess, a little drug running, real estate fraud, night clubs, prostitution and money laundering."

"You did your homework." She clapped softly.

"I have a tendency to obsess over people who try to kill me." Was it too soon to say he'd actually been looking for her?

"Did your research mention that Rushdan Reval has been brokering illegal deals? I never discovered how he got into it. But last year, when his real estate fraud fell apart, he began contact with Public Exposure."

"That's how a low-level fraud group got into the domestic terrorism business?"

"When Megan and Jack stumbled on Rushdan's real estate fraud, it stalled my involvement. At least with his Dallas group. I mainly played go-between on the phone with several of his *business* representatives in San Antonio."

"That's stating it nicely."

"True." She stuffed a yeast roll in her mouth, swishing it down with a cola—not the beer.

"Let me guess… Enter FBI agent Kendall Barlow and her husband Texas Ranger Heath Murray, investigating claims about Public Exposure's fraud."

She pointed at him. "Yes! Bonus points for the

man without a shirt. They really are a good team. Almost too good, since they practically dismantled the Brantley Lourdes end of this thing."

"Brantley Lourdes. Isn't he the guy in charge of Public Exposure? And what do you mean *almost*? We retrieved the algorithm, obtained confessions and nothing happened after all the threats that Dallas citizens would die."

"That's the problem. Rushdan just brokered the deal for Public Exposure. He only had a copy. Someone else developed the algorithm. Sources have verified that he's improved it and bidding for the improved version has begun. We're no longer certain what the algorithm is capable of."

"Son of a biscuit eater!" He picked up his roll. "Lourdes wouldn't tell you who created it? I thought this case was wrapped up. I haven't seen any alerts from local, state or national authorities. Why are your bosses being so secretive?"

"Do you really not know after one of the FBI's Dallas agents was caught in the middle of this?"

"I get it. There might be another traitor around. But you trust me, right? I could have been helping discover who Reval plans to sell to."

"I've already explained why working with you wasn't possible. Besides that information isn't what we're after. We need to discover what it does now. In addition to capturing the geeks who designed an algorithm that can take down a city's electrical grid."

"Every city's worst nightmare."

"Country's worst nightmare. I've been attempting to get back in Rushdan's good graces. He's accused me of helping you escape, but he seems to overlook it."

"Why's that?"

"Maybe he's hoping I'll hang myself and he won't have to give the order to get rid of me. Like other people I won't name…" Therese reached over the tray and brushed crumbs from the corner of his mouth, seductively raising an eyebrow in his direction "…he's sort of sweet on me."

Man alive, he no longer wanted to talk about Rushdan Reval or the FBI or algorithms that could bring down cities or countries. At her touch, he just wanted to pull her to the bed and finish a different discussion.

"You know, it's not too late for you to go back to your regular duties as a Texas Ranger. I can clean this up."

"No. We talked about this." He stood, removing the remnants of dinner to the desk. "I'm going with you and we'll find the threat. I've spoken with Jack. I'll call back. Who should he speak with at the FBI to confirm my involvement?"

"Steve Woods. He's the only person I can trust there who knows about the threat. He's working with Homeland and only providing 'as needed' info to them."

"You don't trust very easily, do you?"

"No," she answered with a whisper. "Rushdan will have a hard time believing a big ol' Texas Ranger is willing to get his hands dirty. Why is that exactly?"

"Money. It's always about money."

"We'll have to convince him you need a lot… and fast."

"Right. Heath will be set before Reval looks into my background." He pushed down the old feelings from his youth. Fright had no place here. He needed confidence and arrogance. "Think I have time for a shower before our location is discovered?"

"Probably. I think I'll try to catch some sleep. After they get here, it might be rough." She draped the robe across the end of the bed, then pulled back the covers. "Thank you."

"For what?" he asked from the bathroom door.

The urge to bring her close was overwhelming. His knuckles turned white as he gripped the door trim and tried to keep himself there instead of at her side. She smiled—completely sexy in his blue shirt that looked better on her than him. That was all she did, but he understood.

He took a quick shower, thinking about the impossible situation the FBI and Homeland had placed on her shoulders. Therese needed help whether anyone admitted it or not.

Her eyes were closed when he locked his phone, gun and creds inside the safe. He called Jack from the hotel line—not only to check in, but to tell him the combination so he could send one of the guys to grab his things.

He scrambled back into his jeans since he knew that at some point a gun would be aimed and they'd be taken to Reval's headquarters. Therese shivered in her sleep. He smoothed the covers and she backed her body close to his. They lay in each other's arms, fitfully resting. He woke with every movement and could tell that she hadn't fallen into a deep sleep, either. He kept her close, whispering again what he would eventually do.

Around four in the morning, Reval's men arrived for the next phase of their undertaking. It was going to be a very long day.

Chapter Six

Rushdan's men used a key to enter the hotel room. Wade covered Therese with the robe as the door burst open, so he hadn't been taken by surprise.

He'd held on to her body until they were yanked apart and his hands tied behind his back, angled to grab her robe before she was shoved through the door.

Therese had never worked with a partner and oddly enjoyed the thought of her first being this tall Texas Ranger. She liked him. A lot.

All those sexy words he'd whispered in her ear as she'd tried to go to sleep still had her body burning. She hadn't dare tell him she wanted the same. She wouldn't have held back. If they survived, being with Wade would be a genuine pleasure.

But one that would wait.

It was infuriating not to be tied up like Wade, not to be considered a threat. But she'd worked hard over the last years not to reveal her strength or quickness to these men. She walked freely as they were taken down the service elevator and escorted into the back of an SUV.

Once they were at Rushdan's new office, one of his hired goons punched Wade hard enough to make him lose his breath. "That was for the six months I served in the county jail."

What had she done by involving Wade? How could she have let her judgment lapse so badly not once but several times? She'd completely lost her mind and would probably lose her job for disclosing everything about her undercover assignment.

But worse…if they beat Wade or tortured him? Would she be able to hold her tongue?

"Just take us to Rushdan," she instructed, stepping in front of Wade. "If you touch my boyfriend again, I guarantee you won't be around tomorrow to regret it."

Therese held her breath, preparing for the punch that never came—not to her and not a second one to Wade, either. Both of them knew the risks. Talking his way into the Reval organization was a long shot. They were both flanked by two men who yanked them through rooms and eventually stood them in front of Rushdan Reval.

"Therese, my darling. Come, let me see you. Untie our guest." Reval instructed his men. "Are you barbarians or something just as awful?"

The goons released her arms when she gave them a shrug. She approached Reval's desk wearing the robe over Wade's shirt, which covered her skimpy underwear.

"Come closer. You know what I want." The pig tugged at the belt at her waist, inching her closer to his chair. She could see his hope of anticipation that she'd let the robe fall open. She dug her fingers into the cotton sides, barely keeping it closed.

Somehow she managed to get into character, the part she played of a dingy woman who was slightly incompetent. The character that all these men thought so little about that they didn't bother to tie her hands.

Tonight was different. Wade watched, as well. His strength could be felt across the room. She saw the worry on the men's faces. Gritting her teeth, she forced herself to tolerate Rushdan as he unbuttoned the top two buttons of the dark blue dress shirt. He skimmed the back of his fingers against her cleavage to cop a filthy feel. She desperately wanted to slap his hands away from her, but she took it.

Just like always.

The men gripping Wade attempted to hold him, but he broke free. He yanked her back to his arms just before the robe fell open.

"So it's true. Our ranger friend has a thing for you. After all this time of you saying no to me, you said yes to someone who can put you behind bars? Do you think he really cares for you?"

"He got me out of jail last year."

"So you finally admit that you had someone with pull to help you. Why not just tell me the multiple times I've asked?"

"He said it was a secret, Rushy, baby. And you told me secrets were important," she sounded more like the confused ditz they were used to. "I told you I was meeting someone last night and you had me followed. I don't understand what I did wrong."

"They ran." The bigger-than-big man tsked at them.

"Only after they began shooting at us," Wade threw out.

"I didn't ask you, ranger boy." Rushdan dug his fingernail into his mouth, picking food from his teeth, then gestured as if shooing a fly. "Take him from my sight while I decide what to do with him. Did you think to bring their clothes?"

"Rushdan, baby." Therese turned and took steps back to her "boss," letting the robe fall open, and purposely tugging the shirt to where it left little to the pig's imagination. "I've been working on this guy for months. I thought you could use his help."

All the men in the room could barely raise their eyes. She had them mesmerized and hoping the shirt would fall completely open. Rushdan had the best seat.

The pig.

"I spent nearly six months in that filthy cell, wearing orange." He shuddered. "Why would you think you could bring your pet in here for me to adopt? I have no use for a Texas Ranger. He can't do anything for me. Even if I thought he really would." Rushdan tried for a whimsical, light voice, but it was countered by the evil in his eyes.

"You're right. I didn't believe Wade at first, either. Now I mainly want the money he owes me."

She leaned forward to whisper. Rushdan bent to look down her shirt. "He has a gambling problem, baby. You can use that against him," she suggested.

"Therese." Once again Wade tugged on her arm to pull her to his side. "I can speak for myself."

"Not if he won't listen, sugar."

"Aww, how sweet. The two lovebirds are fighting," Rushdan said.

"We aren't fighting." Wade buttoned the shirt to cover her cleavage. She spun around while he kept his hands on her shoulders.

"I do so enjoy your little shows, Therese. Too bad it seems your champion has ended this one." He nodded to his men. "I'm busy. Go put them somewhere until I'm not."

"But," she began again.

"By the way, I love the boots. Sal, remind me I need to get me some real Texas boots." He pointed at Wade's Western footwear.

"Yes, sir." Sal pushed at them with a gun.

Rushdan looked at the men in the room. "I said put them somewhere until I can think up an appropriate punishment."

Therese forced Wade to let go of her. "Really, Rushdan. I do a good job for you. Even while you were gone I ran the San Antonio clubs like you wanted. Wade is a fun time, but you know I'm loyal to you. I really thought we could use his connections to widen our prospects."

"Why would you think that?" Rushdan said,

smacking his lips after another bite of breakfast. "Or should I ask why you try to think at all?"

"I thought I could help."

"Therese, you are such a nice-looking broad. But why do you bother?" Rushdan backhanded her, sending her stumbling barefoot against Wade.

She quickly turned around and stopped the ranger from roaring forward. "I warned you about this, Wade," she whispered. "Rushdan is always right and never wrong."

"I can't let him—"

She locked both his hands with hers. But he still managed to swoosh her around and protect her, absorbing Rushdan's next blow across his back.

"I need the money," Wade managed after a couple of seconds. "I admit that. Thing is, Texas Rangers are squeaky clean, man. No one thinks of us as being dishonest. It doesn't happen. You're throwing something special away here, Reval. I'm a one-of-a kind opportunity. Whatever you think up, I can do."

"Wait, wait, wait," Therese said as Sal began pushing them from the room. "Please listen. He can get inside places even the cops you own can't get into. Wade literally works with every agency. Right?"

"All right. Wait. Can you really get inside every building or restricted area?"

Yes! They'd found a reason Wade was unique.

"Sure. No problem." Wade shrugged.

"How do I know this isn't just a very good acting job?" Rushdan swiveled his huge body to sit in his chair. His house slippers slid across the marble floor.

Only the best for Rushdan Reval.

Wade slipped his arm around her waist. "I can't help it. No way can I walk away from this lady. I'm crazy about her. Thing is, she doesn't come cheap. I need money, Reval. If I don't work for you, I'll be working for someone else to get it."

Oh, God, he was about to kiss her. She recognized that smoldering longing in his eyes. How in the world could he do that with threats and guns hanging over them?

"This just might work, but what type of collateral can you give me?" Her enemy interrupted.

"Collateral, sir?"

"Aren't you quaint. *Sir?*" Rushdan looked around at his men. "Listen to that, he called me *sir* and actually means it. Yes, collateral. You don't think I'm going to invest in you so you can steal from me when you're entrusted with something valuable, do you? I don't work that way."

"Me," she answered for Wade. "I'll be his collateral."

"Isn't that sweet." Rushdan used his pinky to pick something from his teeth again, making the nice words turn sour. "Unfortunately Therese, you're already mine. Neither important nor valuable."

"She is to me. I love her."

The words struck something deep inside her. Even knowing they were said in order to save their lives. Coming from his lips after the beautiful night in the hotel…she realized just how much she wanted them to be true.

Chapter Seven

"Take them somewhere." Rushdan shooed his crew away like they were flies. The thud of someone being shoved reminded him to say, "And no punching. At least not yet. Pretty boy might have a job to do."

He caught Sal's look, which certainly questioned his temporary decision. He hated anyone questioning him. What was the harm of considering the ranger's proposition? If he didn't, he'd lose Therese, too.

One person could give him the confirmation he needed. Andrew was faster with a computer than Rushdan was at making money. He silently laughed at his own joke and picked up his normal phone. Then dialed the number on the hidden cell phone in his desk.

The key to everything was right there in plain sight for anyone who wanted to see it. But they wouldn't know what it was and they wouldn't know what to say even if they found a reason to search.

"Money is a pitiless master but a zealous servant." The code quote seemed both stupid and cryptic.

"P.T. Barnum," the voice answered. "Andrew, it's

for you," the voice called from a distance a few seconds later.

He looked around the new office, so close in style to his last. A shame he'd blown up the previous one. All because that badass ranger had brought others to try and take him down. Perhaps this was a mistake and he should just kill him and be done with it.

Therese would need to die, too.

He tapped on the fish tank full of smaller versions of the inhabitants of the one he'd had last year. They'd gain in size, just like his bank roll would after this deal was brokered. The biggest deal of his life.

"Yeah?" Andrew finally said.

"This is Rushdan Reval. I need information on Wade Hamilton. He's a Texas Ranger in Dallas." Rushdan waited for some type of acknowledgment.

"Who is this? JK, I mean…just kidding, Reval. What did you want?" Andrew asked.

"I need information. Today."

"Yeah, on a Texas Ranger. You said that. Why are you bothering, Reval? Does it have anything to do with our deal?"

"As a matter of fact, I either need to kill him or I can use him to help facilitate the exchange."

"I'll get back to you."

The phone went dead. "Thank you, I look forward to hearing from you," he said into the phone, refusing to let anyone working for him know that someone had hung up on him.

Andrew was a rude young man who continued to

call him by his last name. No matter how many times he insisted on being called Rushdan.

"What now?" Sal asked. "I locked them in the sixth-floor storage room."

"Do you have surveillance in that room?"

"That's not up and running yet, boss."

"Dammit, Sal, make that a priority. I want to know if anyone is following our two guests or approaching our building."

"You got it, boss."

"Did anyone pick up his vehicle?"

"Nope."

Rushdan tapped on the glass. He didn't allow anyone else to bother his fish that way, but he loved it. They all swam toward him, expecting food.

"I guess a little more won't hurt you," he said to his fish. "Did you keep someone at the hotel room?"

"No. Want me to send someone back?"

"Why do I surround myself with idiots?"

The exception was Therese. Smart. Competent. Reliable. Even though she pretended to be all too stupid around his men. She had all the qualities that made him question why she worked for him. Even if she did try to hide behind the dumb broad persona she portrayed. He didn't understand why she played that part. It didn't make sense. And that was exactly the reason his men had been following her tonight.

He had suspicions. Too many coincidences for his peace of mind.

If he dwelled on it or questioned her motives too

much, he might let his paranoia get rid of her. But he wanted her in every way.

He should kill the ranger and be done with that specific problem. Sal and others had wanted him to deal with Therese after the Public Exposure episode but he'd ignored them.

The problem with Therese... She was good with the details. He needed her back in the fold and she might leave if anything happened to her "boyfriend."

"Oh, well," he mumbled to the blue fish with dots. "I shall call you Dotty."

If Wade Hamilton hadn't stuck his nose where it didn't belong last year, Rushdan would have his lovely office building, and the program would be complete for the new buyers. The money he would rake in from this deal would easily make up for the past six months of being shut down.

If he had a way to keep the ranger under his control, to assure that he'd behave, then he'd control Therese at the same time.

He tapped on the fish tank glass again. A beautiful blue-and-pink wrasse came to his finger. The blue reminded him of Therese's eyes. He'd have to ask her to streak that dark brown hair of hers pink. That would be interesting...very interesting.

Perhaps keeping the ranger alive could get him benefits of a different, more intimate nature with the smart beauty. Even if it didn't, having someone to offer his new clients assistance with their government endeavors would only help the real operation get up and running again. An inside man always paid off.

"Yes," he answered his beeping cell.

"Your ranger is in debt up to his eyeballs," Andrew said without any greeting. "That should be enough for your purposes. But I went a little deeper, just to make sure. Back to a sealed court case when he was fifteen. Seems he had a very big bad gambler dude for a daddy."

"Is he still alive?"

"Naw. Died in prison. But get why he was in the pen. The dude pulled the trigger on a Texas Ranger when a scam went south."

Blackmail. How convenient.

"Send me details. Everything."

"Look, Reval. My boss overheard the convo. Is the date firm yet?"

"Definitely. I'll have details first thing in the morning. It seems I have a new knight to insert into the game."

"Info is on its way. Did I mention my boss is getting impatient?"

And once again, Andrew disconnected without a proper goodbye, taking him by surprise. It didn't matter since he was alone. Sal had backed out of the room at his earlier irritation. A few arrangements and he'd get his gambling ranger involved so deep that the success of the deal would be guaranteed.

Chapter Eight

One dim yellow light in the back ceiling gave the small room an eerie feel. She sat next to Wade on the unfinished floor. At least it was cool against her bare legs. She pulled the belt on the robe tight again. Thank God Wade had given her his shirt or she might be even more exposed.

"Who has a storage closet that's completely empty?" she asked to break the silence.

"Reval seems to like 'em," Wade said quietly. "I was locked in one just like this."

"Oh, right. Sorry. That's where they kept you in the building that exploded."

"Don't forget I nearly exploded with it." He looped his fingers through hers, drawing her hand to his lips. "I should have said thanks as soon as I saw you again. You know…for getting me rescued."

"Are you really angry about me not calling you?"

"Did behaving like a hurt kid give me away?"

"Sort of." She patted his thigh like they'd been together for months, not hours. "So how do we get out of here?"

The electrical charge she associated with him filled the air as he leaned close enough to kiss her. His warm breath shifted to her neck and close to her ear. "We don't. Remember? We want to be right where we are."

"Don't we need a backup plan or something?"

"Shh." He placed a finger across her lips. "Your boss might be listening."

"I feel like we're wasting time," she whispered back, as close to his ear as he'd been to hers.

"I know a lot of things we can do in the dark."

His whisper sent one of those delicious tingles down her spine, landing in all the right spots.

"You already passed on that, remember?"

"Postponed," he breathed intimately across the top of her ear.

One word of encouragement from him and she melted in anticipation. About to give in, she came to her senses when two unknown somebodies walked past the door. "You're right. They may be watching us. I know surveillance and security increased since you brought the building down. Literally."

"To be fair, I was in no shape to destroy anything." Wade twisted her hair around his finger, trapping her ear close to his face.

"Never mind, you know exactly what I mean." Breathy words escaped and a gasp of expectation as his lips passed across hers once more.

"As a matter of fact, I do," he said louder, leaning away from her.

"Don't sound so surprised." She cut an anxious

giggle short, changing it to a worried tap on his shoulder. *Why am I more nervous with him than the criminal I work for?*

"I am surprised."

"Why? This happens when two people know each other. It's natural."

He laughed so hard he began to choke, coughing into his hand like a man with asthma.

"Why is that so funny?" she asked before she laughed with him.

"Therese, we don't know each other." He shook his head, laughing more. "We have this thing—believe me, it's an attractive thing and I like it. But I don't know if anything about you is even real."

God, he was right. Wade Hamilton was absolutely right. *He* didn't know her, but she'd kept tabs on him, researched him, knew a lot about him.

Not like a stalker or anything—or at least that was what she told herself. But every once in a while she'd see where he was or what he'd been working on. He did good work. He was a good man. The one-sided relationship she'd forged was the main reason she trusted him.

"What do you want to know?" she blurted into the darkness, unafraid of who might hear.

"They're probably listening," he reminded her. "Why not pass the time another way?"

His hand slid around her back, circling her waist, scooting her even closer to him. He didn't have to hit her over the head with the fact that he was attracted. But her real emotions got the best of her and crept through. She wanted a genuine relationship with him. Not a one-sided almost-stalker thing.

"There's no telling how long we'll be left here," she said, trying to play it cool. A real relationship. So that involved talking and not just necking as soon as they were alone. Right?

"To be honest, sitting in the dark next to you— practically naked like you are—isn't that bad." He put space between their hips. "It's not the worst situation I've ever been caught in. This doesn't make the top ten."

She bit back a laugh. "I don't know what possessed me to involve you."

"It's okay. Everybody panics occasionally." He rubbed the back of his neck, then his side.

"Not me."

"I'm not sure I believe you—" He slid a hand across her bare leg. "Instead of debating the ways people react to stress…why don't we just get back to what we can do in a dark room?"

Of all the sexy voices in the world, the owner of the one that affected her in the best way possible flirted with her. In a closet. In a dire situation where they may very well be killed. He bent his head and gave her a perfect kiss. Just enough pressure to suggest to her lips he didn't want to stop. But he did.

"I guess I deserve that after—"

His lips connected again. When they both were breathing extra fast he paused. "After all the teasing?"

"Teasing is what someone does who has no intention of following through," she pointed out.

Both of his strong arms wrapped around her and pulled her across his lap. "I have to say this is the most unusual date I've been on."

"Do you go on many?" She knew the answer.

After checking the bars for her, he sat on the same stool every Friday night for hours. She'd been so tempted to meet him there and talk. Deep down she'd known it would end like this. Okay, not necessarily sitting on a concrete floor as hostages. But definitely sitting on his lap...somewhere.

"I've been doing a lot of late night filing. It's kept me busy."

Huh? Oh, right, they'd been talking about his dating life. She let a nail wander across his collarbone and leaned forward to whisper in *his* ear.

"If we can't really do anything or make *plans*, let's get to know each other for real. Tell me one truth about yourself."

"Like...?"

"Your choice. It can be anything as long as it's the absolute truth," she continued whispering.

"Absolute?" he whispered back.

"No sugarcoating or stretching to make it fit first-date parameters."

He tapped her just above her heart. "Okay, but you go first."

"I hate alarm clocks."

"Doesn't count." He shook his head. "Everybody hates alarm clocks. Getting up in the morning isn't my favorite thing, either."

"Point taken." It had to be more intimate, something she wouldn't share with others. It had been so long since she shared something real. "I love running. Physical training. Give me a long path with no one else around and I'm in heaven. Your turn."

She tapped his knee next to her, afraid to glance directly at him and see an "are you serious?" look on his face. It hadn't been that intimate a gesture. His knee was covered with worn blue denim. Dragging her finger across his chest...*that* was intimate. Kissing him, sitting on his lap...intimate.

So why did she finally feel naked and vulnerable?

Dangerous territory.

She needed a distraction and fingered the strong black rope braided around Wade's left wrist, holding his watch. "I've always wondered about this strange watchband."

"Always?"

"You know what I mean."

She'd noticed it six weeks ago when he'd seen her at the FBI bust. But recognized it from when they'd first met. It wasn't the right time or place to remind him of that meeting. He'd definitely think she was a stalker. Shoot, she was having to convince herself she wasn't.

"I began wearing it again full-time after my capture last year. It's a little insurance policy. It might come in handy one day. Your turn."

"Oh no. It's still round one. That is definitely the same level as my alarm clock and totally not intimate."

"I have a better idea. Let's warm up a little."

One-handedly he unbuttoned the top two buttons of her borrowed shirt, causing her to shiver. Still sorting the emotion shooting through her, she forced herself to return to their lighthearted flirting. "So your motive is purely to get me warm?"

"Warm is good," he teased, winking before his lips captured hers again.

Kissing him was a little bit of heaven.

He behaved, keeping his hands in place, cupping her shoulder with his fingers to entice her to get closer. She tried to be careful not to sweep them up to the next level of desire—which would have been easy to do anywhere else. But he was quickly warming her inside and out. An unshaven cheek tickled a little before he abruptly brought his face away.

The bright light flooded the room when she opened her eyes. Wade quickly helped her to her feet and tucked her close to his side before walking through the hallway to meet Rushdan.

"Well, well, well." Rushdan smiled. "Welcome to the dark side, Ranger Wade." As he looked at their hands and snickered at Wade's obvious protectiveness.

"You came to a decision?" she asked, knowing the answer.

He splayed his hands and shrugged.

"Come on, Rushy, honey. If you intended to kill us, you would never have set eyes on us again." She turned to Wade. "He's sort of squeamish that way."

Wade cleared his throat, but his lips curved in the beginnings of a smile. "What do you want me to do?"

he asked, dropping both his head and his voice, then covering his face with his hand.

Rushdan might actually believe the whole pensive act. But that was all it was with Wade…just an act. He cleared his throat several times like he had after laughing himself into a coughing fit.

"Let's chat while Sal retrieves your first assignment." Rushdan placed his hand on Wade's shoulder.

The ranger stood taller, Rushdan's hand slid down and soon returned to his pocket. Wade continued to hold her hand. She yanked on it, hoping to remind him that Rushdan Reval was in charge. And that they wanted him to be.

If Wade continued to tower over the little fat man, it didn't matter what Wade *might* be able to do for him. When Wade didn't react, she squeezed a little harder and thrust her shoulder into his ribs.

"Rushdan, why not just tell us what you need us to do? Why all the drama and suspense?" she asked.

"Oh, allow me to have a little fun, darling Therese. And you should know by now I never discuss business with witnesses. Sal will inform you of where Texas Ranger man is going and what he'll need to do."

"You mean where *we're* going." She pointed to Wade and then herself. "I go where he goes. What do we need to do? And by when?"

"Today, my darling Therese."

"So it's last-minute, not well planned and no big deal if it goes wrong." She tapped one finger on the back of Wade's hand, hoping he got the message to let her go.

No luck. He squeezed her hand but didn't release it.

Finding and stopping the terrorists—her real assignment—was probably the most important thing she'd ever done. But keeping Wade alive ran a close second.

"Darling, this will be so easy for your boyfriend. It seems he has a very sordid past. At least in his youth. It's admirable that he turned his occupation around to work for him. Using his instinct and certain…skills." Her undercover employer stared again at their hands, fingers laced together.

"Do us all a favor, Rushdan, and stop talking in riddles. We already know Wade has a gambling problem."

"Yes, but do you know about his father?"

"Those records are sealed," Wade said, squeezing her hand tighter.

It was his cover. He didn't have to give her any sign. Had she worried about his ability to act before? Wade was a statue, stiff and unmoving. His eyes were hard like he wanted to rip Rushdan's head off.

"Dear, dear lover boy," Rushdan continued. "Everything can be found if you know how to look."

"I haven't run a game in years. I wouldn't know where to begin," Wade told him.

"Game?" she asked, trying to keep up.

"That's the beauty of today. It's waiting for you. All put together…just waiting." Rushdan clapped his hands together with excitement. "Give yourself credit. You know your way around a track. Who to look for. Where to look. This will be second nature for you."

"What's Rushdan talking about?" she asked, playing her part. "What records were sealed?"

"Mine. My childhood and teen years were filled by feeding my dad's gambling addiction." Wade rubbed his forehead with his free hand. "That is, until we were caught."

"You were in jail?" She heard the amazement in her voice. Not disappointment...more like wonder.

Why would she feel a kinship with him? They barely knew each other. Wait. They didn't know each other at all. And this was a perfect example. He was cute and had been helpful. And somehow she felt closer knowing he had more flaws than just following a hunch and jumping into situations.

Rushdan practically giggled like a girl. "Tell her all of it. Knock all the stars from her eyes."

It wouldn't help. She knew what Rushdan attempted to do. Crime boss Reval wouldn't ever make her his, no matter what she thought of Wade or what he shared from his past. She tucked herself closer into her ranger's side, more comfortable there by the minute.

She'd assumed Wade was an honorable man because of his occupation. But no modern Texas Ranger had been accused of something like this. They were the keepers of law.

"You look betrayed, my darling. Did you think

you were the first to lead this one—" he gestured as if dusting Wade's chest "—off the righteous path?"

Rushdan laughed, dabbing at the corner of his eyes as if tearing up.

"Aw, that's sweet. You were a delinquent, Wade." She rested her head on his arm. "How perfect. Where were you—"

"You've got more skills than I gave you credit," Wade said, finally dropping her hand, circling her waist instead. He hid the surprise of his past being revealed or kept a poker face for another reason.

Oh, Lord. She'd fallen for the fake background his partner had created. She should have known immediately that this man wouldn't have had a gambler for a father.

"That's enough reminiscing about sordid youths," Rushdan commanded. "We need this done quickly. Sal will give you the instructions and will be there to capture it all on video."

"Blackmail?" she asked.

"Insurance policy," Rushdan answered sharply.

"And Sal has all the details? Details that I had nothing to do with." She faced Rushdan straight on, keeping Wade's hand plastered across her stomach. "When are you going to accept me back?"

"If you weren't back, my darling, you wouldn't be in my building." Rushdan's voice held a menacing threat as he swept the bottom of her chin with his pointer finger. "Perk up, Ranger Wade. This should be old hat for you if you remember the racetrack. You do, don't you?"

Wade shrugged. She didn't know if that meant no, yes, or a big fat he-had-no-clue.

Rushdan sped up his short-legged steps and grabbed her upper arm as he began to pass, spinning her to face him. "This money is important, Therese. Don't screw it up." His anger literally spit through the gap in his front teeth.

Chapter Nine

Wade caught Therese as her "boss" thrust her away. Sal tried to grab her, but Wade stepped between them, blocking his reach. A leather bag hit the top of his boots.

"Everything's inside. Cash, names, bets and pay-offs." Sal didn't appear happy at the change of events. "Take the back exit." He glared at Wade before taking a long stare down Therese's robe. "You aren't decent enough for the front."

He drew his arm back ready to throw a punch but stopped himself. Therese stared at his chest, which quickly rose and fell as she tugged a little to get him headed in the right direction. He'd almost lost it from the disgusting look Reval's right-hand man had sent toward Therese.

Dressed like they'd gotten thrown out of a cheap hotel—no money of their own or phones—they watched Sal draw the door closed. "Remember we're watching the whole thing," Sal said through the thick steel.

"No ride?" Wade unzipped the bag, revealing

stacks of cash. "Do they expect us to walk to Lone Star Park?"

"We'll have a ride in a few minutes." She patted his chest with her palm.

Loving the feel of her hand sliding up and around his neck, he didn't wait for her to pull his lips down. He didn't mind kissing her at any time. But he did arch an eyebrow, questioning her timing.

"I could get used to this." He really could.

"You're so cute." She darted her eyes up and to the side of the building. He found the surveillance camera. Right. She was still acting.

"Cute? Not sure anyone's called me that since junior high." He winked and scooped up the bag of cash. "About that ride…"

"It'll require a little walking. At least it's eventually a sidewalk." She led the way out of the alley to a major street, then stepped into a large field.

"The building that looks like a bird's nest…that's the Irving Convention Center? Reval set up shop in Las Colinas. I hope you don't mind waiting a bit to get back to an open restaurant or fast-food joint."

"I think Sal will send a car. And if not, there's a hotel only ten minutes up the street." She pointed south toward the lake. "He's ultimately responsible for that bag you're carrying. I don't think he'll let us out of his sight for long."

To avoid parts of the dirt path, Therese jumped onto the curb occasionally. The late June sun hadn't heated the day completely but probably had made the pavement hot, so she couldn't use the street.

"You were pretty good back there," he said, shifting the bag to rest on his bare back. "Watch out for the broken beer bottles."

"Got it." She sidestepped onto the street, picking her feet up faster.

He could offer to carry her to the hotel, but he didn't think she'd go for it. She hadn't liked him throwing her over his shoulder last night.

He kept searching, but no cars were heading their direction—either from Reval's building or a Company B Ranger. He knew Jack or one of the men had followed them from the hotel. But they would keep out of sight until they were certain no one followed. That meant out of view from the building, leaving them a long walk.

Therese detoured into the street again, hopping from one foot to the other.

"Sure you don't want me to carry you?"

"Did you ask?" She shook her head. "But no thanks. Keeping the robe closed while I'm walking is a challenge. Besides, I think you explored my backside enough last night."

She laughed. He smiled, keeping an eye open for his team. It went without saying that they were close. Jack wouldn't have it any other way. So they were around here somewhere.

"Tell me about Reval." He needed to know more. "Not the paper version. What have you learned about him? Was today a normal reaction? Did he look desperate?"

"You want to know if he'd normally give us a bag

of cash?" She fast-walked a little down the street, avoiding more broken glass, rocks and trash.

"Exactly."

Another hundred yards and the apartments would block anyone watching from Reval's building. They hit the sidewalk and Therese winced, popping her feet up and down off the hot concrete. Wade scooped her up in his arms to get her under some shade a bit farther.

She kissed his cheek, not objecting to being carried. "Short answer…yes. Everything he's done in the past couple of days is within his character. And I promise you, Sal isn't far away. By now, he's in front of us somewhere, just waiting and watching."

"Like at the hotel."

"Probably." She locked her arms around his neck.

"Damn."

"Tell me what I'm missing, please."

Years of approaching vehicles as a highway patrolman had him searching between cars and behind the tiny things considered trees that they passed.

"Let's put the questions on hold a minute." He set her on the manicured grass of the apartment buildings along the road leading to the hotel. He pointed to the bag of money, shook his head, then covered her lips with his finger.

Therese pulled the robe tighter around her body, knelt and helped him look through the entire bag for a listening or tracking device. She also blocked their search from a couple of cars passing by.

"Looks like it's all clear. I'm pretty sure that Jack's at the hotel. At least, I would be there."

"How would he have known—" She put up a hand, realization plainly dawning on her face. "He followed us. That was risky. Why didn't you tell me?"

She lifted the gym bag and took off back to the main road. Wade caught her free arm, spinning her back to face him. The force caught her off balance and she fell into his chest. He slid the bag's strap off her shoulder and onto his own.

"It'll be okay. Trust me." He planted a quick kiss on her lips, receiving a small response. "My partners and I are good. Jack won't do anything to jeopardize putting Rushdan Reval back in jail. For good."

"I don't see Sal," she said.

"It doesn't mean you're wrong." He didn't miss that she hadn't said she trusted him.

Not a lot of vehicles went up and down the street, but he recognized one that pulled into the area reserved for those not staying long. Major Clements was one of the few Company B Rangers who actually drove a car instead of a truck.

He started toward the hotel entrance, but a strong tug on his arm pulled him in another direction.

"Maybe we shouldn't walk in through the *front* door?" Therese laced her fingers through his, heading across the street and into the hotel's parking garage.

She squeezed herself between the oak tree and hedge, waiting for him on the other side. He followed, stepped down from the retaining wall and into the coolness of the covered garage.

He lifted her down, not embarrassed that he drew her body close, wanting the athletic suppleness of her next to him as she slid to reach the concrete.

Her hands remained at his shoulders as she slightly tilted her gorgeous face up to his. "If we go to the lakeside, I think we can sneak over the fence and look like we're on our way to the hotel pool."

"Good idea."

They stayed put, not going where they needed to be. Not looking to see who was around or if anyone followed. It had been a long time since he'd stared into the eyes of a beautiful woman. An equally long time since he'd admired one so completely. Longer than both of those put together since he'd *wanted* to do either.

And whose fault was that?

"Not mine."

"Do all the ideas need to be yours?"

Dammit. The question had been so loud in his head that he'd answered out loud. "Nothing. We should probably get going."

The unbelievable sexual tension passed from his head but left his knees slightly wobbly. Right up to the point he heard the tires squealing on an upper garage floor.

"If it's Sal, we should just wait here."

"Not sure that's a great idea," he answered, securing the gym bag's shoulder strap across his body.

Therese stepped in front of him, stop-signing his

chest for him to quit or give up. "Even if your friends are inside, there's no way for us to explain how they might help us. Rushdan told Sal to give us a ride. He *is* coming and will expect us to be exactly like this, with no money, no cells and basically no clothing."

"And if he finds anything different, he'll be suspicious," he agreed.

"Basically he has permission to kill us and let Rushdan move forward with other plans."

"About those plans—" Wade saw movement out of the corner of his eye at the staircase. A silver-haired man resembling Major Clements.

"He hasn't told me a thing. That's why I risked following him last night," she said.

"Then it's agreed. We stay put and see who's about to drive around the corner any second." He raised his voice so his boss could hear, then tried to angle Therese behind him, but she wouldn't have it.

"I can take care of myself, Ranger."

"I've noticed that."

The car approaching from the upper floor could be a hotel patron, security, his partner or Reval's man, Sal.

"That's him," Therese said, stepping into the open. "Things just got a little bit easier."

Wade didn't have a chance to ask how.

Sal was already next to them, smoke curling from his open window. "Took you long enough. I ran out of cigarettes waiting on you."

"Then maybe you should have given us a ride at

Rushdan's office," Therese said before opening the door and scooting across the seat.

"You know I had to make sure your new boyfriend here wasn't being followed."

"And?" Therese asked.

Sal was silent as he inhaled his last drag on the butt, then threw it out the window.

"And nothing." Wade shoved the money bag between his feet. "Just like I said."

Sal drove too fast out the parking garage and away from the hotel.

At least nothing Sal could spot.

Major Clements dipped his head, hiding his face as they passed. Rushdan and Sal might recognize Jack and Slate, but the major was a different story. Today he looked like a faded old cowboy with a giant belt buckle and an old-fashioned snap shirt.

The tension between his shoulders eased at the knowledge the Rangers were there, trailing them, just out of sight.

"Take us to my apartment," Therese said as if Sal were her chauffer waiting for instructions.

"The boss said I need to—"

"Don't give any excuses, Sal. We all know I can't go to the track dressed in a robe. It's ridiculous to even suggest that Rushdan expects me to go like this." She tugged the hotel robe closed over her knee.

"What about him?" Sal asked. "You giving him back his shirt?"

"I can handle things after you drop us off."

"The boss ain't going to like that."

Wade listened to Therese handle Reval's right-hand man like she'd been ordering him around for years. Come to think about it, she probably had. So he stayed out of it and forced himself to look forward and not see if one of his friends followed.

Traffic was light early Saturday mornings. Sal turned off Northwest Highway and onto a side street soon after. He stopped at the corner, not bothering to take them to the gate. When Therese opened her door, Wade slid across the seat, following her, dragging the money bag with him.

Sal pulled away before the door closed.

Therese pulled the belt tighter and pushed the robe's collar higher on her neck. Wade stuck his head through the strap of the bag and shifted its bulk to his bare back.

"Lead the way. I'm starved. Your friends didn't provide breakfast."

"That's too bad. I don't cook, so I never go to the store." Therese kept a hand at her throat, holding the robe closed. She was actually more covered than she'd been in that yellow dress the night before.

"Not a problem. I know how to order pizza." It was sort of cute watching her be modest in case one of her apartment neighbors looked out their window.

"Pizza? For breakfast? Aren't we a little old for that?" She looked like she believed her words.

"We're not old and pizza delivers. Order the cinnamon breadsticks and it's like having those bite-size things you get at the airport. Shoot, it's too early for delivery. Maybe we could head to a restaurant?"

"I hate to disappoint you, but we don't have time to go out to eat. We have a lot of things to get done before we head out to the races." She passed by the pedestrian gate and crossed the drive toward the leasing office.

"If you're too old for pizza, we can still clean up and grab something. If I'm remembering correctly, there's a mom-and-pop diner back on Webb Chapel. They have terrific breakfast burritos they serve all day—" He grabbed her hand and turned her back to face him. "Isn't your apartment through there?"

"Yes—" Therese arched her eyebrows, waiting for him to catch on "—but I don't have my keys. I need management to unlock my door."

He tugged her toward the pedestrian gate. "Which apartment?"

She pointed to their left. "Twelve twenty-four. We should go to the office. I don't keep a key under the doormat. I don't even have a doormat."

"It'll be unlocked." He pulled her closer, kissing her quickly before she leaned back, trying to see their surroundings.

"Are you implying that one of your colleagues is waiting inside my apartment?"

"If we're lucky, there might even be breakfast. Then again…" He waggled his eyebrows at her while sliding his hands around her waist. "I might be luckier if there's not anyone around."

Chapter Ten

Was there time to get sidetracked? The gorgeous shirtless man caressing Therese around her waist sent an invitation with his eyes that she understood very well.

Wade made her forget about his implication that someone was inside her apartment. Her mind calculated how long they'd need to get ready and get to Lone Star Park. And then flooded with the disappointment that there would people expecting information. Or Sal demanding he escort them to the track.

Shoot! Wade's closeness was a problem…a huge distraction.

She turned the knob and walked inside without preparing herself defensively. Good grief, the door had been unlocked. They weren't alone. Just like Wade had said it would be. Her only thought had been…

Oh, God, she'd been hoping they'd have enough time to satisfy some of those teasing promises they'd been making.

Yeah, huge distraction.

"Did you bring something to eat?" Wade asked the man dressed in an apartment complex work shirt. They clearly knew each other and Wade had expected him to be here.

"No time."

"I was about to ask how you got in, but you must have picked up our things from the safe. Including my keys." Their phones sat on the coffee table along with her scuffed strappy shoes.

"Jack MacKinnon." He extended his hand and she took it. "I'm Wade's partner, mostly errand boy. At least to him."

"Therese Ortis, but you already know that. Normally my apartment is a little bit neater than this."

"Oh, yeah. I brought some of Wade's stuff and made it easy to find if someone checked you out. I also swept for bugs. You're clear, which I didn't think possible." He stuck electronic gear into a workman's bag, holding the straps in his hand.

"I see." She deliberately looked at the small suitcase and three pairs of men's shoes. Her small apartment was even smaller with both men standing in it.

Wade pulled open every cheap cabinet door in the small kitchen, looking inside. "Man, Therese. You really don't have any food here. Not even peanut butter. Who doesn't have peanut butter?"

Jack reached into the bag and brought out two weapons. He set them on the kitchen bar and tried to look casual, leaning against the wall. "Brother, I'm not going to tell you what we've gone through to make this operation happen and cover your you-know-what. After this one's finished, we're going to have a little talk."

"I figured Major Clements would be talking the loudest. I didn't really have a choice. The opportunity happened." His eyes cut to her and back to the fridge. "Once you guys discovered who and what we were dealing with…did you have a problem?" Wade stared into the freezer. "Man alive. There's not even any frozen dinners or ice?"

"Sorry to say you have some very bad friends, ma'am," Jack said, shaking his head at Wade. "Come on, man, contribute to the conversation."

"What?" Wade shrugged and let the freezer shut.

Therese answered with a shrug and mouthed, "I told you so."

"We probably don't have much time," Jack continued. "Slate is keeping an eye on Rushdan's man who dropped you off." He looked at his phone as if expecting an update. "After dropping you, he went to a 7-Eleven. I think the team is getting up to speed on the situation. Anything happen after we spoke last night? That is, anything I should know?"

"The bag I brought in is full of cash and we're due at Lone Star Park as soon as possible," Wade threw out casually. "A lot of cash that Rushdan Reval wants to increase."

"So I guess you don't need any cash. Your truck's back at your place. If anyone was watching it, we had it towed."

Wade gave a few more details but left out how

he'd been used as a punching bag or how she'd tried to leave him in the truck.

"Did you set up the phone to listen in?" Wade asked.

"Yours, yes. The FBI had a few dozen choice words when we tried Miss Ortis's. Yours should be enough to keep tabs on you." Jack pointed to their phones at the end of the kitchen bar.

Wade's partner lifted his cell phone from his back pocket and read a message. "Gotta run. You've got company coming."

Then Texas Ranger Jack MacKinnon slid open the patio door and hopped over the four-foot patio fence with grace.

He'd cut it close.

Sal barely knocked, turned the knob and came inside. "Boss sent me for a walk-through. Believe me, this ain't my idea."

Rushdan's man picked up a pair of slacks from the back of the couch, dropping them immediately. He went as far as to look inside the bathroom cabinet, finding a slightly used toothbrush that didn't belong to her. Their weapons along with a Texas Rangers badge were on the two-person dining table.

"You shouldn't leave those just lying around anywhere," he said, pointing to the credentials and weapons. "You don't know who's going to sneak inside and lift stuff." When he was satisfied, he tossed an envelope in Wade's direction and left, slamming the door.

"Well, that was interesting," Wade said, dropping onto her couch the minute the door closed.

Therese turned the two bolts she'd installed herself, locking everyone out. She wasn't used to anyone being in the small apartment. No one had ever been there other than a maintenance man.

And yet, having Wade there didn't feel strange or awkward.

No distractions. And no thoughts of them together. They had work to do.

She scooped up his clothes, draping them over the end of the couch before reaching for the envelope. But Wade gently tugged on her hand, pulling her onto his lap.

"Don't you think we should open that?" she asked before glancing at the clock radio on the kitchen bar.

He skimmed the side of her knee with one large hand. And kept the envelope behind her back. He pulled her close enough to kiss her neck.

"Maybe you should read what's inside the envelope before we get sidetracked?" she asked while he nibbled.

"You don't think it's the same instructions that are in with the money?" He dropped the sealed brown envelope onto her lap but didn't relinquish his hold.

"I've never done anything like this for Rushdan before, so I really don't know." She ripped the edge open, then slid her finger, opening up the long side. She tipped it up and a cheap cell phone along with a piece of paper fell to her lap. "Maybe I should sit—"

"We can read it together if you stay where you are. Unless you don't feel comfortable?"

"I'm plenty comfortable. Too comfortable." Her

arm brushed the bare skin of his chest, sending her stomach flipping wildly. She got up quickly before she could change her mind about getting even more comfortable.

There would be plenty of time to get to know Wade better. Plenty of time when they weren't due at the racetrack. She flipped the one typewritten page open, holding it by the corner just in case there were fingerprints to process.

"I don't know why I'm being careful. Rushdan doesn't run his *business* with any connections to himself. It's the reason he's out of jail, rebuilding his empire. Lots of non-prosecutable people do the dirty work."

"His cronies don't know what they're writing or what piece of the puzzle they might be acting on. We discovered that last year after he tried to kill me."

"Rushdan is the only person who has an inkling what the whole picture looks like." She stood by the sliding door, searching the edges of buildings to see if anyone lurked about.

"What's it say?" Wade asked.

"These instructions are different than those in the money bag," she said, handing the note to him as he joined her. "Everything he's done so far is part of a test to see where we'd go or who we'd call."

"And who stopped to help," he pointed out, tugging her to the couch again. He flipped the paper to the side table. "Seems awful risky to be switching the plans around from us placing bets to being the ones who pay out the bribes—at least in this version. Damn risky."

"I should grab a quick shower and get some real clothes on. Unless you want to go first?" She stood, tossed the cheap cell phone with the others and tried to pass by Wade. He didn't let her.

He tugged a little on her hand—too gently for her to blame him for keeping her there.

He shook his head. "I want a kiss." He guided her back to his lap, then placed a fingertip under her chin, drawing her lips to his.

The kiss was good, fulfilling, sexy. Long enough for him to maneuver his hands behind her back and press her breasts against his strong chest. More than enough to shoot her senses into overdrive. More than enough for her to potentially forget why they needed to be anywhere else.

Feeling safe within his arms, she found it hard to ease away. Especially when she wanted more of him. Her longing was getting harder and harder to control. And why was she thinking about feeling safe?

Safety wasn't one of her priorities. Putting Reval in prison for good, discovering who the cash was behind Public Exposure and getting the algorithm off the streets—those were her priorities.

Three things that would make a lot of people safe.

She scooted off his lap, pulled his shirt down around her thighs and tightened the sash around her waist. "We can take my car unless you think that's a bad idea. Jack said your truck was at your place. Is it far?"

Liar! It wasn't far at all. About three miles. She'd known exactly where he lived when she'd agreed to rent this place. Being alone, working alone like she had been for so long isolated her. Getting an apartment close to someone she knew—okay, knew of— was her one gift to herself.

She'd given up a lot to work with Homeland. Her parents may have died when she was eighteen, but she had lots of family in the San Antonio area. Tons of relatives who all thought she'd cheated on a test while at the police academy and had been kicked out. Several knew she worked with a small-time crime boss. Not that she worked for the FBI on loan to the Department of Homeland Security.

Shoot. Wade didn't even know that part.

Wade's steel blue eyes searched hers. "Thinking of something you need to tell me? Another truth-or-dare question?"

"I don't remember any dares." She shook her head. "I thought we were getting to know each other."

He tugged on the long lapels of the hotel robe until her hands were supporting her weight, split on either side of his face against the couch. It brought their lips close. So close she could feel him move to form his next words.

"There's another way for us to get to know each other better," he whispered against her lips.

"Do you…ah…want a shower?"

"You go ahead, I need some air." He took a deep breath and exaggeratedly shifted his seating position.

After that kiss, she needed some air, too. She ran

to the bathroom, throwing her back against the door to save herself.

Pure oxygen might help clear her head. She opened the bathroom window and overheard Wade. He was on the small patio, talking into his phone. She had a sneaking suspicion he didn't need *air* as much as a discussion with his fellow Rangers.

So why not just tell her that?

Because he didn't trust her. Not completely.

She gently shut the window to give him his privacy, twisted the lock and began the shower. This time he couldn't "accidentally" open the door and see her in her birthday suit. A girl should leave some mystery. She hadn't last night, but Ranger Wade Hamilton still remained a gentleman. A teasing gentleman, but a gentleman just the same.

After the past two years of being in his life but not being *in* his life... Well, she'd given him no reason to trust her at all. How could she blame him for being hesitant?

The opportunity to come clean, to tell him *why* she trusted him had come and gone. Maybe they would continue the game about getting to know each other. But what if it was just a game for him?

She rinsed out her hair and dropped her forehead to the tile, letting the stream of water pound the back of her neck. It wasn't really sore, she just needed to think. Or think about another subject that wasn't Wade.

They should both be dead.

What was Rushdan Reval really up to? Why did

he need Wade for his plans? He wasn't the sort of guy who easily forgave anyone. Everything he did had a selfish reason attached to it. Everything.

For weeks he'd had his people searching for someone with access to public facilities. Rushdan had never hinted that it had anything to do with Public Exposure. But the speed at which he'd acted today made her think it did.

Wade would help her find out why the domestic terrorism group wanted the algorithm and how it had been improved or upgraded. He was her way inside Rushdan's inner circle. Wade. Again unknowingly playing the part of her hero. But no longer in the teenage-crush way she'd fantasized about for too long.

No, this was worse. He was a nice guy. A considerate person. A competent lawman. Distracting. She could actually fall for the real person she'd discovered him to be.

Chapter Eleven

Wade awoke from the nudge Therese gave him as they exited the highway close to the racetrack. He hadn't slept—or napped—long, but it had been deep and reviving. Something he'd needed after staying awake most of the previous night.

"I think I'm getting too old for hands-on law work," he said.

"Why's that?"

"Maybe too many days behind my desk recently." He stretched and yawned. "I could have stayed up two nights in a row back in my highway patrol days."

Therese looked sort of funny, paused like she was about to speak, and then she looked out her window. What had he missed?

She hadn't complained when he suggested a nap. In fact, she'd told him to close his eyes. He didn't regret it. There was no telling when he'd get the real thing again and he needed to be on his toes.

A long line of cars was turning into Lone Star Park and it was almost ten o'clock. They were running a few minutes behind but it shouldn't be a big deal. She hadn't seemed anxious in any of the life-threatening situations they'd been in before.

He couldn't pin it down. Was she thinking about Reval's elusive comment about his past? Was she catching on? Would it change her opinion if she knew that he'd run scams like this for real until he was fifteen?

"Will it be easy to find the guy the instructions told us to find? Do you think he'll leave if we're a couple of minutes late? I could drop you off and park the car alone if it will save time." Therese tapped her thumbs against the steering wheel, waiting on the light to turn green.

"Are you nervous or something?" he asked, hoping it didn't really have anything to do with his youth.

"I guess. Aren't you? We didn't really talk about what we were going to do to find the guy, bribe him or even get the money inside the park." She paused for traffic and looked at him. "I mean, that's an awful lot of money in that bag. Who pays off a bribe with cash at the actual race track? Our odds of succeeding are not high."

"Trust me. It'll go fine." He shook his head, but some weird business was happening with his stomach. It had nothing to do with pulling off the bribe. He'd taken care of that with a phone call while Therese had showered.

He didn't have to think too hard about what caused his anxiety. It had been in the background since hearing Reval's words that morning. Having the crook tell him to come to the track had his insides bobbing around like a cork on a fishing line.

Every distraction he'd tried at the apartment had been countered by Therese. There had been a new professionalism in her since she'd showered. He'd ordered food while she dried her hair. They ate in separate rooms and hadn't really talked since he'd fallen asleep soon after getting in her car.

Therese signaled and turned into the racing complex, reading all the signs aloud. He pointed to the left lane away from the regular parking area. It was pretty obvious she'd never been to the races before. But he had. A major portion of his misspent youth had been running behind those gates.

But after he'd returned to Dallas as a ranger, he'd avoided setting foot in the place. No concerts. No nights out with the guys. No Triple-A ballgames at the stadium next door. No cases associated with anything to do with racing or betting.

Hell, he didn't even allow himself to drive on the frontage road around the entertainment complex. He'd done pretty good not looking back for his entire adult life. But now...

Now it rushed him like speeding down the hill of the Titan at Six Flags. Riding a roller coaster wasn't something he'd done since he was a kid, either. He had to control the sickening anticipation of what needed to be done. He had to rein it in, use it to his advantage.

This wasn't a theme park with a fake shoot-out in the Wild West. If he screwed up...

He rolled his shoulders—stretching, relaxing, shaking off the nerves. He wouldn't screw up. He wouldn't let Therese down. He wrestled the fifteen-year-old's memories back behind that locked door in his mind.

Therese pulled behind a line of cars for the parking lot. He remembered exactly where he needed to go for the bribes and broke out of his funk. He put a hand on Therese's shoulder, then pointed for her to head straight.

"Keep heading down this road. Enter through the owner/trainer gate. Then we get to the stables and jockey quarters without any real questions."

"Are you sure, the note said to—"

"What if that's just another test? Look, Therese. I've forgotten more about this track than other people can possibly discover. Trust me. If you want to drop off a bribe, you don't take it through the front gate."

"Forgotten? You've done this before?"

She passed the patron parking lots and main entrance of the park, continuing around the curve to an entrance he remembered all too well.

"What do I tell Sal?" she asked.

"Maybe exactly what I just told you. Or you just let me handle it."

She pulled over, parking just inside, next to the fence. The cell given to them in the envelope rang. Wade pressed the speaker button so Therese could hear.

"Where are you?" Sal yelled.

"We're doing what you instructed," she answered before he could open his mouth.

"I'm supposed to be with you," Sal complained.

"Bribing a jockey is going to be a little conspicuous if someone's on our tail with their phone pointed in our direction." Wade covered her hand when she reached for the cell. "We'll catch up with you after we're done."

He clicked the phone off while Therese tried to swipe it from him.

"I'm not sure that was such a great idea," she said.

"Trust me. We'd be arrested within a couple of minutes his way. Come on, let's get this over with."

They might be arrested any way they tried to pull this off. He reached over the seat, grabbed the bag of money and slid out the door. He kept walking. Not waiting on Therese. Not turning around to see if she even followed.

The car lock and beep of her horn told him he could keep striding between the trucks and trailers. But all of a sudden he doubled over, unable to catch his breath.

"Wade? Are you okay? What happened?"

Therese's questions swam through his head. He heard them but something kept him from answering. He stood straight, catching the end of a horse trailer before he fell over a second time.

"Oh my God, what's wrong with you?" Therese rubbed his back and gripped his upper arm so tight it just might have held him up.

What's wrong? Images swam in front of his eyes,

obliterating the real parking lot in front of him. Years drifted away and he was a lanky teenager with his hair hanging in his eyes, jeans he barely kept around his hips and a T-shirt that was sure to have some foul writing.

"I'm...uh...not sure." But he knew. He was having a flashback.

"If you can't—"

"I can. I'm okay." He pushed himself to his full height again as he shoved the thoughts of his father's arrest back to the place they'd been locked before.

They didn't stay. But he couldn't allow those memories to interfere with today. Everything he saw, smelled...hell, even the sizzle of excitement was like stepping back in time. He was fifteen again and throwing up while they cuffed his father and hauled him to jail.

It was the last time he'd seen his father before the trials. The first one had convicted his dad of everything from petty larceny to organized crime. His father never made eye contact during the second trial for child endangerment. Terrence Hamilton had given up his paternal rights and Wade had never seen him again.

"Never look back," he heard himself mumble his father's mantra.

"What? Wade, you've got to clue me in on what's going on." She stopped him from stepping around her by a gentle touch to his chest.

He could see where he needed to go, knew what he needed to do. It was all right there if he kept looking over her head. She softly cupped his cheek and his knees shook.

"We're going to be late," he squeaked out.

"Better late than dead."

"Everything's okay, Therese. I won't let you down." Dammit, she caught his gaze and locked eyes with him.

It felt like she could see through his lies. Her X-ray vision into his soul made her eyes crinkle around the corners. The hand she had on his chest slid to his belt loop and shook him while she released an exasperated "errr."

"You're a very frustrating man. What did you mean when you said you'd forgotten more about this place than others could discover?"

If another woman had been in front of him, he wasn't certain what he would have done. But their get-to-know-each-other game of truthful facts tugged at him to tell her everything, to not hold back.

"I know my way around."

"You didn't have a real gambling problem. Did you?"

"No. Do you think I'd be a ranger— Hell, I'd be out of a job so fast."

"Then what is it?"

His hands found their way to each side of her waist. He was about to physically move her out of his path. But he looked into her eyes and realized his breathing was normal. His knees were rock steady.

The formidable memories of witnessing his father's arrest faded as he looked at a beautiful dark-haired woman. Dressed in lots of…sequins? He hadn't noticed until the sunlight bounced off a couple, making him blink back to reality.

"We need to get moving. Remember that whole thing about our real objective?"

"Hard for me to forget after three years." She stepped aside so they could continue. "You sure you're all right?"

"One of those punches caught up with me, that's all. A momentary thing."

The opportunity to come clean passed by without a second thought. Okay, so he was thinking about it as they walked between the vehicles. It wasn't a big deal. No one in his current world would care.

The guys would slap him on the back and might ask a question or two. He'd proven himself to Company B. He belonged there. They already knew he had their backs and was willing to put himself at risk.

But did Therese? Did she know?

More important, would *she* still trust him or think he'd been lying?

Just say it, man!

"This is probably going to sound funny." Therese laced her fingers through his. "I heard if you want a sure way to tell which horse will win the race, you should watch them before they're saddled. Then bet on the last one that went pee."

"Where the hell did you hear that crock?" He laughed.

She laughed. "My dentist. It's exactly what he does."

"And it works?"

"He swears by it."

"In my experience there's only one sure way that a horse wins." He patted the bag of money. "Bribery."

Chapter Twelve

Not many people gave them a second look as they walked between the buildings housing the horses, jockeys and owners. Therese looked everywhere, taking it in, still hyperaware that Sal could be around any corner. Sal or the police. Getting arrested would blow everything.

She also watched Wade. He didn't seem sick and didn't act like getting punched in the gut hours ago had anything to do with what had happened in the parking lot. Honestly, it seemed like he'd seen a ghost.

She wasn't used to seeing strong men like him stumble. One minute he stood tall and the next he was practically on the ground.

"Any idea where to find this guy we're supposed to pay off?" she whispered.

Wade pointed to a stall where an older cowboy tightened a buckle on a saddle.

"Are you sure? He looks too...tall." Wade arched both of his brows, waiting for her to explain. So she continued in a whisper, "I thought we'd be paying off the jockey like the instructions say."

"We'd be caught faster than any of these horses can run. The jockeys are watched a lot closer than the stable hands. We slip this guy the money, then he'll slip a jigger into the race."

"I have no idea what you just said." He tried to step around her, but she moved in front of him. She needed an answer. "He's also not the man Rushdan wants us to contact. Why not just do things his way?"

"A jigger is kind of like a small cattle prod they use to get extra speed at the last minute." His confidence looked to be back. "This is something I know, Therese. Trust me."

Wade took a step forward again, but she latched on to his arm to stop him. *Trust him?* Everything she'd sacrificed clawed its way to the surface from somewhere deep down where it had been buried for years.

Fear. Apprehension. Doubt. Especially doubt…

The self-assured character she presented to the world shrank back, giving way to the lonely undercover agent. The real her sat alone way too often, questioning every move she made.

What in the world was wrong with her? She'd never hesitated as much as in the past twenty-four hours.

"Oh sssugar!"

Yeah, she'd said it loud enough for everyone around them to hear. She got a confused expression from Wade and had startled the man he'd been watching. The stall cleaner's face changed from surprise to recognition when he concentrated on Wade.

"Well, I'll be a horse's patootie. As I live and breathe. Is that you, Wade? You've kind of filled out." He carefully tipped the pitchfork behind him and spread his arms wide.

"It has been fifteen years, Joey. I remember you as older." Wade walked into the old man's embrace.

"True. Every word, true."

Therese watched in silence and wonder. Wade Hamilton had a past. A real one with…regular people. People who matched the sealed files Rushdan had discovered. The Rangers hadn't built this background. It was real. Wade Hamilton had a sealed juvie record. The fact sort of stunned her. No wonder he'd laughed so hard when she'd said they'd known each other.

"Who's your friend?" Joey asked as the two men separated.

"This is Therese."

She stepped forward to shake his hand but he held it up to stop her.

"Mind your step, Miss Therese. Maybe I should come your direction."

Therese mumbled a "nice to meet you" and stayed put just inside the stall's entrance. But as Joey took a step, her new partner reached in front of him, grabbing the pitchfork.

"We should stand over here, out of sight." He quickly moved the horse poo to the far wall, making room for them.

There was a story there. Some bond between the two men that she really wanted to understand. It was a story for another time. Joey was more than just Wade's friend. But her curiosity would have to wait.

"You in trouble again?"

"No, sir, but I have a favor that might bring some your way."

"I heard you'd gotten out of the game, gone straight, were making something of yourself."

There was suddenly a great deal of tension charging the musky air. She sensed Wade respected the older man and wanted to be straight with him. His jaw muscles visibly flexed. But he knew they couldn't. It would put everything at risk…including Joey.

Someone out there had an algorithm that could potentially harm thousands. The organizers they'd caught from the domestic terrorist group Public Exposure had promised a catastrophe would happen in Dallas. That specific threat had been thwarted by capturing the group's FBI contact six weeks ago. Only a copy of the program had been found…not the original or the person who had developed it.

The programmer put the algorithm on the market again. Rushdan Reval was facilitating a new sale to the highest bidder. He claimed this version was more destructive than the original.

If Wade couldn't guarantee a win for one of these races Rushdan wouldn't get the cash he needed to proceed. Or he wouldn't have the leverage he wanted to include Wade in the plan.

Then they'd be back to square one.

"I wish I could explain, sir."

The older man shook his head.

"It's a matter of life and death." She heard the words fly from her lips.

Joey's eyes grew big and round in his weathered face. He shifted from foot to foot, clearly conflicted about lending aid.

She moved closer and took Joey's hand between hers. "Wade says you're the one who can help, I know you can. You probably think I'm exaggerating. I mean, life and death, who even says that? You have absolutely no reason to trust me. Please help us."

God, she hoped he would.

They needed a break.

"I suppose that's a lot of cash in that bag," Joey said.

Wade nodded.

"I hate to ask—"

"To tell the truth I had high hopes for you, son. I thought that lawman straightened you out. I've been on a narrow path of redemption for a while myself."

"This is a bad idea," Wade said flatly.

"I won't tell you the thought hasn't crossed my mind once or twice. Make a killin' and retire on some island paradise. I wouldn't go up against the real mobsters out here. Look at what happened to your old man."

"You're right. It's too dangerous," Wade said. "I don't know what I was thinking. Forget it."

Therese watched the genuine emotion on both

men's faces. The admiration, then sadness in Wade's eyes. The disappointment in Joey's. She wanted to jump in and tell Joey about the good man Wade had become.

Had she been worried about Wade's ability to keep their objective secret? He was about to let this man think the worst possible things about him.

She pressed herself into the stable wall covering her mouth with her hand. It was the only way she could keep herself from blurting out the real reason they were there.

"Well, I can't rightly do that," Joey pushed his hat off his forehead and smiled. "Thankfully, no one will be expecting me to rig anything."

He walked to the stall door and stuck his head out, looking both directions.

"You'll help us?" she asked, surprised by the man's agreement.

"Rightly so, little lady. I should have helped this boy when he was twelve and didn't. No way am I standing around like a wallflower again." He shut the door behind him as he spoke, enclosing them in the tight space. He sniffed a little—not at the smell but wiped away the sign of a tear—before cupping Wade's shoulder in a manly acknowledgment.

Joey claimed to be an upstanding citizen, but he knew exactly which jockey or horse owner was open to accepting a bribe. In a few short sentences he laid it all out for Wade. It was a shorthand she couldn't completely follow, but something Wade had no problem deciphering.

After accepting a couple of stacks of the cash to bribe the jockey, Joey pushed them both out of the stall.

"I'll send note when everything's set. You know it'll be best if I disappear for a while 'til things are cleared up."

"Take this," Wade said trying to give Joey another stack of cash.

"No thanks. Favors don't come with price tags. Come back around when all the dust settles. Don't be a stranger." He patted them both on the back before he swaggered bowlegged past the other open stalls.

Wade took her hand in his and led them in the opposite direction.

"That's it?"

"Yeah. Well, we still have to place some bets. And I know right where to find the people we need."

"I bet you do." She had a long stride, but she practically ran to keep up with Wade. "You weren't kidding when you said you've done this before. If I didn't know better, I'd say you have real-life experience as a gambler. You have the lingo down perfect. No wonder they established your background so quickly."

Was that what Rushdan had been hinting at? Did Wade have some sort of juvie record? Joey had spoken of letting Wade down when he was twelve.

"Therese, if we had more time I'd explain. But we don't."

"I know. I know. I'll have to *trust* you."

Her words didn't get any reaction. They reached

a corner close to where the crowds clamored around and he dropped the bag on her shoulder.

"Stay back where those two hallways meet, out of the line of cameras. I'll be sending several people to you. They'll all say I did. You give them a couple of grand each."

"Tell me one thing that's personal—and relevant—and I promise not to bombard you with questions of how this is possibly going to work."

She swore his eyes rolled as he tipped his white felt hat to the crown of his head.

"One thing." He held up his index finger before leaning in close next to her ear. "It's true. My father was a gambler and con artist. He was in jail several years and I put him there when I was fifteen."

He pivoted and hurried away before she could draw breath to whisper, "Wow."

The bundles of cash weren't in stacks of thousands, so she darted into the closest family restroom and locked the door. She counted quickly, not allowing herself to think about a fifteen-year-old Wade turning his father in to the police.

Of course she thought about it. But she got the money ready and took her place to wait. Several minutes passed before the first person stood next to her against the wall and said, "Wade sent me."

Nine men and women stopped next to her and inconspicuously flattened their palm to collect the money just out of view of the cameras monitoring everything. She gave it to them without questions or even direct eye contact.

"Well, lookie here." Sal stepped from around the corner. "You're finally showing up and you still got the money? What the hell are you playing at? You're going to get us both killed."

He reached for the almost empty bag but she twisted the strap around her wrist. If he pulled at it, he'd make a scene.

"We've got it under control." Her calm, confident voice didn't reflect her jumping insides. She tried to see past Sal but he blocked her view of the main area where Wade and the people he'd been sending were located.

Sal turned quickly, pinning her to the wall, his finger poking deep into the fleshy part of her shoulder.

"I've never understood why the boss keeps you around. You ain't smarter than any of the rest of us. Just remember that this cop's severed head rests on your shoulders. Totally your fault when he disappears."

She let him poke her. Let him push her back into the wall until her bare skin pinched. Let him get in her face without loosening her grip on the bag. She stood firm, raising her chin a little more defiantly while staring into his watery, sad eyes and smelling his bad breath.

Whatever doubt had been tugging at her brain had fled. She was once again in the moment and remembering that she *had* done this job alone for a very long time. Wade might have the upper hand on fixing a horse race but she could navigate Rushdan's men.

An arm dropped across Sal's shoulders. He im-

mediately stepped back but he couldn't free himself
from Wade's embrace.

"Funny seeing you here, Sal. Checking up on us?"

Sal ducked his head, slipping from Wade's grip.
"Man, you don't know who you're messin' with!"

"Calm down, Sal." Wade shifted his weight, draping his arm around her shoulders. "Babe, this is my
buddy, Dale Beauchamp. He'll be taking that bag
off our hands. Don't worry. He also placed our bet
for us."

She didn't want to give Sal any reason to report to
Rushdan that something was wrong. She swallowed
her nerves—the ones that increased her breathing
each time Wade stood next to her.

The strap of the bag slid off her shoulder and into
the hands of a good-looking man about the same
build and age as Wade. If he was from her partner's
time here as a child she couldn't tell. More likely he
was another part of the rangers' plan that she didn't
know.

Dale eased the bag from her, holding the handle as
he smiled and winked. "See you 'round, Hamilton."

Sal took a step in the same direction. Just one
step before Wade slammed his palm into his chest,
stopping him cold.

"You should hang around for the fun, Sal. Winning big calls for a celebration."

"You better win big, Hamilton. The boss expects
his investment to mature. Keep the phone. Someone
will be in touch." Sal walked away, obviously searching for the direction Dale Beauchamp had gone with

the cash before lifting his hand to hide his face from the cameras.

Therese couldn't believe so much had happened in such a short time. Whatever respect she'd held for the Texas Rangers before, it didn't compare to how high she held them now.

They worked fast. About as fast as she was falling for the strong man beside her.

Chapter Thirteen

Wade saw the security guard passing to Sal's right. He remembered the old familiar rush, felt the adrenaline surge through him again.

"Well, that was easy," Therese said, heading toward the track.

Wade stood there a moment, tamping down the shakiness in his arms and legs. He snapped a picture of Dale walking away, fingers gripped around the bag handle. No one was taking the rest of the money from that Texas Ranger.

How many times had Wade been the handoff, receiving his father's payoff. Or more accurately the winnings of whatever group his dad was fronting for. Wade should make certain Therese understood the truth. He'd confessed haphazardly. He made this operation seem easy because it was second nature to him.

Still. Even after all this time.

Calling upon that cocky kid who carried around thousands of dollars, afraid of nothing, had been too easy.

"Wade? Are you coming? Do we get to watch which horse wins? I mean…we *are* here." Therese asked.

"Sure."

She waited until he stood beside her again. Lacing her fingers through his, she smiled at him as they headed through the crowd, back to the track's rail. They looked like any other couple betting a few bucks on a few horse races. He didn't have to work at keeping her close to his side. He wanted her there.

Dammit. Why had he allowed being here to hit him so hard? He'd controlled the emotions associated with this part of his life for years.

For a couple of panicked minutes he'd actually become that lost fifteen-year-old kid. But he didn't care about the old man who'd taught him to steal and cheat. He didn't. Terrence hadn't been a father to him.

Fred Snell was the only real man who had taken on that role.

Therese tugged on his arm. "Are you feeling sick again? You're looking sort of sick."

He shook his head, dropping his hand on top of hers, gathering warmth for his icy fingers. "I'm good."

"This is so exciting. Even if I know one jockey is—" she dropped her voice so only he could hear through the crowd noise "—you know, going to do whatever to win."

They stood through a couple of races. Each time his sequined companion would turn her face to his and he'd ask her who she'd thought would win. She actually chose one who placed, but not the winner. Then it was time. She asked. He nodded.

Therese didn't need to know specific details. Didn't need to know that the one wearing purple dot silks would send a shock through his horse at the last minute to make it run faster.

The crowd was happy and unworried, waiting for the start of the race as the horses lined up in the gate. The boards reflected great—but not too great—odds for Texas T.

The gates opened and hooves pounded the ground, dirt flew and muscles rippled through the beautiful horseflesh of each mount. Memories of other races rushed through his mind, keeping him silent. Back then he hadn't wanted to draw attention to himself.

Authorities questioned the race when they'd seen him or his father or his father's cronies. It was one of the reasons he'd been so active in delivering money and messages when he was younger, smaller. Then overnight he'd grown tall enough to be spotted.

Then caught.

Therese waved her fingers in front of his nose. "Hey, did we win?"

Damn, it was over? He looked at the board and verified the race results. "Reval will get his money."

"So we're done? I'm sort of confused how we're going to collect the winnings since we didn't place the bets."

"Right." He glanced around. "I don't see anyone

watching us, but it's probably better to have this conversation when no one can overhear."

They'd barely closed the car doors when the phone Sal gave them buzzed inside his back pocket. He pushed the speaker button in time to hear "Money. Mustangs. Las Colinas Boulevard. One hour."

"That's not going to happen. It'll take my guy twenty-four hours to get the cash together for that sum." For the Rangers or Homeland or some other government bureaucracy.

"That wasn't what you were supposed to do," Sal screamed.

"Oh yeah? Neither was going to jail, which is what would have happened if I'd bet that much cash. But that was the real test, right?"

"What?" Therese mouthed.

He waved her off, pointing to the phone. Waiting for a response from Reval's crony.

"Keep the phone handy. The boss will be in touch." The call blinked with a disconnection.

Eyes forward, Therese started the engine, put the car in gear and spun the tires a little as she pulled from the lot full of horse trailers and trucks. He'd read about people's knuckles turning white as they gripped the steering wheel. Therese had a death grip on the plastic and it was hard to miss.

She also wove in and out of traffic like a racing pro. Otherwise anyone watching wouldn't be able to tell she was upset. Her expression was...expressionless. The beautiful smile he'd grown accustomed to in such a short time in just twenty-four hours...

That smile hadn't been there since they'd gotten inside the car.

They seemed to be headed toward her apartment when the route changed, and two turns later they were close to his house. How did she know where he lived? A few minutes later, screeching to a halt, she threw the car into Park and smashed the door unlock button.

"I take it that's my cue," he opened the door, still wondering what he'd said or hadn't said as he stepped out.

"Wade?"

"Therese," he said, leaning to look inside.

She held her palm out and gestured for him to hand something over. "Leave the phone."

"We're not waiting together? Inside?"

She flipped her fingers again and he complied, handing over the phone.

"I'll be in touch." She revved the engine, waiting.

"Dammit, Therese. What did I do?" Had he pushed the "I know what I'm doing bit" too far? He could concede that he had. He'd tell her that if he knew they weren't being watched. Watched by either side—Reval's men or the rangers. "Come on inside and I'll explain."

"Don't try to smooth this over by throwing me your all-innocent look. It sounds petty when I say this is my operation. But dammit, Wade, it is. You can't unilaterally make decisions and think I'm okay with it. I'm not. My supervisors won't be. This is way too complicated. There's more at risk than just bringing Rushdan Reval to his knees."

THERESE WANTED TO peel out. Wanted to leave him standing curbside with that complete look of bewilderment on his face. But she couldn't. He'd made sure that they were tied together waiting for the operation's next move.

"You seriously don't get it?"

"What?" he asked, shrugging his sturdy shoulders up into his neck. "Come inside and let's…talk."

Right. Like talking was what he'd want to do if they were alone. Sure, she wanted answers. More than just one at a time from their little game. But more important, she had to make him understand how critical this assignment was. Its completion was her way back. Back to a normal life. Back to friends. Back home.

"We could continue the Q and A you began this morning. The place is clean. No bugs—at least electronic ones—so, it's safe to talk," he said in a persuasive tone. But he didn't look too thrilled about another round of talking. He shut the car door and ambled across his lawn anyway. Yeah, she'd just thought he "ambled" across his lawn.

Must be his boots.

Wade wasn't like any man she'd dealt with. Granted, most of the men in her adult life had been criminals—were criminals. Then again, it turned out Wade had been, too.

So she followed.

Once inside, she took in the sparse surroundings as he set his hat on the rack near the door. She'd seen bachelor apartments with little furnishings before, but this was worse. There was a leather-looking recliner and a television wider than she was tall in the living room. A folding table with four folding chairs was near the kitchen.

"The first thing people ask is if I just moved in. Answer is no. I just don't need a lot of stuff. I only have the house for a tax break."

"Accumulating things takes time. You haven't even been here two years." He raised a questioning eyebrow and she realized her mistake. She shouldn't know that information.

"Speaking of where I live…how did you know? You drove straight here without my directions."

She fingered the closed blinds and peered between them to see if anyone was on the street. No one looked suspicious. A couple of men walked casually behind their self-propelled mowers on a Saturday afternoon, but no one else hung around.

"Oh, I keep tabs on people who owe me favors." That answer would have to do. But she needed to tell him how she really knew. Soon, but not now. She was still a little upset. "You aren't going to change the subject. I think you already know what I'm going to ask."

"Maybe. But why don't you ask anyway?" He brought one of the folding chairs from the kitchen and gestured for her to take the recliner. "We can go back and forth again like when you were sitting on my lap. That was fun."

Wade's tone was sort of casual, but she saw the curiosity in his eyes. She also didn't believe for a minute that it was the questions he found fun—maybe the sitting together. He was willing to share, but he wanted to know something. The look tempted her to spill everything before he could ask. But she had her own agenda and would have to take her chances.

"The world of gambling is more than familiar to you."

"That isn't a question, but the answer is yes. What I said at the track is true. Not a cover story."

His confession should have shocked her. But it fit him. Part of his charm was the way he talked people into situations. All three of the men he worked closely with had fallen for it. Shoot, she had fallen. It was why they were in this mess together.

"Like I said, I was raised by a gambler, a con man," he continued. "A bad one. A cheat. One who got caught. And caught often. Both by the law and the people he stole from."

Of all the things she'd imagined about him when she was younger or after he'd come back into her life again, the possibility of him being the son of a con artist had never ventured onto the radar. She had a thousand questions, but she sat silently and let him talk.

"When he wasn't picked up by the cops, we lived in cheap motels or crashed with one of his girlfriends. I wasn't much different. Not from him or the men who cheated him. That is, with the exception that when I got caught, I turned in my old man to stay out of jail. What does that make me?"

"Smart," she said without hesitation. "How did you get away?"

"From jail or the life?" He flipped the chair around and crossed his arms over the back. "An investigation that involved the state of Texas and a ranger who didn't give up. On anyone. Even me."

He looked relaxed now. Not ill like at the track, not anxious. Just comfortable.

"So that's why you applied to be a Texas Ranger?" It all made sense. "And that's how you got into law enforcement. Because the ranger who put your father in jail had your record sealed and raised you?"

He shook his head. "No." He sprang up and took down the only picture hanging on any wall.

"This is Fred and his wife, Faye." He tapped the people in the photo before handing it to her. "Somewhere they found money to send me to boarding school. It straightened me out. Changed that resentful fifteen-year-old kid to a man who wanted more. And yes, he wrote a letter of recommendation when I told him I wanted to make up for my misspent youth."

"That explains so much about you. Not this house, mind you." She looked around at all the space. "I still don't get why you don't have a couch."

"Are you going to tell me how you knew I lived here?" He'd sat backward on the chair again and tapped his fingers on his forearm, seemingly counting off the seconds until it was his turn to interrogate her.

"One more thing. Explain what happened at the track. Where's the money?" She'd almost been distracted enough to completely forget that she'd been upset regarding him taking over.

"Oh, yeah. Sorry I couldn't really explain everything when it was happening. But there was no way we could rig the race and actually collect that money."

"I wondered about that. So Dale Beauchamp works with you?"

"Yes. If Reval asks, we can say that we sort of cleaned the cash by placing the bet outside of the law's eyes. Sort of like structuring money or exchanging it for money orders, keeping the limits under ten grand. You know the routine."

"I'm halfway glad I don't. I'll trust you that the next time he asks for the money your associates will have it ready. But the last part... What makes you think they were trying to get us caught?"

"There would be an awful lot of questions if we placed a large bet—in cash—and then we won. So that had to be the real test. If we placed the bet and *didn't* get thrown in jail or at least detained, Reval would have known I'm undercover."

"Next time fill me in on the details. You took a risk that could have blown more than three years of my life."

"Promise." He stood, moved in front of her chair

and extended his hands. "This trust thing works both ways, you know."

She shamelessly placed her hands in his, letting him pull her to her feet. "Obviously I just proved that I trusted you by letting you take the lead at the track."

A good, solid answer. One that should deflect her earlier mistake about knowing where he lived. God, being in his arms sent shivers throughout her body. It was mind-blowing how primitively she reacted when he touched her.

He encircled her and tilted his head like he was about to kiss her, then raised it. This kiss might actually get them to the only real piece of furniture in the house...the bed.

Soft lips barely touched the sensitive skin where her neck met her shoulder. His teeth grazed her on the way to her earlobe. Then he stopped and so did the sizzle.

It was about to get real. Very real if he circled back to how she'd driven straight here without directions.

"Why do I have the feeling you know more about me than I do you?" he whispered. "Is Therese Ortis even your real name?"

Chapter Fourteen

Wade kept Therese close to him. He raised his head only long enough to ask his question. When she stiffened in his arms, he put his lips to work. Maybe the attempt to break through her resistance could be approached a different way. The direct questioning route sure wasn't working.

"My real name is Therese Maria Elisabeth Ortis. Born and raised in San Antonio." She stretched her neck back, giving him more access.

Wanting answers, but also wanting more of her bare skin against him, he continued his lips' quest across her shoulder.

"Is this going to be that back-and-forth thing you started? Am I supposed to admit something now?" He kept his words low and in between each nip along her skin.

"If you…want to," she said, sounding out of breath.

"You don't sound mad anymore."

"Concerned. I was…"

His fingertips found the edge of her shirt and

quickly shot underneath, taking in her smooth skin, pressing her breasts even closer to his chest.

"I think—" he planted his lips in the curve of her neck again "—that I—"

He raked the edge of his teeth up to her ear, following it with circles on her back.

Therese shivered against him.

Who the hell was he kidding? His actions weren't an interrogation—as if he ever thought they could be. He wanted her. She knew the truth about his history and still wanted him, too.

Dammit, he'd never felt like this. Open. Real. Excited about what came next. He drew back, staring at her beautiful face, waiting for her eyes to open and acknowledge the real him.

God, he'd turned into a sap. That was what nearly a year of desk duty and seeing his best friends find the women they love had done.

Therese opened her eyes. He waited for her to kiss him or at least expose her neck for him to take up his teasing again.

"Is this a good idea?" she asked instead.

"Getting to...um...know each other?" He slid his fingertips over the clasp of her bra. "Honestly, I think it's been a little one-sided."

Smiling, she drug a fingernail across his neck, then up and around the edge of his ear. His muscles tensed.

"You know that's not what I meant."

"I think you're assuming I can still think." He

lifted her off the floor, letting her body mold against him. "I am a man, you know."

Wade flexed his jaw along with other muscles as he tried to let Therese down. Her arms were around his shoulders, but she moved, resting more against him. She reached up to stroke his temple gently. He couldn't let her go.

"I think you're right about the talking. Let's chat with our bodies."

He was at a crossroads. The do-or-don't sign flashed on and off, on and off. One decision would keep him in a perpetual teasing state and the other led to sweet relief. But along with that relief came a commitment he'd never made or wanted before.

The pledge was right there, ready for him. The weight of Therese in his arms was less than the weight of that promise he wanted. Yeah, he wanted it all. Relief, connection, possible love.

Hell's bells, he had a beautiful woman in his arms and he was thinking about tomorrow. And the next day.

He shifted to keep her next to him, but with a little pop off the ground she lifted herself, wrapping her legs around him, and he kept her there. The movement hiked the small stretchy skirt she'd worn to the racetrack higher on her thighs. Closer to his face, she smiled before kissing him—winding her tongue around his.

Two seconds. That was all it took to make every bit of him rock-hard for her. It was like she'd read his thoughts and given her answer.

He was no longer questioning if he should or shouldn't. She'd made the decision when she settled her practically naked bottom against the skin of his forearm.

Wanting the bedroom, he stepped in its direction, but the lounge chair was closer. He got near and plopped his backside down, sinking into the leather. Therese stayed as close as possible until she shimmied onto her knees, placing them on either side of his thighs.

"Help me with this," she said, then laughed when she met his eyes.

He probably looked like a man who hadn't thought the chair all the way through. She continued to work at the zipper of her skirt, tugging, her arms behind her, thrusting her soft breasts closer to his face.

A man could only take so much cleavage that close before he had to…

Wade got out of the chair as fast as possible with Therese precariously balancing on his chest. Somehow in his rush, he scooped Therese into his arms instead of splaying her on the carpet. He bolted down the hallway, ready to drop her on the bed and devour every morsel of her delicious skin.

All of it. Every last inch of her.

"This is not good," he said stepping foot into the room.

With her arms around his neck, she burst out in a full-blown laugh. Her head dangled back, enticing him with more skin and sparkling eyes.

"I'm assuming there isn't a bed in the spare room with no clothes on top?"

Normally stacked inside his dresser, his clothes looked like they had all been upturned onto the unmade bed. *Jack.* "I don't keep it this way. Really."

"It doesn't matter."

"Jack or one of the other rangers grabbed stuff to leave at your place." He set Therese on her feet.

"It looks more like they took revenge on you for some reason." She spun around. "Unzip that, will you? I think there's a hook at the waistband."

He obliged and was mesmerized at how she gave the material a tug and it fell to her feet. She bent at the waist and picked it up, showing her heart-shaped derriere framed by a couple of strips of lace.

She folded her skirt and set it on the dresser next to his phone charging station. He watched her in the mirror as she crossed her arms and pulled off the matching top. Again he stared as she folded it and placed it with the skirt.

Wade took in her golden skin, the pale color of her lacy bra—even the tiny bows between her cleavage and on each side of her hips.

Therese cleared her throat, "The sooner we get this stuff put away, the sooner we can…get back to where we were. Unless you'd rather go back to the chair."

No chair. He shook his head.

But there was also no way he would wait until things were back where they belonged. No way.

He took giant steps to the end of the bed, pulled

the side of the blanket up and over the clothes and yanked until everything was on the floor.

"That's one way to take care of things."

He had his shirt over his head before she finished speaking. The belt followed while he toed off his boots. Yeah, everything landed on top of the mass of blanket and clothes. He didn't care.

The three triangles of lace beckoned. Teasing. Testing his limits of control. Ripping them off might be considered too…too something rude. His brain wasn't working, so it was probably true.

Man, did he want underneath those triangles.

Chapter Fifteen

Wade reached out, grabbing her hand as he jumped onto the bed, pulling Therese down with him. She giggled like a teenager. Maybe more like a nervous college girl. But she wasn't nervous.

Wade was just…fun. Their circumstances aside, she loved being with him.

He drew her next to him on top of the cool sheets. One arm under her head, the other under his own. She stared at the ceiling fan, spinning and cooling her skin.

Suddenly feeling awkward and not nearly as brave as when she'd disrobed, she tried to cover some of her midriff. But she wasn't going there. She would be bold and decisive with this man. She threw her arm out, landing on his chest.

Still watching the fan spin its blades in a circle, she drew the same shape across Wade's tanned chest, inching lower.

He drew in a deep breath through his teeth and captured her hand in his. "Whoa, how can you be so chilly?" He rubbed the back of her hand, keeping her fingertips just at the top of his jeans.

"Hey, not fair. There's still a major portion of you covered up." She gave a quick tug on a belt loop.

"Right." He popped up and tugged his jeans and socks off like they were on fire.

Maybe he was. She certainly needed the fan to cool off as he sat on the edge of the bed and slipped out of his boxers. The slight darkening of bruises from where he'd been hit by Rushdan's men almost brought her back to reality.

But instead she lay back on the bed on her elbows, watching him. Then he joined her, tangling their bodies together. She marveled at his warm, naked flesh touching every inch of hers.

The warmth soon became volcanic heat as he used all of himself—skin, hands and mouth—to touch most of her. Her cursed underwear was still between them.

"Did you answer your question?" he said before another round of strokes across her good lace bra.

"What?" she barely got out.

"About whether this is a good idea or not." He kissed his way to her belly button.

It is a super good idea. She enjoyed every second of his attention and wanted to be serious. But she laughed. Partly because his fingers slightly tickled and partly because he just made her feel good.

"Yes, my...my own question." *Oh, man.* How could she still think, let alone speak, with what he was accomplishing?

Wade kissed and explored and didn't ask any more questions. Her entire body shattered with reaction and kept her from thinking. Feeling became everything. The man used his hands—belly, hips, top of the lace, sides, bottom, then back to repeat. When his thumbs hooked the edges of the lace across her breasts, she clapped her hands over his to keep them still.

He paused until she slid her hands up his forearms. Then he gently raised her until his teeth could tease her nipples through the lace. Again and again he kissed, nipped and laved. Until...

"Enough!" she shouted, her voice bouncing off the ceiling and four walls. "Enough."

She pushed at Wade's shoulders, rolling him to his back. Sitting up, she bent her arms behind her back and unlatched the device she'd forever remember as being pure torture. She looked back at her partner, hoping she hadn't hurt his feelings.

Wade shamelessly grinned as her bra uncupped her breasts and fell to the bed.

"You did that deliberately." She quickly moved, shoving him deeper into the mattress, then sat across his lap and pinned him to the bed. Her intention had been to tickle him until he begged for mercy but that plan soon changed as they both realized where she was now located.

Wade's laughter became a raspy, long release of breath. His hands reached for her breasts but she leaned back, pushing their bodies closer together.

Then he sucked in a breath, holding it while she controlled their movements.

She allowed his thumbs to trace the remaining lace outline, closing her eyes before they gave away all the emotion she attempted to regulate. His breathing quickened as his hands skidded to her waist. She opened her eyes, seeing his closed as he spread his hands over her hips, pulling her down as his hips thrust upward.

She couldn't believe she was about to climax and technically they hadn't done... Well, technically. His jaw clenched as he kept them together but separate. Her hands slid across his chest, allowing her body to melt into his.

Then she exploded. An outburst that demanded all her energy and concentration. Wade used his body to keep her erupting. Weak with emotion, she collapsed onto his chest.

Wanting the same feeling for him, she pushed her panties aside, but he grabbed her hands, lacing his fingers through hers.

"Wait," he rasped. "We need...on the left."

How he kept his wits about him she'd never know. They needed protection. She rolled off him and scrambled to reach the nightstand. Wade didn't move. His breathing was still ragged or very controlled.

It was her turn to grin.

And drive him wild.

Already so close, she wondered just how long he'd last if she... She didn't need to think it through. Just do it.

She rolled the condom into place and stretched a leg across his, almost back where she'd enjoyed such tremendous pleasure. But she slid onto his thighs, teasing his belly with her fingers. Letting her long hair fall and caress until he swooped it into one hand and held one finger silently out to stop her.

"Therese," he pleaded in a whisper. "Forgive me."

Feeling and emotion rushed over her as Wade flipped her onto her back and they were one in an instant. But it wasn't over. Not for a while.

Wade had asked for forgiveness, but he didn't seem to be in a hurry. His body tensed and pulsed over her, around her, in her. She'd only thought she'd experienced pleasure minutes before.

Again and again he moved until they both reached a place she'd rarely been. They both stilled after one long appreciative kiss.

It was wonderful. Something she'd hold close to her soul for a very long time. She drifted off with the sweet thought of a lifetime of possibilities.

When she awoke, the room had gone from bright afternoon to a shadowy dusk. They'd slept for the past hour. She'd lay there watching the same fan turn in circles, attempting not to truly think about what she wanted. Or how much she hoped the assignment with Rushdan Reval would soon be over.

"Wade?" Therese gently shook his shoulder. "We should probably get up."

"Did you fall asleep?" he mumbled from his pillow.

"A bit. Too much on my mind."

Instead of getting up, Wade lifted her arm, rolled to his stomach and laid his head on her shoulder. He had a perfect view of her breasts, but his eyes had closed again. To his credit, the man was running on less than a couple of hours' sleep.

"My God, is today only Saturday?" she asked.

"Mmm," he sort of agreed. "You hungry?"

"Starving."

"I say we clean up and order some Italian. You like pasta? You aren't afraid of some carbs, are you?"

"I love carbs and I love Italian."

"Nice." He moved his free hand next to her head and played with her hair, bringing it across his face. "God, you smell good. Makes me hungry all over again."

"That's wonderful to hear. I thought I smelled like horses."

"Nope. Like peach ice cream."

"That's my shampoo. Peaches and cream."

His movements stopped and his breathing evened out as he fell back to sleep. Minutes passed and she gently freed her hair and tried to slide from under Wade.

"I'm awake," he said, lifting his head, but quickly dropped it again to her chest along with a quick kiss. "I'll see if Heath can pick up from Mariano's around the corner. He needs to take a look at the phone Sal gave us."

"I should probably get up, then." She tried once again to slide free from Wade's weight.

He moved quickly, placing a hand on either side of

her body and moving his over her completely. "You sure you're hungry?"

He lowered his mouth to hers, tangling their tongues as he tangled their legs. They kissed deeply, continuously as their bodies moved in an age-old rhythm again.

There was so much to talk about, so much to plan, to discover. But it could wait. She'd waited long enough for this human contact…however much he could give her, for however long.

Whatever happened between them, she could only hope it happened again and again.

Chapter Sixteen

Something had changed. Wade had a lump in his gut that had nothing to do with eating. The pasta he'd ordered for dinner had been fine. But somehow, something had changed.

He cared.

Before this afternoon, he had taken a beating to keep her safe. But now... The protectiveness that overwhelmed him could become a problem later on. Hell, he'd already gotten *the look* from Heath.

Heath had played the part of delivery boy. Italian food along with the necessary equipment to clone the burner phone Sal had given them. Not to mention his opinion about the unprecedented interagency cooperation he'd been observing.

But no one had any new information to clue them in on what Rushdan Reval, Public Exposure or another buyer would actually do with the algorithm. Everyone was still in the dark. By cloning the phone, the FBI, Homeland and the Texas Rangers could listen in and get up-to-the-minute knowledge about their movements and any instructions Reval sent.

The time frame Sal had originally set had long come and gone. The phone they'd been given sat between them on a TV tray. Every few minutes, Therese would pick it up, turn the screen on and then set it back down. No messages. No calls.

After Heath left, Wade tried to open his mouth a couple of times to ask what was wrong. Because things between them seemed awkward now. There were lots of reasons he should ask and one big one why he shouldn't. They were on the job. They couldn't afford to become any more distracted than they already were.

Right. No distractions.

Like watching her flip her hair off her shoulder or wanting to wrap the stray strand around his finger or use it to pull her to him for a kiss.

Therese was a helluva distraction. His mind was completely occupied by finding reasons not to take her back to bed. A great idea, but it had to wait until they no longer had to deal with Reval. Or find an algorithm before a domestic terrorist group bought it. An algorithm no one could speculate how dangerous it had become.

At least he hadn't thought about it. He hadn't had time. Since meeting up with Therese the day before, his sole focus had been making it through the next hour.

"What do you think this algorithm has morphed into?" he asked breaking the silence. "Six weeks ago it supposedly could take down an electrical grid."

"Chaos is the word most bandied about on the dark web."

"Chaos on what?"

"People paid a lot more than me only have theories. Most center around reasons terrorists would want a complicated algorithm. We interviewed all the members of Public Exposure without getting any closer. None of them knew specifics and their leader wasn't talking."

"Reval is just the go-between guy?" he asked.

She shook her head. "When he went to jail, I thought my undercover days were done. But I hung around Reval's organization tying up loose ends. Then you guys arrested the leader of Public Exposure six weeks ago. Word got out that the creator of the algorithm was looking for a new buyer. Reval wasn't involved before that."

"Then why is he now?"

"Since I was officially still a part of Reval's group they already had eyes on him. The FBI released him, hoping he could broker a deal. Homeland pushed the potential buyers in his direction by arresting others." She shrugged. "I haven't had any luck discovering details of the sale or exactly what the algorithm is capable of now that the programmer has upgraded it. Rushdan is keeping it very close to his fat chest."

"You think whatever reason he needs me will give you answers."

"Fingers crossed." She made the gesture with both hands. "The team has checked out all his known contacts. All dead ends."

"Does the computer guy who got my juvie records have something to do with it? How do we track him down?"

"We don't."

"What do you mean? It should be easy enough to find the info in Reval's office. Don't you have a warrant for his phone records? Together we should be able to find something written down."

"That's not our job." She gave a little shrug of acceptance—not anxious to explain.

"Wait a minute." He had to be misunderstanding. What the hell was their job if not to put Reval behind bars...for good.

"The team has checked out all his known contacts. All dead ends. Finding who has developed the algorithm is my objective. My primary goal. It won't matter if we stop whatever show they have planned for Dallas if we can't find the programmer."

"Show?"

"That's what they've called it recently. I've overheard Rushdan refer to it that way. The team is certain it's Rushdan's term for the terrorist attack."

"On Dallas? Do the rangers know about this? Local police?"

"I'm not certain. Prevention and cleanup aren't my jobs." She reached for the burner phone, checking it again.

"Wait...what?" He shook his head, unable to clearly comprehend what she'd just said. "What exactly is our job then? I thought we were taking down

Reval's organization and preventing the algorithm from being used."

"I tried to tell you this before, Wade. Sure, I want to put Rushdan Reval behind bars. But they may let his petty crimes go in exchange for the algorithm tech and developer."

"Petty? Rushdan's crime activities are no longer involved just locally. And attempting to kill me or others isn't what I'd call petty."

"You know what I mean. He's only a means for me to find the algorithm and the programmer. That's my objective. I have to find the person who created it. Hopefully before it's disbursed or sold."

The use of her singular "I" throughout her explanation didn't escape him. It stung like nothing he'd experienced before. She'd been in big trouble with Reval's men before she'd cozied up next to him at the bar.

Things like accomplishment credit usually rolled right off his back. Especially since he'd been sitting behind a desk while his fellow rangers had been stopping a serial killer, uncovering subversive FBI plots and keeping state analysts alive—a favor to this woman that had nearly gotten him killed.

Teamwork had resolved those cases and he'd been a part of getting the job done. Just like teamwork had gotten them farther along in this particular case. Or at least he'd thought it had. Dammit, were his feelings hurt? Or his ego?

Whatever it was, he had to let it go.

"I heard you say you were after the algorithm. I

kind of thought that's what I was helping with. One good break and we could grab Reval before he sells anything. Stop the terrorist group before they get started."

"That might not happen." Therese checked the phone, then moved to the window. "You need to get used to that idea."

"I get it. You've been at this a long time and it's hard to accept that you've needed help or that someone might have a different way of doing things."

She squinted in confusion. "*I* needed help? Hard for *me* to accept? Oh, really?" She crossed her arms and pressed her lips together into a straight line.

Damn.

"I just meant that working with me—with the Texas Rangers—might accelerate things a little. And plans might change."

"And you think I don't want to what? Share the credit? Stop acting like a bimbo? Stop having Rushdan or his men leer, touch and pinch me?"

"I didn't mean it like that."

"Oh, I see. Then you think I *like* being undercover. Or maybe I'm afraid to explain to my family exactly what's been going on so they might speak to me again? Or stop wondering if they'll be proud of me for what I've done over the past three years instead of thinking that I cheated on my police academy exam?"

"That's rough. I had no idea your family didn't know." His sympathetic thoughts slipped out. Then he witnessed a reaction that he was familiar with but hadn't seen. The feelings he'd had for so many of the early years with Fred rippled across Therese's face.

"I don't need you to feel sorry for me. This is a job."

"Right. Just a job." He hoped she meant the operation and not what had happened in the other room. For him the other room had been life changing and it was hard to focus on *just the job*.

She backed up and rested on the arm of his lounger but at least her arms weren't crossed in anger. "The FBI and Homeland are after the big fish, Wade. Some of the little ones will be thrown back."

"Meaning, they're already prepared to offer Reval a deal like the last time. Like the jail time he didn't serve for ordering his men to kill me."

"I don't have anything to do with the decision-making. Neither do you."

"Why not arrest him and make him cough up the programmer now? Why are we going through the motions?"

"We did that six weeks ago. The men who call the shots are prepared for the consequences."

"Even if innocent civilians get caught in whatever *show*—" he air-quoted the word to remind her what they were calling a terrorist plot "—Reval's customers are planning?"

"Can you drop this now? As a favor to me."

His hand flew to the pounding pulse in his temple, right above his injured eye. "Another favor? I'm not sure I can afford to. If you kept tabs on me like you said, you'd know how much your favors cost me."

Except no one knew about his loss of vision. Not even the doctors knew how much his peripheral was actually gone because he'd never been back to check. He was afraid they'd bench him. So he'd kept the loss to himself.

"I'm very aware of what happened. And I know how frustrating it must be to hear this. But you have to try to see the big picture. The algorithm is more important than you or me."

"I don't get it, Therese. Why can't the aim be to get both?"

The phone rang as Therese shook her head.

"Preventing a national emergency doesn't take into consideration our personal preferences. I just wanted to warn you that Rushdan Reval might make a deal."

Wade watched Therese click the speaker button knowing they hadn't left their debate in a good place.

"He wants you at his club. Now," Sal's voice boomed through the little cell.

"Wade's proven he knows what he's doing, Sal. Give the phone to Rushdan." Therese had shifted to that bimbo-like tone, coaxing men to comply. "Come on, Rushy, I know you're listening."

"Get here within the hour, Therese," the greedy, double-chinned slob answered. "I have a job for you. Leave the phone with your new boyfriend. We're moving forward."

"But we don't have the money yet. Don't you need me to bring that to you?" Therese asked.

"The money doesn't matter. It never mattered

other than I like to have an abundance. I had to make sure Ranger Wade was sincere and didn't hold any grudge for the boys trying to dispose of him last year."

"Then I'll keep it." Wade threw in to let the man know he'd been listening. "That will just about get the guys I owe off my back."

"Probably. But you still need to earn it." Reval made a disgusting sound, like slurping through his teeth.

"No more tests, please. It's too risky, Rushy. Can't you just tell us what you need?" Therese coaxed.

Listening, someone might get the impression she actually believed those words. But watching her, Wade could see that her body language showed she hated saying them. She was good. Really good at what she did. But what was she up to?

"We ran to the track for you. Then we've been sitting here so long just waiting. There's only so much golf a girl can watch. I got things to do, Rush baby. You don't pay me to be a babysitter," Therese complained.

"Funny you should mention that, Therese. I have another chore for you. Sal will pick you up at the club."

"Is an hour soon enough? I need to swing by my place and change."

Wade stood, searching for a reason he should be going with Therese. They should stay together. Right? Didn't she realize that?

"That'll be fine. And Ranger Wade?" Reval said.

"Yeah?"

"Don't bother following Therese. When I send your instructions they'll be timed from your house. And yes, I know where you live." The phone disconnected.

"What the hell was that?" Wade demanded.

"My job."

"I thought your job was to find the algorithm."

"My job is to do anything Rushdan Reval tells me to do so we'll find the algorithm and programmer."

"You can't go. Not like this." He put his hands out, but she grabbed her purse instead.

"When I'm summoned, I go. That's my role in all this."

"I can call him back, demand that you stay with me. We're a team."

She arched a perfectly shaped eyebrow and pulled her keys from her small purse before hanging the strap across her shoulder. "If there's one thing I've learned being undercover, it's that you're out here on your own. You should get used to it."

She was out the door the next instant. What if that was the last time he saw her? What if she did her disappearing act again? What if Reval…? He yanked the door hard enough to bounce off the wall as he pounced onto the porch.

"Wait!"

By the surprised look on Therese's face, she hadn't thought he'd follow her. But he had—still unsure how to handle their differences and damn sure he didn't want this woman to disappear from his life.

"I took an oath to protect the people of Texas. And I don't take my promises lightly. It's hard for me to let harm come to anyone if I can prevent it. Stop the threat, then find the next. I don't think I can do what you're asking me."

"Don't worry about it, Wade. We aren't really a team but it was fun pretending while it lasted. I'll handle this my way. I can take care of myself." She continued to her car. "Don't forget to watch your back, hon. Since I won't be there to do it."

Smiling at him over the top of the sedan, she opened the door and slid behind the wheel like everything was perfect. Wade watched, completely dumbfounded. Sometime in the last fifteen minutes his heart had been ripped from his chest. There was a big gaping hole making him wonder if it could ever be the same.

Why didn't any of this seem to bother her as much as it bothered him?

Chapter Seventeen

Therese's hands shook so hard she couldn't fit the key in the ignition. She wanted to stay put in her apartment. For the first time, she was actually afraid to face Rushdan. Walking out Wade's door was the second hardest thing she'd ever done. Facing her siblings, aunts, uncles and other family after leaving the San Antonio police academy in disgrace had been the worst.

"I hate this," she shouted as she pounded the steering wheel.

Deciding to be a police officer had cost her all of her friends from high school and college. Being a hot shot at the academy hadn't gotten her any new ones. So leaving them behind for an undercover job had been easy at first. Until the lies became everything her life was based on.

After a while it gets hard to remember there was a different reality.

No one knew the truth except her handler, and that person had changed with each year. Currently it was Steve Woods and Megan who had been in her academy class. None of them really knew the person she'd been before this.

And now Wade. She'd wanted to be truthful with him for a long time. Now he knew. So why did it still feel like she was lying?

What had she expected? Gratitude for all her sacrifice? Maybe empathy or even a big "wow." Any of those would have been better than the stunned silence and pity she'd read on his face.

Dropping her head onto her arms, she wanted to cry. But there wasn't time. She needed to get to Rushdan's club instead of Sal taking her to the office. And only had half an hour to do it.

The end game was in sight and she'd soon be able to put all her own self-pity to rest. She drove quickly to the seedier side of Deep Ellum, close to Second Avenue. The Reveille wasn't the darkest, dankest dive around…but it was close.

Pulling into the gravel parking lot, she noticed several of the street lights were out again. It happened all the time. No big deal, but when she caught the kids throwing rocks at them, they normally received a hefty piece of her mind. That wouldn't be high on her priorities for long.

She glanced at her wrist. Among the many hoop bracelets she'd added to her outfit tonight was a watch. She was on time. Before she patted herself on the back, she noticed movement in the shadows to her left. She had to stay in character, had to ignore Sal and pretend to be oblivious.

Therese forced herself to shrink back when he

finally showed himself. Good grief, she wanted to stand nose-to-nose with Rushdan's go-to man and take him down. Drawing on the desperateness she'd felt earlier, she pushed it to the top of her frayed nerves, faking a little scream.

"Oh my God, Sal. You scared the living daylights out of me."

Whatever Sal was doing, his real intention was to intimidate her, and she had to let him. At least a little. That was her part in all this mess. The end was near. She clung desperately to that.

She looked around for Wade's truck. She hated to confess that she had hoped it would be there. Even as much as she hated involving him the night before, she wanted him there by her side.

Upset, confused. A little scared for what was coming. It all mixed together inside her head, making it hard to think straight. Right. That was it. She didn't need Wade to protect her. But that wasn't the point. It wasn't her need. It was her want, her desire. She wanted Wade nearby and wanted to work with him.

"The boss is waiting inside. You know he don't like to wait." Sal puffed on a cigarette, then tossed it to the ground.

"I got here as quickly as I could. Put that silly thing away." She gestured to the 9mm he had pointed at her. "It might actually go off and hurt someone."

Carefully maneuvering the gravel in three-inch heels, she clicked the alarm on her car and headed to the club. She'd been treating Sal like that since she'd been promoted in Rushdan's organization two years ago.

Blunt force dead center in her back sent her tumbling to her knees. There was no way to stop it. Once on the ground, a booted foot across her shoulder blades kept her there.

Her face had landed on the solid slab of concrete at the club's back entrance instead of the gravel that bit into her flesh. She could feel the sting of scrapes on her knees and the palms of her hands.

Sal pressed his boot into her flesh. The barrel of his handgun pinched the base of her neck.

"You listen real close, bitch. I know something ain't right. You might have the boss wrapped around your finger but you're gonna give me more respect. If ya don't…" He twisted the barrel, tangling the long strands of hair behind her ear. "I'll be explainin' to the boss man how you met with an accident."

"Respect. Got it. May I get up now?"

The vibration through her body thrummed so loud in her ears she was certain Sal could hear it. She'd just thought her hands had been shaking with anger before. Maybe it was good that they physically moved as Sal helped her to her feet. It certainly let him know that he'd scared her.

The heels wobbled under her unsteady legs, forcing her to grab Sal's forearm. She hated to, but it was either that or fall to the gravel a second time. He laughed.

Please let it be me that slaps the cuffs on this waste of skin.

The jerk didn't open the door for her. She hadn't really expected him to, but this time she wrapped her hand around the doorknob and found it locked. Her stomach rolled with uncertainty. She nearly lost it as she bent over to pick up her keys. Sal's smackdown had her spooked.

"What will Rushdan say about this?" she asked, forcing her voice to remain steady and ooze confidence.

Lies and more lies. The barrel against her skin had her more shaken than she liked to admit.

Pull yourself together.

"Go ahead and ask him."

Oh my God. It was last night all over again. And this time, she couldn't run to Wade to save her. She had to face Rushdan and hope there was a reason he wouldn't listen to Sal and allow him to kill her.

Still with a gun pointed at her back, she rounded the corner and saw Rushdan holding court with the young women who served drinks. It was early enough in the evening that the bar wouldn't have very many customers, but she searched the room. The official manager was nowhere in sight.

No other staff. Just the girls. Another glance at the front door and she noticed the bolt.

Sal crossed his arms—gun still in his hand— and planted himself between her and the back exit. No one would get out of the bar unless Rushdan allowed it.

The other women probably didn't realize they were hostages. They were chatting away, fawning over the bar owner, vying for attention or his notice. Hoping they might be the next girl Rushdan brought up the ranks. Someone to be her replacement?

Oh, God. She'd played right into their hands. It wasn't an accident that she'd overheard Rushdan's phone conversation that he needed someone in law enforcement to make sure the show happened. Then the threat had come from the two last night and she'd sailed directly into Wade's arms.

He knew.

She'd been set up. Been used like the pawn she was supposed to be. As much as she hated Rushdan Reval, the man was smart. Now he'd separated them.

Whatever Rushdan needed Wade to do, it was about to happen and she wouldn't be there to make certain it did. Wouldn't be there to make certain Wade chose finding the program and programmer over saving the day. Joining him to follow through on her mission… By the look on Rushdan's face, that wasn't going to happen.

"Sit down, Therese. Join me in a drink."

"What's going on, Rushy?" Her heart raced along with her mind.

"You'll learn soon enough. Get my special phone, Sal." He snapped his fingers like he was summoning a waiter.

The snap brought Therese to focus. Everything she'd been thinking vanished with the look on Rushdan's face. Fury filled his eyes. What had happened?

The right-hand man left through the front door

and a new minion Therese didn't know took his place at the back of the room.

"I thought you needed me for something special."

He stared at her skinned palms she'd placed on top of the table and then he smiled. She slowly drew her hands into her lap to keep his thoughts on the now instead of the previous night. But the two accomplices he'd sent to kill her or chase her into Wade's protection were at the front door.

"You don't think a night out with me is something special, my dear?"

"Of course. But if we're taking over one of your bars for the night, it feels kind of weird to keep all the waitresses around. I can get you whatever you need since I know where it is."

"They're staying." His voice turned dark with an angry vibration. It was one of the rare times she'd seen the horrible man Rushdan Reval actually was erupt to the surface.

"Are they… Rushy, they kind of look like…like hostages."

No. She couldn't let all these women be hurt because of his suspicions.

"They won't be as long as your boyfriend follows through. Right now they're my alibi."

"I could take care of that. You don't really need them."

"Don't test my patience, Therese. Keep everyone in line and you'll all be fine."

The menacing look in his eyes as he'd chimed that they weren't hostages shouted that they actually were. She'd been the only one to see it or it would have scared all the women. It verified one thing she'd known all along. Rushdan wasn't afraid to get rid of them all. Especially if Wade failed.

What if the Texas Ranger followed his conscience or his desire for revenge? What if he told the rangers about whatever Rushdan had planned? There were five souls depending on him and he didn't even know it.

She regretted not talking things through with Wade before she'd left. Her self-righteousness might have just gotten them all killed.

Chapter Eighteen

*Go to the private entrance at Love Field Airport.
You'll be met with instructions.*

Great. Would it be Therese meeting him? Maybe
Sal.

Wade drove past the entrance, searching from his
truck for a possible ambush—nothing in sight, no
one around. The entrance looked normal and deserted for a Saturday night. Deserted might be normal. He didn't know.

He parked across the street, keeping his eyes open
for his backup. He could only assume all the agen-
cies involved in this operation had listened in on the
phone call that gave him the instructions. Major Clements wouldn't send him inside without backup. He
just had to trust it would be there when he needed it.

Two men lurked at the edge of the building shadows. He lifted his hands slightly in the air, waiting
on them to indicate which way he needed to go. One
man he recognized from Reval's office building. The
big guy who'd hit him a couple of times. The other
wore glasses and cradled a laptop in his arms.

Was luck on his side today? Could this be the elusive programmer Therese was so hot to catch? He caught himself cracking a smile and stopped.

"You guys going to tell me what's going on?"

"Should we check him for a wire?" the big guy asked the nerd.

"We don't have time." He began walking to the gate. "Come on. Come on."

"To do what? I haven't been instructed—"

"You just need to get us inside. Then escort us to one of the planes owned by your group," the nerdy guy squeaked.

"Now hold on. You mean a DPS plane? I wouldn't know where the Department of Public Safety keeps part of its fleet. This is a little outside my comfort zone." He needed more information.

"Don't worry, just get us inside."

"Easy for you to say. I need to talk with your boss."

"Mr. Reval isn't available. Just do what you do and get us inside the airport." Rushdan's man pulled up the edge of his shirt, showing the handle of a handgun.

"Is that supposed to intimidate me?" Wade pushed his fingers through his hair, then smoothed it back down. "To get inside, I'll be forced to sign in. That means this is a one-time deal. I think your boss might want to know that."

"Everything's been planned, Hamilton. Just get us through those gates and past the guards," the little nerd demanded.

Wade shrugged. He still didn't have a clue about what would happen. If he had to take down these two, he could. Therese might be angry... Who was he kidding, she'd be furious and that would probably be the end to a relationship that had barely got off the ground. But he couldn't allow these clowns to launch an attack on Dallas.

Right?

With no concrete evidence, he had to play it by ear. Waiting to decide was a logical choice, not just an excuse to try to let it unfold Therese's way. Then why did he feel guilty that he'd be stealing all of Therese's glory?

They approached the gate and Wade took out his badge. The security guard turned out to be an excited kid.

"Evenin'," Wade said, holding his ID up and purposely keeping his fingers over his name. "Mind if we visit our hangar?" Hell, he didn't know if the Rangers had a hangar or not.

The kid pulled out a clipboard. "Not at all. I just need your names." He looked up, pen in hand, ready to write.

"That's the thing. It would be better if we didn't leave the reporters anything to report."

"But I might get into a lot of trouble."

Wade dropped a hand on the kid's shoulder. "I promise after this case breaks open to come back and update your log or talk with your supervisor. I'll be sure to let him know how helpful you were."

"Aw, man, that would be really nice of you. The

hangar's a long way. Do you want to borrow the golf cart?"

"You're all right kid. Thanks," the big guy answered.

"No problem. Here's the key." He took a lanyard from around his neck and held it out.

The big guy snatched it with his thick hands while Wade put his ID away. His two companions got on the front bench, leaving him to sit backward. The big guy took off, pedal to the floor.

"Slow down, Nico. Don't draw attention to us," the nerdy guy insisted.

"That was too easy." What kind of a guard just handed everything over—even young inexperienced ones? "Yeah, way too easy," Wade muttered.

"Just go with the flow, Hamilton." Nico turned to look at him and forgot to steer, sending the cart— and them—swaying back and forth.

Bracing himself between the bars, Wade twisted around to look at the guard's booth. Sure enough, the kid was on the phone, pointing in their direction. *Good for you, kid.* But no luck for him tonight.

"We need to ditch this cart." He could see flashing lights from the opposite end of the airfield. "Ditch it now!"

Nico slammed the cart to a halt, drawing his weapon when his feet hit the ground.

"Put that thing away and get to the side of that hangar."

They ran to the metal hangar wall, Nico pounding into it and making enough noise to wake the dead—

or alert Love Field police—whichever happened first. The nerd panted like he'd run a marathon.

"Take care of those cops," he huffed and puffed through his words, "while we do what we came to do."

Wade couldn't let these guys out of his sight. No way. He had to know what they were implementing with that laptop.

"No." He turned and used both hands to grab the nerd by his shirt collar. "Tell me what you need."

"I can't."

"You should have from the get-go and we wouldn't be in this mess. Now what do you need? What are you trying to do?"

The lights were getting closer. The little man's eyes darted back and forth under his glasses. Nico— the big guy who Wade owed a punch to the gut— tugged at Wade's hands.

"All right. I need to test some software."

"Give it to me. I can get in and out without the two of you slowing me down."

"I… I can't."

"It's either that or we all go to jail. You and Reval should have been upfront about this and I would have come up with a plan. A much better plan." He released the man's collar and backed up. "I should hand you over to the cops and maybe I can talk my way out of this mess."

Nico chambered a round. He made a huge mistake by acting all tough guy and keeping it by Wade's ear. Wade whipped his elbow into Nico's gut, then as Reval's gunman doubled over, Wade shoved a fist into the thug's nose.

Nico dropped his weapon, grabbing his face and moaning.

"Sorry about that, tough guy, but I owed you one." Wade quickly knelt and hid the gun in his boot. "Instructions. Fast. Then get lost. If you're caught by the cops, it's trespassing and Reval can bail you out."

"You can't do this," the nerdy guy said as Wade pulled the laptop from his fingers. "You need my expertise."

"Watch me. Now what do you need?"

With blood smeared across the side of his face, Nico had a recognizable look in his eyes—revenge. But he reached into his pocket and pulled out a folded piece of paper. Nerdy guy watched him, shaking his head from side to side, mumbling something about Wade being not only a cop but a stupid one.

Wade crumpled the paper into his palm and ran. He made it to the corner of the building before looking around. The police cars split in two directions. The men he'd walked through the gate with were nowhere in sight.

Squinting at the paper in the dark shadow of the building, he could see that it was a list for the morons he'd parted ways with. Beginning with meeting him at the west airport gate.

Nerdy guy didn't seem to be the programmer. Wade wasn't lucky—unless he didn't get caught by the police currently circling around every building.

He squatted at the corner and held the note in the edge of the light, barely making out Building Six.

Feeling like he was in a World War II POW movie, he avoided searchlights and the airport police. He finally made it to Building Six and parked himself between the recycling cans and some decorative bushes.

There was no way he had the algorithm on this laptop. The directions said nothing about any kind of attack or uploading any type of file. Waiting for the police searchlights to fade in the distance, he walked up to an unlocked door and went inside the dark office.

"Stay right where you are."

"Don't move."

"Freeze!" Laughter. "You know I've always wanted to say that."

Greeted by three familiar voices…music to his ears. Maybe his luck was holding after all.

Chapter Nineteen

Therese sat at the corner table with the other four women. Regulars came to the door, found it locked and would tap on the window close to her. She could only shrug and smile. She pretended to be just as clueless as to what was going on.

Rushdan had practically admitted that this was his alibi for whatever task he'd sent Wade to complete. So here she sat while he flipped the "special" phone Sal had brought to him. He hadn't used it yet.

It looked like any other cell phone as he dropped it inside his jacket pocket. In fact it was identical to the one he took from another pocket. The special phone could be what he used to contact the programmer. She needed that phone.

"God, I'm hungry. Do you think we could order a pizza, Therese?" Julie Anne asked.

"I'd go in on that," Rachel said.

Therese got up and wove through the empty tables to her boss. "Any chance we could order or have one of the guys pick us up a pizza from around the corner?"

With his back to her, she hadn't noticed he was on the phone.

Rushdan turned on a dime and Therese couldn't avoid the backhand that came along with it. She didn't fake the painful moan that escaped before she had control. The staggering blow was meant to hurt and intimidate. He raised his hand to hit her again but she blocked it.

"I'm not telling you what I want done. If the cops get their grubby paws on that laptop, I'll kill you myself." Rushdan's eyes were huge in his red, puffy face. He looked like he'd pop with the prick of a pin.

If only she had a pin.

Too late she realized that her arm still blocked his second blow. She wasn't supposed to be quick or competent enough to accomplish that. Still rubbing her face where his hand had connected, she tried to drop her arm to her side. It was caught by one of the men she didn't recognize.

"Why are you bothering me, Therese? What did you hope to gain besides irritating me?" Rushdan finally asked before putting his concentration back into his phone.

Therese yanked her arm free. "The girls need a restroom break. And if we're just sitting there, is it okay to order a pizza?"

"I don't have time for this! Your stupid boyfriend can't complete one task I give him. First the money and now this! I expected something. But this is outrageous. Get him on the phone. Now. Immediately."

Rushdan paced the length of the bar. Therese had

never seen him frantic, ranting as he tossed his regular phone to one of the guys to dial. His plans must have gone wrong.

Her mind had been working on a way she could keep her cover if Wade stormed the bar and arrested everyone. He must have somehow stopped the attack. Why would Rushdan look so confused if everything had gone well?

Wade was willing to blow everything—including her cover—to bring down Rushdan. She had to be ready.

"Is there anything I can do to help?" she asked timidly while taking steps away from Rushdan.

"Get me a good shot of whiskey. The stuff that's behind the bar is terrible." It might be watered down, but Rushdan still finished what was in his tumbler.

"I'll need to go in the back for the good stuff."

Rushdan tossed his chin up, essentially giving her permission to walk around Sal. Therese tried to remain confident as she passed him in the narrow hallway that held the restrooms. But Sal stayed where he was as she entered the storeroom and secured the boss man's whiskey.

Wait. If Rushdan knew she and Wade were undercover—wasn't that the reason he was treating her this way? Then why would he be confused if Wade hadn't completed his assignment? Good grief. Wade hadn't thrown her assignment away... he'd completed it. That had to be the reason Rushdan was confused.

Wade had followed through.

She felt the outline of her phone in her trouser pocket and was tempted to call Wade. Tempted, but something didn't feel right. Rushdan was out in the open, something he never did.

She abandoned the idea of phoning Wade, deciding to wait it out. Whatever was going on, her instincts told her it wasn't the big "show." So she'd concentrate on getting the girls pizza and keeping them safe. Keeping her fingers crossed that Wade hadn't taken the easy arrest and would wait to get his revenge.

Bottle in hand, she reached behind the bar on her way past and grabbed a clean tumbler.

Rushdan was on the phone, looking into it like a video call. "Bring the laptop back to me, Hamilton, or I'm afraid Therese will…"

Rushdan pointed the phone at her. Sal stepped in front of Therese and threw a right punch into her stomach. The tumbler rolled free from her hand on one side as the whiskey bottle shattered on the other when she hit the floor.

"You son of a bitch, leave her alone!"

Wade? Not here. Just the phone. He was on the phone.

No acting necessary. She hadn't seen the punch coming and sent a major shock through her body. Julie Anne rushed to her side, helping her into a chair. It took several seconds before she could breathe regularly again or talk.

It wasn't the first time she'd been hit. And from the reactions of the other women, they'd all seen something like it before. It was her fault they were all here. So she was glad to see them retreat farther into the corner. They looked a little more relaxed knowing it was Therese who would take the beating.

Now she knew why they were there...to keep her in line. She may be a hostage he would threaten to kill. But she was the leverage to ensure Wade behaved correctly.

Covered in whiskey, she turned to Julie Anne, "Snag me a couple of clean towels from behind that post, please."

Julie Anne did it in as small a way as possible. Therese didn't blame her. Sal stood close by, ready to attack. Once the towels were in her hands, she waved the young woman back to sit with the others. Dabbing up the whiskey around her face and neck, she hid her eyes and took in where all the men were.

Rushdan pushed a drink into her hands. "This will help, my dear."

She tried to fake some calm. She couldn't, but who would? So she acted naturally and swallowed the cheaper whiskey he'd poured in one long gulp. Then she looked into the face of evil... Rushdan.

"I should have killed that tin star bastard when he showed back up last night. What made me think I could use him?" He paced a few seconds then looked directly at her. "Or you."

Rushdan marched to her and backhanded her again. Her head snapped from right to left but this time she concentrated, keeping her breathing even. At least both cheeks would be equally red and swollen.

"Put her in the car," Rushdan ordered, pulling a stack of cash from his money clip. "I'm sure the rest of you could use a couple of hundred in tips tonight to keep quiet."

At least the women would be okay. Sal tried to jerk her up from the chair. She didn't move. She took deep breaths, controlling the urge to rub the sting away. But it was more than just defiance. She needed to hear everything Rushdan said.

She couldn't do that from the car.

Had Wade called Rushdan or had it been the other way around? She forced herself to think. Right. Rushdan had been screaming for someone to get Wade on the phone. What had happened in those precious minutes she'd been thinking in the storeroom? "I said put her in the car." Rushdan seemed to have control of his voice again.

Sal shrugged as she jerked her elbow from his grasp.

"I can walk all by myself. I've been doing it for years. Even in heels." She stood, catching her hip on the nearby table, but keeping the "ouch" all to herself.

Sal walked closely behind her. She could see him in the bar mirror. Rushdan finished paying the women and hurried them out the front door. None of them picked up their purses from the top of the bar.

Therese raised a finger, trying to catch them, but couldn't say anything. It was hard just putting one foot in front of the other. Each upright step was a major accomplishment. Okay, maybe she was a bit more loopy from the gut punch or that shot of whiskey than she originally thought.

Before she made it to the hallway, Rushdan latched on to her elbow, pulling her to a stop. Her heels were slick on the floor as he spun her around.

"Feeling a bit tipsy, Therese?" he laughed.

She tried to nod, but her vision went a little wonky with a lot of blinking, before the world turned completely black. Wade wouldn't be storming the place coming to her rescue.

But the night was young.

"CAN'T YOU GO any faster?" Wade asked, knowing it was the fifth or sixth time since he'd seen Therese get punched.

"Creating a fake that looks as good as the real thing isn't as easy as I make it seem." The FBI computer specialist returned to clicking away at his keyboard on the other side of the office.

Jack dropped a hand on Wade's shoulder. "I know this is tough, but he's doing the best he can."

"He said I had an hour. I need over half that long to get to that address."

"Reval isn't going to hurt her." Jack grimaced. They all knew she'd been hurt with that punch.

"You're right." Wade continued to stare at his phone, watching the estimated arrival time change on his map app. "He's got guys to do it for him."

"Thinking like that is going to get in your way," Heath said, leaning back in a desk chair in the corner. "I can tell you that from recent experience."

"I think we all can," Slate added.

Wade put the phone in his back pocket. Reval wouldn't call him again. He probably wouldn't hurt Therese. Or have Sal touch her. At least not until Wade arrived with the damn laptop.

Then he might kill them both.

Heath was right. Thinking like this was messing with his mind, his training and any plans that needed to be made to ensure he and Therese weren't killed.

"Look, guys. I appreciate that you're here supporting me. But is it necessary for *all* of you to hang around?"

"You're just lucky Major Clements was required to hang back at the task force headquarters. Talk about impatience. He'd be wondering why all of this wasn't done in advance." They all laughed at Jack's observation.

"I got to ask you guys." Wade looked at his three best friends in the world. "What would you have done if those other two clowns had shown up?"

"Arrested them," they said in unison.

His friends and partners all nodded their heads and stopped talking. Arms crossed, each leaning on something, all more worried than they were letting on. He didn't want to be dramatic, but none of the cases any of them had worked on were as important as this. He wouldn't say it aloud, but they all knew it.

The "show," as potential buyers on the dark web had been referring to it, had the potential to be another 9/11. Therese hadn't been exaggerating. She'd been right about its importance, but wrong that she wasn't a part of the team. There was a huge team of people working on this.

This team. His team.

That was why these men were all here for him. Waiting with him. Keeping him sane.

"Maybe you should go over what the task force has come up with one more time," Heath said, breaking the silence.

"I got it," Wade told him.

"It can't hurt. Remember, Heath couldn't recall which one of us he'd sent to find his daughter," Slate reminded them.

"It can't hurt." Jack slapped Wade's back again. "When the specialist over there is finished, you'll have a fake schedule for the private airplanes arriving at Love Field and the surrounding smaller airports. Reval just clued us in on his buyers and their arrival times."

"I don't get why he needed this. Wouldn't they all contact him?" Wade had listened and accepted the information and reasoning handed to him earlier. But the guys were right, hearing it and then processing it were different. This time around, parts just didn't add up.

"It might be that he doesn't have specific information," Jack told him. "Or maybe he's worried competition might be headed this way, too. Maybe you'll get him to fess up why he needed it."

"Aren't we tipping our hand if he does and knows this one is a fake?"

"Possibly," Jack agreed. "If that happens, we'll ride in to save you and your princess."

"I wouldn't let Therese hear you refer to her as a princess or even a lady in distress," Slate joked, bending his arm to show off his muscles. "Have you seen the guns on that woman's arms? I'm sure she's okay, man."

Heath got that what-if look on his face and raised a finger. "I'm going to have the computer specialist check something. Be right back."

That look—or thought process—had saved them on more than one occasion. If it saved his hide tonight, it would be saving Therese, too.

"What are the three of you going to be doing while I'm risking my neck?"

"Getting the job done," Slate told him with a straight face.

"Don't worry about our end—or the task force— we've got your back. Just like you've had ours," Jack told him.

The words meant more than he'd thought. *Damn*. Therese had never had that. She'd been completely isolated for the past three years. No friends, family or coworkers. It made it easier to accept that she'd walked away from him so quickly that afternoon.

Or at least he'd thought it had been easy for her. Maybe not.

The guys—his fellow Texas Rangers—had him covered. They'd penned him to the wall to keep him in that office after Therese had been hit by Sal.

Maybe that was why two of them were still between him and the exit.

Needing to focus, he brought his phone back to his hand to stare at it once again. Focus evaded him except for one thought. Reval.

He'd been determined to bring Reval down before. There wouldn't be any deals for the common scum. He'd be in front of every judge and prosecutor to make certain that didn't happen.

A year ago he'd felt anger at nearly being blown up. Anger at how stupid he'd been to go at it alone and let Reval's men get the jump on him. But he'd gotten over it. Or at least he thought he had, until he'd found out Reval was out of jail.

The past six weeks hadn't just been about searching for Therese. In the back of his mind, he knew she wouldn't be far from Reval. Someday he'd let her know just how right she'd been to question what his true motivation was today.

Reval was going down. Away. For good. Without parole or deals.

But not before Wade got a piece of him. And not before Wade severely chastised Sal for hitting his girl.

Chapter Twenty

Therese awoke in the dark with a headache the size of Dallas. She was on a couch in Rushdan's office, blinds drawn. Alone. Where would he keep important, secret information? She let her eyes search for obvious cameras. None. Envisioned the sleek glass desk. Limited drawer storage only in the bookcase.

There had to be a safe in the wall, the floor, behind the books. That meant they needed a combination. Three years and she still didn't know. But what was most likely his special phone—as he'd called it—would still be in his pocket.

Swinging her feet to the floor, she slowly pushed herself up and staggered to the private bathroom. Even after shutting and locking the door, she could hear the fish tank gurgling as she examined her split lip and slightly discolored cheeks.

"You look absolutely terrible," she told her reflection.

She quickly washed the blood from her face and pulled her fingers through her hair. The bathroom had as little decor as Rushdan's office. No pictures with glass that she could break. No heavy statues to swing. Just the bare necessities.

"The Bare Necessities."

She returned to the couch, humming the Disney song that had popped into her head. She didn't walk the room physically. It was too dangerous and she didn't know if she could. She should let Rushdan return and see her acting obedient.

God, she felt loopy. Light. No, it was more of a heavy feeling like she couldn't get up. Weird. Or drugged.

That was why she'd passed out so fast.

So she continued to hum and look around the room for any indication of a safe. It had to be here. Rushdan didn't have any other offices. She kept staring at the walls, but her headache distracted her.

The song earworm took her back home to San Antonio. She couldn't shake it out of her mind. She was certain there was something else she should be doing. Being the oldest, she'd been the resident babysitter when her parents took extra shifts or the rare times they went out. Her siblings had watched a ton of sing-along movies. The words drifted through her mind, urging her to close her eyes.

But instead of cartoons or animated images, she was suddenly in the passenger seat of a car. Eighteen. Stuck in her boyfriend's wrecked Camaro. The darkness surrounded her. No dashboard or streetlights. They'd been out in the country on a little known state highway when a deer ran across the road. They'd crashed.

Wade.

She hadn't known him. She didn't know his name until she'd read it in the paper. He wasn't a Texas Ranger at the time, just a Texas Department of Safety highway patrolman. It was the only time in her life she'd been rescued and she'd never forgotten his face. A couple of years later she'd seen it again with his promotion to the Company B Rangers and she'd been following his career ever since.

If it hadn't been for the hero crush she'd had on Wade she would never have joined the police academy or been recruited for this undercover position. So, in a way, all of this was Wade's fault. The bloody lip, the headache, the undercover life-threatening moment... *Yep, all of it.*

She laughed hysterically. Out of control, she couldn't stop.

"Therese, my dear. Wake up."

She opened her eyes from the strange, disturbed sleep. Rushdan had his hand on her shoulder. Sal had his hand on his gun.

"Are you okay, my darling?"

Now she was his darling? Hardly.

"I'm fine. Just a bad dream." She scooted across the white leather sofa, away from Rushdan.

Too late she remembered the phone. Back in his jacket pocket? Back in a safe? They needed that special phone. Before she could return to his side, he stood and went to his desk.

"You've been out for a long time, Therese. I had no idea you were so...delicate." He massaged the back of his hands, then dismissively waved at Sal. "Leave us."

She waited for the door to shut before saying, "You love doing that."

"Yes. I love being in charge and making everyone else scurry around trying to stay on my good side."

"Being the big, important man," she mumbled.

"Don't be afraid to speak up, Therese. Nothing can change our relationship."

Control. Focus. Change the subject.

"I'm afraid to ask, but has Wade returned?"

"We'll be joining everyone shortly. He failed, by the way. I don't know how he pulled off the racetrack, but he failed miserably at the airport."

"Airport?" she squeaked.

"Yes. It was fun discovering just how much you and the authorities knew about the *show*. It seems there's an entire task force assigned to me." He dangled a phone between his fingers. "This is what you've wanted by the way. It has all my real contacts. Potential buyers. Sellers. Records. Secrets. You have that look about you now, Therese."

"What look?" she asked, her throat and mouth suddenly drier than dust.

"The look of desperation has settled in your eyes and caused a crease in your brow. Don't worry. I like you, darling Therese, and you've been a huge help over the years. But because of your betrayal, the end you're facing won't be quick and it definitely won't be painless. I intend for it to be long and humiliating, until you beg to join your ranger friend in death."

Long and humiliating. Beg to join…in death. The words echoed, bouncing from one side of her aching head to the other. He slid the phone back into his jacket and crossed to the door. She darted out, causing Sal to draw his weapon and Rushdan to jump in retreat.

"Sorry, sorry." She slowly reached for her boss's hand. "I trusted him and was duped just like you."

"Don't deny it, sweetheart. You helped him right into my inner circle. And I was never duped."

"When he contacted me weeks ago with his sob story, I had no reason to doubt him. Then Friday night he put it all out there to help me." She used one hand to cover her eyes and hitched her breath a little. "I don't know why I fell for it, Rushy."

"Give her the shot." His hand hesitated on the doorknob before he left. Had she made him doubt her guilt even a little?

Not a chance.

THE DIRECTIONS GIVEN to Wade on the burner phone took him north of Dallas. Straight highway gave him access to an express lane and made up some of the time he'd lost waiting on the FBI specialist to check out the computer.

With Heath's help, they'd discovered the laptop meant nothing to Reval. It was all a ruse. Something to keep him and the task force busy. *While he did what?*

Killed Therese. Sold the algorithm. Set up in a location where he couldn't legally be touched.

Wade had left the task force behind in Dallas waiting for a hint of what they needed to deploy to protect the cities in the metroplex area. The Rangers—his friends—were en route via helicopter to his destination. He still had the cloned phone from Reval and they could hear through it.

If he wasn't shot on sight and if he could get Reval to brag, then the others could relay the info to the rest of the team. They'd all agreed the plan had a lot of holes. Too many what-ifs for any of them to feel comfortable. And they'd all left the most important question unasked...would he be able to hold it together *if* Therese was dead?

He honestly didn't know. He kept telling himself not to go there. Kept repeating that he would be fine. He'd be able to do it for her. He'd finish the job she had begun. But he was also realistic.

Being there might change everything. Seeing her might...

The GPS indicated he should make a left turn, and he slowed to stop on the side of the road. The warehouse wasn't what he'd expected. Damn if it wasn't lit up like a strip mall parking lot. It wasn't old or broken down.

"Why the hell did Reval bring me out here?" He said it for the team to digest even though he couldn't hear their reply. "This place is brand spanking new. At least there seems to be a place for your chopper to land. Open parking lot, open fields around it. And completely in the middle of nowhere. See you on the other side, guys."

He turned into the lot, backing right up to the front door. *Why not?* He unlocked the gun safe built into a panel of his truck then tossed his keys in the cup holder. If they made it out of the building alive, it might help them escape.

Heading to the main door, laptop in hand, he gave it a tug and it opened. An electronic bell alerted anyone who could hear that he'd walked through the front. Security cameras followed him from the entryway down the empty hall of offices.

"Hello?" He raised the laptop over his head and shoved his shoulder into the last door.

Staying in the doorway, he searched the almost-empty warehouse.

"Walk straight ahead."

"They're waiting inside the office."

About halfway to the wall in the middle of the emptiness, the two who had spoken to him stepped from the darkness. One pointed an automatic weapon at his chest while the other frisked him, then pushed him forward again.

"Open the door and go inside."

Sure enough, the wall had a door. He hesitatingly opened it to find an exact replica of the office he'd stood in earlier that morning. Rushdan Reval sat behind his desk. Sal stood on the other side of the door. The two men from the chase the night before were on either end of a fish tank empty of fish.

Therese was on the couch. She sat with her head back as if she'd fallen asleep. She didn't stir and seemed to be out cold.

"I guess the party can get started now that I'm here." Wade held the laptop out in front of him.

The nerdy guy from the airport stepped through the door after him and took it. He opened it on the desk, punched several keys and shook his head. "Just like we thought. Bogus info. No tracker. You still want him to do it?"

"I think with the proper motivation he'll do fine." Reval waved his hand toward the unconscious Therese.

Damn.

Chapter Twenty-One

Wade's mind got stuck on what Reval had done to Therese to keep her so solidly out of commission. He shifted gears to what the criminal who'd escaped the law too many times had planned for them both. Why here in this remote part of Denton County?

"I suppose a good investigator like yourself," Reval said, leaving the comfort of his chair, "wants to know why you're needed."

"You might say that."

"Access, access, access." Reval moved toward Therese, leaning on the arm of the couch closest to her. "I need to get in and out of a place without detection."

Reval flicked his finger in the air and the nerdy man at the laptop crossed the room and held out his hand in front of Wade.

"We'll take the phone back from the racetrack."

Wade pulled it free from his back pocket and handed it over. The younger man pulled a screwdriver from his hip, popped open the cover and removed both the battery and SIM card. One of the what-ifs had just happened.

Wade was cut off from the team. They'd be deaf and blind until they landed and set up some type of surveillance.

"Tell me how much of my plans does the Homeland task force know?"

"Homeland?" Wade tried to play dumb. "I don't work too much with those characters."

Reval slapped Therese's check, snapping her head to the left, but she didn't react.

"Wrong answer, Ranger Wade. You won't get very many, so you might want to be truthful."

"You drugged her. What did you give her?"

"You see my predicament, don't you, Hamilton? You're here and I'm certain you didn't come alone. But I still have a problem." He splayed his hands toward Therese. "I need to know if her task force has discovered my plans."

"There's no reason to hurt Therese. She didn't pass anything to me."

"Oh, she's not hurting. I promise she's not hurting…yet." He pulled a syringe from his jacket pocket. "But we could make certain. Just one more little push and she won't have any pain at all ever again. That the path you want to choose?"

Reval lifted Therese's arm. He'd do it. Wade didn't have any doubts.

"Okay, okay. I believe you. But I honestly don't know what you're talking about. I followed your directions at Love Field and brought the laptop back to you."

"Then why are you so disappointingly late?" He shifted the needle closer to her vein.

"I… I had to hide until the cops searched the entire airport because of your men. I got here as soon as I could get back to my truck. What more do you want me to say?" Dammit. Even he thought he sounded like he was lying.

"Maybe we should try to wake her up?" Reval stood, backed away and slashed a fat finger through the air. Sal and his armed companion moved across the room.

"I don't know anything. Nothing." Could Reval's computer guy tell that the FBI had searched what was on the laptop?

"Don't waste my time, Wade. This isn't a negotiation," Reval continued. "Tell me what I want to know, but you're right. An overdose is such an easy way out for Therese." Another flick of his finger sent Sal and the second man to either side of Therese.

"Wait. Look, I don't know what those two inept morons you sent to Love Field told you, but I followed your instructions. I'll do whatever you need me to get done." Wade's heartbeat skyrocketed. They were going to torture Therese.

He had no way to stop it or let anyone know it was happening. And she was still out cold.

They hooked an arm under Therese's arms, semi-standing her, then dragged her to the fishless tank of water against the wall. Wade hadn't noticed that the tank stood just a little higher than waist level. Not before Therese's head lobbed forward and her long hair fell to drift in the circling water.

Therese was suspended between the two men.

"Stop! What do you want me to tell you? I wouldn't be here if the Rangers knew anything."

"Do it," Rushdan commanded.

They lifted her higher and shoved her head underwater.

"She'll drown. Are you trying to kill her?"

When Therese struggled and kicked to get air, Sal let her catch a short breath before shoving her down again.

"Come on, Reval. This is between us. If you don't believe me, then put my head underwater."

Reval nodded. Sal grabbed Therese's hair and wrenched upward. She spit out tank water as she sucked in air. She tossed her head, waking up from whatever drug Reval had given her.

Therese kicked and twisted to get free. Then they did it again.

And again.

Wade grabbed the edge of the couch and held his breath along with Therese. Each time she got close to getting a deep breath, Reval's men sent her under again.

Reval snapped his fingers and Sal grabbed a fist of her long hair, yanking her back. No one said anything as she slowly recovered.

"W... Wade?" Therese gasped.

"Reval, dammit, stop. I did what you asked. You

want the money. I'll get the money I'll have it first thing in the morning. Just don't do this to her any longer."

The men allowed Therese to collapse on the floor. Wade watched her back rise and fall as they gave her a long break to recuperate.

Reval casually walked back and forth in front of the windows that looked out to an empty warehouse. He flipped his phone between two fingers, then tapped it against his chin.

"Here's the deal, Hamilton. I don't believe you, and Therese shouldn't have, either. If she's not a dirty undercover cop—which, looking back over the past three years, I think she is. Then, she's just plain bad luck. Either way, I need to get rid of her."

"His phone," Therese whispered.

"What was that, my love?" Reval bent and grabbed her hair himself, yanking her head back to see her face.

"Every…thing on phone. Forget me."

"Well, look at that. Seems she is a cop and willing to sacrifice herself for the better good. Are you Ranger Wade? Are you going to insist that you aren't here undercover and you aren't a part of the elite task force set up to stop my show?"

Therese was lifted and shoved under the water again. Once there, her face was jerked toward Wade. Eyes wide and scared, hair swirling around her face, she was upside down, holding whatever breath she could. Then Reval snapped his fingers and Sal grinned.

Sal pushed on her harder, lifting her feet off the soaking wet carpet. She was practically to the bottom of the tank when her air escaped in a large set of bubbles. Wade wouldn't let her die. Not like that. Not because of him.

"All right! Let her up!"

"And what?"

"I'll tell you what I know. But let her breathe."

Reval waited another long second before nodding his head to bring her out of the water. Sal didn't move fast enough. Wade jumped from the couch and shoved Reval's men out of the way. He lifted Therese and laid her on the floor, immediately pushing against her belly.

"God, she's not breathing." He needed to push properly on her diaphragm and get the water out of her lungs.

Wade situated his hands, ready to begin CPR, when both men grabbed his arms. He struggled, pushing them away. He shoved on Therese's chest once, twice. They grabbed him again.

"Enough!" Reval shouted. A weapon was fired into the ceiling, causing his men to freeze. Wade was finally unrestricted and forced pressure on Therese.

Therese coughed. Water spewed from her mouth. She turned on her side, still throwing up water. Wade gave a rough shake with his body when both men grabbed him again. They released him and he gently stroked the hair away from her face and tried to reassure Therese she would be okay.

He loved her so much he'd do anything to keep her

alive. He had his answer. He chose her over everything.

"His…his phone," she struggled to say.

Wade understood. The information they needed was on the phone Rushdan Reval had in his pocket. He helped Therese sit up, his eyes falling to the burner phone left in pieces. Damn, the men of Company B wouldn't know.

Whatever happened, he and Therese were the only hope of stopping this man. Of stopping the terrorists who wanted the algorithm.

With her dying breath she'd been telling him what he needed. And with her dying breath, he'd discovered he'd tell Reval anything to keep it from being the last thing he heard her say.

"So, Ranger Wade, let's hear all about this task force the government has brought together to stop my little show."

Chapter Twenty-Two

They were waiting. At least half an hour. Maybe longer. Therese had no idea.

Rushdan's men had taken their watches and phones, locking them in this fake office. At least they had a working toilet. With Wade's help she'd even rinsed the fish and whiskey smell from her hair in the sink.

"What time was it when you arrived?"

"After ten at night." His eyes were closed as he lounged in the corner of the couch.

"I don't know how you can sleep."

"I'm not. You're doing a good job keeping me awake."

"How can you relax like that?"

Wade sat up, blinked rapidly and pushed his fingers through his hair, making it stick straight into the air. It would have been cute under different circumstances.

"Okay, I'm sitting up so you'll think I'm completely awake."

Shoot, it was cute. She quit her pacing directly in front of him. "You need to fix your hair."

"What's wrong with it?"

"Smooth it down."

He clasped her hand and tugged her to his lap. "Now you can fix it however you want."

"This isn't the time, Wade."

"Of course it is. I'm not going to fight with you, Therese. You can be mad at me, but I'm not flinching."

"I'm not mad at you. I'm..." She covered her bruised cheeks with her fingers, whispering underneath them, "Why aren't we trying to get out of here?"

"I had a good look at this box from the outside. We're covered by men with long guns and there's nothing to hide behind if we do manage to knock down one of the walls." He tugged her fingers from her face.

"Still..."

"You nearly died tonight, sweetheart. I wouldn't have... I mean..." He cleared his throat a couple of times and pulled her into his arms closer.

"I didn't die," she whispered, dropping her head to his shoulder. "How long until your partners come bursting in that door?"

"After they freak—because I'm not there to calm them down," he answered softly into her ear. "They'll find a way to discover what's going on. Then they'll wait because we're all taking our orders from your boss."

"And they're after the programmer."

"And none of them know we could get that information right now off his phone."

"Right." Reluctantly, Therese pushed back to look into Wade's eyes again.

She had no clue what he thought. After being undercover for three lonely years, she still couldn't get a read on this man. Even with time on their hands, she couldn't broach the subject of their differences. Too risky.

"I should probably..." She began to move from his lap. "You know, if they come in... Oh wait, your hair."

Wade used both hands to smooth it down.

The door opened with a grunt from Sal. "Time to go. Hands behind your backs."

They were both handcuffed and walked out the back of the warehouse. Wade had filled her in on their location and his curiosity about it. When they walked outside, why they were there was explained with one word...helicopter.

"We'll make an emergency landing at DFW. Flashing your badge around will get my men where they can have access to the systems they need. After we're done, we'll take off, leaving the two of you behind to do whatever you want."

"That's it? You think I can flash my badge and no one will call for confirmation?"

"If they try, it'll be up to you to make sure they don't." Reval climbed inside next to the pilot. "Let's speak plainly. If I don't get what I want Hamilton, neither do you."

"You'd kill her?"

"You know I will."

Sal placed duct tape over both their mouths. They climbed up and were strapped tightly in.

It wouldn't be a long flight to DFW. The control lights put off enough light for her to watch Wade's eyes move around the small bubble they sat in. She was wedged between the guy with glasses and Wade. Sal on his other side.

The helicopter bobbed up and down and around. She'd never been affected by things like this before, so it was probably the drug Rushdan had given her earlier. Her head spun and she wanted to be sick with the hopelessness consuming her.

Right up to the moment that Wade tapped on her bare foot to get her attention. Just looking in his eyes gave her strength. He gestured with his shoulder and eyes. Looking at his strap and then the pilot. This time she had no trouble discerning what he thought. He wanted to crash the helicopter.

Crash it. Stopping the potential attack. Probably killing everyone on board. She shook her head. No. They needed the programmer. Sure, one of their team members might find an extra phone on Rushdan. But the programmer would be gone as soon as he didn't get his information tonight.

Wade bent his ear to her mouth.

"Too risky," she said under the restrictive tape. "No."

The sounds from the helicopter were extremely loud without a headset, which the others were wearing. But he understood the no. Or at least she hoped he did.

Therese stretched her mouth to loosen the tape around her bottom lip and chin. Then she pulled at it by scraping the corner against Wade's shoulder. He copied her movements until they both had it free enough to talk. No one noticed the loose tape since it still connected on the top.

"Can you hear me okay?" she asked directly in his ear.

He nodded and then turned his mouth to her ear. "So we're not going down in a blaze of glory?"

She shook her head. She'd been willing to die in that fish tank, but knowingly dropping out of the sky... Maybe the drugs had clouded her mind enough then, to where she'd given up hope. But now it was different with Wade next to her.

"We can find a way through this without killing ourselves." She truly believed that.

Wade responded with a raised eyebrow and a look toward the pilot.

She used her chin to get his attention again. "I know what you're thinking," she said, continuing their dialogue directly into his ear. "But circumstances change."

He drew his eyebrows together questioningly before leaning to her. "You didn't do your mind-reading trick. I'm waiting." Then put his ear back to her lips.

Explaining what had been in her mind during the

time she'd been struggling to breathe would take longer than a helicopter ride. And maybe fewer restraints. She wanted to kiss him and tell him how glad she was to still be alive.

It didn't make sense to go there. To tell him how she felt—especially about him. Or did it? Would she get another chance?

"Okay, I'm not a mind reader. But I need to tell you how grateful I am that I found you last night. Sorry to get you involved, but once you were, I've been truly grateful not to be alone."

He nodded but didn't turn to speak.

"You know we actually met a long time ago," she continued.

The young man sitting next to her pulled a white Stetson from a gym bag at his feet.

"What the hell?" Wade shouted.

Apparently it was loud enough for everyone to hear. Rushdan's man slapped his hand across the duct tape again—first hers, then Wade's. It was the first time she'd looked at what the younger man with glasses wore. White dress shirt, slacks, Western boots and a silver star inside a circle. Wade's Texas Ranger badge.

Add the Stetson and people would assume...

So why hadn't they killed her and Wade back at the warehouse? Why did they still need them alive?

The helicopter changed directions. Fast. Then began a spiral. It was dark, but she could tell they were close to DFW. No one around her looked panicked. They were staging an emergency landing.

They would be on the ground and all have their weapons inside the airport perimeter.

Staged or not, it felt real, like an out-of-control roller coaster stuck on the same loop.

The man next to her dropped his headset, placed the Stetson on his head and then loaded a round into the chamber of his handgun.

It seemed like forever but actually only took a few seconds before they landed with a hard thud. Rushdan was out first and opened the door closest to Wade. The man dressed like a Texas Ranger ripped the tape from their mouths and unbuckled her. He tugged until she was sprawled face first on the pavement. Sal did the same with Wade.

The sound of the helicopter winding down was accompanied by the smell of smoke. Nothing was wrong mechanically. They'd just covered their tracks.

"Either of you say a word and we shoot your partner," Rushdan said.

"I would have remembered meeting you, Therese. So what are you talking about?"

She wanted to laugh at what Wade had chosen to whisper next to her. But the boot in her back kept her quiet. That and knowing Rushdan would kill Wade.

"Howdy," the fake Wade greeted the emergency crews. "Sorry for the bit of excitement."

Wade tapped his boot against her leg. "I've never said howdy in my entire life."

Chapter Twenty-Three

Wade had been pulled to his knees. If he'd wanted to tell someone what was going on, he couldn't have. There was no one to tell. Since the helicopter hadn't been on fire, the airport first responders left. Two cop cars were between him and any law enforcement officers.

Reval's plan to get into DFW Airport had worked. The pilot stayed with the helicopter. The computer guy impersonating him—something he'd make sure charges were brought about—stood guard with a handgun and a long gun. They'd done a good job separating him from Therese, who now sat in the locked back seat cage of a black-and-white.

"I'm sorry but our transport can't get here for another fifteen," Reval explained. "I wish we could get out of your way."

"No problem, Deputy," an officer said.

Cargo planes passing by on the local runway drowned out the rest. Reval shook hands and rejoined the computer nerd.

"When are they leaving?" the nerd asked. "Our window is closing."

Reval took the long gun from him, propping it on his hip. "The car with Therese is staying. Make your move after the other one departs."

"Got it."

Wade pulled at the cuffs. Whoever gave the movies the idea that it was easy to dislocate your thumb to slip handcuffs off had to have been crazy. He tried and didn't succeed.

The second unit pulled away and computer nerd removed his handgun, shifting it, ready to bring it up to take aim. He'd obviously had some type of training, and looked military calm. Wade moved slowly, trying not to be seen, shifting one foot from back to front, ready to stand.

The remaining police officer turned to face the computer nerd, who raised his weapon.

"Take cover!" Wade yelled too late.

The officer went down as Wade threw himself into the computer nerd, trying to stop him. The nerd moved but was able to recover before Wade took him to the ground.

Wade ended on his back with a gun barrel under his chin.

"Andrew, put that away and get him up," Reval said, jabbing the long gun and forcing Wade's neck to stretch.

Andrew the nerd guy pulled Wade to his feet and immediately punched him in the kidney. "You can't save anyone, Hamilton."

"Now, Andrew, you know he might be able to save Therese if he does as he's told," Reval said, pointing the gun at the police car.

Getting their attention back on himself, Wade said, "Why do you need me? Not that I'm in a hurry to leave this world, but Andrew thinks he looks pretty good in that hat."

"Make sure Andrew gets what he needs and there's a chance I'll let you both go."

"You really think I believe that?"

"I think *she* does. I don't understand how you turned her after last year. She was so loyal."

He'd let Reval think that was what happened. It would just get bloody sooner if the criminal knew Therese had been undercover this entire time.

"Let her go now and I'll give you my word."

"Your word means nothing to me. And I don't want to let her go." Reval stuck the long gun under his arm and used the nail on his little finger to pick something from between his teeth. "You can earn her freedom or she comes with me. Think about that while you help Andrew."

"At least let me say goodbye."

"No way. We need to get this over with. We've wasted too much time talking," Sal said from behind them.

"I think you might really care about our Therese." Reval used his hands once again and made a sweeping sign toward the police car. "Make it quick."

With a vocal protest heard under the engine of a

freight airliner, Andrew unlocked the back door. Therese got out, but the kid kept a hand on her shoulder.

"So this is goodbye?" she asked.

"I still think you're pulling my leg about our first meeting."

"Really? That's all you have to say?" She laughed a little even as Andrew pushed her back inside the car.

"You go first," he encouraged.

"All right... I love you. Keep yourself alive."

"You owe me an explanation," he shouted as the door slammed.

He could have said he loved her, too. The words were in his heart and on the tip of his tongue. But not like this. Maybe he should, since her admission gave him courage he didn't realize he'd been missing.

Therese placed her forehead against the window. Her long dark hair fell to either side, hiding most of her face. If she looked up...made eye contact with him... But she turned, dropping her head to the back of the seat.

THERESE'S BLOOD PUMPED through her veins, making her lightheaded. She'd said it. Admitted that she loved him in the least romantic setting ever. Captured.

She blinked rapidly to keep away the tears. Yeah, she wasn't a girl who cried. Even when the love crush of her life didn't say he loved her back. *Blink. Blink. Blink.*

There are more important things on our plate.

Like how do we get free and prevent a domestic terrorist strike. Yeah. That.

Rushdan Reval took the keys and opened the driver's door. "You both have twenty minutes. Deploy and get back to Hangar Four," Reval told Sal and the kid. "You know we won't wait for you, Andrew."

Deploy what?

"Don't worry. I could do this in my sleep," Andrew answered.

Deploy what?

The algorithm, naturally. Andrew must be the programmer. She'd already pushed and twisted the handcuffs, making her wrists raw. There was nothing in the back seat of a police vehicle to help her. She wasn't wearing anything useful—not even shoes.

Andrew shoved Wade to get him moving. To where? Too many unanswered questions. After nearly drowning, admitting that she worked with Wade and that she loved him…there was little chance Rushdan would release her.

She needed the handcuff key and had no idea even where to look. The kid Andrew had snapped the metal bracelets on her, but maybe—just maybe—Rushdan had kept the actual key on his person.

Rushdan got behind the wheel and was joined by the pilot. *Curious.* Andrew and Wade ran across the field to a group of buildings.

"Where are we going?" she asked through the police cage.

"We're leaving. For good. After this *show* there won't be a need for any more petty moneymaking schemes. My clients will know what we can do and will be paying anything I ask."

"Aren't we leaving in the helicopter?"

"Why would we do that, my dear? It's so much nicer to fly in a private jet. Especially to South America. You'll love it there."

"You aren't going to kill me?"

They didn't travel far. Across a large parking lot from the building where Wade and the kid were entering. It was too dark and too far to read the name on that building. But by looking above it as she was escorted from the car, she could see a tower.

It must be a control tower for private and cargo planes. By accessing this system, Rushdan could gain access to the main air traffic control network for DFW.

"You're going to crash planes? Are you crazy?"

"By your standards, most definitely." He yanked her along with him through a small door the pilot had already unlocked.

"Please don't do this, Rushdan. So many people could be killed."

"I won't be doing anything except living the high life in Costa Rica or Buenos Aires or the Mediterranean. I haven't really decided." He made his signature disgusting sound as he sucked his teeth open to a smile.

SHOWING THAT HE was entirely out of shape, Andrew uncuffed Wade's hands while continuing to huff, puff and curse as they ran. They waited on a security guard to open the door and then the nerd placed the white Stetson on Wade's head. It sat on the crown instead of his forehead, obviously not fitting.

"Doesn't seem to be my size."

"No one cares. You tell the guard we're here to serve this warrant." The kid pulled a piece of paper from his back pocket. "Don't worry. It looks real and is for one of their people on duty tonight."

"And what if he says no?"

Andrew fingered the handgun holstered on his hip. "Convince him or he dies now. And then your girlfriend, of course."

"You feel like a tough guy? A big shot? Shooting that cop back there is the action of a coward." He waited for his words to rile Andrew.

They apparently did, but as the kid started to unholster his weapon, the door opened. Andrew held up the fake warrant, but he remained silent.

"I'm Texas Ranger Wade Hamilton and this is my partner. We're here to serve a warrant on…"

"David Liteman." Andrew flicked the fake warrant.

"Before you object," Wade cautioned the guard and took a step inside, removing the ill-fitting hat. "We know this is a highly unusual situation. But we wouldn't have been allowed on the grounds if it wasn't all cleared. Right?"

"Somebody should have called me," the guard grumbled. "But hey, it's only my job. What do I know about protocol?" He turned his back on them and went to his desk. "Nobody ever tells me anything."

Wade entered, followed by Andrew. He could take this kid at any point. There wasn't anything tough about him. He was just plain more experienced and knew what opportunities to watch for. The kid didn't.

Point in fact, he could have disarmed the kid coming through the door.

"Is he upstairs?" Andrew asked.

"Yeah. Where did you think he worked, here at my desk? Elevator is around the corner, but if you don't want him to see you coming, the stairs are back this way." The guard pointed back over his shoulder.

Andrew walked into Wade's back. Okay, that was another place to disarm him. Throw one punch and the kid would be out cold. He steadied him, waited for him to turn around and followed him to the stairwell.

Yeah, kid, I'm following you, not the other way around.

Once in the stairwell, Andrew seemed to realize he was vulnerable. He waited until Wade passed him and then left two stairs between them.

"What do you need access to?" Wade asked. "Are we going up to the control windows?"

"Not if there's computer access outside the room."

"Like from the supervisor?" Wade pointed to the sign just under the second-floor symbol.

"That should work."

"Where did you get the idea for this malware thing anyway? You that smart, Andrew?" Wade held the door open, hat still in his hand and waited for the kid.

"I mean, you seem smart and all. But no one does stuff like that alone. Right?"

"Smart?" He waited at the top step. "I take exception to that description. I opened your sealed court records in less than a minute. This algorithm took me years to develop. The sophistication of the decryption capability is insane."

"You developed it all by yourself? That's hard to believe."

Andrew pulled his handgun. "Oh no, you don't." He waved the barrel, indicating Wade should go through the door first. "Why do you want to know about me?"

"Hey kid, I have no clue about computer viruses. Nothing like that. None of it's my cup of coffee." He shrugged, taking a step into the second-floor hallway.

"Coffee? It's your cup of *tea*, you ignorant cowboy." Andrew relaxed his direction with the gun, dropping the barrel toward the floor.

Just another opportunity for someone of Wade's experience. And now that he knew Andrew was the programmer...

Wade tossed the Stetson to the kid, whose natural reaction was to catch it. Then Wade grabbed the kid's arm and used his momentum to flip the gun backward behind Andrew. He turned, pinning him to the open stairwell door, lifted his elbow hard into the man's chin and heard the gun drop to the floor.

Then for good measure, Wade pounded his fist twice into the kid's solar plexus, knocking his breath from him. He dropped him facedown to the floor. Out cold. Wade rolled the kid over, grabbed hold of his collar and slid him across the slick linoleum floor to the elevator.

"But I don't drink tea."

He frisked the kid, looking for a phone. Nothing except a flash drive, which he pocketed. He pulled Andrew onto the elevator. He hated doing it, but if was going to save Therese, leaving this guy with the incompetent guard was his only óption.

"What the hell is going on? Did he fall?"

The guard stood and moved while Wade jerked on the kid, sliding him through the elevator doors. He'd seen an empty office on the way to the stairs, which would be a good place to lock this terrorist up.

"Look, I don't have time to explain. Call 911 and get this man to a secure—"

"Help me," Andrew whimpered.

Wade couldn't finish the sentence. Words and thought left him as something slammed into the side of his head. He hadn't seen it coming. Nothing.

Chapter Twenty-Four

Damn blind spot floated through Wade's mind as he rolled in pain. Blurred vision. Pain. Cool floor against his skin. More pain.

"Yeah, this is Randy Allister in the northwest tower. I need help. I ain't kidding. This is the real thing."

Wade used his arms in an attempt to push himself to an upright position. It didn't work.

"Tell 'em not to come in hot. A woman's life depends on it," Wade said. But he didn't know if the guard listened to him.

Randy Allister seemed to be dancing around the room, gun drawn in one hand, radio in the other. Wade managed to roll over and the guard seemed to move faster or maybe there were two of him. He lifted his hands, trying to calm the inexperienced guard down.

"Listen to me, please." Wade covered his left eye, eliminating the double vision. "Randy, I've got to get to Hangar Four."

"You ain't going anywhere, man. I brought you down, imposter."

"You brought down an authentic Texas Ranger. But I'll forget all that if you just let me get to Hangar Four."

"No way. Capturing you might save my job."

"You mean because you let us in the building to begin with."

"Yeah, well. They'll forget that part when I show 'em I captured you."

Wade rubbed the side of his head, vision clearing a little. "I doubt that. You're letting the real bad guys get away."

"Don't listen to him," Andrew screamed, trying to get up and away from Wade.

"Tell you what, Randy. We'll both sit here in your custody if you just get on the horn and ask the cops to check out Hangar Four." If Wade couldn't get to Therese, maybe other cops could.

"No! You can't!" shouted Andrew. "He's…he's trying to trick you. I watched him shoot one of you in cold blood. He's still lying out there."

Wade used his heels to slowly push himself to the wall next to the desk during Andrew's yelling. He didn't want to injure the guard, but he had to get to Therese.

"You can both stay right where you are until the DFW cops get here. They can decide which of you is lying and which is telling the truth."

"Listen, Randy. What would it hurt to ask your friends not to flash their lights on the way here? I'll wait." He stuck his hands behind his head. "I won't give you any trouble."

"He's right, Randy," Andrew moved to the same position. "Be the hero and save this woman's life. She'll die if the terrorists see the cops."

"Terrorists? What kind of terrorists? Is something going to blow up?" Randy began nervously shifting back and forth, mumbling the word *terrorist* with each step. His movements and chanting made Wade's headache grow exponentially.

"Just get on your radio and call it in."

"No! Don't listen to him," Andrew shouted, drawing Randy's attention. "They'll kill her."

Wade took advantage of the moment and pulled his jeans leg up over the boot with the Love Field guard's weapon. He'd grown used to the weight and almost forgotten it was there until feeling it while lying next to Therese earlier.

If he was lucky, neither the guard nor Andrew would see him remove the handgun. Not that his luck had been holding during the past two days.

The radio squawked and Wade used the distraction to pull the gun. Andrew jumped up, sliding feet first, using the guard's ankles like second base. He popped back to a standing position gun in hand.

Wade stood covering his bad eye to search for the radio.

Andrew roared, dipped his head and charged. He crashed into Wade. The force took both of them rolling into a watercooler stand but they both managed to hold on to their guns.

Back on the floor, they were at a standoff, pointing the guns at each other.

"Find your radio, Randy!" Wade shouted, keeping his gun on Andrew. Then told the kid who pointed the gun at the guard, "Don't do it. Put it down."

The guard crawled on all fours. Andrew's barrel vacillated between Wade's head and the back of the guard.

"Got it!" Randy raised the radio in the air.

The reverb of the shot rang in Wade's ears as he saw the poor guard spinning to the side from the force of the bullet. Wade pulled the trigger. He couldn't allow Andrew to fire again.

Wade's aim was true.

Andrew's eyes were wide and fixed, staring at him as if he didn't understand what had happened.

"Oh my God. I've been shot. I've been shot," Randy kept chanting.

Wade stood and removed the gun from Andrew's death grip. He went to the guard's side, taking the man's free hand and placing it on the wound.

"Keep pressure on it like that. Good. I'm sure someone heard the shot and will be downstairs to help you."

"Are you guys really terrorists?" Randy asked.

Wade grabbed the radio and turned for the door. "He was." He stopped and pulled his badge from Andrew's belt. "This is mine."

He pushed the door open with his shoulder. "This is Texas Ranger Wade Hamilton. Cars approaching northwest DFW, refrain from lights and sirens.

Possible terrorist with hostage at Hangar Four. Be aware am on foot and armed. Ambulance needed at tower. Officer down. I repeat, officer down. Don't run code."

"Hamilton, stand down. Team is on the way," a voice he recognized told him. Recognized as one of the men making decisions about this operation. But Steve Woods had no clue what was actually going on.

Wade dropped the radio and covered his bad eye to limit the double vision. He couldn't be sure which hangar was number four, but directly across the con-crete lot—large enough for two 747s to pass—sat an empty police car.

He had to get to her. So he ran.

THERESE PROPPED HERSELF on an old desk in the corner of the cramped hangar. The airplane took up most of the room. Rushdan and the pilot hadn't threatened her since she'd gotten inside.

They also hadn't seen her pick up a paper clip before she parked herself here. While she fiddled with the handcuffs behind her back, she watched the clock above the door click off the seconds toward twenty minutes.

Maybe they'd forget about her. She wished.

"What happens if the kid can't get it done?" the pilot asked while removing the blocks from in front of the wheels of the plane.

"He'll do it. This is his crowning achievement. He'll get it done or die trying." Rushdan leaned against the plane's stairs.

"That's what I'm afraid of. The kid is a bit trigger-happy."

"He does get a bit…excited."

"It's getting close to time. We going to wait?"

"No. I have what I need. Tested or not, my copy of the algorithm will bring me millions." He laughed. "I told him twenty minutes. If we wait longer, the authorities might find his mistake near the helicopter. Go ahead and open the doors. Let's get in the air."

The pilot pushed a button and the doors began to creak open.

"And don't forget Therese," Rushdan added before climbing the steps.

The pilot waved his hand at her like he was directing traffic. It was her signal to join them on the plane. She stared at him.

"Move it."

"You don't have to do this. There's no reason to take me with you."

"The boss wants you around, so you're going. Now get up the stairs and buckle in."

"Kind of hard to do with the handcuffs." She popped off the corner of the desk and turned around to show him.

"Nice try. It'll give the boss a reason to get close. Come on." He gave her a hard push toward the plane.

The metal rungs of the ladder hurt her bare feet and keeping her balance wasn't easy without her hands. But she stepped inside the small plane, climbing into the seat closest to the door.

God, she hated feeling helpless. Or maybe it was

hopeless. She'd had her fair share of pity parties, but she'd never felt as alone and lost as at this moment. If they took off...

The pilot crawled in behind her, then into the seat to fly.

"Is this it?"

"What do you mean, my dear?" Rushdan answered as if it were any ordinary day. He moved past her to the front.

"You're just going to fly away, taking me along for the ride? Why?"

"I have patiently waited for you to come around, Therese. I hate that you allowed yourself to be taken in by the ranger. I guess he fits every girl's idea of a dream man, doesn't he. I can see why you liked him, so I'll forgive you."

"Forgive me?"

"You're mine now. You belong to me. Wherever I go, you go." He moved from the front of the plane, stopping at the seat opposite her.

"You're crazy," she whispered. And then a little louder, "I don't *belong* to anyone. Especially you."

"I disagree. Once we get to South America, you'll be dependent on me for everything. Water, food, clothes, protection. You'll be grateful then."

"I'll never be grateful, you sicko. Who would be grateful to their kidnapper?"

A loud noise from outside the plane got their attention.

"That must be Sal or Andrew. Looks like you'll have company back here after all."

Body slams, crashes and sounds of a fight grew louder as Therese searched out the windows of both sides of the plane. It had to be Wade. More thuds and metallic slams—someone being thrown into the hangar door.

"Sal? Andrew? What's going on?" Rushdan yelled.

"Pull up the steps, boss. We gotta get out of here," the pilot yelled from up front.

Therese Ortis's family had not raised a helpless girl. She'd never be a woman who was dependent on any man's whim. Especially this terrible, sick man. Her eyes met Rushdan's across the aisle, then darted to the staircase.

The plane rolled forward, leaving the brightness of the hangar, only the dim lights from the controls illuminating the cabin. Rushdan reached for her seat belt. Therese scooted forward in her seat, blocking his hands.

This is going to hurt.

Chapter Twenty-Five

The plane taxied forward from the hangar. Wade had run across the giant parking lot. He was about to pull the door open when someone slammed into him. He hadn't seen anything out his bad eye.

Sal was all over him. Wade kicked out, shoving the crazy man off. Sal turned, jumping on him, forcing the gun from his hand. They both fell to the cement floor and rolled, only stopping when they hit the metal hangar wall.

Wade landed on top and got in the first punch. Sal no longer had a smirk on his face to wipe off. He shoved with both hands and Wade's injured head banged against the wall. Hard. Wade thrust the pain aside and threw his weight into pinning the bigger man down.

The plane kept moving. He could see Reval through the doorway as it passed. Could see Therese through the window.

Sal freed himself by rolling. He wanted on that plane.

"Not so fast." Wade jerked on his legs. Sal kicked

out, keeping Wade a leg length away, then rolled and twisted to his feet.

The man's eyes were narrow slits as he used the back of his hand to remove the blood dropping from the smirky tilt to his mouth.

"You want a rematch? Come on. I'll teach you a thing or two." Sal gestured for Wade to come at him. Taunting.

Wade didn't want to engage. He needed to stop that plane from taking off. He needed to save Therese's life. But this man was in his way.

His fingers curled into fists. Then he relaxed, steadied his breathing, found his center and waited for Sal to advance.

"You think you can beat me?" Sal danced from side to side like they had all the time in the world.

Wade kept his good eye focused on his opponent. He watched for the first kick and deflected it with one of his own. He followed with two punches that connected with the center of Sal's chest. Sal absorbed some of the momentum when he took steps backward but quickly charged.

Wade received a right cross that he hadn't seen coming. It stunned him enough that he staggered, giving Sal time to run to the back corner of the hangar.

RUSHDAN MUST HAVE seen the direction of her gaze and made a move to restrain her. She stood slightly, shoving her shoulder into the fat man, keeping him off balance. She took a step forward and he fell back to the seat he'd been occupying.

She stepped over his sprawled legs and leaned against the doorway. She'd nearly fallen trying to step up. How would she get down now that the plane was on the move?

Worrying about how to get down the gangway was a bit bizarre. She had no way to grip anything, with her hands cuffed behind her back. The plane would only gain in speed. She had to go now.

Two men fought at the edge of light from the hangar. She recognized Wade as he swung, connected with the other man's ribs, spinning him sideways. But the other man countered by slamming the back of Wade's thigh, forcing his knee to the ground.

"Therese," Wade shouted between defensive grunts. "Get out of the plane! Now!"

The other man—Sal—removed something shiny from his waist.

"He has a knife!" she shouted to warn Wade.

It was ridiculous to wait for a better opportunity. Each second seemed to flash by. A huff behind her let her know Rushdan was on the move. She took the first two steps. Then the madman was at the door, trying to grab her.

Sal suddenly soared away from Wade, running to catch up with the plane. Therese took another step down. Sal's arm stretched toward the ramp.

One more step. Just one more step. She had to jump. Before she could, her body lurched in reverse, her back falling across the steps. Rushdan jerked her hair, pulling while she screamed.

Having completed its turn, the plane revved its engine and sped up. Therese had no way to hang on. The handcuffs on her wrists were caught on the metal rungs as she twisted, trying to get free. She tugged and pulled her hair from Rushdan's grasp.

The plane sped up a fraction more and she lost her regained footing. She slid free, slamming to the concrete, taking Sal with her.

He landed an arm's length away. In the time it took for her to get her bearings, he straddled her and had the knife raised.

The knife descended while she rolled to her side, trying to deflect the blade from her chest as much as possible. Pain. Her own hiss and scream blocked out all the other sound.

Then a deep shout of pure rage echoed around her. Sal took it as a warning, jumped up and pulled the knife. Coming out was worse than going in. She screamed again, twisting in pain, blinking away the wetness in her eyes.

"You okay?" Wade asked, his hands gently cupping her face. "You're bleeding. Bad."

"Catch him," she gritted through her teeth.

"I think the help can take care of him," Wade knelt next to her. "I need something to put pressure on the wound. Now, don't think I'm trying to be sexy." He joked as he took off his shirt and stuffed it between her arm and ribs.

Each time she opened her eyes, she could see the

flashing lights of the emergency vehicles. She had to convince Wade to go after Rushdan. "I'm fine. Go. They don't know him," she got out after a groan. "He's crazy."

"The plane's surrounded, sweetheart. He's not going anywhere. Dammit, No one can see us. I need help getting these cuffs off."

"He has a copy of the algorithm." She squeezed her hands into fists, trying to control the stinging pain. "You've got to find it."

"Stay conscious, Therese. You need to tell me when we supposedly met."

WADE RAN AFTER the plane to get help. It was the only reason he left Therese lying alone in front of the hangar. He caught up with the cars that had brought it to a halt and caught his breath on the hood.

"My partner. She's bleeding. Need ambulance." He pointed behind him. "The man…armed with a knife somewhere around that building."

"You Hamilton with the Rangers?"

He nodded. "Yes. Can you take me back? Got a handcuff key and med kit?"

"Your team is almost here."

"I can't wait, man. Get her an ambulance."

"Hello out there," Rushdan called from the plane. "We'll surrender, but only to Ranger Hamilton."

"Aw, hell."

Therese needed him. Rushdan Reval was crazy. She'd said it. He agreed. What could he possibly accomplish by going to that plane and taking the man into custody?

He might be able to save lives. And if he didn't try, he was totally sure about one thing… Therese would never forgive him.

He pulled the DFW police officer in close. "You take this car and find my partner. You get her to the hospital no matter what she says. Got it?"

"Yes, sir."

"I need your restraints and your weapon."

"Ranger Hamilton?" Reval shouted.

"I can't—"

"Yes!" Wade nearly grabbed the officer by his shirt front, but dipped his head and regained control. "Please. I'm trusting you with her life."

The officer moved and moved quickly, handing Wade what he needed and jumping in his car. He pulled away like the plane was about to blow.

Oh, damn. What if the plane was rigged to blow?

Chapter Twenty-Six

Wade stuffed the gun down the back of his pants and slapped together the Velcro of the protective vest the officer had shoved at him. He walked with his hands raised toward the stairs of the plane.

"I'm here. You can come out and surrender. Pull off your jacket, hands on your head so we can see you're unarmed."

"Wade, I can't say it's good to see you alive. Come on in."

"Not gonna happen," Jack said from Wade's right side.

"I guarantee you that ain't happening," Slate said from his left.

Heath nodded from his position, pointing a long gun at the nose of the plane. The pilot cut the engine and placed his hands on his head.

"Time to join the party, Reval!" Wade called out. He had to focus on getting Reval out of the plane and finding the second copy of the algorithm. Get this done. But his real attention was on the ambulance that had pulled next to the police car at Hangar Four.

If he could just finish this, he could center his attention on Therese.

"You are surrounded," a voice called through a bullhorn. "Come to the door with your hands on your head."

Wade took a step forward. Jack and Slate pulled him back.

"Don't, Wade," one of them said.

Wade's mind was with Therese. He looked at the blood on his hands. The man in the plane had caused all this.

"If she dies..." he ground out in anger, marching forward before his fellow Rangers could stop him. "Get out here, you filthy coward."

He stopped at the bottom of the stairway, one hand on the rope that would have pulled them closed, one foot on the bottom rung. Rushdan Reval appeared in the doorway, hands in the air and no longer smiling.

"Get out."

"I'm on my way. Don't let them shoot me." Reval took his time, handling the steps carefully.

A lot more carefully than Therese had been able to manage. If she hadn't fallen onto Sal, she might just have a few scrapes and bruises instead of a deep knife wound.

Wade jerked him from the last step, spun him around and raised his fist. "If anyone was going to shoot you, it would have been me."

"Whoa, buddy," Jack said, blocking Wade's right hand. "I'll take it from here. You go see about your girl."

Jack placed the restraints around Reval's wrists. Then turned him, searching his pockets, pulling the shoulders of his jacket down to limit his movements more.

"Where is it?" Wade shouted.

"What?" all the men asked, including Reval.

"He has a copy of the algorithm. Therese said it was on the plane. And there's a second phone with all his terrorist contacts. He had it on his person before we left in the chopper. So where is it?" Wade demanded of Reval. Dammit, he wanted to leave.

Jack found a phone but not a second. Wade remembered Therese's dying declaration that they needed the phone.

"We'll take it from here." Steve Woods, Therese's handler, stepped forward to take Reval off his hands.

"He's been using a second phone. It's probably hidden somewhere on that plane. I wouldn't trust anyone else to look for it if I were you."

"You're right," Steve answered, handing off their domestic terrorist to another ranger. Then he slapped Wade on the back. "Great job. I'll meet you at the hospital."

"She lost a lot of blood. The officer said they're moving her to Baylor Grapevine. We cleared to go?" Heath asked behind them.

His friends stared at him and he stared at Therese across the parking lot as they strapped her to the gurney. Jack's hand came down on one shoulder, Heath's on the other.

"She'll make it," one of them said.

Wade couldn't speak. He was willing her to beat the odds and survive. She had to live. They were a good team. She thought so, right?

The ambulance doors shut. God, he could only assume she was still alive, because they were rushing away. Lights flashing, sirens loud and fierce.

The idea that she might die hit him. His knees buckled. If his friends hadn't been on either side of him, he would have fallen to the ground.

He fought the emotion to keep it from his voice, "Get me out of here."

"Sure, man. We got a car waiting."

They walked him to a vehicle. At some point during the ride to the hospital, one of them peeled the vest off him and handed him a T-shirt. Major Clements met them at the emergency entrance and told him the tower security guard was fine. He'd be reprimanded, but he would live.

"She's going to be okay, Wade," Clements said.

Sometime in his haze and daze, he began believing they'd both be fine. Even if the eye injury kept him from working as a ranger in the field, things would be great if Therese was with him.

God, he really was in love. They barely knew anything about each other, but they knew enough. She was definitely the woman for him.

Therese would live. He deserved some good luck. They both did.

"IT'S ABOUT TIME you woke up, sleepyhead." Wade's face filled Therese's vision.

"I think that's the first sound sleep I've had in years. Painful but sound. What time is it?"

They were both alive. Wade raised a straw to her lips and she took a long sip. The cool water felt almost as good as his skin next to hers. It was just his arm, but she used her hand to rub it comfortingly.

"You should ask what day. It's been two." Wade scratched his chin covered in stubble. "You're going to be okay. Sal missed everything vital."

"Doesn't feel like it." She tried to joke but the words sounded rough.

"I bet. But before you convince me to play that question and answer game… Or before the nurse comes in here and they kick me out… You'll want to know what happened after you lost consciousness."

"I didn't pass out."

"I assure you that you did." He kissed her quickly on the lips and sat back down, taking her hand into his. "Reval surrendered and they caught Sal trying to climb out over the barbed wire fence of the airport. Steve searched the plane, found the phone with all the contacts and the algorithm. I had Andrew's copy. Reval swears there were only two. Homeland's priority is to verify that."

"That's good, but—"

"Turns out Andrew was the sole programmer—according to him. Something else DHS is checking into. It looks like his algorithm was just a fancy word for a highly capable decryption code that was designed and modified to take over air traffic control stations. If terrorists had gotten their hands on it, they would have brought down planes, or worse. Unfortunately, Andrew didn't make it. He fired on the tower guard and I had to shoot."

"Can we get back to what's important?"

"I can give you more details later. All you need to know is that Reval is going away for a very long time. No deals."

"I'm glad we managed to succeed with both of our goals. Now you owe me…" She couldn't believe he looked puzzled. "You don't remember our first fight? Come on. You wanted him put away. And I wanted the programmer?"

"Oh, yeah. That conversation seems like a life-time ago. Your lifetime, to be exact."

"I wasn't going to die. Not when I finally have the chance to live," she whispered. "Speaking of which. It's your turn."

Wade's face relaxed into a smile. He knew exactly what it was his turn to say.

"And you have a story to finish. Talk about drama. You tell me we met years ago and then you promptly get abducted." He picked up her hand and kissed the back of it.

"You first," she prompted.

"Sorry. When did we meet? Did I pull you over when I was with the highway patrol and issue a ticket?"

"Actually, you pulled me out of a wrecked vehicle nine years ago. It was May 31, near San Antonio."

"Damn. You must have just been a kid. That was a

long time ago. And you knew where I lived because you were keeping tabs on me?"

"I would never," she lied.

"I bet you would, Therese Ortis. I bet you would." He leaned forward to kiss her properly on the lips, then sat again. "I wish I could remember you from back then. How come you kept it a secret? Did you have braces or something like that you didn't want me to remember?"

"I thought I'd find you here. Ranger Hamilton, you have to spend some time in your room for us to check on you," a nurse said, walking to a whiteboard to write.

"But Debbie, she just woke up," Wade whined dramatically and winked at Therese.

"Oh my goodness, you are awake. Fantastic. I'll page your doctor as soon as I get your vitals." The nurse wrapped a blood pressure cuff around Therese's arm but looked at Wade. "Seriously, Ranger Hamilton, they're debating if they should add restraints to your bed. You'll have to go back to your room now." She put her hands on her hips but she still didn't look very authoritative.

"Room?"

"We kept him for observation," the nurse supplied.

"I have a little concussion. Nothing's wrong."

Debbie smiled at Therese. "And yet they've kept him here for two days."

"Two days? Were you shot? You've really been here for two days?"

"Yeah, but you didn't miss anything by getting

some rest. And they're kicking me out today so I can officially sleep on your chair."

Did he really think she was more interested in the task force operation than him?

"I'll be back after the day shift does their poking and prodding." Wade stood and kissed Therese sweetly on her forehead and then her lips. "Don't go anywhere without me this time."

He smiled and left before she could get a word out.

The nurse pumped the blood pressure cuff, shaking her head. "That man is too stubborn for—"

"Oh, yeah." He stuck his head through the door opening. "I love you, too. Hell, I'll even buy a couch."

TRUE TO HIS WORD, Wade brought his cell phone with him when he returned to Therese's room. She didn't realize how touch and go it had been that first night. One day he'd tell her. But today was for celebrating that they were both alive.

"You look different," Therese said groggily when she awoke a second time.

"Yeah, the nurses thought you might like me better if I cleaned up. I told them that was impossible— for you to like me more—but they insisted."

"I think the same thing about me. I must look horrible."

"Well, I won't ever lie to you, sweetheart. The bruising is pretty bad. But I'm good with it." He ran his thumb along the line of deep purple discoloration on her shoulder. "But the nurses might be right about cleaning up. I had the guys stop by your place and get some things."

"I don't know if I'm up for that."

"Come on, honey. There are a couple of big surprises you're going to want your hair combed for." He pointed to her bag.

"Can't it wait?"

"You've got about an hour."

"Wade? What's going on?"

"I had a long talk with Agent Woods. He agreed that your undercover days are done. I mean, our pictures have been all over the news and it wouldn't really work any longer."

"And…"

"There are some very important people on their way to be with you."

Therese's eyes filled with unshed tears. "You called my family?"

"Not me, but I'll take some credit."

"He threatened a lot of people to make it happen," Steve said from the doorway. "If it's something you don't want, blame him."

"Oh, I want it," she whispered. "Thank you, Wade."

"Come on, Wade. The nurses are ready to do their thing."

Wade gently kissed a very happy Therese, reluctantly leaving her room.

He stuck his hands in his jeans pockets and wandered to a pillar to wait. Steve followed.

"Thanks for getting the Ortis family up here. It's

the best way you could have thanked her for the sacrifice she made for this country." Wade stuck out his
hand for Steve to shake.

"I heard what you said. It was the very least we
could do. I also heard your physical didn't go so
well."

"You heard right. I've got some permanent eye
damage." He dropped his head, staring at the floor.
"Looks like a spot will be opening up in Company
B."

"Are they transferring you?"

"I resigned."

"Got something in mind?"

Wade looked up at Steve. "You offering?"

"Actually, Homeland wondered if you and Therese
would be interested."

"I don't know. I just bought a couch."

Steve looked confused. "They move those along
with the other furniture."

"Honestly, I'd be happy sitting around a pool for a
while. Whatever she wants. You know? I'm not willing to give her up yet."

"I bet you aren't. Same thing happened to me a
long time ago. I made that mistake. Let her walk
away. Worst day of my life."

"But you're married now, right?"

"That I am. But this is your story and you've got
time to think about it." Steve shook his hand again
and Wade watched as the agent walked down the
hall to the exit.

The nurses came out of Therese's room, leaving

the door open. Wade's phone vibrated with a message that the family had arrived. He didn't have much time.

He knocked before entering. Therese sat up in bed, ready for visitors.

"They're on their way up," Wade told her. "It took them an extra day to get here. I think Heath told me one of your younger brothers attends Washington State."

"I know." She grinned. "I kept tabs on all the people I loved."

"So you are a stalker." He crept over to her side.

"I said you were more like a hero crush." She held her hand out, wiggling her fingers for him to take hold. Which he did.

"That does sound a lot better than stalker," he teased.

"Why don't we just keep that as our little secret." She slid her finger down his nose, landing across his lips.

"I won't ever tell. But I will be exacting blackmail on a regular basis." He leaned in for the long, extended kiss he'd wanted for days.

She wrapped her arms around him, bringing him to sit on the bed next to her, ending their kiss in each other's arms. He could have stayed there. Finally resting because she was awake. And safe.

But her family was on their way. Jack had picked them up personally. Wade sat back, wondering how he would tell her he'd had to resign. But he had a feeling she wouldn't mind. That she'd support him in whatever he decided to do.

Life after being a Texas Ranger…

"Hey, I ordered a couch."

"Really? That's what you think is important right now."

He turned off all the outward charm and stared at her. It was one of the few times in his life he actually tried to be serious. "I never had a reason to buy a couch before. This is a pretty big deal."

"Wade Hamilton, are you asking me out?"

"Well, I do have a couch we can make out on now."

Therese wrapped her arms around his neck, tugged him close and kissed him again.

"Now we have to rescue a dog."

"Oh no. No animals. This thing is plush leather. The real stuff. Not that fake pleather."

Epilogue

Six weeks later

Wade's heart pounded in his chest. It could probably be heard by the people sitting at the next table. He'd never been this nervous in his life. Time was running out to change his mind. But he didn't want to change his mind.

Nope.

He was frightened about the upcoming situation he let himself be talked into. What had he been thinking?

"Are you okay?" Therese asked, reaching around her now empty plate to grab his hand. "Should we go to the hotel instead of trying to see a late movie?"

"No. No. I'm good. Sorry. I've just been thinking."

"Well, that's obvious. I don't mind heading back if you're tired. You did drive me to Fort Worth for a lovely weekend and brought me here for a very fancy dinner." She squeezed his hand tighter. "You *are* springing for dinner, right? Did you forget your wallet?"

To answer, he drew his hand away, pulled his credit card from his wallet and held it in the air, signaling to the waiter. Therese leaned back, wiping the corner of her luscious mouth one last time with her napkin.

"I didn't need dessert anyway."

"Did you see something you wanted?" He barely got the words out when her foot connected with his. He mouthed an "ouch" but it hadn't hurt.

"No, silly. I'd love to head back, too." She winked.

The waiter came and went with the card and Wade took her hand back into his. Things were good. Great, in fact. But they needed this weekend before he headed out for Homeland training.

All their spare time had been spent together, but that had been limited. Between wrapping up the case, grand jury testimony, paperwork, applications, more interviews... Well, they'd barely seen each other. So, yeah, he got the hint about heading back to the hotel.

But first...

They walked hand in hand from the restaurant toward the hotel.

"Hey, what's up?" She dropped his hand, wrapping both around his biceps and giving him a squeeze. "Are you worried about training? They said your blind spot wouldn't be a problem in your new analyst position."

He shook his head, shrugging, and mumbled that he was fine. He could feel her disappointment as she loosened her grip, letting her hands fall to her sides.

Damn...he could barely swallow and his knees

really felt weak. He was just nervous. He hated to admit it, but if he wasn't careful he would blow all the elaborate plans.

Maybe he should tell her and not find out if she enjoyed surprises. He'd been assured by his best friends' girlfriends, Vivian, Kendall and Megan, that *all* women liked this kind of surprise.

Wade scooped up Therese's hand, raising her arm above her head and forcing her into a twirl in the middle of the sidewalk. She laughed. He did it again until they were both smiling and he could forget his nerves.

A minute later they were there.

Sundance Square.

The fountains glowed with a gold light. He'd been told by Megan, Vivian and Kendall it was the perfect backdrop. Beautiful. Great for pictures. Something they all said was important. New traditions and all that.

Tradition?

He'd never had much of that but wanted it now. Even if Therese hadn't mentioned it. Not once. A sign the major and Fred had both warned him of.

Their friends were all around them. He recognized the men from their hats and the women who ducked behind them. But the one woman he loved hadn't noticed. Or at least she didn't give him any indication she had.

Too enthralled with the kids running through the plaza fountain, she didn't seem to pay attention to anything behind them. She was focused only on walking and being happy. Maybe on seeing the show she'd mentioned or just getting back to their hotel.

He wanted to scoop up Therese and run with her over his shoulder back to the truck. What if she said no? God, what if she said yes?

Before he could confuse himself any further, he dropped down to one knee. Strangers pointed. Mothers pulled their kids from splashing through the fountain. And Therese turned around to stare at him, covering her mouth with her fingers.

"Wade? Are you—"

"Why's everyone looking like that? Can't a guy scratch his leg?" He pulled up his dress jeans and reached inside his best boot. That was a clue for all of their friends to get a little closer. Her family sat just a little behind and Therese hadn't noticed them yet.

Therese released a long breath and spun away from him. He snagged the ring tucked safely inside his sock and worked it onto his little finger before pulling his pants leg over his boot.

He didn't move even as she took a couple of steps away from him.

"Oh, thank God. I thought you were going to pro—"

He stayed put, his arm outstretched with an engagement ring on display to everyone except the one it was intended for. When the woman with a kid in her arms pointed in his direction Therese stopped, hesitatingly turning back toward him.

Her beautiful eyes were huge, and the tips of her fingers covered her lips, which were open and in the shape of an O. She stared into his eyes, then at the ring, then back again. Her unblinking orbs filled with tears, making them sparkle.

"Is this a bad idea? Do I need to put this back in my boot?"

He spoke as softly as he could. If she was going to say no, he didn't need all of Fort Worth along with their family and friends hearing.

"Therese?"

She blinked and the tears swiftly slid down her cheeks.

Crying. She was crying. Of all the scenarios that had played through his head...*this* wasn't one of them. He began shifting, preparing to get to his feet.

He wanted to wipe her tears away, but he was stuck kneeling and quickly feeling like an idiot. All the doubts his friends had talked him out of after buying the ring slammed into him again.

"Wait!" Her hands extended to keep him where he was. "If there's a question in there somewhere... I might have an answer."

Hadn't he asked?

"Damn. Therese Ortis, would you marry me?"

"When you put it like that, how could a girl say no?" She smiled and offered him her hand.

He slipped the ring onto the appropriate finger and got up off his knee. He barely kissed her before his friends were slapping him on the back and welcoming Therese to the fold.

She began crying again when she saw her family along with Fred and his wife. Everyone was there for the important moment. Wade had never felt blessed before, but he did now.

"You had all of us worried there for a minute," Jack said.

"I was totally caught off guard." Therese smiled at Wade again.

He was still recovering from her answer and couldn't really think straight to reply. He could only feel and this…*this* was completely right. No doubts. He hugged Therese and spun around.

"I love you," he whispered into her ear. "You're not alone in life. I'll always have your back."

"I love you, too. You're the best partner I've ever had."

"I'm the only partner you've ever had. And for this—" he kissed her finger with the diamond "—the only partner you'll ever need."

* * * * *

Secret Agent Surrender
Elizabeth Heiter

MILLS & BOON

Elizabeth Heiter likes her suspense to feature strong heroines, chilling villains, psychological twists and a little romance. Her research has taken her into the minds of serial killers, through murder investigations and onto the FBI Academy's shooting range. Elizabeth graduated from the University of Michigan with a degree in English literature. She's a member of International Thriller Writers and Romance Writers of America. Visit Elizabeth at www.elizabethheiter.com.

Dear Reader,

Thanks for joining me for the final book in The Lawmen: Bullets and Brawn miniseries. As children, Cole Walker, Andre Diaz and Marcos Costa formed their own family. Now these brothers try to unravel the secret that separated them so many years ago. Andre's and Cole's stories hit shelves over the last two months, and the miniseries finishes with the youngest brother, Marcos.

If you missed the first Lawmen miniseries, you can find out more about all of the lawmen at my website, www.elizabethheiter.com. You can also learn more about my Profiler series, and my FBI profiler, Evelyn Baine, whose latest case involves the mysterious disappearance of a teenager who left behind a note foretelling her own death.

Thanks for reading! I hope you enjoy Marcos and Brenna's story!

Elizabeth Heiter

DEDICATION

For Andrew—I couldn't have imagined a better real-life hero.
I love you!

ACKNOWLEDGMENTS

Thank you to Paula Eykelhof, Kayla King, Denise Zaza
and everyone involved with *Secret Agent Surrender*
behind the scenes. Thanks to my family and friends
for their endless support, with a special thanks to:
Kevan Lyon, Chris Heiter, Robbie Terman, Andrew
Gulli, Kathryn Merhar, Caroline Heiter, Kristen Kobet,
Ann Forsaith, Charles Shipps, Sasha Orr, Nora Smith
and Mark Nalbach.

CAST OF CHARACTERS

Marcos Costa—Deep undercover on a DEA operation, Marcos crosses paths with his first crush, Brenna Hartwell, and he's smitten all over again. The problem is, she might have set the fire that separated him and his foster brothers as kids—and when this operation is over, he'll have to arrest her.

Brenna Hartwell—The rookie police officer is in way over her head when she runs into Marcos again at a drug lord's hideaway. She's onto something big that could change everything they know about the fire, and getting to the truth means getting close to Marcos. Only, if she gets too close, their covers could be blown—and then they're both dead.

Cole Walker—Marcos's eldest foster brother is a police detective, but the role he's always taken most seriously is "big brother" and he's there whenever Marcos needs him.

Andre Diaz—Marcos's elder foster brother is a sniper for the FBI. Like Cole, he'll do whatever it takes to keep Marcos safe when he tries to unravel a decades-old secret.

Carlton Wayne White—The drug lord has been gaining power for nearly twenty years, and Brenna suspects he's doing it on the backs of foster kids.

Jesse White—Carlton's nephew was orphaned and left in Carlton's care. He's Marcos's in at the drug lord's hideaway, but could a secret from his own past ruin the undercover operation?

Chapter One

"This is a bad idea," Marcos Costa muttered as he drove the flashy convertible the DEA had provided him into the middle of Nowhere, Maryland. Or rather, *up* into the middle of nowhere. He could actually feel the altitude change as he revved the convertible up this unpaved road into the Appalachian Mountains.

"It was your idea," his partner's voice returned over the open cell-phone line.

"Doesn't make it a good one," Marcos joked. The truth was, it was a brilliant idea. So long as he lived through it.

The DEA had been trying to get an in with Carlton Wayne White for years, but the man was paranoid and slippery. Until now, they hadn't even had an address for him.

That was, assuming the address Marcos was heading to now actually did turn out to be Carlton's mansion and not an old coal mine where a drug lord could bury the body of an undercover agent whose cover was blown. Namely, his.

"According to the GPS, I'm close," Marcos told his partner. "I'm going to hide the phone now. I'm only going to contact you on this again if I run into trouble."

"Be careful."

"Will do." Marcos cut the call, hoping he sounded confident. Usually, he loved the thrill of an undercover meet. But this wasn't their usual buy-bust situation, where he'd show up, flash a roll of money, then plan the meet to get the drugs and instead of doing a trade, pull his badge and his weapon. Today, he'd been invited into the home of a major heroin dealer. And if everything went like it was supposed to, he'd spend the entire weekend there, being wined and dined by Carlton.

Because right now, he wasn't Marcos Costa, a rising star in the DEA's ranks. He was Marco Costrales, major player in the drug world. Or, at least, aspiring major player in the drug world, with the kind of money that could buy a front-row seat in the game.

Pulling over, Marcos slid the car into Park and popped open a hidden compartment underneath the passenger seat. Ironically, the car had originally belonged to a dealer down in Florida, and the compartment had been used to hide drugs. Today, Marcos turned off his cell phone to save the battery and slipped it in there, hoping he wouldn't need it again until he was safely out of the Appalachians.

This was way outside normal DEA protocol, but Carlton Wayne White was a big catch, and Marcos's partner was a fifteen-year veteran with a reputation as a maverick who had some major pull. Somehow, he'd convinced their superiors to let them run the kind of op the agency hadn't approved in decades. And the truth was, this was the sort of case Marcos had dreamed about when he'd joined the DEA.

"Let's do this," Marcos muttered, then started the car again. The dense foliage cleared for a minute, giving him an unobstructed view over the edge of the mountain. His breath caught at its beauty. He could see for miles, over peaks and valleys, the setting sun casting a pink-and-orange glow over everything. Carlton Wayne White didn't deserve this kind of view.

Then it was gone again, and Marcos was surrounded by trees. The GPS told him to turn and he almost missed it, spotting a narrow dirt trail at the last second. He swung the wheel right, giving the convertible a little gas as the trail got steeper. It seemed to go on forever, until all of a sudden it leveled out, and there in front of him was an enormous modern home surrounded by an ugly, electrified fence.

Most of the people who lived up here were in that transitional spot between extreme poverty and being able to eke out a living to support themselves. They had a reputation for abhorring outsiders, but rumor had it that Carlton had spread a little cash around to earn loyalty. And from the way the DEA had been stonewalled at every attempt to get information on him, it seemed to have worked.

Marcos pulled up to the gate, rolled down his window and pressed the button on the intercom stationed there. He'd passed a major test to even be given this address, which told him that his instincts about the source he'd been cultivating for months had been worth every minute. "Hey, it's Marco. Here to see Carlton. He's expecting me."

He played it like the wealthy, aspiring drug dealer they expected him to be, entitled and a little arrogant. His cover story was that he came from major family money—old organized crime money—and he was looking to branch out on his own. It was the sort of connection they all hoped Carlton would jump on.

There was no response over the intercom, but almost instantly the gates slid open, and Marcos drove inside. He watched them close behind him and tried to shake off the foreboding that washed over him. The sudden feeling that he was never going to drive out again.

Given the size of his operation, the DEA knew far too little about how Carlton worked, but they did know one thing. The man was a killer. He'd been brought up on charges for it more than once, but each time, the witnesses mysteriously disappeared before he could go to trial.

"You've got this," Marcos told himself as he pulled to a stop and climbed out of the convertible.

He was met by his unwitting source, Jesse White. The man was Carlton's nephew. Jesse's parents had died when he was seventeen and Carlton had taken him in, provided him with a home and pulled him right into the family business. Unlike Carlton, Jesse had a conscience. But he was desperate to prove himself to the uncle who'd given him a home when no one else would. Marcos had spotted it when he'd been poring over documents on all the known players. He'd purposely run into Jesse at a pool bar and slowly built that friendship until he could make his approach.

"Hey, man," Jesse greeted him now. The twenty-four-year-old shifted his weight back and forth, his hands twitching. He was tall and thin, and usually composed. Today, he looked ready to jump at the slightest noise.

Please don't get cold feet, Marcos willed him. Jesse didn't know Marcos's true identity, but that didn't matter. If things went bad and his uncle found out Jesse had brought an undercover agent to his house, being a blood relative wouldn't save the kid.

Marcos tried not to feel guilty about the fact that when this was all over, if things went *his* way, Jesse would be going to jail, too. Because Marcos also saw something in Jesse that reminded him of himself. He knew what it was like to have no one in the world to rely on, and he knew exactly how powerful the loyalty could be when someone filled that void.

In Jesse's case, the person who'd filled it happened to be a deadly criminal.

Marcos had gotten lucky. After spending his entire life in foster care, being shipped from one home to the next and never feeling like he belonged, he'd finally hit the jackpot. In one of those foster homes, he'd met two boys who'd become his chosen brothers. He wasn't sure where he would have wound up without them, but he knew his path could have ended up like Jesse's.

Shaking off the memory, Marcos replied, "How's it going?" He gave Jesse their standard greeting—clasped hands, chest bump.

"Good, good," Jesse said, his gaze darting everywhere. "Come on in and meet my uncle."

For a second, Marcos's instinct was to turn and run, but he ignored it and followed Jesse into the mansion. They walked through a long entryway filled with marble and crystal, where they were greeted by a pair of muscle-bound men wearing all-black cargo pants and T-shirts, with illegally modified AK-47s slung over their backs.

One of them frisked Marcos, holding up the pistol he'd tucked in his waistband with a raised eyebrow.

"Hey, man, I don't go anywhere without it," Marcos said. A real aspiring dealer with mob connections wouldn't come to this meet without a weapon.

The man nodded, like he'd expected it, and shoved the weapon into his own waistband. "You'll get it back when you leave."

Marcos scowled, acting like he was going to argue, then shrugged as if he'd decided to let it go. The reality was that so far, things were going as expected. Still, he felt tense and uneasy.

Then Jesse led him down a maze of hallways probably meant to confuse anyone who didn't know the place well. Finally, the hallway opened into a wide room with a soaring ceiling, filled with modern furniture, artwork and antiques, some of which Marcos could tell with a brief glance had been illegally obtained.

From the opposite hallway, a man Marcos recognized from his case files appeared. Carlton Wayne White was massive, at nearly six-and-a-half-feet tall, with the build of a wrestler. His style was flamboyant, and today he wore an all-white suit, his white-blond hair touching his shoulders. But Marcos knew not to let Carlton's quirks distract him from the fact that the drug dealer was savvy and had a bad temper.

"Marco Costrales," Carlton greeted him, appraising him for a drawn-out moment before he crossed the distance between them and shook Marcos's hand.

Marcos wasn't small—he was five-nine—and made regular use of his gym membership, because he needed to be able to throw armed criminals to the ground and hold them down while he cuffed them. But this guy's gigantic paw made Marcos feel like a child.

"Welcome," Carlton said, his voice a low baritone. "My nephew tells me you're in the market for a business arrangement."

"That's right. I'm looking—"

"No business yet," Carlton cut him off. "This weekend, we get to know one another. Make sure we're on the same page. Things go well, and I'll set you up. Things go poorly?" He shrugged, dropping into a chair and draping his beefy arms over the edges. "You'll never do business again."

He gave a toothy smile, then gestured for Marcos to sit.

That same foreboding rushed over Marcos, stronger this time, like a tidal wave he could never fight. He could only pray the current wouldn't pull him under. He tried to keep his face impassive as he settled onto the couch.

Then Carlton snapped his fingers, and three things happened simultaneously. Jesse sat gingerly on the other side of the couch, a tuxedo-clad man appeared with a tray bearing flutes of champagne and a woman strode into the room from the same direction Marcos had come.

Marcos turned to look at the woman, and he stopped breathing. He actually had to remind himself to start again as he stared at her.

She was petite, probably five-four, with a stylish shoulder-length bob and a killer red dress. She had golden brown skin and dark brown eyes that seemed to stare right inside a man, to his deepest secrets. And this particular woman knew his deepest secret.

Because even though it wasn't possible—it couldn't be—he knew her.

"Meet Brenna Hartwell," Carlton said, his voice bemused. "I can see you're already smitten, Marco, but don't get too attached. Brenna is off-limits."

It *was* her. Marcos flashed back eighteen years. He'd been twelve when Brenna Hartwell had come to the foster home where he'd lived for five years. The moment he'd seen her, he'd had a similar reaction: a sudden certainty that his life would never be the same. His very first crush. And it had been intense.

Too bad a few months later she'd set their house on fire, destroying it and separating him from the only brothers he'd ever known.

After all these years, he couldn't believe he'd recognized her so instantly. He prayed that she wouldn't recognize him, but as her eyes widened, he knew she had.

"Marcos?" she breathed.

And his worst nightmare came true. His cover was blown.

Chapter Two

Marcos Costa.

Brenna couldn't stop herself from staring. Fact was, she might have been drooling a little.

What were the chances? She hadn't seen him since she was eleven years old, a few short months after her whole world had been destroyed and she'd found herself dropped into a foster home. She'd still been reeling from her mother's death, still been physically recovering herself from the car crash that had taken her only family away from her. She'd walked into that foster home, terrified and broken and alone. And the first person she'd seen had been Marcos.

Back then, he'd been twelve, kind of scrawny, with dimples that dominated his face. Even through her devastation, she'd been drawn to him. To this day, she couldn't say quite what it was, except that she'd felt like her soul had recognized him. It sounded corny, even in her own head, but it was the best she'd ever been able to understand it.

Now, there was nothing scrawny about him. Next

to Carlton, sure, anyone looked smaller, but this grown-up version of Marcos was probably average height. It was hard to tell with him sitting, but one thing she could see quite well was that he'd filled out. Arms that had once resembled twigs were now sculpted muscle, easily visible through his polo shirt.

And the dimples? They were still there, like the cherry on top of an ice-cream sundae. The man looked like a movie star, with his full, dark head of hair and blue-gray eyes that popped against his pale skin. And just like when she'd been eleven, she couldn't stop staring into those eyes, feeling like she could happily keep doing it for hours.

"You two know each other?"

Brenna snapped out of her daze, realizing Carlton was glancing between them suspiciously as Marcos told her, "Marc-OH. My name is Marco."

"Marco," she repeated dumbly, still wondering what in the world he was doing here. Of all the ways she'd imagined running into him again, in the middle of the mountains at a drug lord's lair certainly wasn't one of them.

And if she didn't get her act together fast, she was going to get both of them killed.

Brenna tried to clear the dazed expression from her face. "Sort of," she answered Carlton, wishing her voice had come out as breezy as she'd intended, instead of breathless.

She glanced back at Marcos, praying whatever he was doing here, he'd leave before he could ruin things for her. This was a once-in-a-lifetime opportunity, and she wasn't going to let it slip away, not even for the first boy who'd made her heart race and her palms sweat.

She strode through the enormous room, her too-high heels clicking against the marble floor, and then settled onto the chair next to Carlton. "I picked him up at a bar. When was it? A couple of years ago?" She shook her head, letting out a laugh, hoping Marcos would go along with her story.

She could have told them she'd known Marcos from the foster home. Carlton knew her history—at least the version of it she'd chosen to let him hear—and he definitely knew about her time at that foster home. But Marcos was using a fake name, and she didn't know what his game was, but she didn't want to contradict whatever story he'd given Carlton. Because no matter how much her heart hurt at the idea of the adult Marcos being a criminal, she held out hope that he was here for some other reason. And she definitely didn't want to cause his death.

"Sorry for telling you my name was Crystal," she said to Marcos.

Carlton guffawed and relaxed again. "Lucky man," he told Marcos.

Marcos's gaze lingered on her a moment longer before he looked back at Carlton. "Yeah, until she slipped out at dawn. But you never forget a face like that." His eyes darted back to her for a split second, and then he accepted the glass of champagne the butler held out.

Brenna relaxed a tiny bit. She shook her head at the butler when he stopped in front of her and simply watched as Carlton, Jesse and Marcos toasted to a potential friendship.

Disappointment slumped her shoulders. She knew what a "potential friendship" toast meant. Marcos Costa was a drug dealer.

· She should have recognized it instantly. There weren't very many reasons someone would come out to Carlton Wayne White's secret mansion. To even earn an invite, Marcos had to have some serious connections.

But Brenna couldn't help herself. She looked at him now and she still saw the boy who had opened the door for her, taken her pathetic suitcase in one hand, and her hand in the other. That foster home hadn't been anything close to a real second home to her, but she'd realized after being sent away a few months later that she'd gotten very, very lucky at that first introduction to life in the system. She'd gotten very, very lucky meeting Marcos.

She'd spent most of the rest of her life dreaming of him whenever things got tough, creating a fiction where she'd see him again and he'd sweep her off her feet. She knew it was ridiculous, but that didn't matter. The dream of Marcos Costa had gotten her through the worst times in her life.

It made her sad to see that he'd grown up into

someone who'd have a "potential friendship" with the likes of Carlton Wayne White. Of course, what must he think of her? She wondered suddenly if he'd ever suspected she'd set the fire eighteen years ago that had separated them.

Why would he? Brenna shook it off and tried to focus. She couldn't let Marcos Costa—whatever his agenda—distract her.

She'd worked hard to get this invite to Carlton's house. She'd spent weeks planning ways to catch his attention, then even more weeks testing those theories, until finally he'd taken the bait. But Carlton hadn't gotten to where he was by being careless, or being easily distracted by a woman who wanted to trade assets. She knew he didn't trust her yet. And there was only so far she was willing to go to earn that trust.

But she needed to get close to him, so she could dig up his secrets as thoroughly as she knew he'd tried to look into hers. Because the events of that day eighteen years ago, when the study had gone up in flames around her, still haunted her. And she suspected that Carlton Wayne White, whether he knew it or not, was connected to that day. And that meant he was connected to her. He just didn't know it yet.

If everything went as planned, he wouldn't know it until it was far too late.

THREE HOURS LATER, after a ridiculously heavy five-course meal filled with meaningless small talk,

Brenna walked gingerly toward the room Carlton had put her in. Her feet were killing her. The shoes he'd bought her boasted a label she'd never be able to afford, but as good as they looked, they were far from comfortable. Give her tennis shoes over these heels any day of the week. But she'd never tell him that.

Carlton had bought her the dress, too, as well as a necklace that probably cost more than her car. So far, he seemed to be respecting her boundaries: she'd made it clear that she wasn't interested in being anyone's mistress. But she'd also dropped hints that she liked the sort of life her job with the state could never give her.

Slowly, over the course of a series of dinner meetups where she'd pretended to be naive enough to think he was interested in simple friendship, he'd dropped his own hints about what he could offer her. About what she might offer him in return.

And now here she was, at his mansion, far from help if he discovered her real intentions, being "interviewed" as clearly as Carlton was doing to Marcos.

Marcos. It had been hard to keep her eyes off him during dinner, a fact she was sure Carlton hadn't missed. Even if Marcos hadn't been her first childhood crush, he was exactly her type. Or at least, he would have been if he weren't a drug dealer.

Besides his good looks, the man was charming and funny and interesting. Maybe a little more cocky and entitled than she'd have expected, but then again, never in a million years would she have pegged that he'd grow up and fall into crime.

He'd seemed so well-adjusted those few months she'd known him, doing well in his classes, having a clear bond with two older boys in the house, a brotherhood that went beyond blood. What had happened to him after that fire?

She knew he and his brothers had been torn apart. All six foster kids had been sent to different places. But that was all she knew; she'd thought about looking him up more than once over the years, but she'd never done it. Now, she almost wished she didn't know the path he'd chosen.

Was it her fault? If she hadn't walked into the study when she had, if that fire hadn't started, would he have traveled a different path?

"Brenna."

The soft voice behind her startled her, and Brenna stepped sideways on her stiletto. She would have fallen except a strong hand grabbed her waist. For a moment, her back was pressed against a ripped, masculine frame she didn't have to see to instinctively recognize.

She regained her balance, her pulse unsteady as she spun and found Marcos standing inches away from her. This close, she should have seen some imperfection, but the only thing marring those too-handsome features was the furrow between his eyebrows. It sure looked like disappointment.

Her spine stiffened, and she took a small step

backward. "Marcos, uh, Marco." She glanced around, seeing no one, but that didn't mean much. Carlton was notoriously paranoid. For all she knew, he had cameras inside his house as well as around the perimeter.

Marcos must have had the same thought, because his words were careful as he told her, "I never expected to see you again after that night. And now you're with Carlton, huh?"

All through dinner, she could see Marcos trying to figure out her relationship with Carlton. The drug kingpin had seen it, too, because he'd made offhand comments that implied she was his, without being so obvious she'd be forced to correct him. But apparently, Marcos had bought it.

She flushed at the idea that he thought she was sleeping with a drug lord for jewelry and cars. But she also heated at the idea of keeping up the ruse that she'd spent a night in Marcos's bed.

What would that be like? Her thoughts wandered, to the two of them, sweaty, limbs tangled on the huge bed in her room. She shook it off, but it must not have been fast enough, because when she focused on Marcos again, the look he was giving her told her he'd imagined it, too.

"Uh, no. Carlton and I aren't dating, if that's what you're asking."

"I'm not sure that's what I'd call it," Marcos replied softly.

She scowled at him. "We have a business arrangement, and it's not what you think, so stop looking at me like that. The fact is, my arrangement with him is probably not all that different from yours."

Except it was. The ruse she was running with Carlton was about access, not drugs. If she really planned to go through with what she'd promised him, though, it was probably worse than dealing drugs.

His eyes narrowed on her, studying her with a too-keen gaze, and she tried not to squirm. He had the look of a lot of criminals who made it long enough to build an empire—or so she'd come to believe in her limited experience. Oddly, it was a similar probing look that cops used.

"So, Brenna, what do you do when you're not hanging out in Carlton's mansion, wearing spectacular dresses?" Marcos asked, shifting his weight like he was getting comfortable for a long chat.

The urge to fidget grew stronger. Lying didn't come naturally to her, as much as she'd tried to convince her superiors that she could do it—that she could do *this*, come into a drug lord's home and lie to him over an entire weekend, get him to give her insight and access. She'd actually felt pretty confident—well, a careful balance of confidence and determination—until Marcos had shown up. Now, she just felt off balance.

"I work for the foster care system." She kept up the story she'd given Carlton. "I grew up in the system," she added, even though he knew that. But it was more a reminder to herself: always act as though

Carlton or one of his thugs was watching. "And I wanted to be on the other side of it, make some changes."

Marcos tipped his head, his eyes narrowing, like he suspected she was lying, but he wasn't sure about what.

She longed to tell him the whole truth, but that was beyond foolish, and one more sign that her boss was right. She wasn't ready for undercover work, wasn't ready for an assignment like this.

If she told Marcos the truth, she'd be dead by morning.

Still, she couldn't help wondering what he'd say. The words lodged in her throat, and she held them there.

I'm a cop.

Chapter Three

Brenna Hartwell was lying to him.

Marcos didn't know exactly what she was lying about, but he'd been in law enforcement long enough to see when someone was doing it. And not just to him, but to Carlton, too. He prayed the drug boss didn't realize it.

"What do you do for the foster care system?" he asked, wondering if even that much was true.

She fidgeted, drawing his attention to the red dress that fit her like a bandage, highlighting every curve. She was in great shape. Probably a runner. Or maybe a boxer, given the surprising muscle tone he'd felt when he'd grabbed her to keep her from stumbling in her shoes.

"Right now, placement," she said, but something about the way she said it felt rehearsed. "But I'm trying to get them to start a program to help kids transition out of the system."

It was a notoriously tricky time. Kids who spent their lives in foster care hit eighteen and that was it. They were on their own, and they had to learn to sink or swim without any help pretty fast.

Some—like Marcos's oldest brother Cole—did whatever it took. Cole had taken on two jobs, built up his bank account until he could afford an apartment big enough for three. Then when Marcos and his other older brother Andre had been kicked out of the system, they'd actually had a home waiting for them.

But Marcos was lucky. And he knew it. Most foster kids didn't have that. Most kids found themselves suddenly searching for shelter and a job. Tons ended up instantly homeless, and plenty took whatever work they could get, including something criminal.

Had that been what had really happened to Brenna? When she'd shown up on their foster home doorstep that day eighteen years ago, her chin up, blinking back tears, his heart had broken for her. A few months later, she'd been gone. He'd always wondered where she'd ended up, but he'd been too afraid to search for her.

Some kids got lucky, ended up in foster homes with fantastic parents who ultimately adopted them. Others, like him, bounced around from one foster home to the next, from birth until eighteen. He supposed he'd never searched for her because he'd always wanted to believe she'd been one of the lucky ones.

"What about you?" Brenna asked, and he was surprised to hear the wary disappointment in her tone.

She was in Carlton's house because she could offer him something. If it wasn't sex, like Carlton had been implying over dinner, then it was some kind of criminal connection. So, who was she to judge *his* motives?

Still, he felt a little embarrassed as he gave his cover story, the way a real dealer would. "Carlton and I share similar business interests. We're talking about a transaction, but I need to pass his test first." He gave her a lopsided grin. "How do you think I'm doing so far?"

She shrugged. "I wouldn't know. I think you and I are in similar positions."

Interesting. So her association with Carlton was relatively new. He wondered if he could get her out of here when he left, convince her to move her life onto a different track. Maybe all she needed was a little help.

It was a thought Marcos knew could get him killed. Doing anything to disrupt Carlton's life before he committed to the deal and Marcos could slap cuffs on him threatened the whole operation. But the idea hung on, refusing to let go.

For years, he'd had an image of Brenna Hartwell in his mind: a perfect, grown-up version of the little girl who'd made his heart beat faster. And even though she probably couldn't have lived up to that fantasy even if she weren't a criminal, he was still drawn to her in a way he couldn't really explain.

"I should go to bed," Brenna said, interrupting his

thoughts. She stared a minute longer, like she wanted to say something, but finally turned and headed off to her room.

All the while, he longed to call after her, longed to ask her why she'd set that fire eighteen years ago. Instead, he watched her go until the door near the end of the hallway clicked quietly shut behind her.

Then Marcos headed to his own room, down a different hallway. He'd just turned the corner when Carlton pushed away from the wall, out of the shadows, nearly making Marcos jump.

The drug kingpin's eyes were narrowed, his lips tightened into a thin line. "Maybe I didn't make myself clear at dinner," Carlton said, his voice low and menacing, almost a snarl. "So, let me be plain. Stay away from Brenna. Or our business here is finished before we get started."

"She's a rookie!"

"Sir, she's determined. She dug all this up on Carlton Wayne White herself. She's found an angle we never even considered and I think it's going to work. She—"

"She's got no undercover experience."

"No, but we can give her a crash course. She's smart. We've never gotten this close to him before."

"I don't like it. And the DEA wants this guy for themselves. They won't be happy if we jump into their territory."

"So don't tell them. It doesn't have anything to do with drugs anyway. Not really."

"Hartwell could get herself killed."

Brenna had overheard the conversation last month, between the chief at her small police station and her immediate boss, the guy who'd convinced her to join the police force in the first place. Victor Raine was the closest thing she had to a friend on the force. She'd met him years ago, when she'd first gotten out of foster care and gone to a presentation on job opportunities. He'd been there, talking about police work, and she'd gone up and asked him a bunch of questions.

Ultimately, when she'd gotten a surprise college scholarship offer that covered not just her tuition, but also part of her lodging, she'd chosen that instead. But years later, after she'd graduated and bounced from job to job without feeling fulfilled, she'd looked Victor up. She'd visited him at the station, and somehow found herself applying to the police academy.

Before she knew it, she had graduated and was a real, sworn-in police officer. It was scarier—and better—than she'd ever expected. But typical rookie patrol assignments had lost their luster quickly, and she'd started digging for more.

Her plan to infiltrate Carlton's network had come to her by accident. She'd been on foot patrol with her partner, a newbie right out of the academy, barely out of his teens. Next to him, her six months of experience had seemed like a lifetime. They'd gotten a call about a disturbance, and when they'd arrived, they'd found a kid stabbed and left for dead on the street.

She'd cradled his head in her lap while she'd called for help, and tried to put pressure on his wounds. He'd stared up into her eyes, his baby blues filled with tears, silently begging her to help him. But he'd been too far gone. He'd died before the ambulance had gotten there, and she'd been left, bathed in his blood, to answer the detectives' questions.

She'd had nothing to tell them. He hadn't said a word, just looked at her, his gaze forever burned into her memory. So, as they'd dug into his murder, she'd followed the case's progress.

She'd learned the kid's name: Simon Mellor. And she'd discovered he was just eighteen years old, a few months out of the foster care system, probably killed running drugs for someone because he couldn't find any better options for himself.

The fury that had filled her then still heated her up whenever she thought about him. The investigation had stalled out and it looked destined to become a cold case, so Brenna had made it her mission to figure out who'd killed the kid. What she'd discovered had led her back to Victor, to the biggest favor she'd ever asked her mentor.

And he'd agreed, gone to their chief and begged for her chance to go undercover in Carlton's operation. Brenna had stood outside the door, just out of sight, but she'd heard her chief's "no way" coming long before he'd said it.

So when he'd announced, "Hartwell could get herself killed," Brenna had pushed open that door, slapped her hands on her hips and told him, "That's a chance I'm willing to take."

This morning, as she slipped into another slinky dress Carlton had bought her, she realized that was a strong possibility. She was way out of her league here. The quick training she'd received on under-cover work—how to remember a cover story, how to befriend a criminal and keep the disgust she really felt hidden—could only take her so far. And now, with Marcos here, she felt unfocused when she needed every advantage she could get.

Carlton Wayne White was behind Simon Mellor's death. He hadn't held the knife—he was too far up the chain for something like that. But he'd ordered it. And Brenna was determined to make him pay.

But if that was all there was to it, her chief never would have approved this assignment. What Brenna had uncovered went way deeper than one boy's murder. Because he wasn't the only kid who'd wound up dead shortly after getting out of foster care, with rumors of a drug connection surrounding his murder. She didn't know how he was doing it yet, but Carlton was using the foster care system to find pawns for his crimes.

If she was right, he'd been doing it for years, building his empire on the backs of foster care kids.

Most of what she remembered from that horrible night eighteen years ago was the fire. The smell of the smoke, the feel of it in her lungs. The heat of the blaze, reaching for her, swallowing up everything in its path. But one of the things in its path had been papers, and years later, when she'd seen similar papers at the foster system headquarters, she'd known.

Carlton Wayne White was using someone in the system to get names of kids who were turning eighteen. Kids who'd have nothing: no family, no money, no help. He'd swoop in and offer them a chance to put a roof over their head and food in their bellies. And then they'd die for him.

It all ends soon, she promised herself, yanking open her door and striding into the hallway—and smack into Marcos.

What was he doing outside her room?

She didn't actually have to speak the words, because as he steadied her—yet again—he answered. "Carlton told me to come and get you for breakfast."

She couldn't help herself. Her gaze wandered over him, still hungry for another look after so many years. Today, he was dressed in dark-wash jeans and a crewneck sweater that just seemed to emphasize the breadth of his chest.

"Brenna," he said, humor and hunger in his tone.

She looked up, realizing she'd been blatantly ogling him. "Sorry." She flushed.

The hunger didn't fade from his eyes, but his expression grew serious. "Brenna, I want—"

She wanted, too. Maybe it was just the chance to finally do something about her very first crush, or the fact that she'd never expected—but always hoped—to see Marcos again.

It was foolish and wrong for so many reasons, but she couldn't seem to help herself. She leaned up on her tiptoes in another pair of ridiculous shoes and practically fell toward him, looping her arms around his neck.

His hands locked on her waist, and then her lips were on his, just the briefest touch before he set her back on her feet.

"Brenna," he groaned. "We can't do that. Carlton—"

"He's not here right now," she cut him off, not wanting to think about Carlton and the dangerous mission she'd begged to get assigned to. Because all she could think about was Marcos. The boy she'd never been able to forget, morphed into a man she couldn't stop thinking about. She leaned back into him, and she could tell she'd caught him off guard.

Before he could protest again, she fused her lips to his. Just one real taste, she promised herself, and then she'd back away, leave him alone and go back to her mission.

He kissed the way she'd imagined he would in all those childhood fantasies she'd had, where she grew up and got out of those foster homes she'd been sent to after the fire. Like a fairy-tale ending come to life.

Except this wasn't a fairy tale. And Marcos was a drug dealer.

She pulled away, feeling dazed and unsteady. He

didn't look much better; he actually seemed shocked he'd kissed her back at all. But as she stared up at him, breathing hard and trying to pull herself together, she could see it on his face. He was thinking about kissing her again.

And, Lord help her, she wanted him to.

"I warned you to stay away from her!"

Carlton's voice boomed down the hallway, making her jump. She almost fell, but braced herself on the wall as Carlton strode toward them, fury in his expression and ownership in his voice that made a chill run through her.

Then he snapped his fingers and his thugs pounded down the hallway, too.

Marcos put his hands up, trying to placate him, but it didn't matter. One of the guards slung his semiautomatic rifle over his shoulder and punched Marcos in the stomach, making him double over.

As Brenna gasped and yelled for Carlton to stop them, the thugs each took Marcos by an arm and dragged him down the corridor.

And she knew what was going to happen next. They were going to kill him.

Chapter Four

Marcos tensed his muscles, but it didn't stop the pain when one of Carlton's guards slammed an oversize fist into his stomach. The punch doubled him over, his eyes watering. They'd been hitting him for five minutes, and he could feel it all over his body. Gasping for air, he staggered backward, giving himself a few precious seconds to gauge his options.

Fight or flight?

His car was a few feet behind him, his DEA phone secreted in the hidden compartment, his keys always in his pocket. But there was no way he'd make it. Both bodyguards had semiautomatic weapons slung over their backs. He couldn't run faster than they could swing the weapons around and fire.

Fighting was a problem, too. These two might have looked like more brawn than brain, but they weren't stupid. They were staying on either side of him, one at a time stepping forward for a hit, the other keeping enough distance that he couldn't take on one without the other being able to fire.

Besides, Brenna was still inside. He could hear her, screaming at Carlton to stop them. And it didn't matter what deal she had with the drug kingpin. If Carlton was this angry at Marcos for a simple kiss, what would he do to Brenna for choosing Marcos over him? Marcos couldn't leave her.

Not that he was going to have much of a choice, the way things were going. The guy came at him again, before Marcos could fully recover, and swept his feet out from underneath him.

He hit the concrete hard, pain ricocheting through his skull. Black spots formed in front of his eyes and bile burned his throat. His biggest undercover assignment, and he was going to die all alone in the middle of the Appalachians. Would they even find his body? Would his brothers know what had happened to him?

The thought gave him strength, and as he made out a size thirteen crashing toward him through his wavering vision, Marcos rolled right. His stomach and his head rebelled, but he held it together, shoving himself to his feet. He was unsteady, but standing.

And then he spotted her. Brenna stood in the doorway to the house. She was screaming, he realized—it wasn't just his ears ringing. Carlton had his arms wrapped around her, lifting her off the ground, but not moving as she swung her feet frantically, trying to escape.

Fury lit Marcos, and it seemed to intensify the pain in his head. He must have swayed on his feet, because the guards both moved toward him at once, smiling, and Marcos recognized his chance.

The first guard swung a fist. Instinctively, Marcos ducked, then stepped forward fast, getting close enough to slam an uppercut into his chin.

The guard's head snapped backward, but Marcos didn't waste time with a follow-up punch. He twisted right, bringing his palm up this time, right into the second guard's nose. Blood spurted, spraying Marcos as the guy howled and staggered backward, his hands pressed to his face.

In his peripheral vision, he could see Carlton's surprise as he let Brenna go. She stumbled, losing one of her shoes as she came running toward him. Behind her, Marcos could see Carlton's hand reach behind his back—surely where he had his own weapon.

He opened his mouth to warn Brenna to duck when the first guy he'd hit shoved himself to his feet. Marcos barreled into him, taking him to the ground hard, his only hope to grab the guy's weapon and shoot first.

It was a desperate move, and unlikely to work, but he didn't even have a chance to try, because the second guy pulled a pistol that had been hidden under his T-shirt. He was swinging it toward Marcos when Brenna slammed into him, taking the guy down despite the fact that he must have outweighed her by a hundred pounds. They fell to the ground together, but Marcos didn't have time to do more than say a silent prayer neither of them had been shot as the guy underneath him suddenly rolled, bucking Marcos off.

He shoved to his knees, ready to slam into the guy again, but he'd somehow managed to yank his AK-47 up toward Marcos.

Marcos's breath caught and then a gunshot rang out.

Shock slammed through him, and it took several seconds before he could process it. He hadn't been hit. The guy in front of him was down, though, eyes staring blankly at the sky, gun lying uselessly at his side.

Marcos glanced over at Carlton, but the man looked as surprised as Marcos felt. Carlton's weapon dangled in his hand, like he'd been getting ready to use it but hadn't been fast enough.

Swiveling to stare at Brenna, Marcos watched as she slowly lowered the weapon she'd somehow gotten away from Carlton's other bodyguard. He lay half underneath her, moaning in pain.

She was breathing hard, blinking rapidly, and he knew instantly that she'd never killed anyone before.

Marcos saw movement from the corner of his eye, and he knew before he looked up that Carlton was raising his gun hand. Marcos gauged the distance to the nearest AK-47, but it was too far, and he knew it even before Carlton barked, "Don't even think about it."

His gaze lifted, and he readied himself for a second time to be shot, but Carlton wasn't pointing the pistol at him.

He was pointing it at Brenna.

"Do you have some kind of death wish?"

Carlton's voice, usually loud and boisterous, was scarily quiet. But the menace came through as clearly as if he'd screamed at her as he pointed the gun at her head.

Brenna realized her mistake instantly. She shouldn't have lowered her weapon. She should have swung it toward Carlton.

But she'd never shot anyone before. Sure, she'd fired a weapon hundreds of times. In practice. She'd even held a weapon on resisting suspects before. But she'd never had to use it to protect herself or someone else.

Until now.

There was no question Carlton's bodyguards were going to kill Marcos. Nothing she'd said had swayed the drug lord. And when he'd released her, she'd acted on instinct. Instinct and fury, and something fiercely protective that scared her.

And afterward, when the man had dropped to the ground, no dying scream, no time for surprise to register on his face, her hand had just gone slack on her. She hadn't even consciously decided to kill him and now it was over.

She'd just *killed* someone. Regret hit with the force of a tidal wave, but there hadn't been any other way. She couldn't just stand by and watch Marcos die.

Pushing the emotions down, Brenna tried to focus, telling herself she could deal with her regrets later—assuming she lived through the next few minutes.

"Carlton," Brenna said, her voice shaky. "I was just trying to—"

"You'd die for this man?" Carlton boomed, making her flinch. "After just a one-night stand?" His eyes narrowed, and he glanced from her to Marcos and back again, but too fast for her to lift her own weapon.

He suspected she and Marcos had a deeper connection than the lie she'd given about picking him up at a bar. And Carlton was right. But she and Marcos had only known each other for a few months. A few months of the worst pain in her life. A pain that had brought her here.

Resolution overtook her fear. She'd come this far. She wasn't going to die without a fight.

And with Carlton, she knew her best weapon wasn't her fists or the gun clutched in her hand. Tossing the pistol away from her, she lifted her hands in the air and got slowly to her feet, stepping slightly away from the bodyguard moaning on the ground.

Her hair was a disaster; pieces of it stuck to her lipstick, more of it was in her eyes. Her knees were skinned and bloody, her dress hiked up way too high. She ignored all of it, locking her gaze on Carlton and tipping her chin up. "You read my file, right? You know about the fire?"

She sensed Marcos tense, but she couldn't dare glance at him as Carlton gave a brief nod.

"Then you must know the rest of it, too." Her voice hitched, remembering the things that had come after that fire, when she'd been sent to other foster homes. Places without smiling boys with dimples to greet her and hold her hand, but older boys with a scary gleam in their eyes.

Carlton's eyes narrowed even more, but she could tell he was listening. Maybe he even cared.

"If you really looked, then you know this isn't about Marcos. Marco," she corrected herself. "It's about me. I'm here because I want a different life from the one I grew up with. I want security. I want to feel safe." She let the truth of those words ring through in her voice. "So, I'll work with you, but you don't own me. If that's what you want, I'm not interested."

A smirk twisted his lips, then faded, and she wasn't sure if she'd just signed her death warrant or gotten through to him.

Beside her, the bodyguard she'd knocked to the ground pulled himself to his knees, snarling at her. For a second, she thought he was going to jump up and tackle her, when Carlton fired his gun, making her jump.

His bodyguard slumped back down, dead.

She stared at Carlton, speechless, and he shrugged. "He failed me. Kind of like you, Brenna."

She hadn't gotten through to him. Brenna took a breath and closed her eyes.

"This is supposed to be a business arrangement, right?" Marcos spoke up.

Brenna opened her eyes again, glancing at him, wondering if it was smart of him to remind Carlton of his presence.

"Because I've got to tell you," Marcos continued, getting to his feet, too, and leaving behind the bodyguard's weapon, which had been at arm's length away, "this is how my family did business. All these feuds. It's derailing their business. Why do you think I want to branch out on my own?"

His family? Brenna frowned, wondering what game he was playing. Some of the kids in the foster homes she'd been to had family out there, either people they'd been taken from because of neglect or abuse, or people who'd given them up. But not Marcos. She knew he'd grown up in the system from the time he was an infant, that they'd never been able to find any extended family. Had that changed? Had he found blood relatives after the fire?

"Let me ask you something, Marco," Carlton replied. "Or is it Marcos?" His gaze snuck to Brenna, then returned. "You've met Brenna once? She was that unforgettable?"

Marcos frowned, and a sick feeling formed in her stomach at the way the drug lord's eyes wandered over her, way more blatantly than he'd ever done before. As if she was his, whether she liked it or not.

Carlton Wayne White was a killer. A man who'd use kids with no one to help them as disposable pawns in his business. Why should it surprise her if he was also a rapist?

She'd been clear with him that she didn't want to sleep with him. She'd thought he actually respected that; she'd believed he saw her as a better business partner because of it. But maybe she'd been fooling herself. Maybe he'd never cared because he hadn't planned to ask.

Before Marcos could answer Carlton's question, he continued, "Or you just have a problem with loyalty? Is that why you're dealing with me instead of sticking with family? I looked into you, Costrales. You're the black sheep, aren't you?"

Marcos shrugged, spitting blood onto the ground. "You say black sheep. I say visionary."

Carlton snorted. "You're awfully confident for a man I still might kill."

"My family and I may not always see eye to eye, but they're pretty good at blood feuds."

Carlton nodded slowly and lowered his weapon. "So they are." He gave a slight smile. "I suppose I don't want to have to deal with your entire family coming after me. Too messy for me to clean up." He nodded at Brenna. "I guess this means you're vouching for her?"

Marcos paused a long moment and Brenna held

her breath, not sure what to hope for. Whoever Marcos's family was—if his story was even true—they had sway. But if Marcos vouched for her too quickly, would Carlton really buy that they didn't know one another well? Or would he think the two of them were playing some kind of scam on him, maybe trying to steal away his business?

"I don't really know her," Marcos said, not even glancing her way. "And I don't know what kind of business arrangement you two have. So I'm not sure I can do that. But I'll tell you this much. I betray you? Fine, kill me. I'd do the same. But playing some sort of ownership game with a woman who's not interested and shooting anyone who gets in your way? That's not how I work. So, I tell you what. You leave her alone and so will I."

Carlton tucked his gun back into his waistband and Brenna let out a breath, tugging down her dress and yanking the hair out of her face.

"Well, hasn't the mob gotten progressive?" Carlton asked. "All right. We've got a deal." He glanced at Brenna. "I guess this means our time together is over."

He turned and walked inside, and Brenna stood rooted in place. That was it? All the months of work and she'd let a foolish attraction to a man she hadn't seen in almost two decades ruin everything?

She blinked back tears as Marcos sent her a brief, unreadable glance and followed Carlton, leaving her all alone in the drug lord's driveway.

Chapter Five

When she'd joined the police department, Brenna had known the day might come where she'd have to shoot someone in the line of duty. It was a responsibility she'd accepted, the idea that she might have to take one life to save another.

But nothing could have prepared her for the roll of emotions making her chest feel tight and her stomach churn right now. She pressed a hand to her stomach and tried to calm her breathing as she stood just inside Carlton's mansion.

His two remaining guards had been called up and were dealing with the bodies outside, and then they were supposed to escort her to her car and send her home. But after all the work she'd put in to get here, she couldn't leave. Not like this. Not with Carlton still planning business deals, and Simon Mellor with no one else willing to take up his cause.

The truth was, there were a lot of Simon Mellors out there. Other kids just like him who were getting ready to leave the foster system and had no idea the challenges that awaited them. Kids who Carlton might target by offering them things they couldn't resist, like a way not to be homeless and hungry.

Brenna straightened and strode to her room. She yanked off the dress, heels and diamonds Carlton had been trying to woo her with, and she'd been pretending to be infatuated with, and traded them for her normal clothes. Then she headed to the living room, where Carlton had settled alone after killing one of his own guards. She might have thought he felt some regret, too, but she didn't think the man knew what that meant.

Throwing the clothes and jewelry at him, she planted her hands on her hips and exclaimed, "I thought you were a businessman!"

He shoved the items off him onto the floor and raised an eyebrow. "And I didn't realize that you were a drama queen."

"I came here because of all the things we talked about over the past few months. I came here to start a business deal with you, and this is what you do to me?"

"Careful now," he said, the amusement dropping off his face. "I gave you a second chance today. Don't make me regret it."

"How is this a second chance? Sending me home with nothing?"

"I'm letting you live, aren't I?"

His words stalled her angry tirade, but she

shouldn't have been surprised. She hadn't had enough of a plan when she'd come out here.

Taking a deep breath, Brenna started over. "Look, we each have something the other one wants. You plan to find someone else in the foster care system who can do this for you? Fine, give it your best shot. Most of them are overworked and underpaid and are either there because it's what they can get, or because they want to make a difference. You approach the first type and yeah, you might get a bite, but they won't be as aggressive about this as I will. You approach the second type, and you'll get turned in to the police so fast your head will spin."

"The police," Carlton mocked. "They're not smart enough to prove anything."

But she could see on his face that her words were getting through to him, that he wanted her connections more than he was showing, so she pressed on. "I started working in the system because I thought maybe I could make things better for kids like me. But the truth is, that will never happen. Someone like *you* is their best chance. And you're mine, too, because I might not have had control over my life since I was thrown into the system, but I do now. And I plan to make the most of it."

A slow smile spread over Carlton's face. "I may have acted too hastily, Brenna. Consider your invitation to stay here extended, and our business deal back on." He looked her over, from her well-used tennis shoes to her inexpensive T-shirt. "But before I hand over any more benefits like diamonds and clothes, you're going to have to prove yourself."

She nodded, elation and disgust with herself at the tactics she was using fighting for control. In the end, determination won out. Before this weekend was over, she was going to have Carlton on the hook with a plan he couldn't resist.

And that would be the beginning of his downfall.

"WHAT ARE YOU doing here?" Marcos had been sitting on a bench outside, but he lurched to his feet, nearly groaning aloud at the pain that spiked all over his body. He almost thought the hits he'd taken to the head were giving him hallucinations.

But there was no way even his mind could conjure up Brenna like this. She looked antsy in a pair of jeans and a loose aqua T-shirt that made her brown skin seem to glow and brought out the caramel highlights in her hair. Instead of the stilettos she'd been wearing all weekend, she wore a pair of hot pink gym shoes. The outfit looked way more natural on her than the skintight dresses and ridiculous heels.

She was also teary-eyed as she looked him over, her gaze lingering on his myriad of bruises that had turned a dark purple since this morning. But she didn't say a word about them, just took a deep breath.

He'd expected her to be long gone by now. And he'd been equal parts relieved and depressed over it all morning.

"I convinced Carlton that we should still be working together."

A million dark thoughts ran through Marcos's mind as he lowered himself carefully back onto the bench. "How?"

"Carlton might have a bad temper—and apparently a possessive streak—but at heart, he's a businessman."

Marcos felt himself scowl and tried to hide it. A real drug dealer would think of himself as a businessman, not a criminal.

By the expression on her face, she'd seen it, but she didn't say anything, just continued, "I have access that he wants. And he's better off with someone who will do the job without a personal distraction."

He held in the slew of swear words that wanted to escape and instead asked calmly, "You sure it's a good idea after what happened today?"

"No." She let out a humorless laugh and sank onto the bench across from him. "But I've come too far to give up now."

What did that mean? He suddenly realized he'd been so distracted by seeing her again that he'd failed to dig into why she was here. He knew what Carlton could offer Brenna: money. But what could she offer him, especially now that she'd made it clear sex was off the table? She said she worked in the foster care system, not exactly the sort of connection Carlton would need.

"What exactly is your arrangement with Carlton?" Marcos asked.

She fidgeted, as though she'd been hoping to avoid this question. "I can get him information he needs."

The answer was purposely vague and Marcos raised an eyebrow.

"How about you, Marc-O?" she pressed. "What can you give him?"

"A new network," Marcos answered simply, wishing he didn't have to lie to her. Wishing it didn't come so easily. But that was good—it meant all his training had worked if he could even lie to Brenna.

"For drugs? How?"

It was time to get off this topic and convince Brenna to rethink her decision to stay here. "Carlton is dangerous," Marcos said softly.

"Yeah, no kidding," she replied, looking him over again.

Her voice cracked as she asked, "How badly are you hurt?"

"Could have been worse. Thank you for that. Where'd you learn to fight?"

Her legs jiggled a little, a clear sign he was about to get less than the full truth. "Foster care." She glanced around, then lowered her voice. "Not all of us can find long-lost family."

"Yeah, well…" Now it was his turn to feel antsy, but he'd had a lot of practice being undercover. So why did lying to her feel so wrong? "Carlton doesn't know about my years in foster care, and I'd like to keep it that way."

She tipped her head, like she was waiting for more details, but he stayed silent. Better if she just kept her mouth shut about his past altogether. Because the story Carlton knew didn't match up with Marcos *ever* having been in foster care.

As far as Carlton knew, he'd grown up in the massive Costrales family, where joining organized crime was in the blood. The DEA had backstopped a story for him that involved being a bit estranged from his family, but still on the payroll. As far as they could tell, Carlton's empire didn't yet stretch to the area the Costrales family ran, but there was no way to prepare for all possible overlap.

On paper, Marco Costrales was the youngest son of Bennie Costrales, born of a mistress. He hadn't grown up with the Costrales name, but he'd been given it—and a large sum of money to build his own empire—when he'd hit eighteen. On paper, Marco had gone to jail a few times, but never for anything major. Just enough to show he was in deep to something the Feds couldn't prove.

It was their best way in, because years of trying to infiltrate Carlton's organization had proved he wasn't willing to work with anyone he didn't know. This was the DEA's way of upping the ante, because they knew Carlton had always wanted to expand his connections. The problem was, if Carlton had a personal connection to the Costrales family they didn't know about and he asked about Marco, he'd quickly find there was no such person.

And then today's beating would look like a party in comparison to what would happen to Marcos.

"How are Cole and Andre?" Brenna asked, bringing him back to the present. "The three of you are still family, too, I assume? Even after your biological family came into the picture?"

Was that wistfulness in her voice? Had she never found anyone to call family in all her years in the system?

He knew it happened. He'd bounced around from one foster home to the next from birth until he was seven. Then he'd landed in the foster home with Cole Walker and Andre Diaz, and for the first time in his life, he'd realized how little blood mattered. These were the brothers of his heart. Five years later, when their house had burned down, they'd been split up until each of them had turned eighteen. And now they lived within an hour of one another and saw each other all the time. The way real brothers would.

"They're doing good. Both are getting married in the next year." He didn't mention their profession, because how could he explain being a drug dealer if he told her Cole was a police detective and Andre an FBI agent?

"Did they ever put you back together?" She twisted her hands together, like she knew she was getting into dangerous territory.

"You mean after you set the house on fire?"

She flushed. "I didn't know you realized... I was young. It was stupid."

"Why was our foster father in the back of the house with you when that fire started?" It was something he'd been wondering—and dreading finding the answer to—for months. He'd never expected to be able to ask Brenna herself.

"What?"

Brenna's eyes widened, and she had to be wondering how he'd known that when he shouldn't have even known she'd set the fire in the first place. At the time, all the reports on the fire had called it an accident. Only recently had he seen an unsealed juvenile record showing that Brenna had set the fire. But it had been his brother who'd remembered that neither Brenna nor their foster father had been where they should have been when the fire started.

The rest of the family had been upstairs in bed, asleep. So why had Brenna and their foster father been downstairs, in the back of the house, in his study?

"How did you know that?"

"Was he hurting you?" Marcos's chest actually hurt as he waited for the answer.

She shook her head. "No. It was...look, he found me in his office. I'd lit the candle, and he came in and I tossed it."

Why was he positive she was lying? "I don't believe you."

She looked ready to run away on those more sensible shoes. "Why not? You said you knew I'd set the fire."

Marcos leaned back, studying her, wondering why she'd lie about the reasons for setting the fire, the reasons for his foster father being nearby, when she so easily admitted to setting it. His agent instincts were going crazy, but he wasn't sure about what. "I meant, I didn't believe you about why he was there." There was way more here than he'd ever realized. "I think you owe me the truth."

"You, Cole and Andre were reunited, right? What does it matter now? I was upset about my mom's death. I—"

"I almost didn't make it out of that house." The fact was, it was amazing none of them had died in there that day.

She sucked in an audible gasp.

Those moments after he'd dived through the living-room window came back to him, Cole slamming into him, knocking him to the ground and patting out the fire that had caught the back of his pajamas. He remembered Brenna running around the side of the house a minute later, just as the ambulance doors had closed. He didn't think she'd seen him, but it was the last memory he had of that day.

Brenna's terrified face, their house burning to the ground behind her.

"STAY HERE!"

Her foster father's voice rang in her ears now as

clearly as if he was sitting right beside her, as clearly as if it was eighteen years ago. But back then, she couldn't have moved if she'd tried.

She'd been dry heaving into the grass, her lungs burning from all the smoke, her eyes swollen almost shut. The fire had caught fast. She wouldn't have made it out of there at all if he hadn't screamed at her, then yanked her right off her feet and ran for the back door.

He'd practically flung her on the grass, then turned back, surely to return for his wife and the other foster kids in the house. But the door they'd come through had been engulfed by then. She'd watched through watery eyes as he'd tried to break a window, searched for another way in. She didn't know how long he'd contemplated, before he took off running for the front of the house.

She'd picked herself off the ground and limped after him and relief had overtaken her. Their foster mother was clutching two of the foster kids close. Three more were huddled together closer to the house. Only—

No, it wasn't three. It was two, with a paramedic tending to one of them.

Panic had started anew because Marcos had been missing. Then she'd seen the ambulance as it flew away from the house. She'd started screaming then, and hadn't stopped until someone had told her over and over again that Marcos was okay.

Within hours, she'd been at the hospital herself,

getting checked out, then hustled off to a new foster home. She'd never seen anyone from that house again. The truth was, she'd never expected to.

"I saw the ambulance," she told Marcos now. "But they told me you were okay, that it was just a precaution."

She must have looked panicked, because he got up and sat beside her, taking her hand in his. And it should have felt very, very wrong so close to Carlton's house, after what had just happened, but instead it felt right. Her fingers curled into his.

"I'm okay. But I spent years wondering what bad luck it was that I'd finally found my family, only to have them torn away from me."

Tears pricked the backs of her eyes. She knew exactly how that felt, only in a different order. All her life, it had just been her and her mom. They'd been more than family; they'd been best friends, the two of them against the world. And then one drunk driver, one slippery patch of road, had taken her whole life away.

"At least you got them back," she whispered, even though she knew it was an unfair thing to say. It wasn't his fault her mom had died. And it wasn't his fault he believed she was to blame for splitting up him and his brothers. She'd told him as much.

"I did, eventually," he said softly. "What about you? You never found anyone to call family after you left that house? I'd always hoped you would."

Her hand tightened instinctively in his. She didn't

like to think about those days. They were long gone now. "No."

"And what you were telling Carlton, about why you wouldn't sleep with him? About your file? You want to tell me about that?"

His voice was softer, wary, like he was afraid what she might say, and she hesitated. It was in her file in the foster system, because back then, she'd been stupid enough to think that if she could just get out of that house, the next one would be okay. Maybe it would be like the one with Marcos. Maybe they'd even move her wherever they'd sent Marcos. But they hadn't. And she'd learned to take care of herself.

She was going to shake her head, but when she glanced at him, she realized if she didn't tell him, he'd think the worst. And somehow, even after believing she'd purposely set fire to their house and almost killed him, he still cared what had happened to her.

"The place I was sent to next, there were two older boys who lived there. One was in foster care, like me. The other was the foster parents' son. The first night I was there, they came into my room, and they told me they owned me now."

Marcos didn't say anything, but his jaw tightened. "You were eleven."

"Yeah. Not all foster homes were like the one we were in." As she said it, she realized the irony. In his mind, she'd been the one to destroy that.

But all he said was, "I know."

"It was bad." She glossed through the rest of it. "They came after me, and I got lucky. And after that, I learned how to fight. That's what you saw today."

A shiver went through her at the memory. Those boys had been fifteen and sixteen, and much bigger than her. They'd come toward her, and she'd screamed her head off. One of them had tried to smother her with a pillow while the other yanked at her clothes. She'd expected her new foster parents to come running into the room, because she knew they were home, but they hadn't. Luck had been on her side, though, because police officers happened to be on a traffic stop down the street and heard her screaming.

She'd told the cops what had happened, she'd told the foster care workers what had happened, and instead of looking as horrified as she'd felt, they'd looked resigned. They'd moved her to a new foster home, and the first thing she'd done was to steal a steak knife and hide it under her pillow. That year, she'd stolen money from those foster parents to pay off some older kids at school to teach her to fight.

"And now?" he asked. "You didn't find family growing up, but what about afterward? You must have a circle of friends, a boyfriend?"

She shrugged. "Sure. Not a boyfriend," she added quickly, though it would probably be better for both of them if he thought she did. "But friends, sure." Sort of. She only let them get so close, though. Foster care had taught her how quickly people came and went, and it was usually easier to keep them at a distance.

"Are you sure this is the direction you want to go? Working with Carlton? There's still time to back out."

She shook her head. "No, there's not. He and I have a deal. And I might not be totally convinced he won't turn on me anyway, but I know one thing for sure. If I back out now, he *will* kill me."

Chapter Six

Brenna looked around the garden. It was late November, and what had apparently been a flower garden was now bare vines and plants. Around them, fir trees rose a hundred feet in the air, mixed with trees in various stages of losing their leaves. Everything was orange and red, and it reminded her of fire.

It reminded her of *the* fire. She wanted desperately to tell Marcos the truth, but that would blow her cover. And even though she couldn't reconcile the sweet boy with the huge dimples with the mob-connected man jumping into the drug business, she needed to remember he was a criminal. But *how* had he ended up with a mafia family?

"I thought you were Greek," she blurted.

"Yeah, well, apparently I got renamed when I entered the system," Marcos said as he pulled his hand free and stood. "My biological family tracked me down later. I went to live with my mom, and then my dad came into the picture, got me connected."

It made sense, and she knew it happened—people who'd lost their kids to the system reconnecting years later. So why did she feel like he was making up this story on the fly? Surely Carlton would know if he wasn't part of a Mafia family.

But he was backing away from her slowly, and she knew whatever his story, asking about it was driving him away. And he might be her best bet for information right now.

"Have you met any of Carlton's other business partners?" It wasn't her best segue, but he stopped moving.

"Not really. Just his nephew. That's how I got invited."

"His nephew." Brenna nodded, disappointed. She knew Jesse, too, and she felt sorry for the kid. Fact was, she felt a bit of a kinship with him. His family died, and he got thrown in with Carlton. What choice had the kid really had? Probably fall in line with Carlton or get tossed into the cold—or worse.

Anger heated her, the reminder of why she was here. It wasn't about Marcos Costa. It was about Simon Mellor, the eighteen-year-old boy who'd died in her arms.

"So you haven't seen Carlton with kids?"

"Kids?" Marcos frowned. "What do you mean?"

"Eighteen, nineteen. Kids who work for him?" The words poured out, even though she knew she was stepping in dangerous territory. If she wasn't careful, she was going to sound like a cop interrogating a suspect. Her heart rate picked up as he continued to stare at her, those gorgeous blue-gray eyes narrowed.

"I've never met Carlton before yesterday," Marcos said slowly.

She held in a curse. She should have realized this was a first meeting. She'd just assumed they'd had others and that this weekend was a final test.

"Why do you want to know about kids who work for Carlton? And what exactly do you think they do for him?"

She tried to look nonchalant, even though her blood pressure had to be going crazy right now. "I'm just trying to figure out how his business works, what I'm getting into here."

He wasn't buying it. He didn't have to say a word for her to know she'd made him suspicious.

"What are you getting into, Brenna? You never did tell me exactly what kind of access you could offer Carlton."

In this moment, all the years they hadn't seen each other didn't matter. The fact that he was an aspiring drug lord with mob connections didn't matter. Because she knew without a doubt that if he figured out what she was pretending to do, he'd hate her. And he'd do whatever he could to stop her from working with Carlton.

He'd been in the system since he was an infant. And even at twelve years old, he'd talked to her about the plans he and his brothers had—plans to look out for one another when they left the system. He'd known there was no net for foster care kids. And the fact that she was pretending to take advantage of that would be a worse sin than anything he was doing.

"You work in the foster care system," he said before she could come up with a believable lie. "You said you wanted to start a program to help kids make the transition to the real world." He shook his head, looking disgusted. "What does that mean, really? Carlton sets up front businesses and you populate them with foster kids to do his dirty work?"

"I..." She faltered, trying to figure out how to smooth this over without risking him hearing the truth from Carlton anyway.

Then his eyes narrowed, and he took a step closer until she was forced to lean back to look at him. "What aren't you telling me, Brenna? Why are you really here?"

"You're a cop, aren't you?"

It made total sense, Marcos realized, instantly relieved. Except if a police department was running an operation on Carlton, the DEA would know about it. Anything to do with drug operations by any organization went into a system the DEA could access. And they'd made very sure before he came here. There was nothing.

She stared at him, her lips parted like she wanted to say something but couldn't figure out what, silently shaking her head. There was panic in her eyes. But was it because he'd uncovered the truth? Or because she was afraid he'd peg her as a cop when she wasn't and Carlton would kill her for it?

As much as he wanted to believe she was here with noble intentions, the truth was that his judgment was compromised when it came to Brenna. His feelings for her were all tangled up in the past, in the first girl who'd ever made his heart beat faster. In the fantasies he'd had growing up, of one day seeing her again. The fact was, he'd never really given up on those dreams.

"No." She'd finally found her voice. "Why would you think that? Anyway, you really think a police department would hire someone who'd set a house on fire?"

"Probably depends on the department and the circumstances of that fire," he replied evenly, still studying her. She was flushed, nervous. If she was a cop, she had limited experience undercover—and what police department would send a rookie into an operation like Carlton Wayne White's? Still, his instincts were buzzing, telling him something here wasn't as it seemed. "That record just got unsealed. Why?"

"You saw it."

It wasn't a question, but it probably should have been, because there weren't a lot of reasons a criminal would have been able to access that record. He silently cursed himself. If he wasn't careful, Brenna's mere presence was going to make him blow his own cover.

"Yeah, I saw it." And it hadn't occurred to him before—why was it unsealed all of a sudden? "It was a trap," he realized. "A way to backstop you as a foster care worker with the right motivations to work with him, but that easily fit into your actual identity. Someone who had criminal actions in her past. And you must be new, if there's no easy way to track you as a cop. So, what department do you work for?"

"Stop saying that!" She jumped up, jammed her hands on her hips and got in his face, despite being a solid five inches shorter than he was. "If I'm a cop, then you're—" She went pale and swayed, then whispered, "No way. You're...what? DEA?"

He smirked at her, though inside his brain was screaming at him. "Don't try to turn this around on me."

Brenna took a few steps backward, still staring at him contemplatively. What she was trying to decide was written all over her face: could she trust him?

And that told him everything he needed to know.

He swore, harshly enough that she flinched in surprise. "You're going to get yourself killed," he snapped at her. "How many undercover operations have you run? You shouldn't even play poker!"

"Hey!" she snapped back. "Don't be a jerk! I'm not a cop, and I don't know what you're trying to—"

"You're right," he told her, breaking every rule in undercover work. "The mob story was backstopping, okay? I'm DEA."

Her lips parted and relief flashed in her eyes, followed by uncertainty. "Is this some kind of—"

"I'm not trying to trick you. You think I'd risk my life for that?"

"And it's perfectly safe to tell a criminal that you're an undercover agent?"

Marcos smiled. "It is when the criminal I'm telling is really a cop. Let's work together. We're after Carlton for pretty obvious reasons—he's got control of a big chunk of the heroin supply. What about you? Because if it was drugs, it should have been put in the system so exactly this didn't happen."

He held his breath as she stayed silent, clearly torn. He was pretty sure he was right, but if not…

"Yes, I'm a police officer. Out of West Virginia. And you're right, it's not in your system because this isn't about drugs. I'm after him for murder."

There was a long silence as they stared at each other. She looked as relieved as he felt, but he couldn't say exactly why. Probably because she had some form of backup now. His relief should have been the same, but the truth was, he was used to going into meets with drug dealers by himself. Maybe not for so long or this far from help, but it was a normal part of the job. And besides, it was clear she was a rookie, at least when it came to undercover work. No, his relief was all about Brenna the woman.

The fact that she wasn't using the foster care system to lure newly released kids to Carlton meant he didn't need to feel guilty that the attraction he'd felt for her as a kid wasn't gone. Not even close. Because even when he'd believed she was here for no good, he'd been drawn to her.

But maybe that guilt was a good thing, because now keeping his distance was going to be a real challenge.

"Just remember Carlton will kill you."

"What?" Brenna squeaked.

"Sorry." He couldn't believe he'd said that out loud. He'd meant it as an internal warning to himself. Maybe the hits to his head really had impacted his judgment. "Just be careful," he amended.

She sank back to the bench. "So what now?"

"Well, you know pretty much all there is to know about why the DEA is after Carlton—we have been for years, and it's straightforward. He's a drug dealer, and we want him gone. I want your story."

She glanced around, reminding him that despite being several hundred feet from the house, with no good way to sneak up without being seen, they were still on Carlton's property.

"You're right about me being a rookie, and you're right that it's the reason I'm using my real name. They scrubbed me from the police records anyway, but there wasn't much, and my department isn't big on putting our faces on a website, thank goodness. So it worked out when I brought them this plan to come in and play to Carlton's weakness."

"What's that? Beautiful women?"

Her cheeks went deep red. "Thanks, but no." She

locked her hands together. "Six months ago, I was on foot patrol when a kid died in my arms. He was eighteen, barely out of foster care. And he was running drugs for Carlton."

Marcos nodded slowly. He understood that sort of motivation for pushing an undercover op, but her superiors were doing her a disservice by letting her follow through, with what had to be minimal training and experience. "So, you're here trying to prove Carlton ordered the hit? Because he's careful. I don't think—"

"Not exactly. What you guessed about what I was offering him is right. But I'm not the first one to do it."

Marcos leaned forward, grimacing as his entire left side protested. "Who?"

"I don't know. But I think Carlton has been using foster care kids just out of the system for a long time."

"We haven't seen evidence of that," Marcos said slowly. And yet, it made sense. The DEA's method when grabbing a low-level dealer was usually to try to flip the person to go higher. But with Carlton, that hadn't worked because no one had ever flipped on him, so they couldn't identify who his dealers were. Foster kids with no one in the world except a man who'd given them a roof and a job wouldn't turn on him. And if they'd tried, Marcos was pretty sure Carlton had gotten to them before they could get to the police.

He swore. "How did you get wind of this? The kid talked to you before he died?"

"No. And his case went cold. But I followed the progress. I looked into his life, saw some evidence that he'd approached the station a few times, indicating he might have some information on a dealer. But he never gave it up, so no file was opened. Eventually I tracked down an address he shared with a couple other kids, also out of the system. They wouldn't talk to me. But as I was leaving, I saw him. Carlton. And I knew. I mean, what better drug runners than kids coming out of foster care with no home, no money, no family? And who's going to push for answers if they get killed?"

Marcos nodded slowly. It was flimsy, so flimsy most departments wouldn't have even let her pursue it as a case, let alone an undercover operation. But he'd been doing this a long time, and he could feel it. She was right.

"There's more," Brenna said, taking his hand in both of hers.

He squeezed back, momentarily distracted by the softness of her skin. It was deceiving, because he'd seen her take down a man almost twice her size.

"The fire—"

"I know. The juvenile file was faked, right? You didn't set the fire." He prayed she was going to confirm it, but from the look on her face, he wasn't going to like her answer.

"No, I didn't set it. My department faked the file.

We wanted to blend my real past with something that would make me seem as though I could be paid off. But I saw our foster father set the fire."

Marcos tried to line that up with what he remembered. "Why? He burned down his own house, risked all of our lives, his wife's life?"

"It wasn't on purpose. I don't think he expected me to be awake. I startled him when I came into his office—I was confused. I hadn't been in the house long, and I was practically sleepwalking, used to the layout of my mom's house." She let out a breath. "I'd been headed to the kitchen for a drink. But then he spotted me and jumped up. He knocked over a candle on his desk. He had so many papers, spread out all over it. The fire caught really fast. At first, he tried to put it out, but it jumped, and then he grabbed me and ran."

"It was an accident." All those years, the original accounts had been right—sort of. They'd assumed everyone had gone to sleep and someone had left a candle burning. But it was still an accident. A simple mistake that had cost him the presence of his brothers for six years. And Brenna.

"Yes, but the papers, Marcos. I saw them as we were trying to get out. I didn't put it together for years, but then I had to go to the foster system headquarters when I was trying to track down Simon—the kid who died—any family he might have had. I saw similar papers."

"Our foster dad was just fostering kids. He didn't

work for them," Marcos said, confused. "Are you sure—"

"Yeah, I'm sure. That night is burned in my mind. He shouldn't have had those papers, and I don't know how he got them, but they weren't on us. There were other names on them. I couldn't tell you the names, but I know this much—"

"You think he was Carlton's connection, eighteen years ago?"

"Yes. I looked into it and from what I can tell, Carlton was just getting started then."

"And he built an empire on the backs of foster kids," Marcos said darkly.

He'd wanted to bring down Carlton before, but now that desire intensified until it became a smoldering hate in his gut. If this man held the truth to why he'd spent six years being tossed from home to home, always hoping to see Cole and Andre again, Marcos was going to get it. No matter what it took.

Chapter Seven

Dinner was uncomfortable.

Brenna kept her attention on her plate as she picked at her food. Across from her, Carlton's nephew Jesse did the same, clearly sensing the tension even though he'd managed to miss the beating and screaming and gunshots that afternoon. Apparently, he'd been in the basement, in Carlton's personal soundproofed gun range. Beside her, she felt Carlton's presence like a tornado on the horizon.

She'd been avoiding looking at Marcos all night. He sat on her other side, and he almost made her more nervous than Carlton, though for a completely different reason. DEA. Two days ago, if she'd been asked to guess what Marcos Costa was doing these days, neither mob-connected drug dealer nor DEA agent would have made the list. But it fit.

Now that she thought about it, it wouldn't surprise her if both of his brothers had gone into law enforcement, too. They'd been so different in the foster home: Cole, the oldest, reliable and even-tempered,

the one everyone turned to if they needed something. Andre, the middle of the three, easygoing,
but with intensity in his gaze, quick to stand by his
brothers. And Marcos, the youngest, who could be
quietly watchful or funny and gregarious, depending
on his mood. But they'd had a core goodness to them
that had her sticking close when she'd found herself
all alone. And they hadn't let her down back then.
They'd stood up for her, too, when she needed them.

She could imagine them all still living by that
motto: helping people, defending people. Joining the
police force was something that had ultimately pulled
her back in, partly because she'd thought if she could
return to her eleven-year-old self and tell Marcos,
Cole and Andre she wanted to be a cop, they would
have been proud.

"Don't be so glum," Carlton boomed, making
Brenna jump in her seat. "Just because I tried to
have you killed isn't a reason not to enjoy your filet."

He grinned, and Brenna was struck again by how
much of a caricature he seemed, in his standard all-
white suit with that white-blond hair brushing his
shoulders. He probably had to have the suits spe-
cially made, given his size. He might have been in his
midforties, but he looked a decade younger, probably
from all the hours he spent in a gym. But it wasn't
his size that made Brenna nervous. It was the contrast between his usually jolly nature and his quick
temper.

Even without his two primary bodyguards, Carl-

ton was still surrounded by protection. His chef—
whom Carlton had apparently lured away from a
five-star restaurant—was also a mixed martial artist
who carried a Glock on his hip and constantly had a
sharp knife in his hand. Another pair of guards had
quickly taken the place of the first two, though she
had no idea if they'd driven in or had been here the
whole time. And then there was Jesse, who looked
as nervous as she felt, but still reached instinctively
for his gun whenever there was a loud noise.

"Don't worry about that," Marcos replied evenly,
sounding like a seasoned dealer—or a really practiced undercover agent. "I won't take it personally
unless you try it again."

Carlton guffawed. "Don't cross me and it won't
be a problem. I'll make you rich."

Brenna glanced at Marcos as he smiled and took
a bite of steak. "That's why I'm here."

Carlton tapped her hand, and Brenna resisted the
urge to yank it away. "I'd planned to take you down
to my gun range and teach you to shoot tonight, but
since it appears you already know your way around
a gun, perhaps we can talk business."

Her pulse picked up and she nodded.

Carlton slowly rubbed his fingers over her hand.
"Who taught you to shoot, by the way?"

She pulled her hand free. "I taught myself. A couple hundred hours at a gun range, and you eventually pick it up."

"But today was the first time you killed anyone, wasn't it?" he pressed.

She looked him in the eyes. "Yes."

"And how did it feel?"

"What?"

Carlton leaned closer, a smile playing on one side of his mouth. "There's nothing like the power of choosing life and death, is there?"

She held back the shiver, but she didn't think it mattered—he'd seen it in her gaze. "That's not really my idea of fun," she said, her voice shaky. "I'd prefer to stick to paperwork."

Carlton leaned back, and she could see on his face that he'd gotten what he'd wanted from her. But what exactly that was, she couldn't tell.

"Do enough paperwork and the diamonds I let you wear earlier can be yours to keep."

She nodded, setting down her fork. "That's why I'm here. But as much as I love jewelry, I'd like to know how to turn it into cash without anyone being the wiser."

Carlton snorted. "You're looking for a tutorial from me on how to hide money?"

She shrugged. "You're going to pay me for a job. Obviously you don't want anyone to notice my new funds. And neither do I. What I want is a nest egg, so that I never have to rely on anyone ever again."

"I knew there was a reason I'd picked you," Carlton said, and Brenna could practically feel Marcos hiding a smile beside her.

Marcos had been right about her minimal training for undercover work. The fact was, this was her first undercover assignment. But the reason they'd gone with her real name was so she could stick as close to the truth as possible. Her trainer had told her to take her real emotions and channel them a different way—if she hadn't chosen law enforcement, if morals weren't an issue, what would matter to her most?

This kind of fiction was easy to remember, but it sure played havoc on her mental state. Because safety and security really *were* two of her life goals. She lived minimally, socking away her savings so that she'd always have a safety net. She relied only on herself, because that way she wouldn't be let down.

How different was she from the character she was pretending to be? And if Carlton found out the truth—or turned on her again at random—and she died out here, what would she be leaving behind?

It terrified her that the answer might be nothing.

THE MEETING WITH Carlton had been a bust.

Sure, he'd given her a rundown on a million different ways to hide money from authorities—some she'd never seen before, even on the other side of the law. But whenever she tried to broach details on next steps with the foster system, he'd pushed her off, telling her they'd get to that later.

This had always been a long-term plan. No one at her police station who knew about the operation—which were very few, to avoid potential leaks—

thought they'd get enough on Carlton over just one weekend. Talk had been of her keeping up her cover at the foster care system for months, maybe even years.

But she just had one more day to go at Carlton's hidden mansion, and already she was itching to return to her normal life, to take a dozen showers and wash off the filth she felt being surrounded by this much evil. And she wasn't sure she could wait a year to nail him for Simon's death. How many more boys and girls would die in that year?

Which was why, once Carlton had given her a lingering kiss on the cheek, shooed her out the door of his office and called Marcos in, she hadn't headed to her room to sleep. Instead, she was walking down the long hallway toward where she suspected Carlton slept and trying to look natural. Because though he might have been down two guards, he had two more who seemed anxious to prove themselves. And they eyed her with suspicion and distrust.

Besides, she knew it wouldn't take much to push Carlton back over the edge.

She shot one more glance at the ceiling, on careful watch for any cameras, and then slipped into the room she'd seen Carlton enter last night after he thought she was asleep. Blinking in the darkness, she let her eyes adjust and then gasped. This wasn't Carlton's bedroom. She'd just hit the jackpot. This was a second office.

Rushing over to the massive desk dominating the

center of the room, Brenna almost tripped on a bear rug that looked real. She tried not to think about the poor creature who'd given his life to be walked on and went for the top drawer of the desk, heart pounding. It was locked.

She tried the rest of them, but they were all locked. There was no key in any of the obvious hiding spots and no papers lying on his desk. She swore under her breath, then hurried to the filing cabinet, with the same luck. It figured he'd be careful—if rumors were right, he'd been in the drug business for twenty years, and he'd never done hard time.

She might be able to pick the locks, but it would take her a while, and every second she spent in here could be the difference between making it back to her room safely or being dragged outside and shot. Still, she couldn't leave with nothing.

Then, she spotted it. The pad of paper on his desk was blank, but maybe… She ran back over there, happy to be in her regular gym shoes instead of those embarrassingly unsteady heels. She ran her fingers over the top sheet, and her pulse picked up for a new reason. Indentations.

Rather than trying to figure them out, she just ripped the page off and shoved it in her pocket. She was reaching for the door handle when the door opened, almost slamming into her. Brenna jerked backward, out of the way, but there was no time to hide.

She braced herself for Carlton's wrath.

CARLTON WAYNE WHITE'S office was dressed in all white, just like him. It was an odd room, with a huge white desk that actually made Carlton look normal-size, and all white cabinets behind him. There was a framed blueprint of his mansion on the wall, the design signed by Carlton himself. Apparently the man had other hobbies besides watching his thugs beat up disobedient would-be business partners.

Marcos sat on the other side of the desk, feeling like he'd wandered into the twilight zone. This didn't feel like a drug lord's office. Then again, most of his meetings were with dealers out on the streets. They did business out of the back of a car, a hotel room or a fast-food joint. On the rare but wonderful occasions he got to arrest a big player, it still didn't tend to be in an office like this.

He'd done deals on luxury yachts, in luxury homes and in opulent clubs. But never in an office that looked like it could belong to an obsessive-compulsive architect.

"I thought we said no business this weekend," Carlton reminded him as Marcos pressed for the third time about details.

So far, the meeting in Carlton's office had been nothing but a test, Carlton asking questions about Marcos to make sure his story was consistent. Given the stakes—his life—Marcos should have been nervous. But he trusted his training, and so far, he hadn't stumbled once. And he was getting tired of the third degree.

"And I thought I'd come here for a deal, not a beating and the runaround," Marcos replied, staying casual with his legs crossed in front of him while he slouched in the chair. The attitude of a man who'd grown up with a crime family guaranteeing power and money, but where danger was common, too. The real Costrales family had been known to take out their own for any kind of betrayal.

Carlton practically snarled as he leaned toward Marcos across the enormous desk. "I'd advise you to watch your tone."

"Look," Marcos said, straightening in his chair, "if you want to play games, fine, but I'm giving up a weekend for this. And I don't give up a weekend for anyone. Time is money, my friend, and if it's not going to be yours, it'll be someone else's. Now, I think you and I can build a great partnership here, but considering that you set your goons loose on me and I didn't walk, I'd like a little good faith in return."

Carlton stared at him a long minute and then nodded. "Fair enough. You've got balls, Costrales, and you'll need them in this business. But this vetting process isn't over, so I tell you what. You get one question."

One question. Marcos knew he should ask about distribution or sources, something they could use to find a leak in the organization if this operation didn't go as planned. But instead, he found himself asking,

"If you and I go into business together, what guarantees do I have that nothing will come back to me?"

Not giving Carlton a chance to answer, he continued, "Because from what I can tell, what usually does people in with this sort of *business*," he said, grinning, "are the low-level dealers. It's why I've avoided getting involved before, despite the obvious cash flow. But your business intrigued me, because you don't seem to have that problem. So tell me this—how do you keep them from turning on you?"

Carlton gave a smug grin. "That's why Brenna is here."

Marcos's pulse picked up. This was exactly where he'd hoped Carlton would go with his answer. He feigned confusion. "Brenna? What does she have to do with anything? I mean, she said you two had business, but honestly, I figured it was minor. Doesn't she work for foster care? What can she offer you?" Carlton lifted an eyebrow, and Marcos let realization slowly show on his features. "You're using foster care kids? That's brilliant," he said, forcing admiration instead of disgust and anger into his voice. "But I thought Brenna grew up in the system? Now she's turning on it, handing over kids?"

How had his foster father gotten involved all those years ago? In retrospect, Marcos realized that the home office where the fire had started was a little strange for a factory worker to need—unless he was involved in some other business, too. But it was hardly a smoking gun. Had their foster father been an indirect connection—had he somehow gotten files on kids by pretending to be interested in helping them after they got out of the system? If so, maybe the system had started to get suspicious. Maybe Carlton hoped Brenna would be a more direct route.

"Not yet," Carlton said. "But the source we've always used is getting ready to retire." He laughed. "And she doesn't even know she's a source! And this time, I'm going to be in charge of the source directly. Brenna still needs testing, but I've dug into her. She's got an angry streak, and we just need to pull it out, use it to our advantage."

Marcos nodded slowly, pretending to consider, when inside he was marveling at how wrong Carlton had it. Brenna didn't have an angry streak; she had a compassionate streak. And that was going to be Carlton's undoing.

"Happy now?" Carlton asked, standing. "You got your question. And I got some answers. Now head to bed. We have an early morning."

"Wait," Marcos pressed. "I said the idea was brilliant, not that it was a guarantee. How can—"

"These kids have no one," Carlton said. "I fill that void, but of course, not directly. They can't identify me even if they wanted to, and they're not about to turn on the one person who's offered them help."

"None of them can identify you? You use a middleman?"

"Something like that," Carlton said.

The brief hesitation told Marcos *some* of those

kids could identify him, which matched Brenna's story that she'd first identified Carlton leaving Simon Mellor's place.

"Besides," Carlton said, "what you got this morning was a second chance. You're one of the few. I don't offer those to dealers who screw up."

"You kill them?"

Carlton smiled. "I've never killed anyone."

Right, Marcos thought.

Carlton held out a hand, gesturing to the door. As Marcos was walking through it, Carlton reminded him, "Early tomorrow. You've got one last test, and then the real fun begins."

Marcos said goodnight and hurried to his room, feeling the same foreboding as when he'd first arrived. Did Carlton suspect something? He'd seemed satisfied enough to give Marcos details, and Marcos knew he hadn't misspoken on any of his backstory. But he didn't like the sound of Carlton's morning "test."

Stripping down to his boxer briefs, he yanked back the covers on his bed. And then he swore loudly enough that he worried for a moment he'd bring Carlton from across the house.

Because curled up under his covers was Brenna.

Chapter Eight

"Are you crazy?" Marcos demanded.

Brenna blinked up at him, too distracted by the wide, bare expanse of his chest to really comprehend his words. He wore nothing but a pair of snug boxer briefs, and even in the dim light of the one lamp lit in the room, she could see he took good care of himself. The man was covered in muscles that seemed to tense as her gaze shifted over them. Even the big bruise snaking up the right side of his stomach and the matching bruises on his arms didn't detract from how attractive he was.

"Brenna," Marcos snapped, grabbing his jeans off the floor and yanking them back on. Instead of buttoning them, he took her arm and pulled her out of his bed.

She hadn't intended to fall asleep. Really, she'd had no intention of going anywhere near Marcos's bed, with or without him in it. And from the way he was glaring at her now, he didn't want that, either.

She flushed, because with his obvious anger,

she should have been less attracted to him. Instead, standing this close to him, she felt like she couldn't get enough air into her lungs.

And when she finally lifted her gaze to his eyes, she realized beneath the anger at her being in his room was something else. Something he was clearly trying to hide. Maybe it was the undercover training that made him so good at concealing his emotions, but even that didn't eliminate the desire in his eyes as he stared back at her.

A smile trembled on the corners of her lips.

"This isn't funny," he whispered. "If Carlton catches you in here, he's going to lose it. And I'm still healing from the first beating."

Any amusement instantly fled. Her free hand lifted, pressing flat against his abdomen, where that nasty purple bruise marred the perfection of his body.

He hissed in a breath.

"Did I hurt you?"

"No," he groaned, pulling her hand away. "Brenna, what are you doing in here?"

"Sorry." She stepped back, trying to regain her equilibrium, and bumped the bed. She swallowed, sidestepping it and crossing her arms over her chest. "Look, I—I messed up."

"Yeah, well, slip back to your room now, and it should be fine. Just don't get caught."

"It's too late."

"Someone saw you come in here?" he demanded.

"No. But while you were meeting with Carlton, I thought I'd take a peek in his bedroom."

Marcos sighed. "Why? What did you expect to find in there?"

"Something," Brenna replied, frustrated that he was angry with her for doing her job. "Anything. I can't take years of this, tiptoeing around Carlton's interest in me, pretending to leak him information so we can catch him. What happens in the meantime? I want to bring him down *now*."

"Yeah, I get that."

"I don't think you do. You got a family out of foster care. Even with the fire, even being split up, you and Cole and Andre found each other again. Me, I got ripped out of there and—"

Emotions overwhelmed her, the memory of standing in that hospital, watching them take Cole into a room beside her, his hands blistering and red, with Andre running after him. Begging the nurse to tell her where Marcos was, and hearing only that he was okay. Being shuttled into a car with some woman from Child and Family Services she'd never met. She'd watched out the window of that sedan until the hospital disappeared. She'd never seen any of them again. Not Marcos, Cole or Andre. Not the other two foster boys who'd lived at that house, or their foster parents, the Pikes. From that moment on, she'd really, truly been alone.

It had been nothing compared to the complete devastation of losing her mom a few months before that, of waking up in the wrecked car off the side of the road, bleeding and cold. Rescue workers telling her she'd be okay. But she'd seen her mom in the front seat, her head slumped sideways, no one helping her because it was already too late.

A few months later, she'd just started to come out of the numbness that had filled her. She'd just begun to feel like maybe one day she'd smile again. It had been Marcos who'd made her feel that way, and then he'd been ripped away, too.

"Brenna," Marcos whispered, his tone softer now, his hand palming her cheek.

She stepped quickly out of his reach, sucking in a calming breath, and spoke the other part of what had brought her here. "A kid died in my arms, Marcos. Eighteen. He was too far gone to even tell me his name." Sitting on the cold pavement, cradling his head in her lap as his blood soaked through her clothes, had taken her instantly back to those moments in the car with her mom, helpless to do anything.

She was going to lose it. *Don't cry*, Brenna pleaded with herself, shoving the memories into the back of her mind, where they were least likely to ambush her.

Marcos had stepped closer again, and Brenna held out her hand, flat-palmed against the center of his bare chest. "Don't. I'm fine. Look, I just—"

"This is personal," Marcos finished for her.

"Yes."

"For me, too," Marcos said, reaching up and taking the hand she was holding him away with and twining his fingers with hers. "You say this is connected to our past, and I want to know how. Because Carlton told me the reason he needs you is that his connection in foster care is retiring. That she doesn't even know she's his source."

"She," Brenna repeated.

"Yeah, *she*. Which means it can't be our foster father."

"THAT CAN'T BE RIGHT," Brenna insisted. "I know what I saw."

"It was a long time ago," Marcos reminded her, still way too distracted by her nearness. She had such soft, tiny hands, and there'd been so much vulnerability in her eyes when she'd talked about her past. And yet, she was here, in the den of a sociopath drug lord, risking her life. She was way stronger than she looked.

"Yeah, well, that day is pretty stamped in my memory."

"Mine, too," Marcos replied. "But maybe the papers aren't what you thought they were." When she tried to interrupt, he said over her, "Or maybe they weren't his."

"You think they were our foster mother's? That he found them, and that's why he was looking at them late at night?"

"Maybe."

"But she didn't work for the foster system, either."

"No," Marcos agreed. "Not that we know of. But she did work out of the house, part-time. Maybe her work was somehow connected."

Brenna shook her head. "No, I double-checked all of that. I can't find any connection between either of them to the system. Not to their biological son, either—he owns his own business, nothing to do with foster care."

Marcos frowned at her. "Then why are you so convinced our foster father is connected? That was a long time ago, and Carlton's operation was just getting off the ground back then. And I have to tell you, the way Carlton talked about the whole thing, I'm not even sure he's the one who found the source. Sounds like it was someone else in his organization, and that this time, he's happy because you're going to be *his* in directly." The thought gave Marcos pause—the way Carlton had said it, it had sounded almost like there was someone else who had as much, or more, power than him and he wanted to steal it. But that didn't make any sense, and he shook it off as Brenna jumped in.

"I know what I saw back then," Brenna insisted. "And I don't know how our foster father is connected, but I know he is."

Marcos nodded slowly. Logically, it seemed like a stretch, but he could see how strongly Brenna believed it. Sometimes memories could betray you—gaining conviction over time, twisting and becoming unreliable. But he'd been an agent for a long time, and he also knew the power of a cop's gut. "Okay, I believe you."

She seemed surprised. "You do?"

"Yeah." He grinned at her, less stressed now that the initial surprise of finding her in his bed had worn off, and more intrigued. He was still holding her hand, and he turned it palm up and stroked the sensitive skin with his fingers. "Now, why don't you tell me what you were doing in my bed?"

Her fingers twitched, then curled inward. Her gaze dipped, lingering on his bare chest before meeting his again. "Uh—"

He took a step closer, suddenly uncaring that they were in Carlton's house. The drug lord had gone to bed. The guards he had left—hopefully—had gone to bed, too. No one had to know Brenna wasn't in her own room.

And it didn't matter how many years had passed, how much he still didn't know about her. He recalled the power of that first crush eighteen years ago. It had been sudden, like a sucker punch to the gut, only instead of leaving him in pain, it had made the world seem wonderful. Seeing her again, even under these circumstances, and he had that very same feeling.

"Marcos," she whispered, her eyes dilating as she tipped her head back.

He kept hold of her hand, sliding his other one around her waist and pulling her close. She gasped at the full-body contact, and he swallowed it, pressing his lips to hers as her free hand wound around his neck.

She fit. The words rattled in his desire-fogged brain, and he knew it was more than the way her body molded so perfectly to his.

Eighteen years should have been more than enough time to move on. They'd both changed so much since those brief months they'd spent together, just trying to understand their place in the world, to find a real connection. Somehow, they'd both ended up in law enforcement, and when she'd said she didn't have a boyfriend, he'd known instantly that it was the same reason he'd never stuck around in a serious relationship. If he was being honest with himself, it was fear. Fear of a real connection that would disappear the way everything seemed to in his childhood.

But he wasn't a child anymore, and neither was she. He tilted his head, trying to get better access as her mouth glided over his again and again. The instant he slipped his tongue past the seam of her lips, she moaned and arched up, freeing their linked hands and grasping his back for better leverage.

He reached for her hand, hoping to redirect it around his neck, but it was too late. She froze and pulled her head away, her eyes wide.

"Marcos," she whispered, stepping out of his embrace and trying to turn him.

He planted his feet and refused to let himself be moved. "It was a long time ago."

Tears welled up in her eyes and one of them slipped free, running down her cheek and getting caught in the Cupid's bow above her mouth.

He reached out and swiped it free, taking her hands in his and trying to pull them up around his neck. "Come here."

She resisted. "Show me."

"It's not pretty," he warned her, nervous even though he knew physical scars wouldn't scare her off. People had seen the scars before, and he'd given the quick, easy truth: "Burns from a fire, a long time ago."

But it was different when he was showing someone who had been in that fire with him. Someone who—whether she admitted it or not—already felt guilty about the way the fire had started.

This time, he let her turn him slowly. She gasped when she saw his back, but he'd expected as much. What he didn't expect was to feel her fingertips glide over the mass of scar tissue that covered his back and then her lips to follow.

He drew in a breath. The pajama pants he'd worn to bed the night of the fire had been cotton—they'd caught fire, but not badly. But his top had been synthetic. The fire had sucked that material right into his skin.

The doctors had done their best, and the scars on other parts of his body—the ones the fire had left on the backs of his legs, the ones the glass had left on his face and hands when he'd dived through the window to escape—were almost entirely gone now. But his back?

He recalled the moment he'd tripped on those stairs, running down from the bedroom he'd shared with Cole and Andre. One minute they'd been in front of him. When he'd pushed back to his feet, they'd been gone, through a doorway he couldn't follow because flames leaped in their place. He'd gone the other way, the fire chasing him, and done the only thing he could do as it finally caught up to him: dived through the living room window.

When he'd landed on the grass in front of the house, he'd thought he was dying. He'd sensed Andre talking to him through his own tears, felt the weight of Cole's hands as they patted out the fire. Then he'd been loaded into an ambulance and passed out.

He'd woken in the hospital, a pain more intense than he'd ever known that seemed to heat every part of his body. But it was centered on his back. After a few months, he'd actually felt less on his back, from the nerve damage. But right now, despite how thick the scar tissue was, each light touch of Brenna's lips made his nerves wake up, sent desire spiraling through his body.

Marcos closed his eyes and let himself feel, then spun back around and captured her lips with his again. They tasted salty now, and he realized she'd been crying.

Instead of the frantic kisses from earlier, this time was slower, sweeter. When her arms went back around him, settling around his waist, it didn't bother him. In fact, it felt right. He pressed his mouth to hers, ready to stay there for a long, long time, when she pulled free.

"Marcos, I need to tell you something."

His fingers slipped under the hem of her T-shirt, discovering the skin there was somehow even softer than her palm. "Mmm. Can you tell me later?"

"No." She slipped out of his arms, stepping back and bumping the bed. Her voice was throaty, her lips swollen from his kisses. "Marcos, I just got tired waiting for you. I didn't mean to fall asleep. I didn't intend for you to find me in your bed."

"Okay," he replied slowly. Was she trying to tell him she didn't want to jump into bed? "That's all right. We don't have to rush into anything." He moved toward her. "I just want to kiss you for a few hours."

She let out a noise that could have been anticipation, could have been surprise. But she put her hand up on his chest again. "No, I mean, I was waiting here to tell you something."

"Okay." He took her hand the way he had before, smiling at her, hoping it would work a second time as he drew circles on her palm. He was about to lower his head and trace them with his tongue when her words stopped him.

"Carlton's nephew caught me in the office."

Chapter Nine

"What happened?" Marcos demanded.

Brenna tried to focus, but her lips still tingled from his mouth and her fingertips still felt the uneven surface of his back. If only she hadn't gone downstairs for a drink of water in the middle of the night all those years ago. Things might have been so different.

Marcos wouldn't have the scars. It made her want to cry all over again, thinking of the pain he must have gone through. Maybe, if the fire had never happened, they all would have stayed together.

What had Marcos looked like as a teenager? What had he done when he hit eighteen and been kicked out of the system? What had made him decide to go into law enforcement? She wished she'd been there for all of those things.

But she couldn't go back and change any of it. All she could hope to do was make some kind of restitution now, by ensuring whatever her foster father had been doing that night ended.

"Brenna," Marcos prompted, and she forced her mind back on the present. "I thought you said you looked in Carlton's bedroom?"

"I thought that's what it was. But he has a second office." She could see Marcos's instant interest and she nodded. "Lots of desk drawers and file cabinets, but they were all locked. I didn't have time to pick them. I'm not sure I got anything useful." She was about to tell him about the paper she'd grabbed when he spoke.

"What did you tell Jesse?"

"I said I got confused, that the house is like a maze. I wasn't in there very long, and I know he wasn't following me. He looked really surprised to see me when he flipped the light on."

"Well, that's believable. The house *is* like a maze, I think on purpose. But what was *Jesse* doing in there? Carlton doesn't seem like the type of guy who'd let people hang out in his personal office."

"I don't know." After her immediate relief that it wasn't Carlton, she'd wondered the same thing. "He didn't say."

"Did he buy your explanation?"

"I think so. I asked him not to tell Carlton—played it like I was nervous about what happened earlier, that it was an accident, but I didn't want him mad at me. Jesse seemed to understand that concept really well. Honestly, I got the impression he didn't want Carlton to know he'd been in there, either."

"So, you think you're safe? Or do we need to run now?"

She gaped at him. "We?" She shook her head. "Even if I'm compromised, you didn't vouch for me. Whatever happens to me, I won't betray your cover. This is about me."

"No, it's not." She realized he'd never let go of her hand as his fingers tightened around hers. "We're a team now, you and me."

The idea flooded her with warmth, made her feel more secure and more afraid at the same time. She'd never let herself lean on someone, and the idea of leaning on Marcos now was way too tempting, for too many reasons. But the opposite was also true. If she didn't rely on anyone but herself and messed up, then no one else would get hurt.

If this were just about her, she wouldn't have hesitated. It was worth the risk.

But it was no longer just about her. "I don't think he's going to say anything, but I can't be positive."

Marcos nodded, stepping a little closer. "Nothing in life is a guarantee, especially in undercover work."

Her pulse picked up again at his nearness, her body wanting to lean into him. She stiffened, trying to let her mind rule. "What do you think we should do?"

"If you don't think you're compromised, we stay."

If she stayed here much longer, she was definitely going to be compromised, but in a completely different way.

As if Marcos could read her thoughts, a little smile tipped the corners of his lips, and then he was lowering his head to hers again. He tasted like the Bordeaux they'd drunk with dinner, intoxicating and rich. He tasted like every dream she'd had as an eleven-year-old girl, discovering her very first taste of love.

Love. The idea had her stumbling backward.

"What's wrong?" Marcos asked.

The concern on his face made her want to touch him even more. She folded her hands behind her back. "I should go." She sounded breathy and nervous, and silently she cursed herself. "I want to get back to my room before Carlton's other bodyguards start their nightly rounds."

"They have nightly rounds?" Marcos asked, but he seemed way more interested in letting his eyes roam over her than the answer.

"Yes." Or if they didn't, someone had a serious sleepwalking problem, because she'd heard footsteps pass her room regularly last night. She glanced down at her watch, realizing that she really did need to slip back to her room soon.

On impulse, she leaned forward and pressed a brief, last kiss to his lips, then ran to the door. Peeking through it, her heart thundered in her chest, but not because she was afraid of getting caught so much as she was afraid to stay.

Puppy love was completely different from real love, she reminded herself. And that's what she had with Marcos—a lingering infatuation she'd never really been able to get out of her system. It was made worse because he'd been the thing that kept her going all those years in foster care. The idea of one day emerging on the other side of the system, to find him waiting for her.

But that's all it had been—a perfect, impossible idea. That's all Marcos was right now, too. She didn't really know the man, just the pedestal she'd put him on all her life.

She glanced back at him one last time, then darted into the empty hallway. All the way back to her room, she wondered if going undercover in the lair of a crazy drug lord wasn't the most dangerous thing she'd done this weekend. It was being in close proximity to Marcos that could really be her undoing.

"We have a traitor in our midst," Carlton announced calmly at breakfast.

Marcos paused, a bite of Parisian omelet halfway to his mouth. He let his gaze move slowly over to Carlton, not to dart around the room and linger on Brenna the way instinct would have him do. Which one of them had Carlton discovered? Marcos prayed it was him.

All last night, after Brenna had left his room, he'd tossed and turned, unable to sleep. He couldn't keep his mind from wandering to the sweetness of her mouth, the softness of her skin under his hands. He couldn't keep from thinking about what an amazing woman she'd become, from wondering about all the years in between now and when he'd last seen her.

"What are you talking about?" Brenna asked when the silence dragged out.

She sounded nervous, a little defiant, but those should have been believable reactions even if she was completely innocent. Because the reality was, *completely innocent* was a stretch for the person she was pretending to be.

"Why don't you tell her, Marco?" Carlton asked, his cold blue gaze locking on Marcos.

He should have felt terrified. Out in the Appalachians without a weapon and surrounded by Carlton and all the guards he had left—which, from what Marcos could tell, were the two regular guards standing against the wall, plus the knife-wielding chef in the kitchen, and Jesse.

Instead, he was relieved. As long as Brenna's cover wasn't blown, maybe he could talk his way out of this. It wouldn't be the first time a drug lord had suspected he was in law enforcement. Actually, any drug lord with any sense at all would suspect everyone he did business with could be an undercover agent. Besides, Carlton hadn't used Marcos's real name, which meant whatever he thought he knew, he didn't have the full truth.

Marcos calmly set down his fork. He didn't have to look around the table to sense the tension increase. Jesse was a ball of nerves at all times, and Brenna was new to undercover. She wouldn't be used to this kind of constant testing.

Marcos prayed that's all it was, that Carlton hadn't discovered his real identity. But Carlton had promised him one last test this morning, and Marcos hoped this was it.

"I'm not sure I can," Marcos replied.

Carlton smiled, but there was nothing happy about it. He looked like a snake ready to pounce. "No?"

His attention shifted to Brenna, across the table from Marcos. "How about you?"

Marcos let his gaze shift to her, watched her narrowing eyes as she folded her arms across her chest. She was dressed in jeans and a long-sleeved red shirt today, and it looked so much more natural on her than the skintight dresses. Although he couldn't say he minded the dresses, this felt like the real Brenna. And the real Brenna was a lot harder to resist than the person she was pretending to be.

"This isn't what I signed up for," Brenna said, her tone a mix of fear and defiance. "This was supposed to be simple business, not beatings and accusations and…" Her voice trailed off, then she finished, "I had to shoot someone, Carlton, and whether it was your intention or not, I felt like I didn't have a choice. I'm looking for security. I'm not some kind of crazy adrenaline junkie."

"Don't forget that was my man you shot," Carlton said.

She set her napkin over her half-eaten omelet and stood. "I don't think I'm cut out for this."

"Sit down," Carlton snapped.

When she didn't immediately comply, one of his guards stepped forward from the corner and put his hands on her shoulders, shoving her back down.

Marcos felt his entire body tense, wanting to lay the man out for touching her, but he tried to keep the fury off his face. If this *was* a test, Brenna was playing it exactly right.

She glared up at the guard but kept quiet.

"It's too late to back out now, my dear. You're going to be *my* ticket," Carlton told her.

Marcos frowned, wondering once again if Carlton had someone else in the organization they didn't know about, perhaps a second in command who ran the current foster care connection. Maybe Carlton wanted to handle it himself. It would mean more possibilities for leaks to law enforcement, but also more power.

"And anyway, you're not the one I'm worried about," Carlton said. "I've got security cameras at my front door. I've got your little shooting on tape. Some creative editing, darling, and unless you want to try to explain murder to the police, I *own* you."

She stiffened, her fingers curling around the tabletop until they turned white, but she still didn't say a word.

This time, Carlton's smile was more genuine.

"Don't worry. You'll still have your *security*. I just like some extra insurance, and your little display yesterday made it simple. It wasn't exactly what I had planned, but—" he shrugged "—you showed me I need to be more careful who I hire to keep me safe."

The guards behind Brenna stood straighter, their muscles tensing at the implication they might be on the chopping block, too.

"So, you think *I'm* a traitor?" Marcos spoke up, wanting to get Carlton's attention off Brenna. "Why, exactly? Because all I've done is try to talk about getting some of your product to my networks. Is this your idea of one last test? Call me a traitor and see if I lose it? My family has done worse than that."

Carlton sneered. "Your family can't protect you here. And I see I haven't underestimated your intelligence, Marco. This *is* one last test. Because I'm not accusing you, either."

"Then who, exactly?" Marcos asked, but he suddenly dreaded the answer, because he knew what Carlton was going to say before he spoke.

Carlton's gaze moved to the last person seated at the table. "I never thought I'd have to eliminate yet another person of my own flesh and blood."

Jesse stood, shaking his head. His face flushed a deep, angry red—but from fear or anger, Marcos wasn't sure.

What did Carlton mean by *another* person? The

DEA knew Carlton was a killer, but they had no intel on the man taking out anyone in his own family.

Marcos glanced from Carlton back to Jesse and realization made the omelet flip in his stomach. The car accident that had killed Jesse's parents and left the kid in Carlton's care. It had been deemed an accident. Lots of snow, slippery roads, combined with a blown tire had been fatal. But maybe that blown tire hadn't been an accident. What had Jesse discovered?

He held in a string of curses as Jesse insisted, "Uncle Carlton, I swear, I didn't betray you. Please—"

"You think I don't know you've been in my office?" Carlton boomed.

Both Jesse and Brenna jerked, and Marcos hoped Carlton hadn't also realized Brenna had been in his office.

"I doubt—" Marcos started.

"Did I ask your opinion?" Carlton yelled.

"Uncle—" Jesse begged.

"Stop! You can't explain this away," Carlton said, suddenly calm.

"He brought me here to you, to do business," Marcos said. "Why would he do that if he was betraying you?" He knew he was stepping into dangerous territory, opening the door to the idea that he was also a traitor, but Marcos couldn't stand by and watch Carlton kill his nephew.

Carlton's shrewd gaze shifted to Marcos, and he

pressed his luck. "He's practically still a kid. There's no need to hurt him."

"Oh, I'm not going to hurt him," Carlton replied evenly. "This is your test. You're going to do it for me."

Chapter Ten

"I'm not the only one who was in—" Jesse started.

Marcos cut him off fast, before he finished that sentence and told his uncle that Brenna had also been in his office. "This is crazy," Marcos said. "Just because the kid was in your office isn't a sign of betrayal. I did the same thing to my dad—I wanted to know more about his business than he was willing to tell me."

The "kid" was twenty-four—only six years younger than Marcos. But for some reason, every time Marcos looked at him, he saw a scared boy pretending to be a badass.

Carlton's eyes narrowed on him, and Marcos couldn't tell if he was pissing the drug lord off or getting through to him, so he rushed on. "It wasn't betrayal for me, either. I just wanted to be part of it. I wanted to be like him."

Marcos nodded at Jesse and watched Carlton's gaze follow.

Jesse was sweating, his entire body shaking. He

had a deer-in-the-headlights look, but at least the fear was keeping him quiet, giving Marcos a chance to talk.

"Your nephew and I met up and played pool about a million times before I got the invite up here," Marcos continued. "And all he did was brag about you. No details, of course, but he didn't need to do that. I already knew who you were. Just hero worship."

It wasn't exactly true, but it was close. Jesse adored the uncle who had taken him in after his parents died. But the adoration had felt a little forced, as though Jesse knew he shouldn't put his lot in with a criminal.

"Is that right?" Carlton asked, crossing his beefy arms over his chest and leaning back in his chair.

Was he pushing too much? Marcos wondered. Was Carlton about to turn on both of them? Only one way to know for sure.

"Yes. And look, I know you wanted me to vouch for Brenna here." He glanced at her, shrugged in feigned apology. "But I couldn't—don't know her well enough. But your nephew? I'd vouch for him. No way would he turn on you."

"That seems awfully foolish," Carlton said, as Jesse glanced between them hopefully. "For all you know, I have absolute proof of his betrayal and you've just signed your own death warrant alongside him."

Jesse went so pale Marcos thought he was going to pass out. One of the guards must have expected

Jesse to run, because the guard stepped in front of the doorway, blocking the exit.

"I don't think you do," Marcos said, keeping his tone casual, almost cocky.

"No? And why exactly would the son of an organized crime boss vouch for an orphan?"

Jesse jerked, then pulled himself straighter, like he'd been insulted by his uncle's categorization of him, then gotten defiant. But thank goodness, he was keeping his mouth shut about one thing he'd seen in his uncle's office: Brenna.

Marcos shrugged. "I don't know how you get your kicks, but I don't kill kids. If you're looking for leverage on me, you'll have to find it some other way."

Carlton's expression got so dark so fast that Marcos knew he'd just pushed the drug lord too far.

"I don't think so," Carlton said, standing and snapping his fingers.

His guards' weapons came out, pointed at Marcos.

Carlton reached behind his back and revealed his own pistol. He emptied all the bullets on the table, except the one in the chamber, then handed it to Marcos. "Either you kill him, or they kill you."

BRENNA'S HAND CURLED around the butter knife she'd palmed almost as soon as she'd sat down for breakfast. It was instinct—had been for years, ever since that third foster home. She couldn't help herself.

The urge had faded as she'd gotten older. Instead of stealing dull knives everywhere she went, she'd started carrying a tactical knife on her at all times. Then, she'd joined the police force, and when she was on duty, she had her service pistol.

But up here in the mountains, with Carlton Wayne White, unarmed for her cover, she'd fallen right back into her old habits. She had a collection of Carlton's butter knives in her room. She was sure he—or his chef—had noticed by now, but no one had said anything. They probably figured it was irrelevant, that she either had a theft problem or that it wasn't going to make much difference against a pack of guns.

They were right about that. But as her gaze swiveled from Carlton, smirking from the head of the table, to Marcos, way calmer than he should have been, to Jesse, terrified in the corner as one of Carlton's guards disarmed him, her grip tightened. She'd never live through attacking a pair of guards with a butter knife. And even if she did, she knew for a fact that Carlton was concealing more than just the gun he'd handed to Marcos.

Her heartbeat pounded in her ears as she prepared herself for a last stand. After all these years, she'd finally found Marcos Costa, only to die with him. She blinked back tears, wishing she'd stayed with him last night. Wishing she had at least that memory now.

"This is crazy," she said, needing to give reason one last try. "Why does anyone have to die? I thought this was a professional business operation." Her voice came out too high-pitched and panicky, and she didn't even need to force it.

"You want to play in the big leagues, you'd better get used to it," Carlton told her.

Ever since she'd turned down sleeping with him, he'd been far less interested in keeping her happy. Carlton's temper—and his unpredictability—were legendary. She'd known that before she'd pressed her boss to let her come up here. But she'd never seen him like this. It almost made her wonder if he was using his own product.

But no, the truth was much scarier. The truth was that he was really willing to watch his own nephew—and anyone else in his way—die to protect his business.

She stared at Marcos, praying that his years at the DEA, which involved a lot of undercover work, had given him practice in situations like this. That maybe he had a way out.

But he seemed as shocked as she felt. He glanced down at the pistol in his hand, then back up at Carlton. The cocky, drug-dealer expression he wore around Carlton was gone, replaced by a seriousness she'd only seen when they were alone.

"Uncle Carlton," Jesse pleaded, his voice barely more than a whisper. "I was just looking for—"

"I know what you were looking for," Carlton replied. "And I'm sorry, kid. I really was hoping to groom you to work with me at a higher level." He shrugged. "But if I can't trust you, there's no way I can let you disrupt everything I've worked for all these years."

Jesse glanced at Marcos, then at her, like he was hoping one of them would come to his rescue, but all Brenna could do was stare back at him, helpless.

His gaze swung quickly back to his uncle, and Brenna thought he was going to blurt out that he'd seen her in Carlton's office, too. Instead, he asked softly, "Did you really kill my parents?"

"Nah, I didn't kill them," Carlton said, but there was nothing truthful in his voice.

He turned to Marcos. "Let's do this outside. I don't need a mess in here."

Carlton nodded at a guard, who grabbed Jesse and forced him to the door. He nodded for Marcos to follow, and when Brenna didn't move, he told her, "Let's go."

"I'm not watching this." Her feet felt glued to the floor. She couldn't just watch Jesse die, no matter what he did for a living. But how could she prevent it? If she went after a guard again, she'd be shot by the second one or by Carlton. This time, no one was going to underestimate her.

"Yes, you are," Carlton said, gripping the top of her arm so hard she knew it would leave a bruise.

She kept the knife flat against the inside of her arm, letting him drag her outside, because the truth was, she couldn't hide from this, either. Panic set in as they all stepped into the wilderness surrounding Carlton's home.

No one would hear the shot. And Marcos would become a killer.

"I HAVE A better idea," Marcos announced, taking in the gorgeous wilderness that surrounded Carlton's home.

The trees were really changing color now, fiery reds and oranges, with greens mixed in from the fir trees. He could hear birds in the distance, and the crisp air seemed to clear his mind.

"I'm getting tired of your stalling," Carlton said. He had a tight grip on Brenna, keeping her close, as though she might run and take out another of his guards.

The two guards had positioned themselves on opposite sides of Marcos, and the one who'd been holding on to Jesse shoved him, sending him sprawling to the ground.

Jesse skidded through a pile of dead leaves, but didn't bother trying to get up. He was crying now, silent sobs that sent tears and snot running down his face. But he'd stopped begging, probably knowing his uncle too well.

"Hear me out," Marcos insisted, the plan forming in his head as he spoke. It was a long shot, but he'd spent months reading up on everything the DEA knew about Carlton Wayne White before he'd even approached Jesse.

No one could identify how exactly Carlton had gotten started, but he was a perfect fit as a drug lord. Not only did he look the part—like someone no one would want to mess with—but even before he hit the DEA's radar, he'd had a reputation. As a kid, he'd been to juvie a few times, but he'd learned fast how to hide what he was doing.

In his early twenties, he'd become a boxer, and he'd been the guy who went for the KO right away and then immediately wanted a new opponent. His trainers had spent a long time convincing him to draw out the fight, to make it a show. But when he'd finally agreed to do it, he'd clearly gotten joy out of taunting the poor sucker scheduled to fight him.

Marcos knew Carlton liked the lead-up as much as the knockout, maybe even more so. "Even though I still think this is unnecessary, what's the fun of shooting someone in the head?"

Carlton smirked. "If you have to ask, you're not doing it right."

Beside him, Brenna was unnaturally still, her arm up at a weird angle as Carlton kept a grip on it. But that wasn't entirely why, Marcos realized. She was holding her arm awkwardly because she was hiding something.

No way had she gotten a gun into Carlton's mansion without it being taken away from her immediately, so what? He tried to figure it out, but gave up after a few seconds. He had more important things to worry about right now.

Jesse had picked himself off the ground, wiped his face on his sleeve and was now standing defiantly, his chin up as he stared at his uncle.

"Come on," Marcos said, moving in a slow circle,

gesturing to the nature around them. "You have all *this* and you want to use a gun?"

Carlton's eyes narrowed. He was either intrigued or starting to get suspicious about why Marcos wasn't pulling the trigger.

Marcos spoke quickly. "Let me work him over, then send him off. No one's going to help him, right? Not if he shows up with a shiner. They'd never mess with you by taking him in. And it took me forever to get up here, find this place. He's not making it back to civilization. It'll be starvation or hypothermia or some animal attracted to the blood."

Brenna's mouth dropped open, and she shook her head, like she couldn't believe what he was saying.

He avoided her gaze, not wanting her to think less of him. If Carlton went for his plan, it wouldn't be pretty. But at least it would keep the kid alive for the immediate future, give him a chance, unlike a bullet to the head—inevitable even if Marcos refused. Then it would be up to Jesse.

Carlton's gaze dropped to Brenna, then back up to Marcos, a slow smile spreading. "You're a lot crueler than I'd figured, Marco."

He shrugged, hoping he looked blasé with his heart racing, a pistol with one bullet clutched in a death grip in his hand. "Yeah, well, I come by it naturally. You know who my family is." It was a subtle reminder not to push him too far.

The drug lord nodded slowly, and Marcos held his breath, hoping he'd agree. It wasn't an ideal solution, but it was better than a shoot-out with one bullet on his side and whatever Brenna had clutched in her hand.

"Okay," Carlton agreed, and Marcos let out the breath he'd been holding. "Do it, but hand over that gun first."

Hoping Carlton hadn't just decided to shoot *him* in the head instead, Marcos held out the pistol.

Carlton had to step forward to grab it, and he let go of Brenna's arm. She tucked that arm close to her, confirming Marcos's suspicion that she had some kind of weapon.

"Now do it," Carlton said, holding the gun on him.

Marcos turned toward Jesse, who'd stiffened his spine and his jaw. He wanted to mouth an apology to the kid, but although Carlton was at his back, the guards would see it.

So, instead he pulled back his fist and swung. It landed with a solid crack, and Jesse flew backward into one of the guards.

The guard shoved him away, and Jesse fell face-first onto the ground as Brenna gasped.

It couldn't have gone better if Marcos had planned it that way. He got down next to Jesse, yanking him back to his feet with one hand, and slipping his car keys into the kid's hoodie pocket with the other. Then, he hit the kid again, pain knotting his stomach as if he were taking the punch instead of giving it.

Jesse went down again without a fight, just another grunt of pain. This time, he pushed himself to his feet, blood dripping from one corner of his mouth.

"Again," Carlton ordered.

"Carlton," Brenna protested.

"Again!"

"Stop!" Brenna yelled.

Marcos swung again. He tried to aim for places that would split skin and cause bleeding, but wouldn't do too much other damage, but he had to be careful. Carlton had been a boxer—he knew his punches.

This time, when Jesse went down, he pushed himself to his knees, then flopped to the ground again. He tried to get up again and stumbled into Marcos, who shoved him away, making sure to push the keys into the kid's stomach through his hoodie.

Please get the message, Marcos willed. Carlton's guards had moved Marcos's car into an outbuilding, then returned the keys to him with a warning not to go anywhere without Carlton's say-so. It was far enough away that Jesse could circle back and take it, hopefully after dark when there was less of a chance of one of Carlton's guards spotting him.

Once the car made it to civilization and Marcos didn't check in, a pack of DEA agents would surround it, since the phone tucked into the car's hidey-hole was tagged with a GPS tracker. When they found Jesse inside instead of him, they'd protect him. They'd also send a bunch of armed agents to retrieve Marcos.

Which meant time was running out if he wanted

to gather evidence on Carlton. This was about to be the end of his undercover operation.

"Now, go," Carlton told his nephew.

Jesse gave his uncle one last lingering glance, full of betrayal and pain and hatred, then turned and walked into the wilderness.

Chapter Eleven

"Congratulations," Carlton told Marcos. "You passed my last test. You're in."

Marcos grinned as he walked by Brenna and headed back toward the house, but she could see the discomfort in his eyes, what it had cost him to beat up Jesse and send him to his death.

Bile gathered in Brenna's throat. Was this what it took to succeed undercover? In order to take down men like Carlton Wayne White, you had to become like them?

She couldn't do it.

How many times had Marcos faced similar situations undercover? How many decisions just like this one had he made over the years? And what had it done to him, having to make the choice between saving himself and saving a kid? Because it didn't matter that Jesse certainly belonged in jail himself for the things he'd done under his uncle's orders. At the end of the day, he was still young enough, probably hadn't yet crossed a line he couldn't come back from, that he had a chance to turn his life around. Or he might have, if he hadn't been sent out into the Appalachians to die.

"Brenna," Carlton snapped, bringing her attention back to him.

He was smirking at her, clearly amused by her reaction. But he didn't seem surprised; after all, she was pretending to be a foster care worker. She might have been willing to make a deal with the devil in exchange for her own security, but a woman like that still wouldn't be immune to violence.

Taking a deep breath of the bitterly cold air, Brenna tried to calm her racing heart. She couldn't stop herself from glancing back in the direction Jesse had gone, deeper into the mountains instead of toward civilization. Not that it would have mattered. It was a several-hour drive just to get out of the mountains, and even then, there was nothing around for miles, unless you could hot-wire a car someone had left before taking a wilderness hike.

And the threats were everywhere. Hypothermia was probably the biggest one, but the threat of other humans might not be far behind. Up here, people didn't ask questions first; trespassers were simply shot.

Marcos had been right when he'd listed Jesse's chances; the kid would never make it.

The desire to run after him, to try to help him, rose up hard, but Carlton was staring at her, one eyebrow raised and that pistol still clutched in his hand.

She had no doubt he'd use it on her if she tried. And what could she really do, with no way to communicate with her fellow officers and no supplies other than a butter knife?

Failure and pain mixed together, reminding her of the day she'd knelt on the cold ground next to Simon Mellor and rested the kid's head in her lap. She'd ignored protocol and tried to stem his bleeding with her bare hands, even though she knew it was too late to save him.

With one last glance into the wilderness, Brenna walked back toward the house. Before she made it, Carlton grabbed her arm again.

Instinctively, she tried to jerk away, but his size wasn't for show. The guy was incredibly strong.

"I've been pretty understanding about your eccentricities, but that's an expensive set of flatware and I'm running out of knives."

She flushed and flipped her hand over, revealing the knife tucked against her arm. "It's—"

"Self-preservation," he finished for her. "Believe me, I understand the concept." He stared at her a minute longer, and she wasn't sure what he saw—probably fear and sadness and self-disgust—and then he told her, "Never mind. You keep it if it makes you feel better."

Then, he actually patted her on the back with his enormous paw, and she saw a flash of matching sadness in his eyes. Some part of him hadn't wanted to

kill Jesse, she realized. But that brief hint of human-
ity didn't matter.

She nodded her thanks and turned away from
him, striding into his house before he saw any other
emotion on her face. Because her determination
to bring him down had just doubled. And now she
needed to do it fast, find a way to get out of here and
get help before Jesse died in the Appalachian Mountains all alone.

"I DIDN'T MAKE the decision about Jesse lightly," Carlton told them, settling into the big chair in his living room and draping his arms over the edges. "But
I want you to understand what happens to traitors.
You're committed now, so I expect one hundred percent loyalty from here on out."

Marcos nodded solemnly as he sat across from
Carlton, then glanced at Brenna. She stood frozen
in the doorway. The expression on her face was unreadable, but her eyes were blazing with anger, fear
and determination. He prayed that Carlton misun-
derstood which emotion was winning.

Her gaze met his only briefly before she ducked
her head and took the remaining chair. She didn't
have to say a word for him to know what had happened in those moments outside the house: she'd lost
all respect for him.

The idea hurt more than it should have, and he
wanted to explain his reasoning, but all he could do
was continue his ruse with Carlton. At least it was

working, because if Jesse was smart—if he waited until the cover of darkness and then took Marcos's car and booked it for civilization, then Marcos had until evening to make this happen.

The plan had always been to head home tonight. Although he'd hoped to be able to wrap up the weekend with enough for an arrest that would send Carlton away for the rest of his life, the truth was, it was unlikely. A smart drug lord would start out with a small transaction, give him just enough product to prove himself before moving to a bigger shipment. And Marcos needed serious quantity to put Carlton away for good.

He had no real hope of sticking with that plan now. Even if the DEA didn't swarm after Jesse showed up, if the kid had gotten the message, then Marcos had no vehicle. And while he was sure Brenna would give him a ride, it wasn't likely to go unnoticed that his car was missing from Carlton's outbuilding. If he left too early, it would be Carlton and his guards searching for Jesse instead of the DEA.

So, he needed to time this exactly right. Set up a deal with Carlton and get out of there in time to stop the DEA from blowing his cover, but still give Jesse a chance to escape.

He settled into his chair and crossed his legs at the ankles. He pasted a semi-bored expression on his face, as if beating up people and sending them to certain death was well within his comfort zone. Inside, though, he felt physically ill.

"What now?" Brenna asked, speaking up before he could.

Carlton smiled. "Now we make your boy toy over here happy. We talk business."

"Boy toy?" Marcos replied, trying to stay in character, trying not to imagine Jesse's eyes as he'd taken that final hit. Resolute to his fate, but determined to go out standing. "Sounds fun, but I'm no one's toy."

"We'll see," Carlton said.

Marcos could guess what he was thinking. To Carlton, Marcos was nothing but a chess piece on a much bigger board. Little did Carlton know, Marcos felt the same way about him.

Some of his colleagues at the DEA had questioned the intelligence of an operation that sent him alone into the home of a man as unpredictable as Carlton Wayne White. Carlton was flat-out crazy. If the DEA came in to rescue him and things went south, Marcos didn't doubt he'd go out in a blaze of glory if it meant taking out cops with him.

Marcos needed something substantial, and soon. He didn't want to risk having to bring Carlton in without enough. Flipping him to get to his suppliers wasn't an option as far as Marcos was concerned. If Carlton was making money on the backs of foster kids, then Marcos wanted him to rot in prison for the rest of his life now more than ever. Not making a deal with the DEA and skating by in a cushy minimum-security federal penitentiary.

So, right now, Marcos let the insult go and leaned

forward. "All right, Carlton. Let's get down to it. I passed your test, and I know why we did it in front of your house. It had nothing to do with bloodying up your marble floors."

Carlton grinned and shrugged. "Hope you smiled for the cameras."

"You've got your leverage and that's fine," Marcos said. "It wouldn't exactly be the first time—my family plays similar games. Now let's skip over some BS small-level deal. You've got this area locked up, but I can move you into New York, get you hooked up with my existing networks. We work together and in a few years, we'll both be tripling our income."

Carlton grinned, and Marcos could practically see the dollar signs flashing in his eyes. Carlton glanced over at Brenna. "What do you think, my dear? You ready for the big leagues?"

Brenna's eyes sparked at the endearment, and Marcos was pretty sure that was why the drug lord did it. He knew it pissed her off, and he liked seeing just how far he could push people.

"I set you up, and you do the same for me," she said flatly. But there was a dark undercurrent to her voice that made Marcos nervous.

What she'd seen with Jesse had tapped into that compassionate streak she had, and he knew it had just made her drive to bring the drug lord down even stronger. But she didn't know his plan, couldn't know they needed to stretch out the timeline.

Even before she spoke, he knew she was going to

go the other way—try to rush Carlton into a deal and get out of there, and go looking for help for Jesse. And that would destroy any chance Marcos had of getting Jesse to safety while still keeping his cover intact with Carlton.

"What do you say you work out the smaller details with Brenna later?" Marcos jumped in. "To start, I'm looking for twenty-five kilograms. I'll bring the cash at the same time, but we do the trade on neutral territory."

"What?" Carlton mocked, not even blinking at the size of the deal. "You afraid I'll rip you off?"

"Nah," Marcos replied, refusing to be baited. "If you're smart—and I know you are—you're looking for a long-term relationship, not a one-off deal. But that doesn't mean I'm letting your goons take a piece of me again."

Carlton's guards tensed from where they'd taken up position near the doorway, and Carlton scowled.

"Glad you reminded me of that, Marco. Because you're going to add the cost of two new *goons* to the price of the shipment." Carlton glanced from him to Brenna. "Unless you think Brenna here should split the cost with you."

Not liking the implication Carlton put behind the word *cost*, Marcos shook his head. "It's fine. What's another fifty grand? But we do that, and the initial shipment goes up, too. Thirty kilos."

Carlton smiled slowly. "You really live up to the

Costrales name, Marco." He leaned forward, held out a beefy hand. When Marcos took it, he said, "You've got yourself a deal."

BRENNA TOOK A sip of the champagne Carlton's chef handed her. The bottle cost a couple hundred dollars, but the liquid felt caustic on her tongue.

Across from her, Marcos and Carlton clinked glasses, both smiling. Carlton was surely dreaming of the windfall he expected to come his way, Marcos silently gloating over being able to bring Carlton down soon. And even though Carlton had finished discussing business with Marcos and then made her an offer that she could try to build a case on, she didn't feel any cause for celebration. All she felt was slightly ill.

Morning had rapidly passed, and no matter how many hints she'd dropped about needing to head out, Carlton wasn't letting her go anywhere. It had been six hours since Jesse had stumbled into the wilderness, bleeding and alone. Was he already dead? Even if he wasn't, did she have any chance of finding him? The fact was, simply following her own tracks back to civilization was going to take all of her concentration. Carlton's mansion was purposely well off the beaten trail. And by the time she made the long drive back to the station for help, chances were the temperatures would be down below twenty. How long could Jesse hold out, even if they could locate him?

"Don't you like the bubbly?" Carlton asked. "This is from my private collection."

She forced a smile. "It's very good. But I really should leave soon. I don't want to be navigating the Appalachian roads in the dark."

Carlton gave her a slimy smile. "You could always wait until morning."

"No." She took a breath, tried to modulate her tone. "I've got work tomorrow. And I want to propose this new plan of ours, for helping kids make the transition out of foster care. I want to be at my best."

Carlton nodded soberly, and Brenna kicked herself for not using this excuse hours ago. She'd been so distracted by her fear for Jesse, by trying to hide her disgust for Carlton—even for Marcos—that she hadn't been thinking straight. Of course the best way to get Carlton to agree was to appeal to his own interests.

"That's a good point," Carlton said. "Finish your champagne, and I'll have my guards bring your car."

"We can get them," Marcos jumped in, so quickly Brenna frowned.

He'd been so determined to hang around Carlton's place, dragging out their discussion for hours, that it was strange he suddenly wanted to go, too.

Carlton shrugged. "Suit yourself. My guards will take you out there, then. I'm not sharing the lock code with anyone."

Marcos seemed to pale a little and Brenna studied him, trying to figure out what was going on with him. But she shook it off; it didn't matter. All that mattered was getting back to the station and sending resources to find the kid wandering around the Appalachian Mountains before it was too late.

She tipped back the glass and drank her champagne in several long gulps. When she set it down, empty, Carlton laughed.

"Okay," he said. "Guess that means you're ready to pack your bags. I have to say—" he looked her up and down "—I'm a little disappointed. But you remember the lesson you learned today about betrayal, and everything will go just fine. I'll give you your security and you give me what I really need."

Brenna kept her jaw tightly locked and simply nodded. What he really thought he needed were more impressionable kids to do his bidding. Kids he figured were expendable. Kids he wouldn't hesitate to kill if they interfered with his plans. Just like Jesse.

"Don't be so sensitive," Carlton said, clearly not fooled by her attempt to hide her true feelings. "Just ask Marco here. Over time, you'll get used to it. And believe me, the money you'll get in return is more than worth it."

Tears pricked her eyes. Was that how Marcos felt about what he did? That trading the life of a kid who'd already made the wrong choices was a small price to pay to bring down someone like Carlton? Was that what she'd have to accept to do the same?

She didn't think she could. And she didn't want

to become someone who was okay with that sort of trade. But where did that leave her?

Pull it together, Brenna told herself. She could figure out the rest of her life once she made it out of here.

"I'll be in touch tomorrow," she told Carlton, amazed that her voice actually sounded normal. "Expect good news about the program."

He grinned. "I knew I chose you for a reason."

She nodded, anxious to get out of there. She didn't look back as she hurried to her room to shove her belongings into the small bag she'd brought with her. She was practically running as she returned to the living room, ready to go to her car and get out of this soul-stealing place.

But she skidded to a halt when she reached the living room, because instead of finding Carlton and Marcos happily sipping champagne like she'd left them, Carlton was fuming. And his guards were both pointing guns at Marcos.

She looked over at Carlton, her desperation turning into dread. "What's going on?"

"You tell me, *Officer* Hartwell."

Chapter Twelve

"What are you talking about?" Brenna demanded, a beat too late.

Not that it would have mattered if she'd denied it instantly. A minute after she'd left the room, Marcos had watched Carlton take a phone call. He'd glanced at the readout and then picked it up so quickly Marcos had known it was important. As the person on the other end spoke, Carlton's expression had gotten darker and darker, then his gaze had flicked to Marcos and he'd known the game was up.

Carlton knew the truth.

"You're a rookie," Carlton said now, sauntering over to Brenna, where she stood clutching a duffel bag and looking dangerously pale. "And your station let you come here?" He tilted his head, frowning. "You *are* a natural, I'll give you that."

Without warning, before Marcos could do anything to stop it—not that he could with a guard locked on each arm—Carlton's fist shot out, catching Brenna under the chin.

Marcos yelled and tried to yank himself free, but the guards had a tight grip on him, and all he managed to do was wrench his shoulders in their sockets. On the other side of the room, Brenna's head snapped back and she went flying. She slammed into the wall and then slumped to the ground.

Fury and panic mingled as she lay there unmoving.

Carlton sidestepped the duffel bag she'd dropped and started to walk toward her again, an angry purpose in his stride.

Marcos ignored the throbbing in his shoulders, tensed his muscles and dropped to the ground. The action caught the guards by surprise and they jolted toward him, falling with him in a tumbled mass of arms and legs and guns.

Sweeping his legs out wildly, Marcos lurched toward the guard to his right, trying to grab his weapon. Before he could get free of the second guard, who'd wrapped his arms around Marcos's shoulders, trying to pin him in place, Carlton ran over and lifted his own pistol.

He shoved the barrel against Marcos's head and snarled, "Try it again."

Marcos froze, and he could actually see the struggle in Carlton's eyes. The man wanted to kill him right now but knew it wasn't smart.

Time seemed to move in slow motion. It felt like hours, but surely had been less than a minute until Carlton slowly backed away and his guards stood.

"Get up," Carlton demanded.

Marcos did as he was told, his gaze going to Brenna, who was still out cold on the ground. He couldn't tell how badly she was hurt, but he knew one thing: Brenna couldn't weigh more than 120 pounds, and Carlton had once been a semiprofessional boxer.

He kept his hands up, submissive, willing Carlton to control his temper, praying Jesse had already gotten away. That the DEA would burst through the doors any second. That Brenna would open her eyes and tell him she was fine.

But it was all wishful thinking, and he knew it. He had no idea how Carlton had discovered the truth, but the drug lord had shown him the images someone had texted him: Brenna in police blues, out on the street, and him in a DEA jacket at a crime scene. Whoever Carlton's contact was, he had inside access. *Too* inside, because although Brenna had been using her own name, Marcos wasn't. And yet, Carlton had gotten off that call, looked him in the eyes and said, "Well, *Special Agent* Marcos Costa, after I kill you, I'm going to find your *actual* family and take care of them, too."

Marcos wanted to believe it was a bluff meant to scare him more than his own impending death. He wanted to believe that the fact that Cole and Andre didn't share his last name, weren't genetically related, would keep them safe. But Carlton had proved his source was way too good. And Marcos already knew he was a killer.

In that instant, he wished he could take back every decision he'd made in the past few months. He'd come here with noble intentions: to get a dangerous drug lord off the street. He'd known—and accepted—the dangers to himself. But *never* would he have done it if he'd thought he'd be putting his brothers—or Brenna—in danger.

Now they were all in the crosshairs of a killer. And it was entirely his fault.

IT FELT LIKE fireworks were going off inside her brain, each one bouncing off her skull before exploding. Brenna squeezed her eyes shut tighter, fighting the pain, when her whole body seemed to slam into something metal, then slide into a warm body.

A warm, *familiar* body.

She struggled for consciousness. Ignoring the new pain it caused, she forced her eyes open, but that didn't change the darkness. Panic threatened, and then Marcos—the warm body pressed against her— whispered, "Brenna? Are you okay?"

He sounded both relieved and worried, and she resisted the urge to press closer to him and give in to the blackness threatening again.

Instead, she tried to get her bearings and figure out what had happened. She remembered Carlton striding toward her. She'd felt rooted in place with shock, and then it was too late. She'd barely even seen his fist coming and then it had landed. The pain had been instantaneous and intense. After that… nothing but blackness.

"Where are we?" She thought she was whispering, but her head protested like she'd screamed the words. She tasted blood and realized she'd bitten hard on her tongue when she'd taken the hit.

"We're in a covered truck bed. It belongs to one of Carlton's guards," Marcos whispered.

Now that he said it, Brenna realized they were moving—it wasn't just her own nausea. The ground underneath them was bumpy, and whoever was driving wasn't trying to avoid a rough ride. She also realized why she was pressed between Marcos and the cold metal of the side of the truck bed. He was trying to keep her from further injury.

She tried to move around and discovered her hands were tied behind her back. Panic threatened anew, and Marcos shifted even closer to her, probably sensing it.

How he could control his movements at all, she wasn't sure. As much as she tried to hold herself in place, whenever the truck took a turn, she slid forward or backward. Without her hands free to brace herself, all she could do was hope she didn't hit too hard. Or that the impact wouldn't roll her over entirely. Because she wasn't sure she could take another bump to her face, no matter how small.

"Where are they taking us?" It was a stupid question; it was obvious Carlton wanted them dead. Knowing how or where wasn't going to change anything.

She struggled against the rope around her wrists, but her frantic movements just gave her rope burn and made her shoulders ache. Her breathing came faster, and she knew she was on the verge of hyperventilating.

"Try to breathe slowly. Relax," Marcos said in the same calm tone, and she wanted to scream at him.

How was she supposed to relax when a drug lord's thugs were about to kill them? But she closed her eyes and tried, breathing in frigid air through her nose until her pulse calmed. When she felt marginally in control again, she asked, "How long have we been driving? And how long was I out?"

"You were probably only unconscious for five minutes before they moved us to the truck. At first, Carlton was going to use my own idea against me and send us out into the Appalachians like Jesse."

Before he could say more, Brenna blurted what she'd been thinking ever since he'd suggested it that morning, "Wasn't there some other way? You sent the kid off to die."

"I gave him my car keys, Brenna," Marcos told her. "And when the guards took us to the outbuilding, my car was gone. He got the message. Hopefully, he's made it out of the mountains by now. If we're really lucky, the DEA has already found him and they're on their way up here. But Carlton and his chef took another car and headed down the mountain to try to intercept him. Carlton sent us with his guards instead of just leaving us to wander the wilderness."

Brenna let the information about Jesse sink in, and relief followed. She tried not to dwell on the part about where they were going.

"You really thought I'd just let Jesse die?"

"I thought it was the only option you saw," Brenna replied, but she felt guilty, because even though her words were true, she *had* thought it. That, given the impossible option of him or Jesse, Marcos had chosen himself.

"It's not ideal, I admit it. And I don't think Carlton realizes I gave him the keys. He seemed to think Jesse had hot-wired it on his own, but that's why we're here. He'd figured Jesse had no shot, and he wasn't about to take that chance with us."

"No," Brenna whispered. Of course he wouldn't. He'd discovered their true identities—she still didn't know how—so the only option was for them to disappear, with no way to tie it back to him. Which meant wherever the guards were taking them, Carlton figured no one would ever find their bodies.

That depressing thought had barely taken shape when the truck pulled to a stop and doors slammed from the front cab.

Brenna renewed her efforts to loosen the ties on her wrists, rubbing them frantically against a rough spot in the truck bed, but it was far too little and far too late.

The cover over the truck bed was pulled back and the guards stared down at them, wearing furious expressions and pointing semiautomatic weapons at their heads.

"Get out," one of the guards said, and the other grabbed her by the elbow and pulled her to a sitting position.

The world around her tilted and spun, and when it finally settled, she glanced around. Nothing but trees as far as she could see to her right. And when she looked left…terror lodged in her throat.

A sharp drop off the side of the mountain.

Chapter Thirteen

They were out of time.

Marcos locked his hands together behind his back as he climbed awkwardly out of the truck. Somehow, it was even colder here than inside that truck bed, lying on the cold metal. Wind whipped around him, raising goose bumps all over his body. Or maybe that was due to their current predicament.

He'd managed to saw the ropes against a rusted-out spot in the truck bed, fraying them enough while they'd driven that he thought a hard yank might break them the rest of the way. Not that it mattered with two guards, each holding semiautomatic weapons.

Behind him, Brenna was trying—and failing—to climb out of the truck bed by herself. She was hunched over the edge, one leg dangling down, her face pressed to the metal like she was trying not to throw up.

One of the guards swore and went to yank her the rest of the way when the second one warned, "Don't. You want her puking on you? Wait a second unless you want to burn your clothes when we get out of here. Carlton said not to bring any DNA back with us."

Stay calm, Marcos reminded himself, standing beside the truck, pasting a dazed expression on his own face and hoping they'd think he was disoriented from the rough ride. He was closer to the tree line; Brenna was closer to the edge of the cliff. He wanted to step toward her, terrified one of those guards was going to just give her a hard shove and send her over.

But he didn't move, because he knew any fast movement on his part might cause them to do the same thing. Instead, he spoke. "You drive us out of here instead, and the DEA will pay a hefty reward."

The guards looked at each other and laughed, but Marcos had already known it was a losing play. He just wanted their attention off Brenna long enough for her to move on her own—preferably closer to him.

And finally, she did. She took a deep breath and hauled herself the rest of the way out of the truck bed, stumbling over and then slumping to the ground beside him.

"Shouldn't have messed with Carlton," one of the guards mocked her, striding over and putting his face near hers.

Marcos's pulse picked up. The guards were just like Carlton. And they were high on their new roles as his first line of defense since Carlton and Brenna had taken out the others.

He purposely didn't look at the second guard, just addressed the one leaning over Brenna. "Come on, man. He outweighs her by at least double. That wasn't exactly a fair fight."

Get closer, he silently willed the second guard, even as he tried to fight with his bonds behind his back. He kept his movements small, not wanting to alert them to what he was doing. But if Carlton wanted no DNA, that meant he probably didn't want them shot. No chance of blood splatter if they just jumped off the cliff on their own. Marcos was pretty sure that was the choice they'd be offered very soon: either jump or be filled with lead.

He needed to distract them long enough to give him a fighting chance. But even if he got his hands free, it was a long shot. Brenna was clearly out of the fight, hurt worse than he'd realized. And he was unarmed against two trained guards with weapons.

"No?" the guard continued to mock. "I guess all that police training is pretty useless, huh?" He nudged her side with the toe of his boot.

The second guard rolled his eyes and took a step closer. "Come on, let's get this over with."

The first guard smiled, a slimy grin that sent a different kind of fear through Marcos. "Don't you want to play a little before the kill?" He got down on his knees next to Brenna and took some of her hair between his fingers, sniffing it.

She turned her head a little, her lips trembling

with a suppressed snarl as she pushed herself to her feet.

"Hey," the second guy said, grabbing his friend.

The first guard turned to shove him, and Marcos knew it was his moment. There was no time even for a quick prayer as he yanked his arms as hard as he could away from each other. There was a loud *rip* and then his hands were free.

"Watch out!" the first guard screamed, jumping backward and raising his weapon again.

Marcos leaped toward him, praying the second guard would spin to help and leave Brenna alone. He fell on top of the first guard, slapping the gun away from him.

It went off, a *boom* that sent the gun in an upward arc as the guard tried to control the kick and fight Marcos off at the same time.

Using the gun's momentum, Marcos shoved it upward, slamming the weapon into the guard's face. He went down and Marcos hesitated, glancing backward. Continue fighting this one or go for the other?

Behind him, Brenna suddenly spun away from the second guard, as though she was going to make a run for it. The guard grinned, starting to lift his gun as Marcos screamed a warning and tried to leap on him.

Before he could, Brenna slammed her tied hands toward the guard and ran backward instead of forward, straight into him. Marcos saw a flash of metal—was that a *butter* knife?—then the guard screamed, and Marcos landed on top of him.

The guard had dropped the butt of his weapon in favor of clutching his bleeding leg, trying to pull out the butter knife Brenna had somehow lodged pretty far into his thigh. Marcos went for the gun dangling from the strap over his shoulder, but he knew he wouldn't get control of it fast enough.

The guard he'd dropped was getting up, lifting his own weapon, his finger sliding beneath the trigger.

Abandoning his plan to fight, Marcos spun away from them both and grabbed Brenna around the waist, redirecting her. Then he ran straight ahead, shoving her toward the downward sloping tree line.

Marcos picked up his pace. This was going to hurt, but hopefully not as much as a bullet.

The blast of one gun quickly became two as bullets whistled past, close enough for him to feel the displaced air. He increased his pace, his strides dangerously long in the slippery, dead leaves. Then his right foot lifted off the ground and didn't come back down onto anything solid again, and he was hurtling through the air, Brenna beside him.

ONE SECOND, SHE'D been running. The next second, there was nothing underneath her but air.

Brenna's stomach leaped into her throat, leaving no room for her to get a breath as she pinwheeled her legs uselessly. She yanked at the bonds holding her arms together, needing to get them free if she had any chance of bracing herself for the inevitable fall, but it was no use.

The ground came up at her hard and Brenna squeezed her eyes shut, curling into a ball at the last second. She slammed into the partially frozen ground, bounced off a tree and continued sliding down the steep hill.

It was better than the complete drop off the cliff in the other direction, but pain exploded behind Brenna's eyes at every jolt, reawakening the pain from Carlton's hit. Although she'd been playing up how badly she was hurt with the guards, it hadn't been far from the truth. It had been sheer will to survive—to make sure Marcos survived—that had given her the strength to jam the butter knife she'd hidden in her sock into the guard's leg.

She felt as if she bounced against every tree on that hill, like she was in a pinball machine, before she finally rolled to a stop at the bottom. Her vision still rolled along with the pain in her head.

"We have to move," Marcos said, and she tried, but when she attempted to get to her feet, she stumbled back to the ground.

Up felt like down and down, up. The attempt to stand sent everything spinning again.

In the distance, the shooting resumed, and bark kicked off a tree ten feet away. "Go," she managed to tell Marcos.

Instead, he picked her up, tossing her over his shoulder in a move that had her clenching her teeth to stop from throwing up. Then they were moving again, zigzagging through the forest, and all she could do was pray he held on to her.

It felt like hours, but Brenna was sure it was much less when Marcos finally stopped, lowering her carefully off his shoulder. Her whole body ached: her head, from Carlton's punch; her stomach, from bouncing on Marcos's muscled shoulder; the rest of her, from bumping every tree on the hill. She couldn't keep from groaning at the bliss of lying still for a minute on the cold forest floor, dead leaves scratching her face.

Brenna focused on breathing without throwing up while Marcos went to work on the ropes around her wrists. A minute later, her hands tingled at the sudden rush of blood flow, and her hands were free. Her shoulders ached as she shifted awkwardly on her side, getting them in a more comfortable position. Her eyes were still closed, but she could see her pulse pounding underneath her eyelids.

"How are you doing?" Marcos asked, his voice soft with concern as he brushed hair out of her eyes.

"I'm alive," she groaned, then cracked her eyes open, testing how badly it hurt. Realizing the trees actually blocked out a lot of the sun and that the world was settling around her, she opened them the rest of the way. "Did we lose them?"

"For the moment," Marcos answered. "But we'd better keep moving."

Brenna wanted to nod and climb to her feet, but everything hurt. She'd used the last of her reserves trying to take down the guard, and when she told her body to move, nothing happened.

"I think we can pause for a minute," Marcos finally said.

She closed her eyes again, wanting to just rest, and then he was lifting her carefully into his lap, tucking her head against his chest. His warmth seeped through her shirt, and she suddenly realized how cold she was.

Marcos's warmth seemed to replenish her strength, and Brenna sucked in a deep breath of the bitterly cold air. "You're right. We'd better go. If we get stuck out here overnight..."

He didn't finish her sentence, but he didn't have to. He had to know that if they were still here when the sun went down, their chances of surviving dropped even lower than the temperatures would.

Chapter Fourteen

Marcos glanced over at Brenna, trying to be subtle about it. He'd already asked her three times how she was doing since they'd started moving again, even offered to carry her again once. Each time, she'd responded in brief monosyllabic replies that made it clear she was doing this on her own.

But it wasn't her annoyance that concerned him. He knew she hadn't been short with him because she was mad; it was taking everything she had just to keep putting one foot in front of the other. He could see it in the tense way she gritted her jaw, in the careful steps, the glazed-over stare focused straight ahead.

She'd been unconscious for too many minutes after Carlton had punched her. Add the tumble down the hill, and he was worried her injuries were more dangerous than they appeared. He'd watched a friend in the DEA take a blow to the head and seemingly bounce back, only to die from it hours later. The idea of losing Brenna that way terrified him.

After all the years apart, he'd accepted that she was part of his past. That she was never going to be more than his first crush, and any imagining who she'd turned out to be was simple fantasy.

But now that she was in front of him again? The truth was, even though he barely knew her still, the fantasy couldn't even begin to compare with the reality. And he had a pretty vivid imagination.

Now, he was determined to do whatever it took to get them both out of this, so that he'd get a chance to really know her. To see if maybe they'd always been meant to have more than just a shared past.

Still, he respected her determination to survive this, to make it on her own. And the truth was, between bouncing down that hill and the beating he'd taken from Carlton's guards just yesterday, running with her for the few miles earlier had taken a lot out of him. He could probably carry her again for a while, but he wasn't sure how long. All he knew was, it wouldn't be long enough to make it back to civilization.

He glanced up at the setting sun. It had to be closing in on 5:00 p.m. now, and the sky was streaked in pinks and purples. Over the fiery shades of orange and red in the trees, it was gorgeous, but the sight made fear ball up in his gut. They weren't going to make it out of here before nightfall.

And as dangerous as the Appalachians were in the day, they were a thousand times worse in the dark. Especially with no flashlights to lead their way.

"We'd better look for a place to hunker down for the night soon." He finally spoke what he'd been thinking for the past hour.

Brenna slowed to a stop, turning to face him. "Shouldn't we push on? Those guards are still out there, still hunting us."

"Yeah, well, one of them is limping now." He stared at her, leaning close until a shaky smile stretched her lips.

"What are you doing?"

"Checking your pupils." Thank goodness, they looked normal. He reached out and stroked his fingers carefully over her cheeks to the back of her head, searching for another bump from when she'd slammed into the wall.

She went completely still as he probed the back of her head, discovering a small goose egg. "Does that hurt?" he asked.

"No," she whispered, staring up at him, her lips slightly parted.

He pulled back quickly. "Good. And your vision is okay?"

She threaded her hand in his, and his pulse picked up at how right it felt. It was ridiculous, given their situation, but he couldn't help it.

"Yes, I'm okay. I have a killer headache, but my vision is back to normal. I haven't thrown up or lost consciousness again. I'm okay."

He nodded, recognizing that she was listing the possible signs of a concussion. "Yeah, well, you were out for a while in the truck." He squeezed her hand and admitted, "You scared me."

She grinned. "None of this is a ball of laughs."

"True."

She looked skyward and bit her lip. "You're right. Wandering around in the dark probably isn't a good idea." Then her gaze swept the trees surrounding them, and he knew she had to be thinking about the animals that lived in these woods. "But are we any safer stopping? The guards might call it a night when it gets dark, but Carlton will probably have reinforcements by morning."

"We're at least a couple of miles east of Carlton's place now," Marcos told her.

"Really?" She let out a long breath. "I'm glad you know that, because I feel like we could be wandering in circles for all I can tell. Any idea how far we are from getting out of here?"

"Too far," he replied, and she didn't look surprised.

"Let's see if we can put a little more distance between us and them," she suggested.

He nodded, letting go of her hand as they started up an incline. He stayed slightly behind her, in case she slid backward.

He knew there were houses out here, but he hadn't seen a single one since they'd run from the guards a few hours ago. Which was probably good—Carlton's money had purchased plenty of loyalty. If someone in a house *had* spotted them, chances were that they'd tell Carlton—or simply shoot on sight—rather than offer help.

It had been nothing but dense woods. Mostly they'd been traveling slowly downhill, but every once in a while, they'd have to climb up to go back down again. He'd seen a trail at one point, but avoided it. No sense walking a path where they'd be easier to spot.

So far, they'd been keeping a brisk enough pace to help warm them slightly, but Marcos knew it would be a whole different story once they found a spot to settle in for the night. He wondered if Brenna was right about them keeping moving.

"Hey," she asked, turning to face him, walking backward now. "Do you hear that? I think—"

Her words ended on a shriek, and she suddenly dropped out of his sight.

"Brenna!" He ran forward, and as he emerged at the top of the incline, he realized two things simultaneously: Brenna had heard the guards, whom he suddenly spotted in the distance off to the left, and they'd reached a summit.

Brenna had just dropped off the side of a cliff.

THE WIND SWALLOWED Brenna's scream as the ground disappeared beneath her, and then she was falling fast. Frantically, she grabbed for something, anything, and snagged a tree root.

The impact of holding it nearly yanked her shoulder out of its socket, but she squeezed tighter, her body swinging as she reached up with her other hand and held on with both. She took a few panicked breaths as her hands slipped a little...and then held.

Slowly, she looked down, and the vertigo she'd fought earlier struck again. This time, though, it wasn't because of the blow to her head. It was because solid ground seemed *miles* below her.

Holding tighter to the root and praying it wouldn't break, Brenna looked up. She'd fallen at least a foot off the edge of the cliff before she'd grabbed on to something. Above her, Marcos's terrified face came into view.

When he spotted her, instant relief rushed over his features, but new panic assailed her. Because off in the distance, she heard shooting. The guards had found them.

"Go," she told Marcos. "Run!" Maybe she could hang here until they passed, then find something else above this root to yank herself up with. But in the meantime, Marcos was right in the line of fire, an obvious target at the edge of a cliff.

She pushed off her disbelief, because it didn't matter now. What were the chances she'd turn just as the ground dropped away? Yeah, it was stupid, she realized now. She'd been cresting what she'd assumed was another hill. Not the top of a cliff. But the Appalachians were deceiving.

Instead of running, Marcos dropped flat on his stomach, and then he was dangling over the edge of the cliff, holding his hand out to her. "Give me your hand."

Brenna hesitated. Did he have hold of something with his other hand? Was he hanging too far off the edge to hold both their weight?

"Brenna!" Marcos insisted, his fingertips brushing hers.

The gunfire in the distance got closer, and now she could hear the guards yelling at each other, sounding triumphant.

Tightening her grip with her left hand, she hauled herself higher, reaching up with her right. And then she was soaring upward as Marcos hauled her over the edge like she weighed nothing.

As she crested the top, he hooked a hand in the waistband of her jeans and pulled her the rest of the way. She realized he *was* bracing himself with his other hand, using a tree he was lucky hadn't snapped with their combined weight. But there was no time to celebrate, because she could see the guards getting closer.

She started to get up, and Marcos pushed her back down, shoving her back the way they'd come, so she slid down the incline on her belly, making her body less of a target. She could hear him right behind her, and the guards coming from off to their left. Once the guards got to the edge of the cliff where she and Marcos had just been standing, they'd have a clear line of sight down below.

"Go," Marcos said as soon as she hit the bottom of the slope they'd just trekked up.

She lurched to her feet and ran, dodging trees and slipping in the dead leaves, only to regain her footing again. She had no goal, other than to run *away* from the bullets, but in the back of her mind, she realized she was probably heading straight back toward Carlton's mansion.

Changing direction, Brenna ran downhill instead of across. Her feet slid even more until she lost her balance. She caught herself on a tree, slowing, then took off again, trusting that Marcos was right behind her. She risked a glance backward and discovered that he was—in fact, he was *directly* behind her. As if he was trying to block her body from a bullet with his own.

How had she thought for a second that he'd let Jesse walk into the mountains to his death, without at least trying to do something? If she'd learned anything about this grown-up version of Marcos Costa, it was that he wasn't just brave. He was also smart. Every time they'd faced possible danger, instead of jumping to the gut reaction of fight or flight, he'd stayed in character and tried to reason his way out of it. Only when he'd absolutely had to had he fought.

And right now, if a bullet managed to find them through the trees, it would hit Marcos instead of her.

Brenna picked up her pace. Her feet barely seemed to touch ground and then they were up again, until she knew she was out of control, half falling down the incline and praying there wouldn't be another sudden drop-off ahead.

But it was working. She could still hear Marcos, staying on her heels. But the sounds of the gunshots were fading, and the guards' voices were distant now.

"Zag," Marcos instructed.

"What?" She glanced back at him and would have run smack into a tree if he hadn't grabbed her arm, redirecting her.

She ran the way he indicated, panting. Now that the threat was less immediate, her adrenaline started to fade. She realized her legs were burning from running, and she could feel every bruise covering her body. It was getting harder and harder to see, and Brenna slowed a little.

Then, Marcos's hand was on her arm again, and he pulled her to a stop. "I think we lost them."

He sounded out of breath, too, and he rested his arms on his thighs, just breathing heavily for a moment.

She leaned against the tree and did the same, watching him. He hadn't left her. Not that she'd expected him to, even when she was telling him to go. But she'd needed to at least try.

"You could have left me."

He swore and straightened. "Not a chance. We're a team, remember?"

"Yeah." She palmed his cheek, running her fingers over the scruff starting to come in. It was so dark against his pale skin, and the contrast fascinated her for some reason. Or maybe it was just the man who fascinated her. The truth was, he always had.

He pulled away. "We should keep moving, try to get a bit more distance from the guards."

"You still hear them?" She strained to listen.

"No, but I don't want to take any chances. I doubt we have more than twenty minutes before we're completely out of light. So, let's get as far as we can and then find a spot to hunker down for the night."

Brenna glanced around her. As far as she could see, everything was the same. Towering trees with bare branches that cast ominous shadows in the semidarkness. Slippery leaves underfoot. In the distance—the opposite direction she knew the guards were—a big branch snapped, making her jump.

What animals were out here in the mountains? Bears, for sure. Maybe wolves?

Brenna shivered and moved forward, a little more cautiously, Marcos right behind her, as the night grew blacker and blacker around them.

Chapter Fifteen

Under any other circumstances, huddled in the dark with Brenna Hartwell sitting between his legs, her back against his chest and her head tucked under his chin, would be heaven.

Marcos had done the best he could, imitating what he'd seen his brother Andre do in practice before: camouflage them with their natural surroundings. Andre worked for the FBI as a sniper, but he'd trained with the military's best Special Operations groups, and he could make a hide pretty much anywhere.

Without Andre's training, Marcos knew his hidey-hole wasn't perfect. But ten minutes before the light would be completely gone, he'd pulled Brenna to a stop beside a huge, fallen fir tree. After checking carefully to verify that no animal had already claimed it, he went to work creating a space underneath it for them to wait out the night. He'd layered fir branches as a pseudo-carpet, to keep them off the cold ground. Then, he'd piled more tree branches around it, hoping to keep in as much warmth as possible, knowing the temperatures were supposed to drop well below freezing overnight.

Neither of them was dressed for it. He was slightly better off than she was, in jeans and a crew-neck wool sweater. Brenna had topped her jeans off with a lightweight T-shirt. Huddling close together and sharing their body heat was the smart move, but the feel of her body against his was distracting. Being in the dark, not being able to see her, seemed to make him hyperaware to every tiny movement she made.

"How are you feeling?" he whispered.

They'd been silent for the past twenty minutes, listening to a pair of owls that had claimed a spot somewhere in the trees above them. They hadn't heard the guards, but Marcos figured they'd returned to the mansion and would regroup in the morning. Which meant he and Brenna needed to start out again at first light.

"I'm fine," she whispered back, sounding like she was trying to be patient with his new favorite question.

Chances were slim that the guards were still searching, but they were keeping their voices low just in case. Especially since there was the possibility the guards would be afraid to return to face Carlton's wrath without having taken care of them for good.

"We should try to get some sleep," he told her, but ruined his own plan when a minute later, he couldn't help but ask, "What's your life like now, Brenna?"

He'd been wondering ever since he'd realized her true identity. Most of what he knew about her came from those few months when she was eleven years old. Although he'd tried to get close to her then, it had been in the innocent ways of a boy with a crush, and he'd mostly tried to support her in her grief.

During the five years he'd lived in that foster home with Cole and Andre, other kids had come and gone. The two boys who'd also lived there during the time of the fire he'd barely known more than the Pikes' biological son, Trent—grown and long gone before he'd moved in. But Brenna had always been different, and he didn't think a year had gone by since then that he hadn't wondered what she was doing.

It was hard to imagine the little Brenna Hartwell he'd known growing up to become a cop, and yet, somehow it seemed perfectly natural. The picture Carlton had flashed on his phone of Brenna wearing her police blues, looking so serious and focused, was such a contrast to the woman who'd attacked a guard to save his life, to the woman who'd melted in his arms that first night. He wanted to know all the different sides to her, and he was certain he'd only scratched the surface.

She shifted a little, the outsides of her thighs rubbing the inside of his. He looped his arms around her waist, holding her still, pretending he was just trying to keep her warm.

"What do you mean?" She sounded tentative, like maybe she didn't want to discuss real life with him.

But there was no need for cover stories anymore, and although he'd seen plenty of glimpses of the real Brenna, he wanted to know more. A lot more.

"What's your life like when you're not out here in a drug lord's house, playing a role?"

"I don't know."

She squirmed a little more until he laughed and told her, "You've got to stop doing that."

"Oh." He didn't need to be able to see her to sense her flush. "Sorry."

"Okay, I'll start," he said. "I work out of the DEA's district office in West Virginia. I've been there about five years, joined pretty soon after I finished school."

He paused, remembering the guilt he'd felt when he'd first started college. He'd wanted to go so badly, had been willing to work to put himself through, but his oldest brother Cole had insisted he focus on school. So while Marcos had worked part-time, Cole had taken on two jobs. Both Marcos and Andre had gone to college, while Cole had worked to make sure they had the life they might have gotten if they'd grown up under normal circumstances, instead of foster care.

"Where'd you go just now?" Brenna asked.

"Just thinking about how lucky I got. The day I turned eighteen, Cole had a home waiting for me."

Her fingers twined with his in her lap. They were icy cold, and he held tight, trying to warm them.

"Most kids in foster care just suddenly end up on the street. Even though they've known it's been coming, they don't have a plan," she said. "But it doesn't surprise me what Cole did for you and Andre. Cole was always looking after everyone. And I might have only known you a few months, Marcos, but I know that even without him and Andre, you would have ended up somewhere like the DEA."

"Maybe. But what about you?"

"No one was waiting for me."

He'd expected as much, from some of the things she'd said in Carlton's mansion, but the thought physically pained him. He wished he could rewind eleven years and be standing on her porch the way Cole had been standing on his the day she'd turned eighteen. Except he hadn't known where she'd ended up. And the truth was, he'd been afraid to look, afraid where she might have gone after that fire, how she might have turned out. It was easier to imagine her happy than risk finding her not.

"You're sitting there feeling guilty about that, aren't you?" she asked incredulously. "I didn't come looking for you either, Marcos. We only knew each other for a few months."

"Yeah, but I never forgot you."

His words hung in the air a long moment before she replied softly, "I never forgot you, either."

BRENNA JOLTED AWAKE, freezing and disoriented.

Slowly, awareness returned: the scent of pine and

old leaves surrounding her; the heat of Marcos's body against her back; blackness so complete she wasn't completely sure her eyes were open. Then, she realized what had woken her: branches cracking.

She twitched as the sound came again, and Marcos's breath whispered across her neck, then his arms closed tighter around her. "Deer," he said softly.

"Are you sure?" Her voice was so low it could barely be called a whisper, but somehow he heard her.

"Yeah. I peeked through the branches a minute ago. There's a little family of them."

She relaxed against him. "How can you see anything?"

"It's darker in here than when you look out. There are some stars."

"Enough to see a trail by? Maybe we should start moving again." She knew if the guards weren't still out there searching, they'd be looking again by morning light. And she was pretty sure that she'd actually run closer to Carlton's mansion when they were trying to escape the gunfire last night.

Realizing she'd lost all sense of time, she asked, "Is it still night?"

"Yeah, you slept about four hours."

"Did you sleep?"

"Some."

She had a feeling that meant only enough to rest his eyes for a few minutes and keep watch the remainder of the time. "We can take turns, you know."

"I'm not worried about Carlton's guards. I may not make the world's best hide, but it's good enough to fool those two. If they're still out there, they're not close by. But I think we should stay where we are for now. If you're cold in here, it's a good ten degrees colder outside."

We are *outside*, she wanted to say. But the truth was, the canopy of branches did give the illusion of being indoors. If indoors had a broken heater. She couldn't stop the shiver that worked through her, and Marcos pressed his arms and legs closer to her.

"Aren't you cold?" she asked.

"Yeah."

"You don't seem cold." In fact, compared to her, he felt downright toasty.

"I'm keeping warm imagining the two of us being back at my house, with the heat blasting on high."

His house. "What's that like?" Even as she asked it, she realized it was unfair to probe into his life when she hadn't been willing to tell him about hers.

Not giving him time to answer, she said, "Never mind. None of my business."

"It is if you want it to be," Marcos said softly, making her intensely aware of the hardness of his chest against her back, the muscled thighs pressed tightly to hers.

Brenna couldn't stop herself from tensing, and there was no way he wouldn't feel it, the way they were pressed so closely together. Did she want Marcos Costa to be her business? Probably more than she'd wanted almost anything else in her life.

But the Marcos of her fantasies wasn't the real thing. The man behind her was way more complicated, way more terrifying to her heart than she could have imagined. Because a fantasy she could hold on to all her life, a stabilizing force in a world she couldn't control, was one thing. Taking a chance on the real man and risking failure? She wasn't sure she could handle that.

Especially not now, when—even if they made it out of the mountains alive—her future seemed murky once again. Did she really belong in police work? Even though Marcos had made the choice that gave Jesse the best chance of survival, the question remained about her. Would undercover work—would any kind of work that involved regularly dealing with someone like Carlton Wayne White—change her in ways she didn't want to be changed?

She felt lost, not unlike the way she'd felt when that foster home had burned down all those years ago, or when the woman from Child and Family Services had showed up at the hospital a few months before that, right after her mother had died, telling Brenna she was going into the system. Over the years, she'd learned how to be alone. It was isolating, yes, but it was safe, too.

In some of those foster homes, it was the only way to survive unharmed. In others, she'd sensed a chance to make real friends, maybe even another person to consider family the way Marcos had found with Cole and Andre. But she'd never reached out, never taken that step, because it was too risky. And, if she was being honest with herself, even the idea had felt somehow like a betrayal to the mom who had done her best for Brenna, whose only failure was dying in that car without her.

The thought jolted her. Did she really think, all these years later, she should have died beside her mom in that car? Tears pricked the backs of her eyes, because she honestly wasn't sure. She missed her mom every day, but it hit now with a strength similar to the days after it had happened.

Was she willing to let anyone into her life? Willing to risk losing them? Even if that someone was the man she'd dreamed of since she was eleven years old?

"You're awfully quiet," Marcos said, making Brenna realize she let his statement go unanswered far too long.

Before she could figure out what to say, he continued. "We don't need to figure anything out here. How about this? You tell me about your place, and I'll tell you about mine. That's not too hard, right?"

"It's not about the house," she said, and cursed the crack in her voice.

"I know," he said softly. "You probably think that because I found Cole and Andre, my experience was really different than yours. And you're right."

She started to speak, but he kept going. "For five

years, Cole and Andre and I were inseparable. And even after that house burned down and we were split up, in my heart I knew I was just biding time until each of us hit eighteen and we were back together. But I came to that house when I was seven. I was in foster care since I was born. They always say that babies have a better chance of being adopted, but when I was little, I had some issues with my heart. Gone now, but by the time they realized it wasn't a major issue, I was getting older. No one wanted me."

She tightened her hold on his hands, hurting for the little boy who probably hadn't understood why he didn't have a real family.

He was right about their experiences being different. She might have spent her life since her mom died feeling totally alone in the world, but that's how he'd entered it.

They'd chosen different paths. He'd let Andre and Cole in, made his own family when he'd had none. And she'd pushed everyone away, because she was too afraid of losing them to give anyone a chance. Maybe it was time to finally change that.

"I want you," she whispered.

Chapter Sixteen

I want you.

Brenna's words from a few hours earlier rattled around in Marcos's brain as he held her hand tightly in his, grabbing tree trunks for stability with his other hand as they picked their way down a steep incline. Snow had started falling sometime after she'd said those words, and now the ground was slick and he could see his breath.

She'd gone silent after that, and he hadn't pushed her, because he'd sensed in the tone of her voice that something important had just changed. Instead, he'd just held her, and eventually she'd drifted back off to sleep. He'd woken her a few hours later, battling his fears of venturing back out into the cold or waiting until it warmed up a little more and risking Carlton sending reinforcements on the mountain.

They'd been up now for a few hours, moving at a brisk jog most of the time. But this incline was slippery enough with the light snowfall that they were moving more carefully. The sun was starting to come up, and he'd been hoping it would bring warmth, but instead, the sky was hazy, threatening more snow. He prayed they were going the right way; his internal sense of direction was usually good, but they'd definitely veered off course running from the guards last night.

"We have to be getting close," Brenna said, every word puffing clouds of white into the air. Her cheeks and nose were bright red, and her fingers felt like icicles in his.

He'd stopped feeling his toes an hour ago, which made him worry how she was faring in her much lighter top. But whenever he'd asked, she'd given him a patient-looking smile and told him she was a skier and used to the cold.

"Yeah, I hope we're close," Marcos replied. The truth was, if they didn't emerge from the forest and onto flat ground soon, he was going to worry that this off-the-trail route he'd picked out for them wasn't as straight a shot as staying on the road. Of course, they couldn't stay on the road or they'd risk running right into Carlton. And while he hoped the DEA was also on that road by now, he didn't want to take the chance.

"You're a worrier," Brenna said.

"This seems like a good time to worry." He kept the rest of it to himself. He was mostly worried about *her*, that she was warm enough, that her head was okay after the hit she'd taken yesterday.

"Well, sure. But I feel a lot safer right now with

you than I did in that mansion with Carlton." He must have still looked concerned, because she squeezed his hand and added, "We have to be close. Once we make it to civilization, then we worry about bringing down Carlton."

"I'm hoping the DEA is already there, and he's in handcuffs. Because if they didn't get the message and Carlton hasn't found us…"

"He's going to run."

"It's his best bet. He assaulted a police officer and a DEA agent—and killed one of his own guards in front of us. Besides, I heard him order his guards to kill us, so he can claim all he likes that they acted alone, but his testimony isn't going to sound better than mine."

Brenna picked up the pace. "Then let's make sure we beat him."

Her feet started to slide out from underneath her and he gripped the tree trunk, pulling her back toward him before she fell in the snow. She grabbed his shoulder with her free hand to brace herself, and then they were pressed tightly together, reminding him of the first night he'd seen her.

He must have telegraphed what he was thinking with his eyes, because her eyes dilated. All of a sudden, he felt like he was the one whose world was sliding out from underneath him as she leaned up and pressed her lips to his.

Her lips were cold, and so was the tip of her nose as it pressed against his cheek, but his must have been the same, because she leaned back for a second and whispered, "You're cold."

Then her tongue was in his mouth, and he didn't feel cold at all. He let go of the tree trunk and wrapped his free hand around her waist, bringing her closer still. And somehow, even in the frigid mountains with a drug lord out to kill him, he knew he was exactly where he was supposed to be.

For a few blissful moments, he let himself forget everything else and just *feel*. The way her fingers curled into his shoulder. The way she arched toward him whenever his tongue stroked the inside of her lip. The strength of her body underneath his hand as he palmed her lower back. For a few moments, there was nothing but Brenna.

In some ways, he knew nothing about her. He had no idea how she drank her coffee, what she liked to read, where she saw herself in five years. In others, he knew her better than most of the people he saw every day: the pain she'd survived; her determination in her job; her compassion for those she tried to help.

And yet, it wasn't anywhere near enough. Not the little bit she'd let him into her world and not this amazing kiss with both of them in too many clothes and with too many secrets still between them. Because what did she really know about him, either? Once they got back to real life, would they have anything in common?

If the answer was no, he half wanted to stay exactly where they were, no matter the consequences.

As if she could read his mind, Brenna pulled back and echoed his words from the other night. "I tell you what, when we get out of here, you show me your place and I'll show you mine."

She spoke fast, as though if she didn't get it out quickly, she wouldn't say it at all, and Marcos nodded just as fast. "It's a deal."

Then he grabbed the tree in front of him, keeping a tight hold on Brenna with his other hand, and started moving again.

CIVILIZATION HAD TO be close.

Brenna had been thinking it for more than an hour and, as big snowflakes started to plop on her head, she finally gave in to the worry that something had gone wrong. That getting out of the mountains would take longer than they'd estimated. Because although she'd been telling Marcos otherwise for hours, the cold was starting to affect her.

Now, when she grabbed the trees they passed for stability, she had to squeeze a little tighter in order to feel the bark. Her fingers were getting clumsy and numb, and her shivering had become erratic and violent. It hadn't warmed up, though, and her mind was still sharp enough to know her body was beginning to shut down.

Glancing up at the sky as another fat snowflake landed on her face and then slid down her neck, Brenna frowned and gave voice to her fears. "I think a storm is coming."

"I know." Marcos sounded as worried as she felt. "We either need to find shelter now and wait it out, or press on and get to help."

She looked over at him, noticing that his lips were tinged just slightly blue. "We might not make it to help if it gets much colder."

"A hide isn't going to keep us much warmer," Marcos said. "I did my best last night, but I'm not sure we can risk stopping. If we stop moving, we're going to lose body heat."

"If this snow keeps up, we've got the same problem. It's going to soak us."

"Let's try—" Abruptly, Marcos cut off, then pulled her another few steps forward, peering into the distance. "Is that—"

"A parking lot," Brenna realized. "And cars. Maybe someone will be there. Or there will be an emergency phone."

She moved faster, half speed-walking, half-sliding down the hill, Marcos's hand somehow still holding tight to hers. The descent felt only partly in her control, partly a dangerous slide she'd never come out of—much like her feelings for the man next to her.

Finally, they reached the bottom of the incline and Brenna might have cried tears of joy—except she was pretty sure they would have frozen the instant they touched her skin. The trees thinned out here, and then the end was finally in sight.

She glanced at Marcos, who was staring at the parking lot at the end of the expanse of woods with similar disbelief. He grinned at her, a full, dimpled smile that sent warmth back into her, and then they took off running.

Brenna had an instant flashback to being eleven years old. She'd been watching as Marcos, Cole, Andre and the other two kids in the foster home had played a game of touch football. They'd invited her, but she'd declined. Even after she'd healed from her injuries in the car crash, she'd felt like her world was in slow motion. Later, she'd recognized that she'd been in a deep depression, but at the time, she'd just felt dazed, unable to really connect with anyone around her.

Only Marcos had made her feel like she would ever come out of that daze. That day, in the middle of the game, he'd run over to the sidelines and handed her the football he'd just caught. Then he'd grabbed her hand and raced with her across the goal line. For a few brief moments, Brenna had felt her childhood return. She'd felt free, even happy.

The same feeling rose up now, and Brenna let out a joyful laugh. They were so close. She could see that the cars were empty, but there *was* an emergency phone, and it was in a little glass enclosure that would keep the wet snow off their faces and the wind off their backs. Then it would be a matter of half an hour—tops—and they'd be in a warm car and heading home.

And then what? she wondered, feeling her feet slow just a little. Would she and Marcos simply go their own ways? She'd invited him into her home—into her life—but soon, they'd have cases to finish, real life to resume. Even if he still wanted to take her up on her offer, would he like what he discovered?

Up in Carlton's mansion, she'd been playing a role. Although parts of the person she'd been pretending to be—someone who would take advantage of kids, who would work with a drug dealer—were despicable, other parts were who she *wished* she could be. Someone confident, the kind of woman who'd walk up to a man she hadn't seen in eighteen years and kiss him as if the next logical step was to yank him into her bed.

The real Brenna was different. More measured, careful about everything she did. Part of what appealed to her about police work were the rules and boundaries. And she sensed Marcos loved undercover work at the DEA for the exact opposite reasons. Would she measure up to whatever he expected her to be?

There was only one way to find out. As Marcos glanced at her questioningly, Brenna picked up her pace again, holding even tighter to his hand.

"Stop right there!"

The voice came out of nowhere and seemed to echo off the mountain behind them.

Brenna jumped and would have fallen if Marcos didn't have such a tight grip on her. Together, they spun, and disbelief and dread slumped her shoulders.

Carlton's guards had caught up to them.

Chapter Seventeen

No way were they going to die this close to freedom.

Marcos stared at the furious guards as they moved in, keeping their rifles leveled on him and Brenna. The anger on their faces was personal this time, and Marcos instantly knew why. Both of them were sporting shiners that matched the nasty bruise underneath Brenna's chin. Apparently, Carlton hadn't been happy when they'd returned last night and had to explain his and Brenna's escape. Not to mention the man Brenna had stabbed was limping, a little blood seeping through his camo pants.

"Very soon, you're going to wish we'd dropped you off that mountain last night," the guard who'd taunted Brenna after taking them out of the truck said darkly.

"That'll seem like a peaceful way to go compared to what Carlton will do to you," the other guard added, then gestured back up the mountain with his weapon. "Let's go."

"I don't think so," Marcos said, keeping hold of

Brenna's hand and taking a step away from them, slightly closer to the parking lot.

"Don't move!" the second guard yelled as the first one moved quickly around to the other side, so they were bracketing him and Brenna.

"You try anything, and we'll shoot you right here," the guard near Brenna warned.

"Really?" Marcos asked, keeping his tone confident as he turned to face the guard closer to him—the one in charge, the one less focused on Brenna. "On camera? You think that's a good idea?"

"What camera?" the second guard demanded, even as the first one swore.

"In the parking lot," Marcos said. "Right above that emergency phone. It's meant to prevent car theft, but believe me, the cops who monitor it will be really interested in automatic gunfire."

"So, move," the first guard demanded.

Marcos took a step backward, and Brenna did the same. He felt her back press against his, and he didn't have to turn to know—she'd lifted her fists, just like him.

"Are you kidding?" the second guard mocked. "You don't stand a chance. We're the ones with weapons."

"Sure," Marcos agreed. "And you use them here, and you're going straight to jail. I'm not following you anywhere. You want to take us back to Carlton, you're going to have to drag us. And incidentally, I don't think Carlton will be happy if you take us out."

He grinned, back in character. "I'm pretty sure he wants to do it himself now. Am I right?"

It was a desperate play, and he knew it. But it was probably his only play. Following the guards meant waiting for a time to attack and hope to overpower them a second time, and it was unlikely. They wouldn't be so easily surprised a second time, and the cold had sapped most of his strength. The fact was, he wasn't sure he and Brenna would even live through a trek back up the mountain.

The first guard snarled, glancing from him and Brenna back to his friend. "Guess we have no choice." He shrugged, but there was glee underneath it as he centered his weapon on Brenna's head. "The cops want to arrest me for this? They'll have to find me first."

"Let's do this," the second guard agreed, lifting his weapon on Marcos.

"Wait!" Brenna yelled, but they ignored her, nodding to one another.

Just before the guards' fingers depressed on the triggers, Marcos shoved Brenna to the ground.

BRENNA SHRIEKED AS she hit the wet ground and Marcos landed on top of her, knocking all the air from her lungs. It was only a temporary reprieve, and she knew it. Marcos had gambled—it had been their only option—but they'd both lost.

She'd never get the chance to figure out where this new connection with him was going. Never get to see his house, reconnect with his brothers, all grown up. Never get to see Marcos in real life, when he didn't have to spend half their time together playing a role. Never get to find out if the way she felt about him now was a leftover childhood crush or the real thing.

She braced herself for the feel of bullets, but instead, she heard cars screeching to a halt, and then voices shouting over each other. "DEA! Drop your weapons!"

Then the gunfire came, and dirt and snow smacked her in the face as some of those bullets struck too close to her. All she could do was curl up smaller, pray Marcos was unharmed on top of her, and wait.

As suddenly as it had started, it was over. Marcos was standing, pulling her to her feet and away from the guards, who were down for good. Red sprayed across the white snow, and Brenna fixated on it instead of looking at the guards as agents ran toward them.

A pair of agents confirmed the guards were dead, and then more agents were leading her and Marcos down to the parking lot, as if they were incapable of making it there themselves.

"You okay, man?" an older agent, wearing a DEA jacket, his hair more salt than pepper, asked Marcos.

"Now I am." Marcos pulled Brenna closer, and she realized she was wedged in the crook of his shoulder.

Odder still, she couldn't imagine being anywhere else right now.

The agent glanced from Marcos to her, then stripped off his jacket and wrapped it around her. "Let's get you in the car. Heat's still on," he told her, gesturing for Marcos to follow.

She glanced back at him, and he smiled at her. "Meet my partner, Jim Holohan. Jim, this is Brenna Hartwell. She's undercover with..." He frowned. "Which department, exactly?"

"Harrisburg, West Virginia."

"Long way from home," Jim commented, opening the door and ushering her into the back of a sedan.

A contented sigh escaped the second she sat down. Although she suspected it would take hours for her to defrost, it was warm in here. Now that she wasn't standing, she realized just how exhausted she was. Hopefully, in a few minutes, she'd start to feel her fingers and toes again.

She started to scoot over for Marcos to join her, but Jim slammed the door behind her. "Hey." She rolled down the window.

"She's okay," Marcos told his partner.

Jim seemed a little skeptical, but he nodded at Marcos and the two of them hopped into the front seat.

"Did you find Jesse?" Marcos asked.

"Yeah. Gave us a good scare when we spotted him racing out of the mountains in your car. We got him some medical treatment, and he's under arrest. Technically, we're holding him because he was driving a DEA car without authorization, but as soon as we have something more to make it stick, we'll be adding charges related to the drug-running operations. Me and a few of the other agents went straight up to Carlton's mansion, but it was empty."

"He was gone?" Brenna asked, surprised. "But his guards said they were taking us back to him."

Jim shrugged. "Our guess is he hasn't gone far. We're watching the airports, but a guy like that has resources."

"Are agents still there?" Marcos asked. "He's got a *lot* of filing cabinets."

Jim grimaced. "He *had* a lot of filing cabinets. Well, I guess he still does, but they've been totally emptied out. Security footage and computers are gone, too. Everything else, he left."

"You're kidding me," Marcos said. "How'd he do that so fast?"

Jim shrugged, then gripped Marcos's arm. "We're glad you're okay."

Brenna could tell the two of them were close. But she supposed that was to be expected; who wouldn't get along with Marcos?

"We had a couple of close calls." Marcos told him about being driven out into the wilderness and escaping.

"About this *we*," Jim said, glancing at her. "You want to tell me exactly what you were doing in Carlton Wayne White's mansion without giving us a heads-up?"

"We can get into all of that later," Marcos said softly.

"He's a known dealer. Anything to do with him should have gone into our system," Jim insisted. "Her very presence could have gotten you killed!"

"Go easy," Marcos started, but Brenna spoke over him.

"My investigation wasn't about drugs. It was about murder. And it's not over."

SHE WAS HOME.

Brenna looked around her little bungalow. She'd lived here for almost a year, and it had always felt comfortable. A place to get away from the world and recharge, just her. It was the first place she'd actually owned, and she'd taken joy in painting the walls cheery colors, in picking out furniture she'd get to keep. She'd figured if she was really going to put down roots, it was time to stop living like she was still a part of the system, being hustled from one place to the next with her single duffel bag.

Back then, the only things she'd cared about were the belongings she'd managed to bring along from her real home. Pictures of her and her mom, her mom's locket, a cherished stuffed animal her dad had bought her when she was a baby, back before he'd taken off for good.

She'd always thought that the day she'd turned

eighteen, she'd start collecting things that were really *hers*. Instead, she'd clung to that old life, something in her unable or unwilling to create anything that might be taken away from her.

But when she'd started this job, she'd decided to make a change. Real job. Real life.

Except now, looking around her, it felt empty. And she realized what was missing was Marcos.

She let out a burst of laughter to calm her raging emotions. That was ridiculous. In her entire life, she'd spent a few months with him. And only three and a half days of that time was as an adult.

It wasn't him she needed, she told herself as she sank into a big, cushy chair she'd bought because it was something her mom would have chosen. But maybe this was a wake-up call. It was time to stop living such an isolated life.

Even now, after almost being killed by a crazy drug lord, she was here, alone. The chief had offered her protection, but they'd both agreed it was probably unnecessary. Carlton was crazy, but crazy enough to seek revenge against an armed cop on her own turf when the whole force was looking for him and getting caught surely meant a life in jail? She felt safe enough, but for once, the isolation itself bothered her.

Sure, her chief had called to make sure she was okay—and to find out what they had on Carlton. And her mentor at the station had called, too. Victor's call was a lot more genuine, and she knew if she hadn't insisted she wanted to be alone, he would have already been at her house with his wife and their four kids. The same was probably true of some of the other officers she worked with, but it had been second nature to insist she was fine by herself.

She'd always been a loner. She had friends at work, but not the kind of friends she spent a lot of time with outside the job. And away from work? She had a few friends, but it was hard to maintain friendships when you didn't stay long in one place.

She should shower and change, maybe even go into the station and come up with a plan to get Carlton before he disappeared for good. But as the sun had started to set on the day, she'd discovered she had no energy left.

Marcos's partner had driven both of them to the hospital to get checked out. No surprise, they'd both been close to hypothermia. Even now, her fingers and toes throbbed. But at least she could feel them again. The doctor hadn't seen any sign of a concussion on her, and Marcos hadn't suffered any internal issues that they could tell from his beating. They were both going to be fine. Yet she was antsy, like her entire world had been upset and she'd never really be fine again.

Or maybe she hadn't really been fine since she'd been eleven years old.

"You're being a drama queen," Brenna muttered, forcing herself out of the chair. She was starving, but first she needed a shower and then, if she didn't fall asleep, food was next on the agenda.

She kicked off her shoes as she headed to her bedroom, and as she was shimmying out of her jeans, she realized there was something in the pocket. Pulling out the crumpled piece of paper, Brenna's heart rate picked up.

She'd forgotten all about the page she'd ripped out of the top of Carlton's pad in his office. Hurrying to the kitchen in her T-shirt and underwear, Brenna grabbed a pencil and shaded carefully across the page, hoping...

"Yes!" Indentations were on the page, and as Brenna squinted at it, she realized it was a phone number.

She probably should have called it in to her chief, have him run it, but she didn't want to wait. Carlton was out there somewhere, probably looking for a way out of the country if he wasn't already gone. And although her plan had been to get some sleep and go into the office as early as possible, when Jim and Marcos had dropped her off, she'd had no real leads.

She'd watched Marcos's curious gaze take in the outside of her little bungalow and bitten her tongue instead of asking him to come in with her. She'd half hoped he would ask—take her up on the promise she'd made on the mountain—but he'd just given her a quick hug goodbye. He and Jim had already been talking about the case as they'd backed out of her driveway.

Shaking off the disappointment that hit all over again, Brenna grabbed the cell phone she hadn't bothered to take with her to Carlton's mansion—not only would she not get service up there, she didn't want him looking through it. With fingers that felt oversize and clumsy, she dialed the number from the paper and held her breath.

It only took two rings and then a woman answered. "Hello?

Brenna drew in a sharp breath as the woman repeated her greeting twice more, then finally hung up. Then she sank into a kitchen chair in disbelief.

She knew that voice. She knew who Carlton's contact in the foster system had been all these years.

Chapter Eighteen

"Brenna Hartwell? From the foster home? Seriously?"

Marcos wrapped the blanket he'd grabbed as soon as he'd gotten home more tightly around himself. It didn't seem to matter how high he cranked the heat or how many hours it had been since he'd left the mountains. He couldn't seem to get warm.

His older brother Andre was still staring at him in disbelief. His oldest brother, Cole, frowned, watching him huddle more deeply into the blanket.

"Yes, that Brenna," Marcos said. "She's an undercover cop." His brothers had arrived an hour ago, after he'd spent several hours with Jim at the DEA office going over the weekend at Carlton's mansion.

His colleagues were busy trying to track Carlton and getting his picture out to anyplace he might try to travel. Eventually, once Marcos had given all the details he could, he'd known as well as they did that there was no reason for him to stay. Nothing besides his burning desire to be the one to slap handcuffs on Carlton.

But he wouldn't be any good to anyone if he couldn't function, and so he'd made Jim promise to call if they got a solid lead and had his partner drop him at home. The entire drive, he'd been wishing Brenna was still beside him.

When they'd dropped her off at her cute little bungalow, he'd been shocked at how close they lived without realizing when he'd spent so many years wondering what had happened to her. He'd desperately wanted to tell Jim to forget the debrief and follow her inside. But time was essential if they wanted to find Carlton, and the truth was, if he'd followed Brenna inside, he'd be tempted to distract her from what she needed to be doing now too: resting and healing.

He hadn't expected to find his brothers waiting for him in his house, but he hadn't been surprised, either. When Jesse had shown up instead of him, the first thing Jim had done before racing up to the mansion was to call Cole and Andre, in case he'd contacted one of them. It wouldn't have been protocol, but Jim knew how close he was with his brothers. Besides, Cole was a detective and Andre was FBI, so they definitely had the resources to help him.

For the past hour, though, they'd both been in pure overprotective brother mode. Only now that he'd gone through the whole story with them—leaving out certain details between him and Brenna—was their concern shifting into something else.

Andre grinned at him. "You don't even have to say it. I see it all over your face. You're in love with this girl as much now as you were when you were twelve."

"I don't think…that's not…" Marcos stumbled, actually feeling the flush climb up his cheeks. Of all the times to suddenly get warm, this was just going to feed Andre's teasing. And that was usually Marcos's job.

He'd gotten used to teasing his older brothers, both of whom had dived headfirst into relationships over the past few months. He didn't like being on the other side of it. And Andre's word choice…

"I only spent a few days with her," he blurted. He couldn't be in love with her. He barely knew her. Except this overpowering mix of emotions he felt every time he so much as heard her name sure seemed like more than a simple crush.

Even Cole, who rarely resorted to teasing, was failing to hide his smile. "Well, at least now we know she didn't actually set that fire."

His words instantly changed the mood in the room, and his brothers got somber again.

"It sounds like it was just an accident, after all," Andre said.

"Yeah. It's still bugging me a little that Brenna was at Carlton's mansion because of what she thought she saw all those years ago, and now we know it wasn't our foster father."

"Well, are you sure?" Cole asked.

"Carlton talked about a woman as his contact."

"Maybe he was lying," Andre said.

Marcos slowly nodded. Carlton wasn't exactly a reliable source of information. There'd be no reason for him to lie about that and yet, the man was mercurial. Anyone who'd turn on a potential investor as fast as he had could easily lie about details of his operation just because he was paranoid. "Maybe."

"Maybe we should—" Cole started.

The ringing of Marcos's phone cut him off. He didn't recognize the number, but he picked up immediately, because he'd given Brenna his contact information before dropping her off. "Hello?"

"Marcos? It's Brenna."

"Brenna," he saw Andre mouth to Cole, and he realized he'd started grinning as soon as he'd heard her voice. He blanked his expression, but it was too late. His brothers were both hiding laughter.

"I thought you'd be asleep by now," he blurted.

There was a long pause, and then she said, "Marcos, do you remember how I told you I found something in Carlton's second office?"

Marcos sat straighter, dropping hold of the blanket. "No. What did you find?"

"Just a piece of paper. Turns out there was the indentation of a phone number on it. I called the number and I recognized the person who answered."

"Who?" Marcos glanced at his brothers, who both leaned forward as he asked, "Was it our foster father?"

"No. It's a woman who works in the Child and Family Services Division—not the location where I was pretending to work, but I've met her while setting up my undercover role."

"She knew you were a cop?" Marcos interrupted. Could that be how their covers were blown?

"No. She thought I was who I told Carlton I was. But it fits. She's set to retire in a few months. Carlton was recruiting me to replace her."

"Okay, I'll let my partner know. He can bring this woman in. What's her name?"

"I just wanted to give you the heads-up first," Brenna said, a stubborn undercurrent to her voice. "I'm going to get my department involved."

"Brenna, why don't you let the DEA handle this? We have more resources, and we've been working the Carlton Wayne White case for years."

Across from him, his brothers both cringed and shook their heads at him, but he didn't need them to tell him Brenna wasn't going to like that suggestion. And he didn't care. When he'd seen her slam into that wall in Carlton's mansion and then slide to the floor unconscious, he'd never felt more powerless or afraid. He didn't want her anywhere near this.

"This is my case, too, Marcos," she said softly, angrily. "I'm not stepping aside."

He sighed, knowing it didn't matter what he said.

She was going to stick to the case. And although he admired her for it, he also didn't want her doing it on her own.

"Tell you what. Why don't we join forces?" He pinched the bridge of his nose, wishing he could just keep her out of it, keep her safe. "Andre and Cole are at my house. Want to come over and figure out a plan?"

"I'll be there in twenty minutes."

"Brenna," he said quickly before she hung up.

"What?"

"What's this woman's name? The foster care connection?"

"Sara Lansky." Somehow, she must have heard his surprise in his silence, because she asked, "You know her?"

"I know the name," Marcos said grimly. "And you were right all along about our foster father. He is involved. Back when we lived in that foster home, he was having an affair with a Sara Lansky."

"Are you sure?"

"Yes. And it explains what Carlton said about his source not even knowing she was his source. It's because she wasn't. She was giving the information to our foster father. *He* was passing it on to Carlton."

His brothers both swore softly, and Brenna insisted, "Don't go anywhere without me. I'll be there soon."

Then she hung up and he stared back at his brothers, anger warming him faster than hours inside, almost faster than thinking about Brenna. He'd nearly died in that fire.

It didn't matter that the foster home had given him Cole and Andre. His foster father was going to pay for what he'd done.

Sara Lansky. If the woman hadn't had such a distinctive voice, low and gravelly from years of smoking, Brenna wouldn't have recognized her so quickly. She barely knew the woman, after all. But Marcos's words rang in her head.

It made sense. Not just the way their foster father had gotten the records back then, but also the secretive way he'd slip down the stairs to his office in the middle of the night. Probably to call this woman.

Brenna had barely slept during those months at the foster home with Marcos and his brothers. A side effect of grief was that she startled to attention at every little noise. Twice, she'd crept down the stairs after their foster father, to see what he'd been doing. Once, she'd heard him open the back door and talk angrily to someone she'd later learned was his only nonfoster son, Trent, already grown and living elsewhere. The other time, he'd gotten on the phone and the conversation had quickly turned to things that at eleven years old, she hadn't understood. Now, she realized it must have been Sara on the line.

But how had their foster father gotten connected

with Carlton in the first place to be passing information to him?

Brenna paused in lathering her hair, leaning against the wall of the shower. She'd spent so many years knowing that something had been wrong with what their foster father was doing that night, and determined to figure out what it was. Once she'd suspected the connection to Carlton, she'd been so focused on finding a way to bring Carlton down, she'd never stopped to wonder how they'd met.

Their foster father had to be at least twenty years older than Carlton, probably more. Eighteen years ago, he'd lived in a lower middle-class neighborhood, working a blue collar job. Apparently, he'd been cheating on his wife, but he'd come home to her every night. To her and their six foster kids, crammed into two of the four tiny bedrooms—plus her, as the only girl, stuck in a converted walk-in closet. They'd kept the third bedroom a shrine to Trent in case he ever wanted to come home. While she'd been there, he never had.

She'd never seen any evidence that their foster father was using drugs. And she couldn't imagine that he'd met Carlton—then a semiprofessional boxer—while at work at the factory. So, where?

Shivering, Brenna realized the water was starting to get cold, and she'd only planned to take a fast shower and change before heading to Marcos's place. She ran her hands through her hair, rinsing out the rest of the suds, then turned it off and stepped onto her rug as a soft noise sounded in the distance.

She froze, straining to listen. Was it her imagination?

After a minute of dripping onto her bathroom floor, attuned to any sound, Brenna let out a heavy breath and dried off. Grabbing a pair of jeans and a sweatshirt, she debated whether to waste time with makeup.

Just lipstick, she decided, swiping some bright red across her lips. As she was flipping the switch on her hair dryer, there was another sound, like something sliding softly across her kitchen floor.

Dropping the hair dryer, Brenna raced around her bed to the nightstand where she'd left her service pistol. From behind her, whoever was in her house must have realized she'd heard and no longer tried to be quiet. Footsteps pounded toward her, and the bedroom door was flung open.

Carlton stood in the doorway, looking larger than life in all black, his white-blond hair tied back, and fury in his eyes.

Brenna scrambled to open the drawer, then Carlton was on her. His massive hands closed around her shoulders, and he tossed her away from the table as if she weighed nothing.

She landed on the edge of the bed, then tumbled off the other side. Her body, already sore from running through the mountains, protested at the hard landing, but she pushed to her feet fast.

It didn't matter. He was already in front of her, blocking her exit.

He didn't have a weapon that she could see, but that didn't matter, either. Brenna knew what one hit from this man could do.

Holding up her hands in front of her, Brenna warned him, "If you're trying to silence me, it's too late. We've already found your real connection in foster care, and he's going to dismantle the whole thing."

Confusion passed over Carlton's face, then he shook it off. "It doesn't matter what you think you know. I'm not here to stop you from talking to your department." He cracked his knuckles. "We both know it's too late for that. I'm here to make you pay."

Chapter Nineteen

"How did you know about Sara Lansky?" Andre asked. "I don't remember her."

"Phone bills," Marcos replied, checking his watch again discreetly. It had been almost twenty minutes, and he was anxious to see Brenna again, even though his heart was telling him to keep her as far away from this case—and the danger—as possible. "Our foster mother was going through them one day. There were all these late-night calls to the same number. She'd circled it and written the name there."

"Did she confront him?" Cole asked.

Marcos shrugged. "I don't know. She saw me looking and covered them up, but by then, I'd realized what it meant."

"If you're right about this, then our foster father started giving Carlton information on foster kids eighteen years ago," Cole said.

"Yeah." Marcos considered what that meant. Eighteen years ago, Carlton had been just starting out, but he'd become a major player in the DC area pretty quickly. And that meant major money.

"They kept fostering after that house burned down," Andre spoke up. "I asked about them a few times over the years. I guess early on, I was hoping that they'd want us back. That the three of us would wind up back together."

Cole nodded. "I think we all hoped that."

"Did he keep working?" Marcos asked. "Maybe they just fostered so he'd have a connection to Sara."

Andre shrugged. "I always assumed so, but I don't know."

"Let's find out," Marcos said, booting up his laptop and doing a search. A minute later, he leaned back and frowned. "Huh."

"What?" Cole asked.

"I can't find anything for at least a decade. It doesn't look like he's at the factory anymore, and he hasn't been for a while."

"Did he move somewhere else?" Andre wondered.

"I can't tell," Marcos replied. "I somehow doubt the foster care system wouldn't get suspicious if he stopped working all of a sudden, but I don't see anything."

"Well, what about the fostering?" Cole asked. "Is he still doing it? Because I always got the feeling they went into it because their own son was so distant, not totally for the money."

"Yeah, me too, not that they really jumped into parenting," Marcos replied. His memories of that house had been happy because of Cole and Andre. The foster parents had just been there; not bad, not good. They'd put a roof over his head and food in his belly and not a lot else, though they'd been far better than some of the other homes he'd lived in over the years.

But he remembered when he'd first arrived, his foster mother talking about her son, Trent, who was grown and had been out of their house for five years. According to the stories, he'd been a genius, but a troublemaker who hung out with the wrong crowd. She'd spent so much energy trying to steer him in the right direction that once he was gone, she'd claimed she'd wanted a second chance. She'd also claimed she had nothing left to give.

Marcos had met Trent a handful of times over the years. He'd swing by for an hour or so, watch the foster kids with what looked like disdain, chat with his parents for a while, then head out again. With a son like that, it didn't surprise Marcos that they might want to try again, except they never really had.

"Maybe that was just an excuse," Marcos said. "Maybe she was in on it, too."

"I doubt it," Andre replied. "Not if the connection was through a woman he was having an affair with."

"Good point." Marcos glanced at his watch again and frowned.

Cole did the same. "Brenna should be here by now, shouldn't she?"

"I'm going to call her," Marcos said, already dialing. But it went straight to voice mail and a bad feeling came over him.

His brothers were already on their feet before Marcos realized he'd jumped up and grabbed his car keys.

Cole took them out of his hand. "I'll drive. You direct."

Marcos nodded his thanks, dread propelling him into a run. "Let's hurry."

ONE HIT AND it was all over. One hit and Carlton could knock her out and then kill her before she even had a chance to fight back.

Panic made Brenna breathe faster as Carlton took a slow step toward her, a gleam in his eyes that told her he was going to enjoy hurting her. She had good reflexes—her years in foster care, some in houses with abuse—had taught her to dodge a blow instinctively. But he'd boxed semiprofessionally, and he'd already proved his fists could be faster than her reflexes.

But up in his mansion, she hadn't been expecting the hit. Right now, she was.

"You shouldn't have let Marcos drop you off and drive away," Carlton mocked her. "Maybe then you would have stood a chance. But I appreciate you sticking around while I learned where he lives."

Brenna's lungs tensed up, panic making it hard to breathe. After he killed her, he was going after Marcos. She forced the distraction to the back of her mind, knowing it was why he'd told her. Not just to torture her even more, but to keep her unfocused, unbalanced.

He proved it when he darted toward her, fist-first. Instead of an uppercut to her chin like last time, he went for her chest. Apparently this time, he didn't want her out of the fight right away—he wanted her to suffer.

She jerked sideways quickly and his fist soared past her, surprise in his gaze. Brenna changed direction just as fast, punching wildly, one fist after the other, both aimed at his throat. The first one bounced off, but the second one scored a solid hit.

He made a choking sound and stumbled back a step, but he regrouped quickly, and she hadn't expected anything less. With a past as a boxer, he knew how to take a hit and keep coming. Surprise would only get her so far. She needed a plan, or a weapon. Something. Because eventually, she wouldn't dodge fast enough and he'd take her down—or he'd decide to use brute strength and barrel into her.

Now, he gazed at her with a mixture of surprise, anger and a hint of respect. He smiled, and it was like a cat that knew it had a mouse cornered, but wanted to play with it awhile before making the kill.

"Not bad," he told her, and the way his voice came out broken told her she'd scored a better hit than she'd thought. "But not good enough," he added and swung his fist again.

This time his hand glanced off her side, but she

knew if she lived through this there'd be a sizable bruise. She leaped right, and like a bizarre dance, he shuffled to face her.

Frantic, she worked through her options. Her gun was too far away. The hair dryer was discarded on the floor, running on low heat. Maybe she could yank the cord up and around him? There was a snow globe on her dresser that might do some damage if she could smash it against the side of his head.

Carlton was swinging again before she could decide, and she jerked right, almost stumbling over the hair dryer cord. She caught herself on the dresser at the last second, and then he was swinging again, and she knew she wasn't going to avoid this one.

Brenna ducked anyway, praying to minimize the damage, but before his fist landed, a crash sounded from behind them, startling him into pausing mid-swing and glancing back.

Not wasting any time, Brenna yanked the snow globe off the dresser and slammed it into the side of his head. The glass broke, cutting her hand and slicing into his scalp, making him yelp, but he was already swinging back toward her, fury in his gaze.

Then Marcos was racing through her bedroom door, and he jumped onto Carlton's back, sending the drug lord to the ground. Two men were right behind Marcos, and despite the passing of eighteen years, Brenna recognized them. Cole and Andre.

Before Brenna could fully wrap her mind around the fact that Marcos was here, he, Cole and Andre had Carlton pinned to the ground. Andre slapped a pair of handcuffs onto the drug lord, and then Cole was on the phone, calling for backup.

Andre and Cole literally sat on Carlton to keep him from racing out the door, handcuffs and all, and Marcos gripped her by the upper arm, looking her over carefully. "Are you okay?"

"I'm fine." She stared back at him, still in disbelief that he was here, in her house. "How did you know?"

"You took too long to get to my house." He pulled her to him, wrapping her in a hug tight enough that it made her side—where Carlton had gotten in a glancing blow—twinge.

But she ignored it, because the pain was worth it to be in Marcos's arms. She rested her head against his chest and closed her eyes, feeling safe despite Carlton still thrashing around on her floor. Feeling content for the first time in years.

Behind them, Andre loudly cleared his throat. "Not to interrupt the reunion, but do you want to give us a little help here?"

Brenna pulled free of Marcos's embrace to discover even with Cole and Andre both shoving him to the ground, Carlton was thrashing around, trying to pull himself free.

Marcos rolled his eyes and went to join them, but Brenna scooted past him, jammed a knee between his brothers on Carlton's back and yanked his cuffed hands straight up behind him.

Carlton roared and went still, and Marcos grinned. "Guess you don't need my help after all."

Then sirens sounded, and DEA agents were piling into her house and dragging Carlton off to their vehicle.

Brenna turned and stared at Marcos and his two brothers, all grown up. Cole and Andre weren't quite what she would have pictured, and yet, she'd recognized them instantly.

"It's good to see you, Brenna," Cole said.

"We've been hearing a lot about you tonight," Andre added, and then they were both hugging her.

It wasn't the sort of brief, polite hug you'd give someone after reconnecting, but a genuine hug, the kind you offered to family. Tears welled up in Brenna's eyes, and she blinked the moisture away before they stepped back.

"At least this is almost over," Marcos said. "With Carlton in custody and only his chef still in the wind from the mansion, now we just need to bring in his foster care connection. Then it will take some time, but the rest of his organization will begin to fall like dominoes."

"That's not all," Brenna said grimly.

"Why not?" Cole asked.

Brenna looked from Marcos to his brothers and back again. "When I told Carlton we were about to bring down his real foster care connection, he looked confused, like he didn't know who I meant."

"Maybe he just thought you meant someone working with Sara," Andre suggested.

Brenna shook her head. "No, I'm pretty sure he genuinely didn't know what I was talking about."

"He said that the foster care connection didn't even know she was his connection," Marcos reminded her. "Maybe he couldn't believe you'd really gotten on to our foster father." He looked pensive. "Although he obviously looked into your past. He knew you'd been in that house, since you specifically mentioned the fire as part of your cover. I'm surprised he wasn't suspicious from the beginning because of that."

"Maybe it's because he didn't know," Brenna replied.

"How could he not know?" Cole asked.

"I think he's the front man," Brenna answered, as the things that had been bothering her since she'd brought it up to Carlton suddenly fell into place. "I think someone else is the real mastermind."

Chapter Twenty

"Who do you think is the mastermind?" Marcos asked.

He and his brothers were sitting in Brenna's living room, and he couldn't stop himself from glancing around again. Just like her bedroom, it was painted with a bright pop of color. The furniture was bright and full of personality, too. It all felt like Brenna and yet, something was off, as if she wasn't fully settled in yet.

Her house was quiet now that his colleagues had cleared out, taking Carlton with them. Normally, Marcos would have insisted on going with them. He'd wanted to be involved in questioning the drug lord, but he knew his partner would do a good job. Jim had more than fifteen years of experience, and if anyone could get Carlton to spill everything, it was Jim.

Still, Marcos knew that wasn't going to be a quick process. He'd told Jim he was exhausted and needed rest. Jim had raised his eyebrows and glanced at

Brenna, like he'd known there was more to Marcos staying away from the initial questioning. And he was right.

It didn't matter that the biggest threat to Brenna's safety was now behind bars. Because she shouldn't have been in danger in the first place. It was completely illogical for Carlton to venture anywhere near the home of an armed police officer when the entire law-enforcement community was searching for him. And right now, Marcos wasn't going to be at ease unless he had her in his sights.

The fact was, he wasn't sure he'd ever be at ease again whenever she was out of his sight.

The thought gave him pause. He was in law enforcement; he knew and accepted the risks he took every day. He knew and accepted those risks with both of his brothers. But the thought of Brenna out on the streets in her police blues, or undercover again, made his entire body clammy with fear.

He knew she was capable. Not as well trained as her department should have ensured before she was sent out on a mission that involved Carlton Wayne White, but she was resourceful and strong. So, why did the thought of her at risk make him want to follow her around?

Marcos glanced over at his brothers, realizing that for all their teasing earlier, they were right. He was falling in love with this woman. No, forget the *falling*. He'd already collapsed at her feet, and he'd probably never get up again.

When he swore under his breath, Brenna gave him a perplexed glance, but his brothers just smirked at him. They knew him too well, and Marcos could just bet they knew exactly what he'd realized.

He was in love with Brenna Hartwell. Now he just had to figure out what he was going to do about it.

"…knew," Brenna said, staring at him as if she expected a response.

"Sorry. What?" he asked, trying to shake himself out of his fog, to focus on truly closing this case instead of on how to convince Brenna to take a chance on him. In the mountains, she'd made a deal with him: she'd show him her house if he showed her his. She'd fulfilled her end of the bargain, intentionally or not. But there was no doubt she was wary of relationships; how did he deal with that? How did he come to terms with dating a woman in law enforcement, who put herself in as much danger as he did every single day? And how did he overcome what had always seemed to be his nature: to only stay in a relationship until it got too serious, and then bail before she could? Because truth be told, he was wary of relationships, too, probably for the same reason she was.

"I said, I wish I knew," Brenna repeated. "Maybe it's our foster father?" She sounded unconvinced.

"We looked into him. It looks like he stopped working at the factory about a decade ago," Marcos told her. "I can't find anything about him working elsewhere, but I assume he was. We'll have to take a lot closer look, but if he was the mastermind, why let Carlton take on the front role? How would he have gotten hooked up with the guy?"

"I've been wondering that myself," she said, then shrugged. "I don't know. Maybe I'm wrong. Maybe Carlton was confused for some other reason, but my gut is telling me there's more here than we're seeing."

"Well, some of the things he said up in the mountains did make me wonder if either there was a second in command we don't know about making a power play, or if Carlton could actually be reporting to someone. If he really isn't the one in charge, then it's somebody pretty brilliant, because it's not just law enforcement who thinks so, but everyone I've talked to in the drug world. And I just don't see our foster father in that role."

"Maybe we need to pay Mr. Pike a visit," Cole suggested.

Andre looked at his watch. "It's almost three in the morning. Why don't we all get some sleep first? We can do it tomorrow after work."

"Or Brenna and I can go in the morning," Marcos suggested, his gaze darting to Brenna's bandaged hand. One of the EMTs who'd shown up with the DEA had stitched up Carlton's head and then wrapped her hand. It wasn't bad, but things could have been so much worse. He wanted to end this, stop any possible threat still out there as soon as possible.

His brothers didn't look thrilled about not being

included, but Marcos didn't want to wait a full day. The fact was, he wanted to charge over to his foster father's house now, but Andre was right about it being a bad time to go knocking on someone's door if they wanted answers, especially when they had no proof of his involvement. And they didn't even know where he lived anymore.

"I wish I could skip out tomorrow and come with you," Cole said, "but I trust you'll keep us updated as soon as you know anything?"

"Of course," Brenna replied before Marcos could answer.

"Good," Andre said, standing and yawning. "Then let's head out. Brenna, you need a bag?"

Brenna stared up at him in confusion. "What?"

"You're staying with Marcos tonight," Cole answered for him. "Even if Carlton is behind bars, he cut a hole in your window that you need replaced. And we kicked down your door to get in. Yes, it's temporarily boarded, but you shouldn't be staying here like that."

"I'm armed," Brenna reminded them.

This time, Marcos didn't let his brothers speak. "You pick. Either you come stay with me or I stay here. But I have to warn you, given the fact that Carlton was here tonight and you think he's got someone pulling his strings, neither of us will sleep much if I stay here because Cole and Andre will be calling all night."

They both nodded, and she rolled her eyes. "All

right. I'll get a bag, but you should know that Carlton must have found my place following us from the parking lot after his guards were taken out. He said he followed you back to your house before returning to mine. He was going to go after you next."

His brothers were instantly frowning again, and Marcos didn't want to drive out to either of their places, so he said, "Okay, we'll be extra cautious and check into a hotel for the night."

Brenna flushed at his words, and Marcos wished either of them were in any shape to do anything besides get a solid eight hours of sleep. But the hours on the mountains were catching up to him fast.

"You sure?" Andre asked. "Because I have room—"

"I'm sure," Marcos cut him off, then stared after Brenna as she disappeared into her room to pack an overnight bag.

And suddenly, he felt twelve years old again, meeting a little girl he was just sure he was going to marry someday.

BRENNA STARED AT the king-size bed in the center of the hotel room, and her heart did a little flip-flop. It didn't matter that she was too tired to do any of the things that instantly came to mind as Marcos sank onto the edge of that bed. And yet, instead of backing away like she should have, she found herself moving toward him.

His head lifted at her movement, those blue-gray

eyes locking on her, hypnotizing. Then his arms were up, reaching for her, and she couldn't help herself from climbing onto his lap and wrapping her arms around his neck.

She'd expected him to pull her head to his, to lock their lips together, for passion to spark instantly like it had that first night she'd seen him. Instead, he gave her a soft smile and cupped her cheek, his thumb stroking her somehow more of a turn-on than full-body contact with any other man.

"You didn't answer your phone, and I don't think I've ever felt so scared. I don't know why, but I just knew something was wrong."

She smiled back at him. "My not answering a phone call was probably the most normal thing that's happened to either of us in the past four days! But I'm glad you came when you did." She shivered, imagining how bad things could have gone if Marcos hadn't worried about her.

Imagine that. Someone worrying about her. It was almost as if they were a real couple, like she had someone in her life again to care what happened to her. The last time she could remember feeling protected and cared about this way was before her mom had died.

Or maybe that was unfair, because she had people in her life she mattered to. And she'd had other men who'd tried to get close, who'd fought for a real relationship with her. But even when she'd felt reciprocal attraction, none of them had offered her something she'd battle for. And now? After four days, she'd found someone worth any fight, because she couldn't imagine her life without Marcos.

As she stared at him with growing awareness, Marcos just kept stroking her cheek, his other hand low on her back. There was something both possessive and familiar about his touch, and Brenna laid her head on his shoulder before he saw panic spark in her eyes.

She'd promised him a trade-off: a look inside each other's houses. But what that really meant to her was much more complicated. She'd been offering him a relationship, a look inside her heart. And while only time would tell how things might work out between them, she was already involved.

What did she know about relationships? She'd avoided them most of her life. Not just the romantic type, but all connections that got too close. Was she even capable of letting someone in?

Growing up in foster care, bouncing from one place to another, always alone, she'd pushed back her fears that her mother's death had damaged her. She'd always figured that she had time to make changes, that eventually life would fall into place and those connections would, too.

But that hadn't happened, and fear rose up hard now that she would always be too broken to offer Marcos anything worth having.

"Hey." Marcos's soft voice penetrated her fears

and he cupped her cheek, shifting her to face him. "What's wrong?"

How did she tell him her fears without scaring him off? Marcos had faced a lot of the same challenges she had, but he hadn't let them close him off. Instead, he'd formed a brotherly bond that was as strong as the blood bond she'd shared with her mom.

So, instead of answering, she pressed her lips to his and kissed him. She poured everything she was feeling into the kiss: her fear; her attraction to him; her admiration for who he'd become; even the love that shouldn't be possible after such a short time, but she could no longer deny. Once upon a time, it might have been a simple crush on a boy who'd shown her kindness when she needed it most in her life. But somehow, in the past few days, it had morphed into something much bigger, something she knew wasn't going to fade no matter what happened between them.

His fingers slid over her face, down the back of her neck, then glided up her arms. His lips caressed hers as though he was feeling the very same things, and hope exploded in Brenna's chest with such intensity that she had to pull back and gulp in a breath.

Then Marcos was scooting them both backward along the bed until they could lay on it, and Brenna suddenly didn't care how tired she was. She slid her fingers up underneath his sweater, loving the way his ab muscles tensed underneath her touch. She fused her lips back to his, and he growled in the back of his throat.

His hands locked on her hips as he pulled her tightly against him and kissed her with such an intensity that the room seemed to spin. Brenna grabbed fistfuls of his sweater and held on, letting the emotions crash over her, letting Marcos further into her heart.

When he finally lifted his head from hers, Brenna had lost all sense of time. He looked just as dazed, but then he gave her that big, dimpled grin that had sucked her in from the very first time she'd seen him.

"What do you say we get some sleep, then head out tomorrow and close this case, put this threat completely behind us? Then I want to come back here and finish this, when I have the strength to love you like you deserve."

Brenna's mouth went dry, and she nodded back at him until he tucked her against his chest. If this was Marcos without full strength, then she was going to need some sleep, too.

As she drifted off to sleep in his arms, she felt a smile tug her lips. Had his word choice been intentional? Because being loved by Marcos Costa was something she wanted desperately, and not just for one night.

For the rest of her life.

Chapter Twenty-One

Marcos woke slowly, becoming aware of bits of sunlight sneaking past the curtains, the unfamiliar bed, the woman curled up in his arms. His arms instinctively tightened, holding Brenna closer, and she stirred a little, only to snuggle closer still.

Every day should be like this. The thought shouldn't have caught him by surprise. He already knew he'd managed to fall in love with her. But it did surprise him. Love was one thing; forever was another. And yet…his heart was telling him Brenna should never have left his life in the first place.

He'd never thought he was a *forever* kind of guy. Marriage and family were fine for Andre and Cole—and he wanted that for both of his brothers. But he'd always figured that he'd spend his life spoiling nieces and nephews rotten, and chasing down bad guys in undercover roles across the world. He'd even applied to an open post in the Middle East a few months ago; now, he knew he'd be retracting it. Suddenly, nowhere seemed like it could possibly be more exciting than right beside Brenna.

Panic threatened and he shoved it down. He went unarmed into the remote hideouts of vicious drug lords. He could handle being in love with a commitment-phobic woman who ran headlong into danger herself.

"Mind over matter," he muttered to himself. He might not be able to change his natural wariness about relationships, but he could choose to jump into one anyway. Because if anyone was worth taking that chance for, it was Brenna Hartwell.

"What?" she mumbled sleepily.

"Nothing." He kissed the top of her head, then let himself hold her a minute longer before slipping out of bed.

Grabbing the cell phone he'd dropped on the dresser last night, Marcos opened the slider to the balcony, and a rush of cold air blasted into the room.

"Brrr," Brenna groaned, sitting up, but hauling the covers with her. "What are you doing?"

"Sorry. I was going to step outside and make a call." He grinned at the tangled mess of her hair, the sleepy half-mast of her eyes. "I didn't mean to wake you."

She made a face at him and finger-combed her hair. "Why are you smiling like that?" Not giving him a chance to answer, she added, "And close the door. I'm up."

He pushed it shut, then strode over to the bed,

leaned across it and planted a kiss on her lips. "I'm smiling because you're ridiculously cute first thing in the morning." And she was.

As for him, he was practically giddy with happiness. His brothers were going to have a field day teasing him. He probably deserved it after the way he'd mercilessly teased them when they'd both fallen in love over the past few months.

She flushed and straightened her hair a little more, then said, "I'm pretty sure this is far from first thing in the morning, but thank you. Who are you calling?"

Marcos glanced at the time on his phone, realizing she was right. It was almost noon. But apparently no one had expected him in the office that morning, and even Jim was giving him a little breathing room. "I'm going to give Jim a call, see what the status is with Carlton."

She let the covers drop away and crawled across the bed toward him as he sat on the edge of the bed. "Speaker?"

"Sure." He let his gaze wander over her. She'd fallen asleep in jeans and a sweatshirt; he was still wearing what he'd had on in the mountains, and he realized he desperately needed a shower.

But she didn't seem to care as she looped her arms around his neck and rested her head against his back. "Maybe he's talking."

There wasn't a lot of hopefulness in her tone, and Marcos doubted Carlton had broken, either. But if he wasn't really in charge, would he be willing to risk going down for another man's empire? "Let's find out," he said, dialing Jim.

His partner picked up on the first ring. "Marcos? I wondered when you were gonna tear yourself away from your lady friend and call in."

Against his back, Marcos felt Brenna muffling her laughter. "You're on Speaker, man."

"Oh. Hi, Brenna. Sorry about that."

"No problem," she said, laughter in her voice.

Marcos got down to business. "So, what's the status?"

Jim sighed. "Well, the good news is that we caught Carlton's last bodyguard-slash-cook. The guy came after us with a butcher's knife, so he's in surgery right now, having a bullet taken out of his chest, but it looks like he'll pull through."

"And what about Carlton?"

"He's not talking. The guy knows he's going to be doing some major time. But I think he figures we've already got him on trying to kill a federal agent and a police officer, and maybe on killing his own guard—although we haven't found a body yet, which always makes a conviction challenging. So I'm sure he's decided, why hand over a drug charge, as well? Because we can try to get him on promises he made to you, but you know how that'll go."

"Yeah." In court, he'd claim that he was talking about some other kind of product, or that he was just joking. With no audio and video evidence like they would have had if the buy had actually gone through, it was unlikely to stick. "What about Jesse? Is he flipping on his uncle?"

"The kid is scared," Jim replied. "Scared of his uncle, scared of doing time, and honestly, at this point, he's scared of his own shadow. But I think you might get through to him. We know he thinks Carlton had his parents killed. That's pretty powerful motivation to turn on the guy."

Brenna's arms tightened around him at the mention of the car crash that had killed Jesse's family, and he didn't think she'd realized she'd done it. "Is there anything there?" Marcos asked. "Can we get that case reopened? Even if we can get Carlton life without parole on everything else, I'd still like him to pay for that, even if it's just another symbolic sentencing."

"We're going to talk to the local police about that. What do you think about coming in and talking to Jesse?"

"Later today," Marcos promised. "First, I need to pay my old foster parents a visit. Did Carlton give any sense that he *wasn't* running the show?"

There was a long pause. "No. You have reason to think he wasn't?"

"Maybe."

When Marcos didn't say more, Jim replied, "All right, well, do what you need to do with your foster parents and then give me a call. Keep me in the loop on this. You taking backup?"

"Yeah, Brenna's coming with me."

"Good. Hey, Brenna?"

She lifted her head from his back. "Yeah?"

"Take care of him for me, will you?"

Marcos twisted his head to look at her, and she smiled at him. "You got it."

THIS WAS HOME ONCE. Sort of.

Marcos stared at the empty lot where their foster home had once stood. Beside him, Brenna folded her uninjured hand in his.

Apparently, their foster parents had never rebuilt here after the fire. Eighteen years later, there was no evidence a house had ever stood there at all, except that it was one bare lot in a row of little houses. The grass was overrun with weeds, but it stood waist-high, browning leaves sprinkled across it in places.

It was hard to picture the worn-down two-story building where he'd come when he was seven years old. His most vivid memories of those days were of his brothers. Meeting them on that very first day when he'd faltered in the doorway, his only belongings clutched in a small backpack. Following them to the backyard when they'd gone to play a game of catch, thinking they hadn't seen him. His surprise and uncertainty when they'd called him over to join them. And then a bond he'd never had in his short years on this Earth.

And then there were the memories of Brenna. He'd known her only a few months, but the time was stamped into his brain. He didn't think he'd ever forget the sight of her on the stoop, tears watering over her eyes, her hair in braids and a nasty gash on her cheek from the car crash. He knew he'd never forget the way it had felt when he'd reached out and taken her hand—as though she was his reason for existing.

He turned to find her staring contemplatively at the empty lot. "It's hard to believe this is where we met," she said softly.

He pressed a kiss to her lips. "Come on. Let's go see our old foster parents."

They'd known before coming here that their foster parents were long gone. But they hadn't moved far, and on the drive over, Marcos had felt his hands turning the wheel onto a familiar street. In the passenger seat, Brenna hadn't said a word, but he'd known she realized exactly where he was taking her.

Silently, they climbed back into his car, and he made the relatively short trip to their foster parents' new house. When he stopped in front of it, Marcos whistled and then double-checked the address he'd written down back at the hotel.

"Awfully nice place for someone who quit his factory job and supposedly just went to work in his son's business part-time," Brenna said, a hard edge to her voice as they climbed out of his car.

Marcos found it hard to believe that the man who'd taken him into his home for those five years was secretly a drug lord. But the house in front of them—easily five times the size of the little house where they'd crammed eight people back then—suggested he was into something more than he was officially reporting on his taxes. Especially since their foster mother had also quit her part-time work a few years later.

"Let's be ready for anything," Marcos said, and Brenna nodded, patting her hip. He knew that concealed under her sweatshirt was her service pistol. He was also carrying. Probably unnecessary with their foster parents, but if they were in league with Carlton in any way, they were more dangerous than they seemed.

They walked up the long entryway, and then Marcos knocked, hoping the Pikes would answer. The plan was to try to play it off as an innocent visit initially, in case their foster parents hadn't heard about Carlton. If necessary, he and Brenna would take a more official route, but right now, they had no evidence and nothing to get an arrest warrant.

The door swung open, and Marcos recognized their foster mother immediately. She'd aged gracefully, with streaks of silver through her light brown hair, and a regal stance to her that Marcos didn't remember from his childhood.

"Can I help you?" she asked.

"Uh, yes. I'm Marcos Costa. This is Brenna Hartwell. We were—"

"Oh my goodness," she cut him off. "From before the fire. Of course! Come in." She held the door wider, letting them pass.

Inside, Marcos glanced around curiously. The

house was a far cry from the small place they'd packed in six foster kids. The floors were expensive, patterned hardwood in the entryway, a huge chandelier overhead. Disappointment filled him at the mounting suspicion that they were involved even more than he'd expected. Passing on foster kid information was bad enough; actually being the mastermind took the betrayal he was feeling to a whole new level. Although he didn't have any real bond with them, he still had fond feelings for the home, because of all that it had given him in his life: Andre, Cole and Brenna.

Their foster mother led them into a huge living room with a wall of windows looking out over a manmade lake, then gestured for them to take a seat on the big white sectional couch.

Brenna sat gingerly at the edge of the couch, and he sat beside her. "Is Mr. Pike here?" he asked.

"Yes, he is. Let me just get him." She fiddled nervously with her hair, then shook her head. "I can't believe you two. All grown up." She glanced between them, and added, "And dating now? Or married? It's a good thing you two didn't stay in that house like siblings."

Brenna nodded noncommittally, and their foster mother backed out of the room. The truth was, none of the kids in that house had felt like siblings to him, except Andre and Cole, no matter how long he'd lived there. Brenna hadn't been there very long, but his connection to her certainly hadn't been familial.

When their foster mother was out of the room, Brenna whispered, "What do you think?"

"She's definitely nervous," he replied, watching the doorway carefully. Although he didn't expect their foster father to suddenly appear with a weapon, he wasn't taking any chances.

But when Mr. Pike did appear a minute later, Marcos worked to keep his jaw from dropping. Their foster mother was leading him into the room, with a supportive hand on his back. Physically, he looked pretty good. A little hunched over from his years of hard labor, but the years didn't show on him otherwise.

Mentally was a different story. Even before his eyes locked on Marcos's, he could tell the man wasn't entirely there.

"Dementia," their foster mother explained, a little teary eyed. "Started about a year ago. He's got good days and bad. Today he probably won't understand who you are, but we'll try." Then she smiled at him and said, "Honey, you remember Marcos Costa— he lived with us about five years, back before the fire? And little Brenna Hartwell? She was there a few months."

"Marcos," he repeated. "And Brenna. Nice to meet you."

Their foster mother shook her head at them, then helped her husband settle into a chair. Then she took a seat and leaned forward, twisting her hands in her lap. "So tell me how you've been. It's so nice to see you after all these years."

Marcos shared a glance with Brenna. If their foster father had ever masterminded anything, that time was long gone. But the house they lived in was nicer than Marcos would have expected for someone who was just passing names for a payoff.

They were missing something. But what?

Chapter Twenty-Two

"Marcos and I just recently ran into each other again," Brenna told them, watching carefully for any reaction. Because *someone* had blown their cover at that mansion with Carlton, and she might have recognized Sara Lansky's voice on the phone, but she doubted the woman would have recognized *her*. And if she had, she would have only known her as a fellow social worker. And she wouldn't have known Marcos at all.

The leak had come from somewhere, and if it wasn't Mr. Pike... Brenna turned her gaze on Mrs. Pike, who was fiddling with the hem of her sweater. She'd been nervous since the moment they'd arrived, but Brenna found it hard to believe she would have collaborated with her husband's mistress. Unless maybe her husband had been in charge until the past year, and then his wife had reluctantly taken over in order to keep up their lifestyle.

Brenna frowned at the idea. It could fit, but she sensed that wasn't right, either.

"Oh, yes?" their foster mother said. "How did you reconnect?" She looked from Brenna to Marcos, seeming genuinely curious.

"Up in the mountains," Marcos said, sounding purposely vague.

"Oh. That's...unusual." Their foster mother returned to fiddling with her sweater. "And what about those other boys, the ones you were so close to?"

"Cole and Andre?" Marcos said. "They went into law enforcement, just like me."

"Law enforcement?" Her voice went up half an octave, then she coughed. "That's great. So, you're a police officer? I never would have imagined that."

"No," Brenna replied. "He's not a police officer. I am. Marcos works for the DEA."

"I see," she replied, and the nervousness seemed to fade, replaced by a wary distrust that blanked the expression on her face.

Next to her, Marcos leaned forward, glancing from Mrs. Pike to her husband, who didn't seem to be following the conversation at all. "So, you know why we're here."

"No," she said, her voice suddenly hard and cold. "I can't say that I do."

"Carlton Wayne White," Brenna supplied.

She shook her head. "I'm not familiar with him."

"How about Sara Lansky?" Brenna asked, and this time she got a reaction.

Mrs. Pike visibly twitched, her gaze darted to her

husband, then back to them as she stood. "I think it's time for you to go."

"If we leave now, we'll be back with a warrant and a whole lot more agents," Marcos promised.

She folded her arms over her chest. "Then I guess that's what you'll have to do."

Marcos stood and Brenna did the same, but before Mrs. Pike shut the door behind them, Brenna told her, "Oh, in case you hadn't heard, we've got Carlton in custody."

The door didn't close fast enough to hide their foster mother's panicked expression.

Brenna stared at Marcos. "Well, she's involved."

"Yeah," Marcos agreed with a sigh. "I guess we'd better give Jim a call. I'm not sure how we're going to get that warrant, but we'd better figure something out before they run."

As they walked toward Marcos's car, Brenna glanced backward and saw their foster mother peeking through the shades, a phone pressed to her ear. When she spotted Brenna, she dropped the shades back into place.

"Something is off here, Marcos. I mean, she obviously recognized Carlton's name, but when we first showed up, she seemed to genuinely want to know how we'd reconnected."

Marcos nodded grimly as they climbed back into his car. "I know. And if she was the one who'd blown our covers, then she'd already know exactly how that had happened."

"I THINK JESSE is going to work with us," Jim announced as soon as Marcos called him.

"That's good news," Brenna said, listening over the speaker, one eye still on the Pikes' house behind them. Marcos hadn't started his car, but had decided to sit out front for a while and see how the investigation at the DEA office was going, then plan their next move.

And it really was going to be *their* next move. She knew Marcos wasn't comfortable working with her yet—that he was resisting his natural urge to keep her as far away from danger as possible—but she also knew that if things were going to go anywhere between them, he'd have to get used to her job.

She was going to stay. She'd realized it while they were inside the Pikes' house, working together. She didn't think she'd be going back undercover anytime soon, but *detective* was an idea that was gaining traction in her mind. Her mentor had been pushing her in that direction since the beginning, telling her that was where she belonged, and she was starting to think he was right.

As for the other place she belonged? She glanced at Marcos, looking serious as he listened to Jim explain that the kid hadn't made any promises, but had been asking about him. Jim felt confident he'd turn if Marcos could give him some guarantees. And she knew Marcos wanted to help the kid turn his life around.

She smiled and twined her hand with his, and he

squeezed back as he told Jim, "We'll come into the office in a few minutes and talk to him then. We just got finished at our old foster parents' house."

"How'd that go?" Jim asked.

"Strange," Brenna supplied. "Our foster father has dementia. He wasn't following the conversation, but our foster mother definitely knew something. As for how much they were involved? We're not really sure."

"We're going to need to bring them both in," Marcos said.

"If he's sick—" Jim started.

"This man was up late at night, going over the names of foster kids he could sell out to a drug dealer in exchange for a cushy life. It may have been an accident, but he still started that fire."

In the pause that followed, Brenna could tell that Jim knew a lot about what had happened the night of the fire. How it had separated Marcos and his brothers, the scars it had left on his back.

But when he finally spoke, his words left her speechless. "It changed your life. You lost Brenna."

Marcos pressed his lips to her hand. "And now that I've found her again, I want to get some closure on the past. Whatever our foster father did, he still needs to pay for it."

"I understand," Jim said. "We're going to need more than a hunch, and Jesse never said anything about someone involved besides Carlton. But if we can flip Jesse…"

"It gives us leverage on Carlton," Marcos finished. "And he'll want to share the jail time if he can, rather than take the heat for everything himself."

"Exactly," Jim agreed.

"We're on our way," Marcos told him, disconnecting the call and pulling on his seat belt.

Brenna was doing the same when a Hummer squealed to a stop in front of them, blocking their exit. The driver got out, slammed the door and strode toward them, a furious expression on his face.

"He looks a lot like—" Brenna started.

"It's the Pikes' son," Marcos finished. "Trent."

"She must have called him when we left the house," Brenna said, watching Trent approach and doing the math. He'd be in his early forties now. He looked ageless, one of those guys who could be anywhere between thirty and fifty, with perfectly styled blond hair, chiseled cheekbones and an expensive wool coat. He'd managed to get the best of both parents' features, and apparently things had changed in eighteen years, because now he was showing up.

Trent stopped next to Marcos's window and knocked on it until Marcos rolled it down.

"What's wrong with you?" he yelled. "You come over here and harass my parents, accuse them of working with *drug dealers*? Are you crazy?"

"We're not harassing anyone," Marcos replied calmly. "We just needed explanations for some inconsistencies about your father's access to the foster care system."

"Foster care! Right. So, this is the thanks you give them for taking you into their home, raising you like you were actually their kids instead of street trash no one wanted?"

"Street trash?" Marcos repeated, sounding both offended and incredulous. "Is that what you think of foster kids? Is that why you think it's fine to use them however you want?"

Trent jerked backward, but recovered quickly. "I don't know what you're talking about, and I want you out of here, now."

"Let me ask you something, Trent. Does the name Sara Lanksy mean anything to you?"

"Yeah, my father's mistress. So my dad's not perfect. Guess what? No one is." He stabbed a finger toward Marcos's face. "You leave them alone. I just left my wife by herself at brunch to deal with this nonsense. If I have to do it again, you're going to regret it. And your little badge there isn't going to save you this time."

He stomped back to his vehicle and peeled away, leaving Brenna to stare at Marcos in disbelief. "Did he really just say *this time*?"

"Yeah, he did. And if Carlton sent pictures of us from the mansion to anyone in this family, they'd all be able to recognize us."

Brenna frowned. "And get access to what we really do?"

"Someone who's been secretly running a drug operation of this size for twenty years has connections."

Brenna considered that, mulling over the idea of Trent being involved—and whether he'd gotten pulled in because of his father, or vice versa. "He didn't even go inside to check if they were okay."

"Yeah," Marcos agreed, his gaze following the Hummer as it spun around a corner. "And yet, eighteen years ago, I'm not even sure he would have done this much. You think he's protecting them or protecting the business?"

"It sure seems like both," Brenna said. It had never occurred to her to consider Trent, but it made a lot of sense. He could get the information from his dad and pass it on to Carlton, then Carlton could use it to build his empire.

"I agree," Marcos said. "But is he doing Carlton's bidding or is Carlton a figurehead?"

"Hang on," Brenna replied, texting Victor at the station. Less than a minute later he came back with a reply.

"Victor says Trent's lifestyle doesn't come even close to matching his tax returns."

"That was fast," Marcos said.

She grinned. "Yeah, you'll like Victor. He's got a way with computers. And he's the one who convinced me to become a cop."

Marcos leaned toward her, dropping a kiss on her lips that made her anxious to wrap this case up and take him up on his promise from last night. A shiver of anticipation ran through her at the thought, and he grinned, his dimples on full display, like he could read her mind.

"Maybe they're partners," Marcos said. "Carlton is perfect for the front man. He's got the sort of personality that likes being feared. And remember eighteen years ago, the way Mrs. Pike talked about her son? All the bad influences he hung around?"

Brenna nodded. "And how he was a genius."

"Yeah, well, that might have been a bit of an exaggeration, but whoever ran this organization for the past twenty years is really savvy."

Brenna nodded back at him. "Probably savvier than Carlton Wayne White."

"I think we just found our mastermind."

"Then let's go and get him."

"Maybe you should think about making the leap over to DEA," Marcos suggested as he pulled away from the curb. "We could work together like this all the time."

"Yeah, I'm not sure undercover work is for me," Brenna replied.

"Carlton thought you were a natural," Marcos teased, shooting her a smile as he left the Pikes' neighborhood and turned onto the freeway.

"We just decided Carlton wasn't all that smart," Brenna joked. "Besides…" She squeezed his hand, still tucked in his as he drove one-handed. "Doesn't the DEA have rules about coworkers dating?"

"Not to mention spouses," Marcos added, and

he said it so easily, so casually, as if it was a foregone conclusion.

Brenna's head spun at the idea, and panic tightened her chest. Marriage. Was she cut out for that?

Then she glanced over at Marcos's strong profile, and the panic started to subside. If anyone could make her want to promise her life to him, it was Marcos.

In fact, the more she thought about it, the more right it seemed. A smile started to bloom, and the panic in her chest exploded into unfettered joy. Marriage to Marcos. It might be a little scary, but there was suddenly no doubt. That's what she wanted for her future.

She probably should wait until they finished the investigation, until they were back in that hotel, making good on Marcos's promise, to tell him. Not driving on the freeway, knowing in their hearts who all the major players in this drug organization were, but still needing to prove it. But the words wanted to escape, and she couldn't hold them in one minute longer.

"Marcos, I lo—" she started, then her gaze darted up to the rearview mirror and she screamed as a huge dark vehicle raced toward them. "Watch out!" she screamed, but it was too late.

The Hummer slammed into the back of Marcos's car, and everything seemed to move in slow motion as the back end of the car lifted off the ground. Then they were spinning, out of control, heading for the concrete divider in the center of the freeway.

Chapter Twenty-Three

The air bag deployed, smacking her in the face hard enough to disorient her as Brenna clutched the armrests in a death grip and the car spun wildly.

Next to her, Marcos was grappling for control, trying to maneuver around his own airbag and pull the car out of the spin before it slammed into the divider.

It started to slow, and then she saw the Hummer, coming at them again. This time, when she looked behind her, she could actually see Trent behind the wheel, his face twisted in a nasty grimace as he barreled toward them.

The car lurched forward as Marcos gave it a little gas, trying to stop the spin and get out of the way at the same time, but Brenna knew it was too late. She braced for the next hit, but it didn't matter.

The Hummer smacked into them again, squishing her against the air bag before her seat belt yanked her back, making it hard to breathe. Beside her, Marcos made a sound of pain, and then the Hummer hit again.

This time, the car flipped. Her stomach dropped as up became down, and then they slammed back into the ground. She felt the jolt through her entire body, but only once in her life had she felt this help-less as the car slid forward on its roof.

Marcos dangled upside down next to her, his eyes closed, and when she heard a wailing sound, it took a minute to realize it was her. Instantly, she was trans-ported back eighteen years to another car crash, to looking into the front seat and seeing her mom, al-ready gone. She couldn't survive watching another person she loved die.

As the car finally came to a stop, Brenna strug-gled against her seat belt, but thought better of it just before she unsnapped it and fell on her head. Instead, she stretched left, trying to touch Marcos.

"Marcos? Marcos? Are you okay?"

Her voice sounded distant, and she blinked as he went blurry. Swiping her hand over her eyes to wipe away tears, she was surprised when it came back bloody. Her head pounded, and she realized she had a nasty gash in her hairline, but it didn't mat-ter. All that mattered right now was Marcos open-ing his eyes.

"Marcos!" She grabbed his arm, shaking it, hop-ing for a response. When there was none, she fum-bled to press her fingers to his wrist, searching for a pulse. But she couldn't tell over the thundering of her own heart, the pain exploding all over her body.

"Marcos!" she shouted, and this time he groaned in response.

Relief made it hard to breathe, and her hand shook as she took his. "Are you okay?"

His eyes opened and he stared back at her. Pain was reflected in those blue-gray depths, but he was alive.

This wasn't like eighteen years ago. Tears filled her eyes instantly, the rush of them so heavy it was hard to see.

"It's okay," Marcos rasped. "We're okay."

Behind him, through the cracked side window, Brenna spotted cars swerving to a stop. But much closer, a pair of expensive loafers moved leisurely toward the vehicle and Brenna swore. "He's coming."

She braced her hand on the roof, now underneath her, to help break her fall, then pressed down on the seat-belt release. Nothing happened.

Tugging harder, Brenna tried again as Marcos did the same. Beside her, he slammed into the ceiling with a sickening thud, partially bracing his fall, and let out a groan. He was twisting to reach for the weapon he had holstered at his hip, but she could tell something was going wrong even before he lifted his sweatshirt and she could see that the gun had come free during the crash.

Then, Trent's face was filling the side window,

a satisfied grin on his face. He mouthed a mocking *Sorry* as he pulled something from his pocket.

Expecting a gun, Brenna gave up on the seat belt and reached for her own weapon, but it was wedged between her and the seat belt, jammed tight.

Then, Trent's hand came back and Brenna's pulse took off. Instead of a gun, he held a match.

Yanking at the seat belt was useless, so Brenna shoved herself closer toward Marcos, her eyes watering at the intense pain that ripped through her side. Ignoring it, she yanked her gun free and swung it toward Trent, still grinning in the window.

Angling her arms in front of her awkwardly, she fired just as Trent struck the match and tossed it.

Then the front of the car went up in flames.

THE WORLD IN front of him was on fire.

Marcos reacted instinctively as smoke billowed toward him and flames sucked at the windshield. He jerked his feet away from the front of the car and grabbed the door handle, trying to shove it open.

It stuck, refusing to budge, and Marcos gasped in a desperate lungful of air, even though he knew he needed to try not to breathe the smoke. Through the window, he could see Trent on the ground, eyes wide but staring sightlessly at the sky.

But they were still in trouble. The people who'd stopped on the freeway had kept their distance— either because of the gunshot or the fire. The smoke was starting to turn gray, and he could feel the heat seeping in from the hood.

He tried to keep the panic at bay, tried not to remember the feeling when he'd lifted his head in that house all those years ago after falling on the stairs. But it came back to him, the sight of the flames blocking his exit, his brothers both gone.

At least in that terrifying moment, he'd known they'd made it out of the fire, even if he didn't. He turned to look at Brenna, and his fear seemed to quadruple. "Brenna, does your door open?"

She grabbed the handle, twisting awkwardly, still hanging upside down, tethered by her seat belt, trying to kick it when it only moved centimeters.

"I...can't...get...it," she wheezed.

Marcos swore and climbed into the back seat awkwardly, his head throbbing and his vision unsteady. "Come on. Move away from the fire. The back isn't as crumpled. Maybe these doors will...yes!" He shoved the door and it popped open.

"Brenna!" He glanced back, and she twisted her head to look at him, tears in her eyes.

"I'm stuck."

He pushed his head and chest through the small space between the two front seats, reaching around her and grabbing hold of her seat belt. Pressing hard on the release button, he yanked as hard as he could. Nothing.

Bracing his feet on the roof beneath him, Marcos tried again, and this time, Brenna wrapped her hands over his and tugged, too. He sucked in another breath, choking on smoke instead as he yanked again and again. But no matter how hard they pulled, the seat belt didn't come loose.

"Go," Brenna said, her gaze swiveling from the hood of the car, now engulfed in flames, a thick black smoke rising from it, back to him.

"No way," Marcos said, fighting the panic making it hard to breathe. Or maybe that was just the smoke. It no longer seemed to matter that the back door was open, letting in air, because smoke was filling the interior fast.

Way off in the distance, Marcos heard sirens approaching, but he knew they weren't going to make it in time.

"The car's going to blow," Brenna told him, her voice strangely calm, even though there was fear and sadness in her eyes. "You need to get out."

"I don't suppose you have another butter knife on you," he said, ignoring her ridiculous suggestion.

"Marcos, go!" Brenna shouted, then choked on the smoke. She coughed violently, then insisted, "I want you to go. You're not dying in here."

"Neither are you," he promised, searching the car for something—anything—to saw through the seat belt and get her free. But there was nothing.

He kept searching, reaching past her to yank open the glove box, and swearing at the burning heat that seared through his hand. But the only things in his glove box were a compass, a map of the Appalachian Mountains and a spare cell phone.

"Marcos." She grabbed his hand in hers, holding on tight and effectively stopping his desperate search. "I love you. I've loved you since I was eleven years old."

He started to respond, but she kept going. "And I'll never forgive you if you don't get out of this car right now."

"Brenna," he whispered, tears clouding his vision because he knew she was right about one thing. The car was going to blow any second, and he couldn't get her out.

But he wasn't leaving without her, either. "We're a team," he told her, then scooted closer.

She lifted her other hand to shove him away from her, trying to force him to leave, and he spotted it: the gun still clutched in her hand.

Yanking it away from her, he tugged her toward him, then reached around her and aimed the gun at the seat-belt mechanism.

"No!" she yelled. "The fuel. It could spark!"

Marcos fired anyway, and then Brenna fell toward him and he grabbed hold of her and tugged her into the back seat. He could tell he was hurting her—something was wrong with her side—but he kept going, feeling blindly for the open back door as the thick smoke got even blacker.

And then, somehow, they were falling onto the

cold, hard pavement. But Marcos knew that wasn't good enough.

The car was going to go.

He shoved himself to his feet and ran, half carrying Brenna as she stumbled along beside him. Then he pushed them both to the ground and covered her body with his as an explosion *boomed* behind them, and pieces of metal and fire rained from the sky.

Beneath him, Brenna groaned and rolled so she was facing him, the pinched expression on her face telling him she'd broken at least one rib. Then her arms were around his neck as she choked out, "We're a good team."

"I love you, too," he said in return, then wiped soot away from her mouth and kissed her.

Epilogue

The boy in the doorway smiled at her. It was tentative, but understanding, and it made dimples pop on both cheeks. Then he held out his hand and Brenna took it, and somehow, she knew nothing would ever be the same again.

"Marcos."

"I'm here."

Brenna frowned, trying to make sense of what was happening as her past mingled with her present, and she opened her eyes. She was lying in a hospital bed, and Marcos was sitting in a chair beside her, his hand tucked in hers.

"What happened?"

He leaned closer, looking concerned, and she saw the hastily cleaned soot still clinging to the edges of his face and his clothes. "Trent hit our car and—"

"I know that," Brenna rasped. "Why am I in the hospital?" The last thing she remembered was being flattened to the pavement by Marcos, then him whispering something to her before he kissed her.

"You love me." She remembered his words.

He grinned, and there were those dimples. The man was so much more than she ever could have imagined in the eighteen years they'd been separated, and yet, he was exactly how she'd expected him to grow up on that very first day. Strong and kind and exactly who she needed.

"I do," he whispered, then he got serious and told her, "You passed out on the freeway after we hit the ground. They admitted you to check you out, but everything looks okay. You have a few cracked ribs and a lot of bruises. They stitched up a bad cut on your head, and they gave you oxygen because of the smoke inhalation, but you'll be out of here by tomorrow."

"And you?"

"I'm fine. Some burns on one hand, but I've been through this before. They're just covered in ointment and wrapped. Same deal with the smoke inhalation, but nothing that won't heal."

"When we were in that car, I was flashing back to the time with my mom..."

"I know," Marcos said softly. "I'm sorry."

"And then the fire..." It had to be his worst nightmare come back to life, too, and yet, he'd stayed with her.

"We got out," Marcos said simply. "And when Jim told Jesse what had happened to us, the kid spilled everything. He didn't want any part of that, said he knew we'd tried to help him get away."

"So, was Trent in charge or Carlton?"

Marcos shrugged. "Jesse wasn't sure, but he thought they had a dysfunctional partnership that was getting more and more uneven. It sounds like once upon a time, Trent had all the power, but Carlton was trying to make a play for it. And Carlton still isn't talking. Jim agrees with us that they were in it together from the very beginning. Carlton's power came from being the face of the organization, and Trent's came from his foster care connection. It's why Carlton was recruiting you. He knew Trent's connection through his father was retiring, so he wanted to grab some of that power for himself."

"What about the Pikes?"

"They're talking, too, since their son's death. They're claiming they didn't know what he was really doing with the names, but we're not buying it. I'm not sure what's going to happen because of Mr. Pike's medical needs, but they're going to face time."

"Good." She squeezed his hand, and he scooted his chair even closer to the bed. "They should pay for what they did to all those kids. And for what happened to us all those years ago."

"I'm glad we found our way back to each other," Marcos told her. "Because—"

A knock at the door cut him off, and then Cole and Andre peeked in. "How's she doing?"

"Awake," Marcos told them. "Come in."

"Thank goodness," Cole said, and Andre added, "We've got company."

Brenna shifted a little, pressing the button on the remote beside her to lift her bed so she was half sitting. She grimaced at the pain in her ribs, but it was worth it to see everyone right now. "Who?"

"The rest of the family," Cole said. "This is my fiancée, Shaye." He indicated a tall redhead with a friendly smile.

"And this is my fiancée, Juliette," Andre added, gesturing to the brunette holding his hand.

"Nice to meet you both," Brenna said. Normally, she'd be self-conscious about the fact that she was laid out from injuries and still feeling emotionally wrecked from being trapped in that car with Marcos. But somehow, this group made her feel instantly at ease. As if they were her family, too.

"We're glad you're awake," Andre said. "And that the case is finally over."

"Well, we've got all the major players in custody," Marcos corrected him. "But the investigation isn't over. I want the rest of his organization, too."

"And the kids he had running drugs for him," Brenna added. "I don't want them falling through the cracks again. I want to find a way to help them into normal lives, if we can."

Marcos smiled softly at her. "I've been thinking about that transition program you were pretending to set up for Carlton."

"What about it?"

"What if it was real?"

Brenna nodded back at him, knowing that she was

going to find a way to do it. She had a lot of free time outside of the job. It wouldn't be easy, but she had a feeling the things most worth doing weren't easy.

"I think between the two of us, we can garner a lot of support for a program like that," Marcos said.

"Between the six of us," Cole spoke up. "That's how family works. We're a team."

Tears welled up so fast that Brenna couldn't stop them from spilling over. *Family.* It had been eighteen long years since she'd had anyone to call family.

"Hey," Marcos said, wiping the tears away. "Don't start crying yet. I haven't even gotten to tell you what I wanted to say before my brothers came in."

A surprised laugh snuck out. "You're going to make me cry?"

"Happy tears, I hope," Marcos said, suddenly looking nervous. And then he was reaching into his pocket and telling her, "So, I remember you telling Carlton that you liked diamonds…"

He flipped open a box and a ring was staring back at her.

Brenna's mouth dropped open, and she looked up into his eyes, surprised and scared and happier than she thought she'd ever felt in her life. "It's only been a few days," she whispered. "Are you sure?"

"I love you," he answered, as if it was the simplest thing in the world. "And after all these years, after thinking I might lose you in that car, there's one thing I know for sure. It's something I think I knew the minute I saw you in the doorway of that foster house. Home is always going to be wherever you are."

"I love you, too," she said, and she realized it didn't matter that it had been less than a week since she'd first seen him all grown up. She'd never stopped loving that boy with the dimples, and she was never going to stop loving the man he'd become.

She had a lifetime to learn all the little details about him. And she knew it was going to be the best journey she'd ever take.

She held out a shaky hand for the ring and Marcos grinned at her, his dimples popping. "So is that a *yes*?"

"Yes."

Then, the ring was on her finger and Marcos was kissing her and there was a loud *pop* behind him.

When she pulled back, she saw Andre holding up an open bottle of champagne and Cole pulling out glasses.

"To family," Marcos said, his gaze never leaving hers.

"To family," she agreed, and pulled him down for another kiss.

* * * * *

Alpha One
Cynthia Eden

MILLS & BOON

ABOUT THE AUTHOR

USA TODAY bestselling author Cynthia Eden writes tales of romantic suspense and paranormal romance. Her books have received starred reviews from *Publishers Weekly*, and she has received a RITA® Award nomination for best romantic suspense. Cynthia lives in the deep South, loves horror movies and has an addiction to chocolate. More information about Cynthia may be found on her website, www.cynthiaeden.com, or you can follow her on Twitter (www.twitter.com/cynthiaeden).

Books by Cynthia Eden

HARLEQUIN INTRIGUE
1398—ALPHA ONE*

*Shadow Agents

DEDICATION

I've wanted to write a Harlequin Intrigue novel for over ten years. Ten long years. So I'd very much like to thank the wonderful Denise Zaza and the fabulous Dana Hamilton for helping me to achieve this dream. It's been a pleasure to work with you both!

CAST OF CHARACTERS

Logan Quinn—The team leader of the Elite Operations Division's secretive Shadow Agents, Logan is a man who knows all about the darker side of life.

Juliana James—Kidnapped in Mexico, Juliana is terrified as she waits for her abductors to come back for her. The last person that Juliana expects to see in her prison is the one man that she's never been able to forget.

Senator Aaron James—The wealthy and influential senator from Mississippi has deadly secrets that are coming back to haunt him. His secrets may just cost his daughter, Juliana, her life.

Diego Guerrero—Known as "El Diablo" by his enemies, Diego is a man who inspires fear in all who cross his path. He is determined to teach Senator James a lesson, and Diego knows that Juliana can be the perfect instrument of his revenge.

Susan Walker—For years, Susan has worked closely with the senator. She is his most trusted assistant, the person with instant access to all parts of Aaron's life, but does she know the truth about Aaron's ties to Diego?

Jasper Adams—A former army ranger, Jasper isn't afraid to jump into the heart of a battle. But will Jasper's addiction to danger jeopardize the team?

Gunner Ortez—A former SEAL sniper, Gunner is one of the deadliest men in the EOD. Gunner is carrying his own secrets—secrets that he's sworn never to reveal, not even to his own EOD team members.

Sydney Sloan—When it comes to computers, there is no one better able to infiltrate a system than Sydney. Her skills are needed now more than ever, because her team is racing against the clock, and if the Shadow Agents don't stop El Diablo, then Juliana will be dead.

Chapter One

"You don't deserve to die here."

Juliana James looked up at the sound of the quiet voice. She couldn't move her body much because she was still tied hand and foot to the chair in the dimly lit room. Tied with rough ropes that bit into her skin. Though she'd struggled for hours, she hadn't been able to break free. She'd done nothing but slice open her flesh on the ropes.

"If you tell them…what they want to know…" He sighed. "They might let you go."

Juliana swallowed and felt as if she were choking back shards of glass. How long had it been since they'd given her anything to drink? After swallowing a few more times, she managed, "I don't know anything." She was just trapped in a nightmare. One day, she'd been soaking up the sun on a Mexican beach, and the next—

Hello, hell.

It was a nightmare all right, and she desperately wanted to wake up from it. *Ready to wake up—now.*

John Gonzales, the man who'd been held captive with her for—what was it now? Three? Four days?—was slumped in his chair. She'd never met John until they were thrown together in this hell. They'd both been kidnapped from separate areas in Mexico. The men who'd abducted them kept coming and getting John, taking him.

Hurting him.

And she knew her time was coming.

"I'm not…perfect," John's ragged voice whispered to her. "But you…you didn't do anything wrong… It was all your father."

Her father. The not-so-honorable Senator Aaron James. She might not know who had taken her, but once her abductors had started asking their questions, Juliana had figured out fast that the abduction was payback for something the senator had done.

Daddy hadn't raised a fool. Just, apparently, someone to die in his place.

Would he even care when he learned about what had happened to her? Or would he just hold a press conference and *look* appropriately saddened and grievous in front of all the cameras? She didn't know, and that fact made her stomach knot even more.

Juliana exhaled slowly. "Perfect or not…" She didn't know the things that John had done. Right then, they didn't matter. He'd talked to her when she'd been trapped in the dark. He'd kept her sane during all of those long, terrible hours. "We're both going to make it out of here."

His rough laughter called her words a lie.

She'd only seen his face a few times, when the light was bright enough in the early mornings. Appearing a bit younger than her own thirty years, John had the dark good looks that had probably gotten him plenty of female attention since he was a teen.

Not now, though.

"Do you have any…regrets?" John asked her. She saw his head tilt toward her as he waited for her response.

Juliana blinked against the tears that wanted to fill her eyes. *Regrets?* "A few." *One.*

A pause. Then "You ever been in love, Juliana?"

"Once—" and in the dark, with only death waiting for her, she could admit this painful truth "—but Logan didn't love me back." Pity, because she'd never been able to—

The hinges on the door groaned as it opened. Juliana tensed, her whole body going tight with fear. John was already swearing, jerking against his binds, but...

But the men weren't coming for him this time.

They were coming for her.

Juliana screamed.

LOGAN QUINN FELT A TRICKLE of sweat slide down his back. He didn't move, not so much as a muscle twitch. He'd been in position for the past forty-three minutes, waiting for the go-ahead to move.

To storm that building and get Julie out of there.

Hold on, baby.

Not that she was his baby. Not anymore. But the minute Senator James had contacted him, asking for his help and the help of his team, Logan had known that trouble, serious trouble, had come to hunt him down.

Julie's missing. You have to get her back.

That was all it had taken. Two sentences, and Logan had set his team up for a recovery mission in Mexico. His unit, part of the Elite Operations Division, didn't take on just any case.

But for her, he'd do anything.

"There's movement." The words whispered into his ear via the comm link that all members of his recovery team used.

Logan barely breathed.

"I have a visual on the target."

His heart raced faster. This was what they'd been waiting for. Movement and, hopefully...visual confirmation. They wouldn't storm the place, not until—

"I see her. The girl's being led down a hallway. There's a knife at her throat."

Visual confirmation.

Logan held his position even as fury pulsed within him. Juliana would be scared. Terrified. This was so far from the debutante balls in Mississippi that she knew. So far from the safe life she'd always wanted to lead.

He'd get her back to that life, then he'd walk away. Just as he had before.

"South side," that same voice whispered in his ear. Male. Gunner Ortez, the SEAL sniper Uncle Sam had recruited for their black-ops division. A division most said didn't exist.

They were wrong.

"Second door," Gunner said, voice flat and hard as he marked the target location.

Finally, Logan moved. A shadow in the night, he didn't make a single sound as he slipped into the building. To his right, Jasper Adams moved in perfect sync with him. The Ranger knew how to keep quiet just like Logan did. After all their training, stealth was second nature to them now.

Logan came up on the first guard, caught the scent of cigarettes and alcohol. One quick jab, and the guard's body slumped back against him. He pulled the guy into the shadows, dropped him in the corner and signaled for Jasper to keep moving.

Then he heard her scream.

The blood in Logan's body iced over. For a second, his vision seemed to go dark. Pain, fear—he could hear them both in Juliana's scream. He rushed forward, edging fast on Jasper's heels. Jasper knocked out the next guard, barely pausing.

Logan didn't pause at all. He drew out his gun and—

"Please, I don't know!" It was Juliana's desperate

voice. The voice he still heard in his dreams. Not soft with the South now, but high with terror.

They passed the first door. The second was just steps away. *Hold on, hold on...*

"Company!" Gunner's terse warning blasted in his comm link. They barely had time to duck for cover before the *rat-a-tat* of gunfire smashed into the wall above them.

Made. Logan fired back, once, twice, aiming with near-instant precision. He heard a choked cry, then the thud of bodies as two men hit the ground. Jasper covered him, moving quickly, as Logan kicked open lucky door number two. With that gunfire, the men inside would either flee...

Or try to kill their prey.

Option number two damn well wasn't going down on his watch.

But as Logan burst into the room, three men turned toward him. He fired at the guy on the left as the man drew his gun. The guy's body hit the floor. Then Logan drove his fist into the face of the attacker on the right. But the one in the middle...the one with his knife pressed against Juliana's throat...

Logan didn't touch him. Not yet.

"Deje a la mujer ir," Logan barked in perfect Spanish. *Let the woman go.*

Instead, the soon-to-be-dead fool cut her skin. Logan's eyes narrowed. Wrong move.

"Vuelva o ella es muerta," the guy snarled back at him. *Step back or she's dead.*

Logan didn't step back. He'd never been the type to retreat. His gaze darted to Juliana. She stared at him, eyes wide, body frozen. A black ski mask covered his head, so he knew she had no idea who he was. But Logan knew she'd always had a real fine grasp of the Spanish language. She understood exactly what the man had said to him.

"Step back." Her lips moved almost soundlessly. "Please." Then she repeated her plea in Spanish.

Still, he didn't move. Beneath the ski mask, his jaw locked. He kept his gun up and aimed right at her attacker's head. *One shot...*

"Vuelva o ella es muerta!" Now the guy yelled his warning and that knife dug deeper into Juliana's pale throat.

Instead of backing up, Logan stepped forward. Juliana screamed—and then she started fighting. Her nails clawed at her captor's hand, and she drew blood of her own. The guy swore and yanked back on her hair, but that move lifted the knife off her throat. Lifted it off just enough for Logan to attack.

He caught the man's wrist, wrenched it back. Even as Logan yanked Juliana forward, he drove the guy's wrist—and the knife—right back at the bastard's own throat.

When the body hit the floor, Logan didn't glance down. He pulled Juliana closer to him and tried to keep her attention off the dead men on the floor. "It's all right," he told her, attempting to sound soothing in the middle of hell. More gunfire echoed outside the small room. The sound was like the explosion of fireworks. The voice in his ear told him that two more men had just been taken out by Jasper. Good. The guy was clearing the way for their escape. Logan's hands tightened on Juliana, and he said, "I'm gonna—"

She kneed him in the groin.

Logan was so caught off guard by the move that he let her go. She lunged away from him, yelling for all that she was worth.

"Damn it," he growled and hissed out a breath, "I'm not here to hurt you!"

She'd yanked the knife out of the dead man's throat.

She came up with it clutched tightly in her white-knuck-led grip. "You stay away from me!"

"Easy." They didn't have time for this. Logan knew that if he yanked up his mask and revealed his identity, she'd drop the weapon. But he had mission protocol ruling him right then. Their team was to stay covered during this res-cue, until the target had been taken to the designated safe zone. No team member could afford to have his identity compromised at this site. Not until everything was secure.

"Back up and get out of my way," Juliana snapped right back at him, showing the fire that had first drawn him to her years ago.

He hadn't obeyed the dead guy. Did she really think he'd obey her?

But then Jasper leaped into the room at the same instant that Gunner barked on the comm link, *"Extraction. Now."*

Logan caught the whiff of smoke in the air. Smoke... and the crackle of flames. Fire wasn't part of the extrac-tion plan.

"Two hostiles got away," Jasper grunted, shifting his shoulders, and Logan wondered if he'd been hit. He'd seen the Ranger take three bullets before and keep fighting. One hit wouldn't slow him down—Jasper wouldn't let it slow him down. "And I think those fleeing hombres want to make sure we don't get out alive with her."

No, they wouldn't want her escaping. Too bad for them. Logan spun for the window. Using his weapon and his fist, he broke the glass and shattered the old wooden frame. He glanced down at the street below. Second story. He could handle that drop in his sleep, but he'd have to take care with Juliana.

"Clear," Gunner said in his ear, and Logan knew the guy was still tracking the team's movement. "Go now... 'cause that fire is coming hard for you."

Juliana's captors had probably rigged the place for a fast burn. The better to leave no evidence—or witnesses— behind.

Logan grabbed Juliana's hand. She yelped. He hated that sound, hated that he'd had to hurt her, but now wasn't the time for explanations.

The knife clattered to the floor.

Now was the time to get the hell out of there. He wrapped his arm around her waist and pulled her close against his body. "You'll need to hold tight," he told her, voice low and growling.

But Juliana shook her head at him. "I'm not going out that window. I have to—"

"You have to live," Jasper said from his post at the door. "That fire's coming, ma'am, and you need to get through that window *now*."

She blinked. In the faint light, Logan saw the same dark chocolate eyes he remembered. Her face still as pretty. "Fire?" Then she sucked in a deep breath, and Logan knew she'd finally caught the scent of smoke and flames. *"No!"* She tried to rip out of his arms and lunge for the door.

Logan just hauled her right back against him. Now that he had her safe in his arms, he wasn't about to let her get away.

"Area's clear," Gunner said in Logan's earpiece. *"Extract now."*

Logan tried to position Juliana for their drop. The woman twisted against him, moving like a slithering snake as she fought to wrench back and break free. "I'm not leaving!" she snapped at him. "Not without John!"

Who?

"Extract." Gunner's order.

"Stop fighting," Logan told her when she twisted again. "We're the good guys, and we came to take you to safety."

She stilled for a moment. Heaving a deep breath, she said, "Me…and John."

Seriously, who the hell was John?

"He's back there." Her hand lifted and one trembling finger pointed to the doorway. The doorway that was currently filling with smoke. "We have to get him out."

No other civilians were in the building. Only Diego Guerrero's killers. Logan's team members were pulling back and—

"I'm not leaving without him!"

An explosion rocked the building. Juliana fell against Logan's chest.

Jasper staggered. "Go time," Logan heard him say.

And yeah, it was. Keeping a hold on Juliana, Logan tapped his receiver. "Is there another civilian here?" He had to be sure. He wouldn't leave an innocent to burn.

He motioned for Jasper to take the leap out. He had Juliana; there was no need for the other agent to stay any longer. Jasper yanked out a cable from his pack and quickly set up an escape line. In seconds, he began to lower his body to the ground.

"Negative," Gunner responded instantly. "Now move before your butt gets fried."

Gunner wouldn't make a mistake. He and Sydney Sloan had the best intel there was. No way would they send the team in without knowledge of another innocent in the perimeter.

Juliana blinked up at him. "Y-your voice…"

Aw, damn. He'd lost most of his Southern accent over the years, but every now and then, those Mississippi purrs would slip into his voice. Now wasn't a good time for that slip.

"You're goin' out the window…" Another explosion shook the building. Her captors were packing some serious firepower. *Definitely don't want her getting away alive.* "Your choice—you goin' through awake or asleep?"

"There's a man trapped back there! He's tied up—*he'll burn to death.*"

She wasn't listening to him. Fine. He grabbed her, tossed her over his shoulder, held tight and dropped down on the line that Jasper had secured for him.

By the time she'd gotten any breath to scream, they were on the ground.

"Take her," Logan ordered, shoving Juliana into Jasper's arms. "Get her out of here." She was the mission. Her safety was their number one priority.

But…

He'll burn to death.

Logan wasn't leaving a man behind.

He grabbed the cable and started hauling his butt back up into the fire.

"What the hell is he thinking?"

Juliana stared around her with wide eyes. She was surrounded by two men, both big, strong, towering well over her five foot eight inches. They had guns held in their hands, and they both wore black ski masks. Just like the other guy. The guy that, for a moment, had sounded exactly like—

"Alpha One," the hulking shadow to her right said into his wrist. "Get back here before I have to drag you out of that inferno." Wait, no, he wasn't muttering into his wrist. He was talking into some kind of microphone.

Alpha One? That had to be the guy who'd jumped out of the window—with her in his arms. Her heart had stopped when he'd leaped out and she'd felt the rush of air on her body. Then she'd realized…he'd been holding on to some kind of rope. They hadn't crashed into the cement. He'd lowered her, gotten her to safety, then gone back into the fire.

"There's someone else inside… John…" Juliana whispered. The fire was raging now. Blowing out the bottom windows of that big, thick building. Her hell.

They were at least two hundred feet away from the fire now. Encased in shadows. Hidden so well. But…

But she couldn't stop shaking. These men had saved her, and she'd just sent one of them right back to face the flames.

She couldn't even see the men's eyes as they glanced at her. The sky was so dark, starless. The only illumination came from the flames.

Then she heard a growl. A faint purr…and the man to her right yanked her back as a vehicle slid from the shadows. Juliana hadn't even seen the van approaching. No headlights had cut through the night.

The van's back doors flew open. "Let's go!" a woman's sharp voice ordered.

The men pretty much threw Juliana into the van.

"Where's Alpha One?" the woman demanded. Juliana's gaze flew to her. The woman had short hair, a delicate build, but Juliana couldn't really discern anything else about her.

The man climbing in behind Juliana pointed to the blaze.

"Damn it." The woman's fist slammed into the dashboard.

But as Juliana glanced back at the fire, she saw a figure running toward them. His head was down, his body moving fluidly as he leaped across that field.

The van started to accelerate. Juliana grabbed on to

the side of the vehicle. Were they just going to leave him? "Wait!"

"We can't," the woman gritted out as she glanced back from the driver's seat. "That fire will attract every eye in the area. We need to be out of here yesterday."

But—

But the guy was nearly at the van. One of the guys with her reached out a hand, and her "hero" caught it as he leaped toward them. When he landed on the floor of the van, the whole vehicle shuddered.

Juliana's heart nearly pounded right out of her chest. Her hero was alone. "John?"

He shook his head.

"Logan, what the hell?" the woman up front snapped. "You were supposed to be point on extraction, not going back to—"

Logan?

A dull roar began to fill Juliana's ears. There were thousands of Logans in the world. Probably dozens in the military.

Just because her Logan had left her ten years ago that didn't mean...

"There was no sign of another hostage," the guy—Logan—said, and his voice was deep and rumbling.

A shiver worked over her.

Juliana sat on the floor of the van, arms wrapped around her knees. She wanted to see his eyes, needed to, but it was far too dark inside the vehicle.

One of the other men leaned out and yanked the van doors closed. The sound of those metal doors shutting sounded like a scream.

"'Course there wasn't another hostage!" This came from the woman. "She was the only civilian there. I *told* you that. Don't go doubting my intel."

He grunted as he levered himself up. Then he reached for Juliana.

She jerked away from him. "Take off that mask." She could see now. Barely.

He pulled it up and tossed it aside. Not much better. She had a fast impression of close-cropped hair and a strong jaw. Without more light, there was nothing else to see.

She needed to see *more*.

"You're safe now," he told her, and his words were little more than a growl. "They can't hurt you anymore."

His hand lifted, and his fingertips traced over her cheek. Her eyes closed at his touch and Juliana's breath caught because... *His touch is familiar.*

His fingers slid down her cheek. Gentle. Light. It was a caress she'd felt before.

There were some things a woman never forgot—one was the touch of a man who'd left her with a broken heart.

This was her Logan. No, *not* hers. He never had been. "Thank you," she whispered because he'd gotten her out of that nightmare, but she pulled away from his touch. Touching Logan Quinn had always been its own hell for her.

The van rushed along in the night. She didn't know where they were heading. A heavy numbness seemed to have settled over her. John hadn't made it out.

I'm not...perfect.

"We're the good guys," one of the other men said, his voice drawling slightly with the flow of Texas in his words. "Your father sent us after you. Before you know it, you'll be home safe and sound. You'll be—"

Rat-a-tat.

Juliana opened her mouth to scream as gunfire ripped into the vehicle, but in the next instant, she found herself thrown totally onto the floor of the van. Logan's heavy body covered hers, and he trapped her beneath him.

"Get us out of here, Syd!" Texas yelled.

Juliana could barely breathe. Logan's chest shoved down against hers, and the light stubble on his cheek brushed against her face.

"Hold on," he told her, breathing the words into her ear. "Just a few more minutes…"

Air rushed into the van. Someone had opened the back door! Were they crazy? Why not just invite the shooters to aim at them and—

Three fast blasts of thunder—gunfire. Only, those shots came *from* the van. The men weren't just waiting to be targets. They were taking out the shooters after them.

Three bullets. Then…silence.

"Got 'em," Texas said just seconds before she heard the crash. A screech of metal and the shattering of glass.

The van lurched to the left, seeming to race away even faster.

Juliana looked up. Her eyes had adjusted more to the darkness now. She could almost see Logan's features above her. *Almost.*

"Uh, Logan, you can probably get off her now," that same drawling voice mocked.

But Logan didn't move.

And Juliana was still barely breathing.

"Missed you."

The words were so faint, she wasn't even sure that she'd heard them. Actually, no, she *couldn't* have heard them. Imagined them, yes. That had to be it. Because there was no way Logan had actually spoken. Logan Quinn was the big, strong badass who'd left her without a backward glance. He wouldn't say something as sappy as that line.

Backbone, girl. Backbone. She'd survived her hell; no way would she break for a man now. "Are we safe?"

She felt, more than saw, his nod. "For now."

Right. Well, she'd thought they were safe before, until the gunfire had blasted into the back of the van. But Texas had taken out the bad guys who'd managed to follow them. So that had to buy them at least a few minutes. And the way the woman was driving...

Eat our dust, jerks.

"Then, if we're safe..." Juliana brought her hands up and shoved against his chest. Like rock. Some things never changed. "Get off me, Logan, *now.*"

He rose slowly, pulling her with him and then positioning her near the front of the van. Juliana was trembling— her body shaking with fear, fury and an adrenaline burst that she knew would fade soon. When it faded, she'd crash.

"Once we get out of Mexico, they'll stop hunting you," Logan said.

Juliana swallowed. Her throat still felt too parched, as if she'd swallowed broken glass, but now didn't seem the time to ask for water. Maybe once they stopped fleeing through the night. Yes, that would be the better moment. "And...when...exactly...do we get out of Mexico?"

No one spoke. Not a good sign.

"In a little over twenty-four hours," Logan answered.

What? No way. They could drive out of Mexico faster than that. Twenty-four hours didn't even make—

"Guerrero controls the Federales near the border," Logan told her, his voice flat. "No way do we get to just waltz out of this country with you."

"Then...how?"

"We're gonna fly, baby."

Baby. She stiffened. She was *not* his baby, and if the

guy hadn't just saved her, she'd be tearing into him. But a woman had to be grateful...for now.

Without Logan and his team—and who, exactly, were they?—she'd be sampling the torture techniques of those men in that hellhole.

"We'll be going out on a plane that sneaks right past any guards who are waiting. Guerrero's paid cops won't even know when we vanish."

Sounded good, except for the whole waiting-for-twenty-four-hours part. "And until then? What do we do?"

She felt a movement in the dark, as if Logan were going to reach out and touch her, but he stopped. After a tense moment, a moment in which every muscle in her body tightened, he said, "We keep you alive."

Chapter Two

Her scream woke him. Logan jerked awake at the sound, his heart racing. He'd fallen asleep moments before. Gunner and Jasper were on patrol duty around their temporary safe house. He jumped to his feet and raced toward the small "bedroom" area they'd designated for Juliana.

He threw open the door. "Julie!"

She was twisting on the floor, tangled in the one blanket they'd given to her. At his call, her eyes flew open. For a few seconds, she just stared blindly at him. Logan hurried to her. She wasn't seeing him. Trapped in a nightmare, probably remembering the men who'd held her—

He reached out to her.

Juliana shuddered and her eyes squeezed shut. "Sorry."

His hands clenched. The better not to grab her and hold her as tight as he could. But this was a mission. Things weren't supposed to get personal between them.

Even though his body burned just looking at her.

Faint rays of sunlight trickled through the boarded-up window. Sydney had done reconnaissance for them and picked this safe house when they'd been planning the rescue. Secluded, the abandoned property was the perfect temporary base for them. They could hear company approaching from miles away. Since the property was situated on high land, they had the tactical advantage. They also had the firepower ready to knock out any attackers who might come their way.

And with that faint light, finally, he could *see* Juliana. She'd changed a lot over the past ten years. Her long mane was gone. Now the blond hair framed her heart-shaped face. Still as beautiful, to him, with her wide, dark eyes and full lips. She was still curved in all the right places. He'd always loved her lush hips and breasts. The woman could—

"Stop staring at me," she whispered as she sat up.

Hell. He *had* been staring. Like a hungry wolf who wanted a bite so badly he could taste it. Taste her.

She pulled up her knees and wrapped her arms around them. "Is John dead?"

Logan didn't let any expression cross his face. Here, he had to be careful. The team wasn't ready to reveal all the intel they were still gathering. *Another reason we aren't slipping out of Mexico yet.* They could have gotten her out faster, but his team didn't like to leave loose ends behind. So a twenty-four-hour delay was standard protocol for them.

"I searched down that hallway," he told her, and he'd found the room they'd been holding her in. Seen the ropes on the floor near not one, but two chairs. *John had been there.* Only, no one had been in the room by the time Logan got there. "I didn't find another hostage."

"They got him out?"

He didn't want to lie to her. "Maybe." He'd been trained at deception for so long, sometimes he wondered what the truth was.

He took a slow step toward her. She didn't flinch away. That was something. "Did they…hurt you?"

She touched her cheek. He could see the faint bruise on

her flesh. "Not as much as they hurt John. They'd come in and take him away, and later, I'd hear his screams."

Another slow step, almost close enough to touch. "So they took you, but they never questioned you?"

"At first, they did." She licked her lips. Now wasn't the time to notice that her lips were as sexy as ever. It wasn't the time, but he still noticed. He'd always noticed too much with her.

Not for me. Why did he have a problem getting that fact through his head?

They were thrown together at the moment, but once they got back to the United States, they'd be going their separate ways. Nothing had changed for him. The senator's daughter wasn't going to wind up with the son of a killer.

And now he was a killer, too.

Logan glanced down at his hands. No blood to see, but he knew it stained his hands. After all these years, there was no way to ever get his hands clean. Too much death marked him.

He was good at killing. His old man had been right about that. They'd both been good....

Too good.

Logan sucked in a deep breath. *Focus.* The past was buried, just like his father. "So when they were…questioning you…" The team needed this info and he had to ask. "Just what did they want to know?"

Her chin lifted. "They wanted to know about my father." She paused. "What did he do this time?" Pain whispered beneath her words. Logan knew that Juliana had long ago dropped the rose-colored glasses when it came to her father.

As for what the guy had done this time…

Sold out his country, traded with an arms dealer, took

blood money and thought that he'd get away scot-free. A normal day's work for the senator. "I don't know," Logan said. The lies really were too easy. With her, it should have been harder.

She blinked. "You do." She stood slowly and came close to him. Juliana tilted her head back as she looked up at him. At six foot three, he towered over her smaller frame. "But you're not telling me."

Being the guy's daughter didn't give her clearance. Logan was on Uncle Sam's leash. The job was to get her home safely, not blow an operation that had been running in place for almost two years.

"What did you tell them about the senator?" Just how much did she know about his dark deeds?

"Nothing." Her eyes were on his, dark and gorgeous, just like he remembered. "I didn't tell them a thing about my father. I knew that if I talked they would just kill me once they had the information they needed."

Yeah, they would have. He hated that bruise on her cheek. "So you didn't talk, and they just left you alone?" Her story just didn't make sense. Unless Guerrero had been planning to use her as a bargaining tool and the guy had needed to keep her alive.

For a little longer, anyway.

Juliana shook her head and her hair slid against her chin. "When you found me…they'd taken me into the torture room." She laughed, the sound brittle and so at odds with the soft laughter from his memory. "They were going to *make* me talk then. The same way they made John talk."

But they'd waited four days. Not the standard M.O. for Guerrero's group. All the signs were pointing where he *didn't* want them to point. "This John…what did he look like?"

"Tall, dark…late twenties. He kept me sane, kept me talking all through those long hours."

Yes, Logan just bet he had. But "tall and dark" could be anyone. He needed more info than that.

"You get a good look at his face?" Logan asked.

She nodded.

He offered her what he hoped was an easy smile. "Good enough that you could probably talk to a sketch artist back in the States? Get us a clear picture?"

A furrow appeared between her eyes.

"We'll need to search the missing-person's database," he told her. *Liar, liar.* "A close image will help us find out exactly who John was."

She nodded and her lips twisted. "I can do better than meet with your sketch artist." Her shoulders moved in a little roll. "Give me a pencil and a piece of paper, and I'll draw John's image for you."

He tried not to let his satisfaction show. Juliana was an artist; he knew that. Sure, she usually worked with oils, but he remembered a time when she'd always carried a sketchbook with her.

She'd always been able to draw anything or anyone… in an instant.

"We'll want sketches of every man or woman you saw while you were being held."

Now her shoulders straightened. "Done."

Hell, yes. This could be just the break they needed.

"I want these men caught. I want them *stopped.*"

So did he, and Logan wasn't planning on backing off this mission, not until Guerrero was locked up.

The mission wasn't over. In fact, it might just be getting started.

He turned away from her. "Try to get some more sleep." They could take care of the sketches soon enough. For the moment, he needed to go talk with his team to tell them about his suspicions.

But she touched him. Her hand wrapped around his arm and every muscle in Logan's body tightened. "Why did you come for me? Why *you,* Logan?"

He glanced down at her hand. Touching him was dangerous. She should have remembered that. He'd always enjoyed the feel of her flesh against his far too much.

With Juliana, only with her, he'd never been able to hold back.

Maybe that was one of the reasons he'd run so far. He knew just how dangerous he could be to her.

"The senator came to our unit." Yes, that was his voice already hardening with desire—just from her touch. "He wanted you brought to safety."

"Your unit?" Her fingers tightened on him.

He gave a brief nod. "We're not exactly on the books." As far as the rest of the world was concerned, the EOD, or Elite Operations Division, didn't exist. The group, a hybrid formed of recruited navy SEALs, Rangers and intelligence officers from the FBI and CIA, was sent in for the most covert missions. Hostage retrieval. Extreme and unconventional warfare. They were the ones to take lethal, direct attacks...because some targets had to be taken out, no matter the cost.

"Does your unit—your team—have a name?"

Not an official one. "We're called the Shadow Agents." Their code name because their goal was to move as softly as a shadow. To stalk their prey and complete the mission with a minimum amount of exposure.

They always got the job done.

"My father really came to you? How did he even know you were—" Her hand fell away, and he missed her touch. Close enough to kiss, but never close enough to take.

It was the story of his life.

"He didn't come to *me* for help." The senator had nearly doubled over when he'd seen Logan sitting across the desk from him. "He came to my division, the EOD—the Elite Ops Division." Because the FBI had sent him there. The senator still had power and pull in D.C., enough connections to get an appointment with the EOD.

Juliana shook her head. "I didn't think he'd try to get me back." A whisper of the lost girl she'd been, so many years ago, trembled in her words. Lost…but not clueless.

She knew her father too well. The mission to Mexico hadn't just been about her. And if Juliana knew the full truth about the trade-off that had been made in that quiet D.C. office, she'd realize that she'd been betrayed by them both, again.

As if the first betrayal hadn't been hard enough for him to stomach. For years, he'd woken to find himself reaching for her and realizing that she'd forever be out of his hands.

But she's not out of reach right now.

He turned fully toward her, almost helpless, and caught her chin in his fingers. "I was getting you back." Logan recognized his mistake. He was letting this case get personal, and that was the last thing he should be doing.

Hands off. Get her on the plane. Deliver her home. Walk away.

But it had been so long since he'd held her. Even longer since he'd kissed her. One moment of weakness…would it really hurt? Would it really—

She rose onto her toes and kissed him.

Yes.

Logan let his control go. For that moment with her, he just let go. Logan's arms closed around her as he pulled her against him. Her breasts pushed against his chest, and he could feel the tight points of her nipples. She had perfect breasts. He remembered them so well. Pretty and pink and just right for his mouth.

And *her* mouth…nothing was better than her mouth. At twenty, she'd tasted of innocence. Now she tasted of need.

Seduction, at that moment, from her, wasn't what he'd expected. But it sure was what he wanted. His hands tightened around her, and he held her as close as he could. His tongue thrust against hers. The moan, low in her throat, was a sound he'd never forgotten. Arousal hardened his body as her hands slid under his shirt and her nails raked across his flesh.

She was hot. Wild.

But this was *wrong*.

So why wasn't he stopping? Why was he putting his hands on her curving hips and urging her up against the flesh that ached for her? Why was he pushing her back against the wall so that he could trap her there with his body?

Because I need her.

The addiction was just as strong as ever, just as dangerous to them both.

He jerked his head up and stared down at her. Juliana's breath panted out. Her lips were red, swollen from his mouth. He wanted to kiss her again. One hot minute wasn't close to making up for the past ten years.

A taste, when he was starving for the full course.

Get her naked. Take her.

She'd been through hell. She didn't need this. Him.

He sucked in a sharp breath and tasted her. "This can't happen," Logan said, voice growling.

At his words, the hunger, the passion that had been on her face and in her eyes cooled almost instantly.

"Julie—"

But she shoved against him. "Sorry."

He wasn't. Not for the kiss, anyway. For being a jerk and turning away? Yes.

But making love then, with his teammates in the next room? He wouldn't do that to her.

"I don't even know what I'm doing." She walked away from him and didn't look back. "I don't want this. I don't want—"

She broke off, but Logan stiffened because he could too easily finish her sentence.

You.

Adrenaline. The afterburn. He understood it, had been through enough battles and enough desperate hours after them to know what it was like when the spike of adrenaline filled your blood and then burned away.

He headed for the door and kept his shoulders straight, like the good soldier he was supposed to be. "You should try to get some more sleep."

They weren't out of the woods yet. Until they were back in the United States, until death wasn't hanging over her head, he would be her shadow.

That was his job.

Since they'd been forced together, he figured she deserved the warning he'd give her, and he'd tell her only once. "If I get you in my arms again like that…" His hand closed around the old doorknob, tightened, almost broke it off. Logan forced himself to exhale. *If I get you in my arms again…* He glanced back and found her wide, dark eyes on his. "I won't stop. I played the gentleman this time."

Right. Gentleman. Because he knew so much about that bit.

Her eyes said the same.

His jaw clenched. "I'll be damned if I do it again. You offer," he warned, "and I'll take."

Not the smooth words a woman needed to hear after her ordeal in captivity, but there wasn't much more he could say. So he left. While he still could.

And of course, Jasper was waiting for him in the other room. The guy lifted a blond brow. His face, one of those pretty-boy faces that always fooled the enemy, hinted at his amusement. "Now I get it," he drawled.

Angry, aroused, close to desperate, Logan barely bit back the crude retort that rose to his lips. But Jasper was a friend, a teammate.

"You're always looking for the blondes with dark eyes," Jasper teased as he tapped his chin. "Wherever we go, you usually seem to hook up with one."

He was right.

Jasper smirked. "Now I know why." The briefest pause as he studied Logan. "How do they all compare with the original model?"

Logan glared at his friend. *There is no comparison.* Instead of responding to Jasper, Logan stalked off to trade out for his guard shift.

SENATOR AARON JAMES stared down at the gun in his hands. Things weren't supposed to end this way. Not for him. He'd had such big plans.

Easy money. The perfect life. So much power.

And everything was falling apart, slipping away.

The phone on his desk rang. His private line. Jaw clenching, he reached for the receiver. "J-James." He hated the tremble in his voice. He wasn't supposed to be afraid. Everyone else was supposed to fear him.

Once, they had.

Until he'd met Diego Guerrero. Then he'd learned a whole new meaning of fear.

"She's dead." The voice was low, taunting. No accent. Just cold. Deadly.

Diego.

Aaron's hand clenched around the receiver. "Juliana wasn't part of this."

"You made her part of it."

His gaze dropped to the gun. "She's not dead." He'd gotten the intel, knew that Juliana had been rescued. The price for that rescue had been so high.

His life.

"You think this will stop me?" Laughter. "I'll hunt her down. I'll get what I want."

Diego and his men never stopped. Never. They'd once burned a whole village to the ground in order to send a message to rivals. *And I thought I could control him?* Perspiration slicked Aaron's palms. "I made the deals for you. The weapons were transferred. We're clear."

More laughter. "No, we're not. But we will be, once I get back the evidence you've been stashing."

Aaron's heart stopped.

"Did you think I didn't know about that? How else would you have gotten the agents to come for her? You made a trade, didn't you, James?"

"She's my daughter." He hadn't been able to let her just die. Once, she'd run to him, smiling, with her arms open. *I love you, Daddy.* So long ago. He'd wrecked their life together. Thrown it all away but…

I wasn't letting her die.

"I want the evidence."

He'd tried to be so careful. He'd written down the names, the dates of all the deals. He'd gotten recordings and created a safety net for himself.

But now he was realizing that he'd never be safe. Not from Guerrero.

"I'll get the evidence." A deadly promise from his caller. "I'll get you, and I'll *kill* her."

The phone line went dead.

Aaron swallowed once, twice, trying to relieve the dryness in his throat. Things had been going fine with Guerrero until...*I got greedy.*

So he'd taken a little extra money, just twenty million dollars. It had seemed so easy. Sneak a little money away from each deal. Aaron had considered the cash to be a... finder's fee, of sorts.

He'd found the ones who wanted the weapons. He'd set up the deals.

Didn't he deserve a bit of a bonus payment for his work? He'd thought so. But then Guerrero had found out. Guerrero had wanted the money back. When Guerrero started making his demands, Aaron had threatened to use the evidence he had against the arms dealer...

My mistake. Aaron now realized what a fool he'd been. You couldn't bluff against the man called El Diablo. The devil would never back down.

Instead of backing down, Guerrero had taken Juliana.

His eyes squeezed shut. Juliana was safe now, but how long would that safety last?

I'll get you, Guerrero had said. This nightmare wasn't going to end quietly. The press would find out about what he'd done. Everything he'd built—*gone.*

I'll kill her.

Juliana was his regret. He'd pulled her into this war, and she didn't even realize it.

Now she'd die, too.

No one ever really escaped Diego. No matter what promises Logan Quinn had made. You didn't get to cheat the devil and walk away.

The receiver began to hum. Fumbling, Aaron shoved the phone aside. Stared down the dark barrel of the gun.

He wouldn't lose everything, wouldn't be made a mockery on every late-night television show. And even when the public turned on him, Aaron knew he'd still be hunted by Guerrero.

There wasn't a choice. No way out. When Guerrero caught him, El Diablo would torture him. He'd make Aaron suffer for hours, days.

No, no, that wasn't the way that Aaron wanted to go out.

"I'm sorry, Juliana..."

JULIANA HELD HER BREATH as the small plane touched down, bounced and touched down again on a landing strip that she couldn't even see. Her hands were clenched tight in her lap, and she didn't make a sound. Fear churned in her, but she held on to her control with all her strength. The men and the woman with her weren't scared, or if they were, she sure couldn't tell.

The woman was flying them. Sydney—that was her name. Juliana had heard Logan call her Sydney once. The group hadn't exactly been chatty, but that was probably due to the whole life-and-death situation they had going on.

The plane bumped once more and then, thankfully, settled down. She felt the plane's speed begin to slow as it taxied down what she sincerely doubted was a real runway. They'd taken off from some dirt road in Mexico, so she figured they were probably landing in the middle of nowhere.

"And we're back in America," Logan murmured from beside her with a flash that could have been a brief grin.

She pushed her fingers against her jean-clad thighs.

The better to wipe the sweat off her hands. "Does this mean I'm safe again?" she asked. He'd been her shadow nearly every moment. Close but not touching. And that was fine, right? She didn't want him touching her.

"This means..." He leaned forward and unhooked the seat belt that had kept her steady during the bumps and dives of the flight. "It means that it's time for you to get your life back." His face came close to hers. The face that she'd never forgotten. His black hair had once curled lightly but now was cut brutally short.

The old adage was annoyingly true—a girl really did never forget her first lover.

Over the years, Logan had grown harder. A thin scar under his chin looked as if it could have been a knife wound. And his eyes now creased with fine lines. No one else had eyes that shade of bright blue.

Only Logan.

Right then, his lips were only inches away. Had she really kissed him hours before? At the time, it had seemed like a good plan. Some hot, fast action to chase away the chill that had sunk into her bones.

John is dead. She'd left him behind, and he'd died.

She'd almost died, too, and she'd been so scared. Had it been so wrong to want to feel alive? For just a few moments?

Then Logan had pulled away from her.

Again.

Apparently, it had been wrong. Same story, same verse. Logan Quinn wasn't interested.

And she wanted to forget. She wanted passion, not just him.

Not. Just. Him.

They climbed out of the plane. The guy called Gunner went first, sweeping out with his weapon up. Logan stayed by her side. A giant bodyguard who took every step with her.

Two black SUVs waited for them. Logan steered her to the front one. Climbed in and slammed the door behind him.

As soon as he and Gunner were inside, the SUV started moving. The driver tossed back a cell phone to Logan. "Another mission down, Alpha One."

She glanced over and found Logan's eyes on her. Should a man's gaze really feel like a burn? His did.

He had the cell to his ear. Who was he calling already?

"Alpha One checking in," he said into the phone. "Package delivered safely."

Being referred to as a package grated. She wasn't a package. She was a person.

Juliana glanced away from him. Empty landscape flew by them. Miles of dry dirt, dotted occasionally by small bursts of struggling green brush.

"Sir?" Logan's voice was tight as he talked to whoever was on the other end of the line. "Yes, sir. I understand."

The called ended. Short. Sweet.

"Juliana..." He caught her right hand. Oh, now he was back to touching? "I'm sorry," he told her, and he actually sounded as if he was.

Curious now, she glanced over at him. "For what?"

Logan's handsome face was strained and his bright blue eyes told her the news was going to be very bad even before he said, "Senator James is dead."

Chapter Three

The hits just kept on coming for her. Logan watched Juliana, clad in a black dress that skimmed her curves, as she
bent and placed a red rose on her father's closed casket.

No one had been able to glimpse the body—folks didn't
need to witness the sight left after a gunshot blast to the
head.

His team had been with Juliana for the past four days.
They'd stood guard, making sure that she returned to
Jackson, Mississippi, without any further incident. Once
in town, his team had taken over a group of rooms at a
local hotel. He'd insisted that Juliana stay at the hotel, too,
so that his team could keep a better eye on her. At first,
she'd balked, but he hadn't backed down. His instincts
had been screaming at him, and Logan hadn't wanted to
let Juliana out of his sight.

He'd expected her to cry at the news of her father's
death. After all that she'd been through, she was entitled
to her tears.

She hadn't cried once.

Her back was too straight as she walked away from
the casket. Mourners began to file past her. One after the
other. All offering their condolences and stopping to give
her a hug or a pat on the shoulder.

Logan watched from his position underneath the

sweeping branches of a magnolia tree. The fresh scent of the magnolias was in the air. That scent had reminded him of her. The first time they'd kissed, they'd been under a magnolia tree. It had been raining.

She'd trembled against him.

"You know what we have to do," Gunner said from beside him.

Logan spared him a glance. Gunner's gaze was on Juliana, his face tense. Gunner was the quiet type, quiet but deadly. A Spanish father and a Native American mother had given him dark gold skin and the instincts of a hunter. He'd been trained early on a reservation, learned to hunt and stalk prey at his grandfather's knee. A lethal SOB, Gunner was one of the few people on earth who Logan actually called friend. He was also the best SEAL sniper that Logan had ever met.

"Knowing it and liking it…" Logan said with a sigh and tried to force his tense body to relax. "Those are two very different things." But the orders had come down from high above. There wasn't a choice on this one.

With the senator out of the picture, Juliana was now their key to cracking Guerrero.

She'd created the sketches for them. Of Guerrero's goons and of the man she'd called John. Perfect sketches that had even included slight moles on some of the men. Her artist's eyes had noted their every feature. Juliana truly was a perfect witness.

One that Guerrero would never let escape.

It was the picture of John Gonzales that intrigued Logan and his men the most. An innocent man, or so Juliana claimed. Another hostage who'd been taken and tortured by Guerrero.

Except John Gonzales wasn't listed as missing in any database. He wasn't turning up in any intel from the CIA or the FBI. As far as they were concerned, John Gonzales didn't exist.

"You think Guerrero's gonna make a hit on her?" Gunner asked as his gaze swept the crowd.

They weren't there to pay respects to the senator. Neither of them had respected Aaron James worth a damn. They were there for guard duty.

The mission wasn't over. Not by a long shot.

"The boss does." Because Logan wasn't the man in control at the EOD. But this time, he agreed. Every instinct Logan had screamed that Juliana wasn't clear, not yet.

She had to be here today, though. Senator James was being laid to rest. Unfortunately, he wasn't taking his demons with him.

The crowd began to clear away. It was a high-profile funeral, with government officials spilling out for their photo ops. Lots of plainclothes security were scattered around, even some folks Logan recognized from the Secret Service.

In particular, he'd noticed that two men and one woman in black suits stayed close to Juliana. On-loan protection. Those three were so obvious, but maybe that was the point. The Secret Service liked to be in-your-face some days.

"You really up for what you'll have to do?"

Logan paused. He knew what Gunner was asking. Could he look right into Juliana's eyes and lie to her? Over and over again? That was what needed to be done, and because of their past, he was the prime candidate for the job.

The man who was supposed to slip close to Juliana, to stay by her side. He'd be her protection, and she just thought he'd be—

Her lover.

"Yes." His voice dropped to a growl. "I'll do what needs to be done." Another betrayal. But he didn't trust any other agent to get this close to her. Not even Gunner.

Especially not Gunner.

The operative on this mission had to stay with Juliana. Day and night.

Only me.

He headed for her. He knew his glasses covered his eyes, so no one would be able to tell he wasn't exactly in the mourning mood. Good. No need to put on a mask just yet.

A long black limo waited for Juliana. The door was open. She'd already turned away from Logan and headed for the vehicle.

As he closed in on his prey, a woman with blond hair—perfectly twisted at the nape of her neck—and wearing a tight black dress wrapped her arms around Juliana. Logan's eyes narrowed as he recognized Susan Walker, one of the late senator's assistants. Logan's team had questioned her for hours, but she'd seemed clueless about the true nature of the senator's activities.

"I can't believe he's really gone," Susan whispered, and a tremble shook her body. "This shouldn't have happened. We had so many plans…."

A tall, dark-haired male walked up behind her and put a comforting hand on her shoulder. Thin black glasses were perched on his nose. Logan knew him, of course. Ben McLintock. Another assistant to the senator. One who hadn't broken during the interview process, but still… he'd been nervous.

McLintock glanced over his shoulder and spotted Logan. The guy swallowed quickly and bobbed his head. *Too nervous.* The EOD was already ripping into his life.

As soon as they turned over some info they could use, something that would tie him in with the senator's illegal deals...

Then we'll have another talk, McLintock. Logan wouldn't play so nicely during their next little chat.

"Juliana needs to get home," Ben said as he pulled Susan back. "You can both talk more there."

"Yes, yes, you're right." Susan's thin shoulders straightened. She looked toward the casket again. She shook her head and turned away from the limo. "It just seems like a dream."

Ben took her hand but his eyes were on Juliana. "You have my deepest sympathies."

Juliana's eyes were dry. Her face too pale.

"I never...*never*...thought things would end this way."

The senator had surprised them all. Logan wasn't even sure why the guy had done it. Had the senator thought that if he were out of the picture, Guerrero would back off? That Juliana would be safe?

"I'm truly sorry," Ben told her and bent to press a kiss to Juliana's right cheek.

Logan's back teeth locked. Mr. Touchy-Feely could move the hell on anytime. He could spend some quality moments comforting Susan Walker...

And he could stay away from Juliana.

"I need some time...some air..." Susan said, then staggered back as tears trickled down her cheeks. "I can't leave him...."

The woman's body trembled, and Logan wondered if her knees were about to give way. He tensed, preparing to lunge forward.

But it was good old Ben to the rescue. He kept a firm hold on Susan and steered her away from the vehicle. "I'll take care of her." He offered Juliana a firm nod. "We'll meet you back at the house." Then he glanced at Logan.

Logan gave him a shark's smile. "Don't worry, I'll make sure that she arrives home safe and sound."

Other cars began to pull away. Logan spared a glance for the crowd. Juliana still hadn't met his stare, and that fact was pissing him off. He wanted to take her into his arms, hold her, comfort her. But the woman might as well have been wearing a giant keep-away sign.

The trouble was…he'd always had a problem keeping away from her.

Ben and Susan slowly walked away. They stopped under a big oak, and Susan's shoulders shook as she cried.

"I can't do that." Juliana's voice was just a whisper. "Everyone is staring at me, waiting for me to cry, but I can't." Finally, she glanced at him with those dark, steal-a-man's-soul eyes. "What's wrong with me?"

"Not a damn thing." And he didn't care what the others wanted. The reporters—they were just eager for a clip of the grieving daughter so that they could flash her picture all over their TVs. As for all the senator's so-called friends…Logan knew when tears were real and when they weren't.

Better to not cry at all and still feel than to weep when you didn't feel any emotion.

Her lower lip quivered and she caught it between her teeth. Helpless, Logan reached out and caught her hand. "Come with me," he told her.

She stared up at him. Light raindrops began to fall on them. Did she remember the last time they'd stood in the rain?

I need to forget. But that magnolia scent teased his nose.

Sometimes you could never forget.

Logan shrugged out of his jacket and lifted it over Juliana's head. "I want you to come with me."

Juliana didn't move. "You're not supposed to be here." Shaking her head, she said, "I saw you standing under that tree, watching me…but you're not supposed to be here. You should have gone back to Washington or Virginia… or wherever it is that you belong."

For now, he belonged with her.

The rain came down harder now.

"Miss James?" It was the limo driver. He was an older guy with graying red hair. The rain was already dampening his dark suit, but he didn't seem to mind. He stared at Juliana, and there was concern—what looked like *real* concern—in his gaze. Not that fake mask most folks had been sporting for the funeral.

Not hardly.

"She won't be taking the limo," Logan said as he moved in closer to Juliana. "We need to talk," he whispered to her.

She nodded. Drops of rain were on her eyelashes. Or were those tears?

She glanced back at the driver. "Thank you, Charles, but I'll be getting a ride back to the house with Mr. Quinn."

The driver hesitated. "Are you sure?" The look he shot toward Logan was full of suspicion.

After a moment's hesitation, Juliana nodded. "Yes." She cleared her throat. "Thanks for all you've done today… I just… You've always been so good to me."

Charles offered her a sad smile. "And you've been good to me." He gave her a little salute and shoved the back door closed. "Take care of her," he said to Logan.

I intend to do just that.

Logan caught Juliana's hand and steered her away from

the grave. "I'm not leaving town yet," he told her. "In fact, I'm going to be staying in Jackson for a while."

Her eyes widened. "Why?"

They were moving faster now. His truck waited just a few steps away. There was no sign of Gunner. "Because I want to be with you."

Her lips parted in surprise. "But— *What?*"

An engine cranked. The limo. It would be pulling away soon, then they could—

The explosion threw Logan right off his feet. The heat of the fire lanced his skin and lifted him up into the air. He clutched Juliana, holding her as best he could. They flew through the air and slammed against the same magnolia tree he'd stood under moments before.

Son of a bitch.

"Juliana!" Fear nearly froze his heart.

But she was fine. She pushed against him, and he raised up to see a gash bleeding on her forehead. Her eyes were wide and horrified with understanding. "Oh, my God," she whispered and her head turned toward the burning remains of the limo. "The driver..."

There wasn't anything they could do for the poor guy now. Logan didn't waste time speaking. He grabbed Juliana, lifted her into his arms and raced for his pickup.

Gunner was out there. He'd seen what happened—he'd be radioing for backup and making sure EMT personnel were called. There were injured people on the ground, folks who'd been burned and blasted. Law enforcement who'd been at the funeral were swarming as they tried to figure out what was happening.

Chaos. That was happening.

Logan kept running. Right then, Juliana was his only priority. The others would have to attend to the injured. He had to get her out of there.

"Logan, put me down! We've got to help them! Stop it, just *stop!*" Fury thundered in her words as she fought wildly against his hold.

That fury didn't slow him a bit. With one arm, he yanked open the truck's passenger-side door, and with the other, he pushed her inside.

She immediately tried to jump out.

"Don't." A lethal warning. Fury rode him, too. She'd come too close to death. He could have stood there and watched her die. "Who do you think that bomb was meant for? The driver...or you?"

Juliana paled even more and shook her head. "But... the people... They're hurt..."

She'd always had that soft spot. A weakness that just might get her killed one day.

But not today. "Stay in the truck." He slammed the door and raced around to the driver's side. Two seconds later, he was in the truck, and they were roaring away from the scene.

The limo was supposed to have been swept for bombs. Every vehicle linked to her should have been swept. Someone had screwed up, and Juliana had almost paid for that mistake with her life.

The driver had.

"That was...an accident, right?"

The woman was trying to lie to herself. "I don't think so."

Sirens wailed behind them. Logan glanced in his rearview mirror and saw the dark clouds of smoke billowing up into the air. His gaze turned toward the road as he shoved the gas pedal down to the floorboard. The truck's motor roared.

His hands tightened on the wheel. *A deadly mistake.*

"But…it's safe now." She just sounded lost. "It's *supposed* to be safe."

From the corner of his eye, he saw her hands clench in her lap. Her voice came, soft, confused. "You said…you said once I got back to the U.S., I'd be safe."

"I was wrong."

LOGAN TOOK HER to a cheap hotel on the outskirts of Jackson. She didn't talk any more during the drive. She couldn't. Every time she opened her mouth to speak, Juliana could taste ash on her tongue.

I'm sorry, Charles. He'd been with her father for over twenty years. To die like that…

She swallowed. *More ash.*

The truck braked. She followed Logan, feeling like a robot. Only, her steps were slow, wooden. He tossed a wad of cash at the desk clerk and ordered the kid to forget that he ever saw them. Then they pushed inside the last room, the one located at the edge of the parking lot.

A ceiling fan fluttered overhead when Logan flipped the light switch. Juliana's gaze swept around the small room. A sagging bed. *One* bed. A scarred desk. A lumpy chair. The place had *pay-by-the-hour* written all over it.

"You're bleeding."

Juliana glanced over at the sound of Logan's voice. She saw that his stare was focused on her forehead. Lifting her hand, she touched the drying blood. She'd forgotten about that. "It's just a scratch."

Her dress was torn, slitting up a bit at the knee. And said knee felt as if it had slammed into a tree—because it had.

"You're too calm."

What? Was she supposed to be screaming? Breaking

down? She wasn't exactly the breaking-down type. Right then, all she could think was…

What's next?

And how would she handle it?

"Shock." He took her hand and led her to the match-box bathroom. "Let's get you cleaned up."

She wrenched away from him as anger began to finally boil past the numbness holding her in check. "I'm not a child, Logan."

He blinked his sky-blue eyes at her. The brightest blue she'd ever seen. Those eyes could burn hot or flash ice-cold. Right then, they held no emotion at all. "I never said you were."

"I can clean myself up." She took slow, measured steps to the bathroom. Took slow, deep breaths—so she wouldn't scream at him. "Stop acting like I'm about to fall apart."

"Someone just tried to *kill* you. A little falling apart is expected."

Near the chipped bathroom door, Juliana paused and looked back at him. "Why do the expected?"

He stared at her as if he'd never seen her before. Maybe he hadn't. "Your father's gone." Now there was anger punching through his words. "Your car just exploded into a million pieces all over a graveyard. Want to tell me why you're so cool?"

Because if she let the wall inside of herself down, even for a second, Juliana was very afraid that she might start crying and not stop. "Wanna tell me why you're with me now?"

"Because you need someone to keep you alive!" Then he was charging across the room and catching her shoulders in a strong grip. "Or do you not even care about the little matter of living anymore?"

She stared up at him. Just stared. She was finding that being so close to Logan hurt. Over him? Not hardly. Once upon a time, she'd been ready to run away with the jerk.

She'd waited for him in a bus station—waited five hours.

He'd never shown. Too late, she'd learned that he'd left her behind.

Could she really count on him to keep sticking around now? He'd saved her butt in Mexico. Hell, yes, she was grateful, but Logan wasn't the kind to stay forever. Juliana wasn't going to depend on him again. "Call the cops," she told him, weary beyond belief all of a sudden. Her body just wanted to sag, and she wanted to sleep. An adrenaline burst fading? Or just the crash she'd been fighting for days? Either way, the result was the same. "They can keep me safe."

Juliana opened the door and entered the closet that passed for a bathroom.

"Juliana—"

Then she closed the door in his face. She looked in the mirror. Saw the too-pale face, wide eyes and the blood that covered her forehead.

She took another breath. *Ash.* How long would it be until she forgot that taste?

Her eyes squeezed shut. She could still feel the lance of fire on her skin. If Logan hadn't been there, she would've been in that car.

And it would've been pieces of *her* that littered that cemetery.

LOGAN TURNED AWAY when he heard the sound of the shower. He yanked out his phone and punched the number for his boss. "What the hell happened?" he demanded when the line was answered. "The site should have been safe, it should have—"

"You aren't secure." Flat. Bruce Mercer was never the type to waste words or emotion. "We need you to get the woman and get out of that hotel. Backup is en route."

Not secure? For the moment, they were. "No one followed me. No one—"

"There's a leak in the senator's office," Mercer said in his perfectly polished voice. A voice that, right then, gave no hint of his New Jersey roots. Those roots only came out when Mercer was stressed—and very little ever stressed him. "Money talks, and we all know that Guerrero has a ton of money."

More than enough money to make certain one woman died.

"You need to bring her in," the boss ordered. "We're setting up a meet location. Tell her she'll be safe with you. Get her to trust you."

Yes, that had been the plan...until the cemetery caught fire. "We're still going through with this?" He almost crushed the phone. The shower was still running. Juliana couldn't hear him, but just in case, Logan took a few cautious steps across the room.

"The plan remains the same. You know how vital this case is to the department."

"I don't want to put her in the line of fire." She'd come close enough to death.

"That's why you're there, Alpha One. To come between her and any fire...just like you did today."

Yes, he had the burn marks on his skin to prove it.

"Your relationship to her is key. You know that. Get her trust, and we can close this case and finally put Guerrero away."

But could they keep her alive long enough to do it?

A pause hummed on the line. "Does she realize what's happening?" Mercer wanted to know.

"She realizes that she's targeted for death." Any fool would realize that. Juliana wasn't a fool.

Once, she'd been too trusting. Was she still? The idea of using her trust burned almost as much as those flames had.

"Have you told her about John?"

The shower shut off. His jaw clenched. "Not yet."

"Do it. The sooner she realizes that you're her only hope of staying alive, the sooner we get her cooperation."

It wasn't just about keeping her alive. The EOD wanted to use her. They were willing to set her up if it meant getting the job done.

Logan exhaled. "When are we moving her?"

"Ten minutes."

The line died.

Ten minutes. Too little time to convince Juliana that he was the only one she could trust to keep her alive.

JULIANA WAS CLIMBING OUT of the shower when her cell phone rang. She'd washed away the blood and ash, but the icy water had done nothing to soothe the aches and pains in her body. She'd cried beneath that pounding water. Juliana hadn't been able to hold back the tears any longer. Her whole body had trembled as she let her grief and pain pour out of her. Part of Juliana had just wanted to let the grief take control, but she'd fought that instinct. Gathering all of her strength, she'd managed to stop the tears. Managed to get her wall of self-control back in place.

As the phone rang again, she grabbed for the dress

she'd tossed aside moments before and pulled her phone from the near-invisible pocket. Her fingertip slid across the smooth surface. Ben McLintock. Her father's aide. The guy had to be frantic. She answered the call, lifting the phone to her ear as she said, "Ben, listen, I'm all right. I—"

The bathroom door crashed open. Juliana gasped and jumped back. Logan stood in the doorway, eyes fierce. "End the call."

"Juliana!" Ben's voice screeched. "Where are you? I searched for you after the explosion, but you'd vanished! Oh, God, at first—at first I thought you were in the car!"

She almost had been.

"Then a cop remembered seeing you jump into a truck." His breath heaved over the line. "They're saying it looks like a car bomb, it looks like—"

"I'm in a motel, Ben. I—"

Logan took the phone from her. Ended the call with a fast shove of his fingers. A muscle flexed in his jaw. "GPS tracking. Your phone just told him exactly where we are."

His gaze swept over her. Crap, she was just wearing a towel, one that barely skimmed the tops of her thighs even while her breasts pushed against the loose fold she'd made to secure the terry cloth. He'd seen her in less plenty of times, but that had been a long time ago.

Juliana grabbed her dress and held it in front of her body. It was a much better shield than the thin towel. "No one is tracking me, okay, Rambo? That was just Ben. He was worried and wanted to make sure—"

"Guerrero has a man in your father's office. Someone willing to trade you for a thick wad of cash." His eyes blazed hotter, and they were focused right on—

"Eyes up," she told him, aware of the hot burn in her cheeks.

Those eyes, when they met hers, flashed with a need she didn't want to acknowledge right then.

"I know how this works," he told her. "And I sure as hell know that we have to move now."

GPS tracking. Yes, she knew that was possible, but... "Why? Why can't they just let me go?" Her father was dead. Shouldn't that be the end with Guerrero?

Logan didn't speak.

"Turn around," she snapped.

His brows rose but he slowly turned, giving her a view of his broad back. Juliana dropped the dress and towel and yanked on her underwear—a black bra and matching panties—as fast as she could. Her gaze darted to his back and—

Wait, had he been watching her in the mirror? She couldn't tell for certain, but for a moment there, she'd sworn she saw his gaze cut to the mirror.

To her reflection.

"Done yet?" he asked, almost sounding bored. Almost.

Eyes narrowing, Juliana yanked on her dress. With trembling hands, she fumbled and pulled up the zipper. All while Logan stood right there. "Done," she gritted out. *Not even trying to play the gentleman now.* "My father is dead. Why do they want to bury me, too?"

He turned to face her. His gaze swept over her. Made her chilled skin suddenly feel too hot. "Because you're a witness they can't afford." He caught her elbow and led her back through the small hotel room. He paused at the door, glanced outside.

"A witness?" Yes, she'd seen the faces of a few men in Mexico, but...

"Did you know that no witness has ever been able to

positively identify Diego Guerrero? The man's a ghost. The U.S. and Mexican governments both know the hell he brings, but no one has been able to so much as touch him."

She pulled on her pumps. Useless for running but she felt strangely vulnerable in bare feet. "Well, I didn't see the guy, either. The big boss man never came in when I was being held." He'd left the torture for his flunkies.

Logan shot her a fast, hard stare. "Yes, he did come in."

She blinked.

"From what we can tell, he spent more time with you than he ever has with anyone else. You saw his face. You talked to him."

Wrong. "No, I didn't. I—"

"John Gonzales is one of the aliases that Guerrero uses."

My name's...John. John Gonzales. She remembered the voice from the darkness. *Who are you?*

"He didn't need to torture information out of you, Juliana. All he had to do was ask for it in the dark."

And they'd talked for so many hours. Her heart slammed into her chest.

"You weren't talking to another hostage in that hell-hole." Logan exhaled on a low sigh. "My team believes you were talking to the number-one weapons dealer in Mexico—the man his enemies call El Diablo because he never, ever leaves anyone alive who can ID him."

Goose bumps rose on her arms.

"That man with you? The one you were so desperate to save? *That* was Diego Guerrero."

Oh, hell. "Logan..."

A fist pounded on the door.

Logan didn't move but she jumped. "I need you to trust me," he told her. "Whatever happens, you have to stay with me, do you understand? Guerrero's tracked you. He'll use anything and anyone he can in order to get to you."

The door shook again. There was only one entrance and exit to that room. Unless they were going to crawl out that tiny window in the bathroom…

"I can keep you alive," Logan promised, eyes intense. "It's what I do."

Her father had told her that he was an assassin. That for years Logan's job had been to kill.

But he'd saved her life twice already.

"This is the police!" a voice shouted. "Miss James, you need to come out! We're here to help you."

Logan's smile was grim. "It's not the police. When we open that door, it might look like them—"

Nightmare. This is a—

"—but it won't be them. They'll either kill you outright or deliver you to Guerrero." His voice was low, hard with intensity. "I'm your best bet. You might hate me—"

No, she didn't. Never had. Just one of their problems…

"—but you know no matter what you have to face on the other side of that door—"

Cops? Maybe more killers?

"—I'll keep you safe."

"We're comin' in!" the voice shouted. "We're comin'—"

Gunfire exploded. Juliana didn't scream, not this time. She clamped her mouth closed, choked back the scream that rose in her throat and dived for cover.

Logan jumped for the window. He knocked out the glass, took aim and—

Smiled.

From her position on the floor, Juliana watched that cold grin slip over his face. She expected him to start firing, but…

But she heard the sound of a car racing away. Tires squealed.

And Logan stalked to the door. He yanked it open.

The man he'd called Gunner stood on the other side.

Juliana scrambled to her feet. "The cops?"

"Those trigger-happy idiots weren't cops." Gunner shrugged. "A few shots sent them running fast enough, but I'm betting those same shots will have the real cops coming our way soon enough." His eyes, so dark they were almost black, swept over her. "There's a hit on you. A very, very high price on that pretty head. So unless you want the next funeral to be your own…"

"I don't."

Logan offered his hand to her. "Then you'll come with me."

In order to keep living, she'd do anything that she had to do.

Juliana took his hand, and they ran past the now bullet-scarred side of the hotel and toward the waiting SUV.

Trust…it looked as if she had to give it to him.

Because there was no other choice for her.

DIEGO GUERRERO STARED at the television. The pretty, little reporter talked in an excited rush as the camera panned behind her to take in the destruction at the cemetery.

Smoke still drifted lazily in the air.

"Police aren't talking with the media yet," she said, "but a source has revealed that the limousine destroyed in that explosion was the car used by Juliana James, daughter of Senator Aaron James. Juliana was laying her father to rest after his suicide—"

Juliana's old man had been a coward until the end.

"—when the explosion rocked the service."

No, it hadn't rocked the service. The blast had erupted *after* the service. His sources were better than hers.

"One man was killed in the explosion—"

The driver had been collateral damage. There was always collateral damage.

"—while four others were injured. Juliana James left the scene and is now in an undisclosed location."

His eyes narrowed. The reporter rambled on, saying nothing particularly useful. After a moment, he shut off the television, then turned slowly to face his first in command.

Luis Sanchez swallowed, the movement stretching the crisscross of scars on his throat. The man was already sweating.

"Was I not clear?" Diego asked softly.

"Sí," Luis rasped. His damaged voice was often limited to rough rasps and growls.

"Then, if I told you—clearly—that I wanted Juliana James brought back to me alive—" he shrugged, a seemingly careless move, but it still caused Luis to flinch "—why did she nearly die today?"

Luis shifted from his right foot to his left. "I heard… word on the street is that…s-someone else has a hit on her. They're offering top dollar…for her dead body."

Now, that gave him pause. "Who?"

"D-don't know, but I will find out. I will—"

"You will," Diego agreed, "or you'll be the one dying." He never made idle threats. Luis understood that. Luis had been with him for five years—and he'd witnessed Guerrero carry out all of his…*promises* to both friends and enemies.

"Put the word out that Juliana James isn't to be touched." Except by him. They had unfinished business. She couldn't die, not yet. He needed her to keep living a bit longer. "And when you find the one who put out this hit—" he leaned forward and softly ordered "—you make his death hurt."

Because *no one* interfered with Diego's plans. *No one*.

Chapter Four

The place wasn't exactly what she'd expected. Juliana glanced around the small elevator from the corner of her eye. When Logan had said that he was taking her in for a briefing with his team, she'd figured they'd go somewhere that was…official.

Not so much a hole-in-the-wall.

From the outside, the building hadn't even looked inhabited. Just a big, rough wooden building. Maybe three stories.

But Logan had led the way inside, walking with sure steps. Now they were riding up the creaking elevator, and Juliana was forcing herself to take slow, deep breaths.

She'd cried in the shower. She hadn't been able to help herself. But she wouldn't, couldn't cry now. Now wasn't the time for weakness.

The elevator came to a hard stop, jarring Juliana and sending her stumbling into Logan. The guy didn't so much as move an inch, of course, because he was like some kind of military superhuman, but his arms closed around her.

"I've got you."

That was her problem. Being with him—it was just making everything more painful.

She pulled away and saw a muscle flex in his jaw. "I'm fine." The doors were sliding open. Very, very slowly. "Is this the best that the EOD could do?" The EOD. He'd told her a little more about the EOD on the drive over, but the information that he'd given her regarding the Shadow Agents just hadn't been enough to satisfy her curiosity.

When she'd tried to press him, she'd gotten a just-the-facts-ma'am type of routine. That hadn't been good enough. Juliana had kept pressing. The need-to-know routine was getting on her nerves.

Logan had told her that the EOD was composed of individuals from different military and government backgrounds. Their missions were usually highly classified.

And very, very dangerous.

A situation tailor-made for Logan and his team.

"On short notice, this building was the best we could find in terms of providing us with a low-profile base," a woman's voice told her, and Juliana glanced up to see Sydney walking toward them. Sydney stared at Logan with one raised eyebrow. "We were starting to wonder if you'd gotten lost."

He growled. Was that a response? Juliana guessed so, because in the next instant, they were all heading down a narrow hallway. A fast turn, then they entered an office. One that didn't look nearly as run-down as the rest of the place. Two laptops and a stash of weapons were on the right. Some empty chairs waited to the left.

Juliana gladly slumped into the nearest chair.

I can still feel the fire on my skin. Even the cold water from the shower hadn't been able to wash away that memory. Juliana rubbed her hands over her arms and caught Logan's narrow-eyed glance.

The guy watched her too much. Like a hawk.

She cleared her throat, glanced away from him and saw the others file into the room. No masks this time. Just tough, fierce fighters.

The woman was already sitting down near the side of the table. Sydney. Juliana had no idea what the woman's last name was. She was booting up her laptop while a big, blond male leaned over her shoulder.

Gunner closed the door, sealing them inside, and he flashed her a broad grin. Was that grin supposed to be reassuring? It looked like a smile that a tiger would give the prey he was about to eat.

The silence in the room hit her then, and Juliana realized that everyone was just…staring at her. Hell, had she missed something?

"You understand why you must have protection, right?" Sydney pressed. Juliana realized the woman must have asked the question before.

Her breath eased out slowly as her gaze swept over them. "Tell me your names." A simple thing, maybe, but she was tired of being in the dark. From this point on, she expected to be in the loop about everything.

"I'm Sydney," the woman said with a slow blink, "and I…um, believe that you know Logan pretty well."

Too well. She would *not* blush right then. She was way past the blushing point. An exploding car made a woman forget embarrassment.

"I'm Gunner," the big guy to the right said. His dark hair fell longer than Logan's, and his eyes—no eyes should be so dark and so cold.

Juliana glanced at the last man. The blond wasn't leaning over Sydney any longer. He'd taken a seat next to her. His arm brushed against hers.

"Jasper," he said. Just that. More rumble than anything else.

Gunner frowned at the guy, and his dark, cold gaze lingered on the arm that Jasper had pressed against Sydney.

Ah…okay. "First names only, huh?" Juliana murmured. That was nice and anonymous.

"For now, it's safer that way," Logan said.

Right. Though Juliana wasn't even sure any of them had given their real names. She put her fingers into her lap, twisting them together. "How are you going to stop the man who is after me?"

Sydney and Logan shared a brief look. Juliana's shoulders tensed. She wasn't going to like this part; she knew it even before Logan said, "Your father…made a deal with the EOD." Logan's quiet voice shouldn't have grated, but it did.

Juliana forced herself to meet his stare. "What sort of deal?" She needed to know all of her father's dark secrets, whether she wanted to hear them or not. It wasn't the time to wear blinders.

"Your safety, your life, in return for evidence that he had against Diego Guerrero."

Guerrero. Her heart slammed into her ribs. The man that Logan had told her was the same guy she knew as John Gonzales.

"What did my father—" Her voice sounded too weak. *Don't be weak.* Juliana tried again. "Just what was my father doing with this Guerrero?"

"Selling out his country." From the one called Jasper. When he spoke and she heard the drawl of Texas sliding beneath his words, Juliana remembered him.

Maybe he expected her to flinch at the blunt charge, but she didn't. She just sat there. She'd known her father wasn't exactly good for a long time.

"The senator facilitated deals between Guerrero and foreign officials," Jasper said with his eyes narrowed on her. "Your father would find the people who needed the weapons, those desperate for power, those ready to over-throw weak governments…"

Her father had made so many connections over the years. He'd been on dozens of committees, and he'd told her once that he'd been working hard to make the world a better place.

Better? Not from the sound of things. Just more bloody, more dangerous.

"We're talking about billions of dollars' worth of weapons," Jasper continued. "From what we can tell, your father took a nice little finder's fee for every deal he made."

She swallowed and forced her hands to unclench. "You're saying my father took a commission from Guerrero? That every time weapons were sold—" *every time people died when those weapons were used* "—he got a slice of the pie."

Jasper nodded grimly.

"He was a good man," she had to say it. Someone did. He wasn't even cold in the ground. "Once." She could remember it, couldn't she? If she tried hard enough, the memories were there. "Before my mother died. He went to Congress to make the world better."

Only, he'd wound up working to destroy it.

Was that why he'd put the gun to his own head? Because he couldn't live with what he'd done?

You left me behind to deal with everything, all on my own.

Sometimes it seemed as if he'd left her that hot summer night when her mother died in the car accident on a lonely stretch of Mississippi road.

"He wanted to save you," Logan said, the words deep and rumbling. His hand took hers. Almost helplessly, her gaze found his. "He agreed to trade every bit of evidence he had on Guerrero in order to get you home alive."

"So that's why you—your team came for me." In that hell. "Because my father paid you with his evidence."

"He didn't exactly make the payment...." Gunner muttered as he ran an agitated hand through his hair. "He put a bullet in his head instead."

Juliana flinched.

Logan surged to his feet. His chair fell to the floor behind him with a clatter. Logan lunged for the other man. "Gunner..."

Gunner just shrugged, but he hurriedly backed up a few feet. "Payment was due at delivery, right? As soon as you were brought back safe and sound, Senator James was going to give us the intel we needed. Only, instead of delivering, he chose to...renegotiate."

Juliana could only shake her head. This...*this* was the last thing she'd expected when Logan had brought her in to meet with the other agents. "I *buried* him today."

"And because of Guerrero's deals, hundreds of people are buried every single day," Sydney said, her voice soft and lacking the leashed fury that seemed to vibrate beneath Gunner's words. "We have to stop him. You have to help us."

"How? I saw Guerrero, but..." But she'd already told them that. She'd sketched out half a dozen pictures. Done everything that she could. "Now he wants me dead."

Logan shoved Gunner into the nearest wall. "You aren't dying." He tossed that back without glancing her way. His focused fury was on the other man.

Sydney cleared her throat. "Your father...indicated that you had the evidence we need."

Her words had Juliana blinking in surprise. "I don't. I didn't even know about Guerrero until—I just thought I was being held with a man named John Gonzales, until Logan told me the truth! John said that he'd been kidnapped just like me. When those men put me in the room, John was already there. I didn't know he was Guerrero, and I don't know anything about his weapons." She wished that she could help them. She wanted to make this nightmare end, but she just didn't have any evidence.

"Your father left a suicide note."

She didn't want to hear any more. Juliana pushed to her feet, found Logan by her side. For someone so big, he could sure move fast. She stared up at him. "I wasn't told about a note." He hadn't told her.

He glanced back at Sydney. Glared. "We didn't…want that part leaking to the media."

Rage boiled within her. He was so close. In that instant, she wanted to strike out at him. To hurt him, as she was being torn apart. "I'm not the media! I'm his daughter!"

"Exactly." From Jasper, drawling Jasper. Cold Jasper. "In his note, he said you had all the evidence. We kept that bit from the media, but Guerrero would have put a spy in your father's life, someone who could keep close tabs on him. That someone…we believe he told Guerrero about the evidence."

Her head was about to erupt. The throbbing in her temples just wouldn't stop. "I have no evidence." Could she say it any plainer? "I can't give you anything!"

"Guerrero thinks you can. And he's just going to keep coming for you…" Jasper didn't have to finish. She knew what the guy had been about to say….

Until you're dead.

"So you see now why you must have protection," Sydney said with a firm nod. "Until we can recover the information we need, you've got a target on your back."

A giant one. Yes, she got that. "And what happens to my life?"

"With Guerrero out there, you don't have a life." Blunt.

Cold. Sydney could have an edge just as hard as Gunner's—
or Jasper's.

"We're going to get him," Logan promised her.

She wanted to believe him. But then, she'd gone for
his lies before. Juliana wet her lips. Lifted her chin. "This
protection…what does it mean?"

Sydney cast a quick look at Logan before her attention returned to Juliana, then she explained, "It means
an EOD agent is assigned to stay with you 24/7. You'll
be watched, monitored and kept alive," Sydney told her.
"What more could you want?"

Now Juliana's eyes were on Logan. He seemed even
bigger to her in that moment. More dangerous. So far removed from the boy she'd known. Maybe she'd never really known him at all. "Which agent?"

The faint lines around Logan's eyes deepened.

"Which agent?" Juliana demanded again.

A beat of silence, then Sydney said, "Given your…
history with Logan…"

Did everyone know that she'd given the man her vir-
ginity? Had the team been briefed about that? Her breath
heaved in her chest, but Juliana managed to speak from
between her clenched teeth. "There's a thing about history. It's in the past."

Logan's expression didn't change.

"If I'm giving up my life…" For how long? Until they
caught Guerrero? Until the magical evidence turned up?
"Then I want a say on my guard choice."

But Logan was already shaking his head. "No, it's—"

Not wanting anyone else to overhear, she closed in
on him. "We're done, Logan." A whisper that she knew
he'd heard, but hopefully the others hadn't. Juliana turned
away from him. Pointed to the man that Logan had shoved

up against the wall moments before. Gunner. Then, raising her voice once more, she said, "I'll take him."

"Hell." Gunner's shoulders dropped. "I knew this wouldn't be easy."

Juliana stepped toward him. "Actually, all things considered, I think I'm being pretty agreeable." Another step. "If this is going to work, then—"

Logan's hand wrapped around her shoulder, stilling her. "We're not done."

She saw Gunner's gaze dart from Logan's hand back to her face. Juliana wondered just what he saw, because Gunner gave a little whistle.

"No, I don't think you are," Gunner said.

But then Logan was spinning her back around. He leaned in close, and she could feel the force of his fury surrounding her. "Time to get some things clear."

Oh, what, *now* was the time for that?

"I'm lead on this team." Each word was bitten off.

"That's why he's Alpha One," Gunner said from behind her. The guy was so not very helpful.

"You don't give the orders," Logan snapped at her. "I do. When it comes to keeping you alive, I'm the one in charge. I'm the one who is going to stand between you and whatever hell might come." His gaze searched hers. "You might not like me. Hell, you might hate me, but too bad. This isn't about emotion. It's about getting a job done."

Her chest hurt. Juliana forced herself to breathe. "And nobody else here can—"

"I'm your guard. Day and night. Get used to it."

Her jaw clenched. She didn't want to get used to any of this, and Logan was stripping away all of her choices.

"Unless you don't think you can…trust yourself around me…" This line Logan spoke with a slow, sexy grin.

It took a stunned instant for his words to register with

Juliana. "What?" She almost had to pick her jaw off the floor. There was no way he'd just said that.

"Maybe the old feelings are still there." Now he was barely whispering, talking for her alone. Closing in on her just as she'd done with him moments ago. "Is that what scares you? That when we're alone, you might want... more?"

Yes. "No," Juliana denied immediately.

His gaze called her a liar, but he just said, "Then we're set. I'm point. I'll be with you, making sure you're safe. We'll keep you alive."

Promises, promises...

JULIANA STOOD IN THE HALLWAY while Logan and Gunner huddled over a computer screen. They'd called their boss, some guy named Mercer, then they'd gotten busy with their plans.

Plans about her life.

"You're going to be all right."

She jumped a little bit at Sydney's voice. She hadn't even heard the other woman approach, but Sydney was there, watching her with a light green stare.

"Logan's good at his job," Sydney continued, giving a nod toward the men. "The best I've ever seen in the field."

She didn't doubt that.

"He's always cool under fire," Sydney said as she crept closer. "The only time I've ever saw his control crack... it was when we were in Mexico, waiting to get you out." A faint smile curved her lips. "The man wanted to race in, guns blazing, when he knew that wasn't protocol."

Juliana's back was pressed to the wall. Her gaze swept over the other woman. She wasn't sure what to make of Sydney. On the outside, Sydney looked petite, almost breakable, but…but then Juliana looked into her eyes, and she could see the power there.

Sydney was a woman who'd seen dark things, done dark things. It was all there, the memories, the pain, in her eyes.

"I thought he did come in with guns blazing," Juliana said, forcing herself to speak. She remembered him rushing into that room, nearly ripping the door away. Clad in the black ski mask with the big gun in his hands, he'd looked so deadly.

She hadn't known who she should fear more. The man with the knife at her throat or the masked man who promised hell.

"Does he scare you?"

Juliana's lashes flickered. She'd have to remember just how observant Sydney could be. Nothing seemed to slip past the woman. "No." And it was the truth, mostly. No matter how deadly Logan was, she never thought he would physically hurt her.

But she did fear the way he could make her feel. He stirred too much lust in her. Made her want things she couldn't have.

Sometimes he scares me.

But the full truth was…*sometimes I scare myself.*

"Good." Sydney's gaze darted back to the men. "And Gunner?"

Yes. He made her nervous. So did Jasper.

Her silence must have been answer enough because Sydney gave a little shrug that seemed to say she understood. "Gunner has a special grudge against Guerrero. We were…we were in South America about two years ago. Came on a village that was supposed to be a safe haven for us and for the hostage we'd rescued."

"You do that a lot?" Juliana asked. "Rescue people?"

"We do what needs to be done." Sydney rubbed her palm over her heart in an almost unconscious motion. "The village... I was the one doing intel. I thought it was safe. I didn't realize Guerrero had made a deal with a rebel leader in the area. The gunfire started. It was a bloodbath."

Juliana glanced at Sydney's hand. "You were shot."

Sydney's hand dropped. "Gunner was the one who took four bullets, but he still kept fighting. He and I—we were the extraction team. He got me out, too."

"And the hostage?"

Sydney gave a small shake of her head. "Gunner's brother didn't make it out."

Oh, hell.

"So you can see why he might seem...determined... to get Guerrero."

The men were finished talking. They were heading back toward them. Juliana glanced at Gunner's eyes. Still dark. Still cold. But...she could have sworn she now saw the echo of pain in his gaze.

"It wasn't a sanctioned mission." Now Sydney was whispering. "We went in, just the two of us, because we had to get him out."

There was something there in Sydney's voice. Something... "Who was the hostage to you?" Juliana asked. Gunner's brother, but maybe more.

Sydney just gave her a sad smile. "We all want Guerrero stopped."

Juliana nodded.

"Don't give up," Sydney told her. "Whatever happens, keep fighting, keep working with us. Help us take him out."

Staring into Sydney's gaze and seeing the struggle on her face, Juliana realized that walking away from the EOD wasn't an option. "I will." She'd do her part. Guerrero was a monster, one who was destroying lives left and right.

He had to be stopped.

Logan's arm brushed hers.

We'll stop him.

JULIANA WASN'T GOING to like this walk down memory lane. Logan knew it even before the woman's body tensed up, boardlike, in the seat beside his.

"Why the hell are we here?"

The *here* in question would be in the middle of nowhere—or rather, in the middle of the woods in Mississippi. Pulling in front of an old cabin that had seen so many better days, long ago.

A familiar cabin.

He pulled the SUV around back. Made sure that it was hidden. There was only one dirt road that led to this cabin. So when the men hunting Juliana came calling, his team would know.

Logan climbed from the vehicle, swept his gaze past the trees. Jasper and Gunner would be setting up watch points out there, securing the perimeter.

The location was the perfect trap. And Juliana...

"Logan, *why here?*"

She was the perfect bait.

He forced a careless grin to his face. "Because the cabin's secluded. It's secure. And no one in Guerrero's team would think to look for you here."

True enough. They wouldn't think to look for her there, not until they were hand-fed the info.

Sorry, Juliana. And he was. He didn't like lying to her, setting her up. But no matter what else happened, he would keep her safe.

That part hadn't been a lie.

She was already out of the SUV, heading up the old wooden steps that led to the front of the cabin. The steps creaked beneath her feet.

Logan followed her. When she paused on the slightly sagging porch, he opened the door for her with a sweep of his hand, and he remembered the past.

No one's here, Julie. Come inside.

Logan, are you sure?

The cabin's mine. No one will find us here. It's just you...and me.

For an instant, he could feel her mouth beneath his. The memory was so strong. Her lips had been soft, silken. Her body had been a perfect temptation under his.

Here. It had all happened here.

Locking his jaw, Logan slammed the door shut behind him and secured the lock. Because the team had been planning this move in advance—for days, actually, even before the hit in the cemetery—the cabin was already wired. Cameras had been set up to scan the cabin's exterior. Alarms and sensors were strategically placed outside.

The feed would all go back to Sydney, since she was their tech queen. But Logan had a few monitors set up inside the cabin, too. He liked to keep his eyes open. Being blind in the field had never suited him.

He turned and found Juliana's dark eyes on him. There were smudges beneath her eyes. Exhaustion. She looked so fragile, so very breakable, that his body tensed.

Go to her, every instinct he had screamed at him, but he knew Juliana didn't want his comfort. The stiff lines of her body said she didn't want him at all.

The kiss in Mexico had been a fluke. She hadn't come looking for seconds, and she'd been very clear when she told him they were done.

Not yet.

So he'd just hold on to his fantasies. They'd gotten him through plenty of long nights, and he could keep his hands off her. He'd try to keep them off, anyway.

"You can take the room at the top of the stairs," he said. It was the only bedroom there and—

Her gaze darted to the staircase. "I'd, um, rather not."

The memories were hitting her, too. He'd pushed her back at the EOD meeting. The idea of her being so close to one of the other agents—*hell, no.* He didn't want her spending any nights alone with Gunner or Jasper. So he'd pushed to see what she'd do.

And maybe because he hoped that deep down she still wanted him. He was on fire for her.

Only, Juliana was turning away. "I'll take the couch."

"Take the bed." He'd gotten a new bed for her. New sheets. New covers. She could rest, take it easy and—

"I'm not getting into your bed," she snapped. Her temper was back. Probably the wrong time to mention he'd always found her sexy when temper spiked her blood and heated her voice. "I might have to stay with you, but I don't have to—"

"You kissed me in Mexico." His words stopped her, but he regretted them the minute they left his mouth. He didn't want to make her mad. He just wanted...

Juliana heaved out a long sigh. "I was half-awake. I didn't know what I was doing." No emotion in her words. "Don't worry, I won't make that mistake again."

If only. "Maybe I want you to do it again." Because they were alone, for the moment. And he was tired of pretending that he didn't ache just looking at her. That her scent didn't make him hard. That her voice—husky, soft—didn't turn him on.

Everything about her got to him. Always had.

Logan was afraid that it always would.

Juliana glanced back over her shoulder at him. A guy could only take so much. She stood there looking so beautiful, reminding him of all the dreams he'd had—dreams that had started right there—and what, was he really not supposed to touch?

He wasn't that strong.

He stalked toward her.

The bag he'd brought in—a bag of clothes that Gunner had prepared for them both—fell at his feet.

"Logan…" She held up her hands. "I said another agent should come. I told you—"

He wasn't touching her, not yet. But he sure wanted to. "You're a liar, Julie." He knew—he'd been lying for so long that it was now easy to spot the lies that others told.

And he'd been watching her eyes when she lied to him. He said, "You don't trust yourself around me. After all this time, you still want me."

She backed up a step. "You're guarding me. Nothing else. Got it? *Nothing…*"

"I remember what you taste like. For years after I left, I remembered…" She'd given him another taste just days ago. For a man who was starving, that taste had been bounty.

But Juliana had stiffened before him. There was a stark flash of pain in her eyes. "But you were the one who left, Logan. I was at the bus stop. Standing there for hours because I was so sure that you wouldn't just abandon me. That you wouldn't walk away and leave me there alone…"

He'd seen her at the bus stop. He'd had to go. She'd held a small black bag in her hands. Her gaze had swept the station. Left to right. A smile had trembled on her lips every time the station's main doors swung open.

Eventually, the smile had faded. When the last train left, tears had been on her cheeks. She'd walked away then.

And I felt like my heart had been cut out.

She didn't understand. There were some secrets that he couldn't share.

Because the truth would hurt her too much.

"You always looked at me like I was some kind of hero." A dangerous look, that. It had made him want to be more. Do more.

But the truth, the sad, sick truth, was that he'd never been a hero. He'd been a killer, even back then. And not good enough for her.

I walked away once. I can do this again.

So he didn't kiss her, didn't stroke her skin. He sucked in a breath, pulled her sweet scent into his lungs and moved back. "The bed is yours. I'll take the couch." He turned away.

A man could only resist for so long, and if he didn't put some space between himself and the biggest temptation that he'd ever faced, Logan knew his control would shatter.

He could already feel the cracks.

"Juliana James has disappeared."

Diego turned away from the window and its perfect view of the small city below. A city that still slept, for the moment. "That's not what I wanted to hear." He wasn't paying his men for failure. He paid no one for failure.

Diego walked slowly toward Luis, deliberately keeping a faint grin on his face. Luis knew he didn't accept failure.

Those who failed him paid with their lives.

And often the lives of their family members.

"One of those agents...he took her from the *cementerio,* stopped her from entering the car."

Sí, he already knew this. He'd seen the video clips. The

cameras had been rolling when the limo exploded, and Juliana James had been tossed back into the air.

The press had all wanted to be there when Senator James was laid to rest. Then when the car had exploded, the reporters had closed in even tighter.

Those reporters had done him a favor, though. They'd shown him the face of Juliana's rescuer.

Diego strolled to his desk and picked up the photo that he'd had enlarged. The photo that his team had used to track down Juliana's anonymous protector.

Only, the man wasn't so anonymous any longer.

Logan Quinn. A SEAL. A SEAL who hadn't been listed as officially in action for the past three years.

But I bet you are in action, hombre, under the radar, fighting dirty.

Diego could almost respect that. Almost. He didn't actually respect anyone. What was the point?

"He's the one we need to track." Diego tapped the photo. This wasn't some random agent. Just a man doing his job by protecting his charge. This was…more.

Diego knew how to get information out of people. Sometimes you used torture. Sometimes lies. With Juliana, he'd enjoyed a game of lies. The torture would have come, of course, but he hadn't been ready to kill her.

He *couldn't* kill her, not until he'd gotten the evidence back. A dead daughter wouldn't have encouraged the senator to give up the secrets he'd stashed away. But a living daughter…one who spilled all her secrets so easily…she'd been a tool that he used.

Logan. Perhaps that had been her most important secret to reveal. He just hadn't realized it at the time.

Everyone had a weakness. It was a lesson he'd learned so very long ago. Diego slanted a fast glance at Luis, not surprised to see the man shifting nervously. *I know his weakness all too well.*

The agent, Juliana—they both had weaknesses, too. *Weaknesses that I already understand.*

Juliana had revealed so much to him in those hours spent in the darkness. Sometimes torture wasn't the most effective means of getting what you wanted. Sometimes... sometimes you had to make your target trust you.

Only then could you go in for the kill.

"When we find Logan Quinn, we'll find Juliana." Simple. Diego dropped the photo. *Weaknesses.* They were so easy to exploit.

"You ever been in love, Juliana?" It had been a question he had to ask. If she loved, then she was weak. He could use her loved ones against her. So he'd waited, trying not to look eager, then Juliana had said...

"Once." Pain had trembled in her voice. A longing for what couldn't be. Juliana had been so sure that death waited for her. And it had. She'd drawn in a ragged breath and said, *"But Logan didn't love me back."*

Diego stared down at the picture. Tough SEALs weren't supposed to show fear. Not any emotion. But... right there, on Logan Quinn's face, Diego saw that the man had been afraid.

Not for himself.

For the woman he held so tightly. The woman he'd shielded with his own body when the car exploded, and Diego knew he was staring at—

Her Logan.

Ah, Juliana, I'm not so sure he didn't love you back.

Diego picked up a red marker and circled the face of his target. "You have six hours to find Quinn." The man wouldn't have left the area with Juliana, not yet.

Not...yet.

Diego glanced back up at Luis. "You know what happens if you fail."

Luis gave a grim nod. Then he grabbed for the photo and hurried toward the door.

"Your daughter..." Diego called after him softly. "She's six now, isn't she?"

Luis's shoulders stiffened. *"Si."* More growl than anything else.

"I'll have to make sure to send her an extra-special gift to celebrate her next birthday."

Luis glanced back. Ah, there it was. The fear. Flashing in the man's dark eyes. "Not necessary." His Spanish accent thickened with the broken rasp of his voice. "You've done enough for her. For me."

Diego's gaze fell to the rough scars on Luis's throat, then after a moment, he looked back up into the other man's eyes. Let the tension stretch. Then he smiled. "She's such a pretty little girl. So delicate. But then, children are always so fragile, aren't they?"

Luis lifted the photo. "Do you want him dead?"

Now the man was showing the proper motivation. Diego considered his question, then nodded. "Once you have Juliana in your custody, kill the agent. Do it in front of her." The better to break her.

Luis's fingers whitened around the photo. *"Si."*

Diego watched him walk away, satisfaction filling him. His resources were nearly limitless. With Diego's power behind him, there would be no stopping Luis. Money could motivate anyone. The right targets taken out—the right information gained, and Luis could attack.

If someone else was trying to kill Juliana, then they'd just offer more to keep her alive. An insurance policy. Diego liked to have backup plans in place.

And as for the SEAL, they wouldn't need others to kill

him. Luis could send out near-instant checks on Quinn, find any property he had. Find his friends, his family.

Hunt the bastard.

Then kill him.

Luis might be a good father, but he was an even better killer.

Especially when the man was properly motivated...

Logan Quinn was already dead; the fool just didn't know it.

Chapter Five

"It wasn't Guerrero."

Juliana blinked at the rough words and tried to push away the heavy darkness of sleep that covered her. She blinked a few more times, letting her eyes adjust to the faint light.

Where am I?

She glanced around. Saw the old, gleaming wood. Felt the lumpy couch beneath her.

Met Logan's bright stare.

The cabin.

The memories flooded back. Fire. Death. A nightmare that she wouldn't be waking up from anytime soon.

She pulled the blanket closer. "What? What are you talking about?"

He sat on the couch, his legs brushing her thighs. The move made her too aware of him, but then, she always felt too aware when he was close.

And he expected me to sleep in that bed upstairs? Oh, no. She wasn't up for that kind of punishment. Too much pleasure. Too much pain waited up there.

She'd bunked on the couch. She wasn't even sure where he'd gone.

"I got a call from Sydney."

Juliana scrambled to a sitting position. Okay, maybe

she was just trying to put some distance between her body and his.

Logan shook his head. "There's a price on your head. Damn high."

"We already knew that...."

The faint lines around his mouth deepened. "The money is being offered if you are taken in alive."

"What?" No, that didn't make any sense. "The car exploded. That's not exactly a way guaranteed to keep me breathing." Or Charles. Poor Charles. Dead in an instant, for no reason.

He ran a hand through his hair. "That hit...Sydney doesn't think it was from Guerrero's crew. The chatter she's hearing all indicates that was from...someone else."

Her heart slammed into her ribs. "You're telling me that *two* people want me dead?" Could this get any worse for her?

Logan touched her. *It could.* The heat of his touch burned through her. His fingers wrapped around her arms. "Guerrero doesn't want you dead. Syd is sure that he wants you brought in alive. And he's willing to pay top dollar to make sure you arrive breathing."

Her breath whispered out. "Because he thinks I have the evidence?"

A slow nod. Did he realize that his fingers were caressing her arms? Moving in small, light strokes against her skin. "I don't have it," she whispered. If she did, then maybe this could all end.

Logan could go back to his life.

She'd go back to hers.

"Syd is working with local law enforcement. They're gonna find out who rigged the car." He exhaled on a rough breath but didn't release her. "The limo was swept before it left the senator's house. It was cleared."

But then it had still exploded.

She'd never forget the fury of the fire sweeping over her.

"I'll be with you. Don't worry. You'll stay safe."

Easy for him to say. He wasn't the one being targeted by two killers. She stared into his eyes.

But...

But Logan had been targeted for death plenty of times before. She knew it. Death was his life. His job.

He was a survivor. A fighter.

If something were to happen, if one of those men hunting her came too close...

I don't want to be helpless. "Teach me," she said, pushing away the covers.

Logan blinked in surprise. "Uh, Julie..."

Under the blanket, she wore a loose T-shirt and a pair of jogging shorts. Not exactly sexy, but his gaze still dropped to her legs, lingered.

Her heartbeat kicked up a beat. "Teach me to *fight,* Logan." He'd already taught her to make love years before. *Upstairs.*

When the pleasure had hit her, she'd said that she loved him.

He'd never told her the same.

Maybe there was one thing he couldn't lie about.

Juliana shoved those memories back into the box in her mind. "I want to be able to defend myself if...if—"

"When a bullet or a bomb is coming, there's not much defense."

No. "But when you're trapped in some hellhole and the enemy is coming at you because he wants to *torture* information out of you—information that you don't have— then being able to fight back matters." She'd been helpless in Mexico. If something happened and Guerrero got her again… *I won't be helpless.* "You can teach me some defensive moves. I know you can."

His gaze wasn't on her legs any longer. That too-intense stare raked her face.

"I need this," she told him. She had to have some control, some power.

His nod was grim.

He rose, backing up.

The drumming of Juliana's heartbeat echoed in her ears. She followed him into the opening in the middle of the room. Her toes curled over the old, faded rug.

Light flickered on when Logan bent toward the lamp at his right. Juliana finally started focusing enough to realize that Logan wore no shirt. Just a pair of loose sweatpants. His chest, ripped with muscles, was bare. Only…

Logan was sporting a tattoo now.

She hadn't noticed the tattoo back in Mexico. But then, he'd kept his clothes on there. *Thank goodness.* Now it was tempting…all that bare flesh.

Juliana licked her lips. *Down, girl.*

Her gaze focused on the tattoo. The ink was black, dark, sliding up a few inches over his heart.

Forming a trident.

Why did that symbol look so sexy on him?

Why did she always have to want him?

"I use a mix of martial arts," he told her as he came closer, positioning his body just a few inches from hers on that rug. "I can teach you a few moves to help with CQC."

"Um, CQC?" No clue.

"Close-quarters combat." His words were quiet. His body was too big. She was too aware of his every breath. "You want to be able to kill quickly, efficiently."

She didn't exactly want to kill, just stay alive. But Juliana nodded. She'd never heard him sound so cold before. Her hands pressed against her stomach. "And have you done that?"

He didn't answer. She knew he had. Probably more times than he could count.

Not the boy you knew.

She wasn't sure she'd ever known him.

"Can we...can we start easier? I mean..." *I'm not ready to kill.*

He must have read the truth in her eyes. A muscle jerked in his jaw. "When it comes down to it, if it's your life or your attacker's, you'll be ready." Then he moved in a flash, almost too fast for her to see, and in the next breath, Logan's hand was around her throat. "If you hesitate, you can die." His big fingers surrounded her neck, seemed to brand her flesh. She knew with one twist of his hand, he could kill her.

Logan stepped back. "But we'll start easy, if that's what you want."

Had his voice roughened? His eyes had hardened, his body seemed to have tensed.

"Go for your attacker's weak spots. Always make them your targets."

Juliana forced her own body to ease its stiffness.

"When you attack—" Logan was circling her now, making her nervous "—use the strongest part of your body." He stood behind her, came closer. His body brushed against hers. His arm slid around her, and his fingers curled over her hand. "Use your fists." He lifted her hand, punched out with it and turned her arm. "Your elbows." He surrounded her. So big and solid behind her, his arms sweeping out.

He spun her around so that she faced him. His fingers still curled over her fist. He lifted her fist toward his neck.

"Punch at your attacker's throat. Hit hard, with every bit of strength that you have."

His gaze blazed down at her. "You have to be ready to take your attacker out," Logan said.

She tugged her hand. He didn't let go. Her eyes narrowed. "What if I'm just trying to get away?"

Another spin, and her back was to him again. He'd freed her, and she stood there, her body too tense and aware.

"I'll be the attacker," he said.

Her mouth went dry.

"If I come at you from behind…" And he did. In a rush, he had her. His arms wrapped around her body and he hauled her back against him. Juliana struggled, twisting and straining forward, but she couldn't get free of his hold. Her struggles just strained her against him.

He was getting turned on.

Juliana froze.

"Hunch your shoulders," he told her, voice gruff. "Don't try to lunge away. Curl in…"

She did, hunching her shoulders.

"Then drop."

She slid out of his grasp. She twisted and turned back up. Her hand fisted, ready to punch.

"When you're free, go for my eyes. My throat." His lips twisted. "My groin."

She *wasn't* going there. Not then. With an effort, she kept her eyes up.

"Use your elbow or fist in a groin attack. Hard as you can hit…"

She managed a slow nod.

"But if I come at you straight on…" And he did. He advanced and those big hands came for her throat once more. His fingers wrapped around her neck. Not hurting her. Again, she felt the ghost of a caress against her skin. "Then shove your fingers into my eyes."

Vicious. Juliana swallowed and nodded. She would do whatever she had to do.

He didn't drop his hand. Just stared at her. The air seemed to thicken with the tension between them.

"I'm not going to let them get you again."

His fingers were behind her ear, caressing. She shivered at the touch and the memories it stirred. In the past, he'd liked to kiss her in just that spot.

"I'll stand between you and any person who comes for you."

She believed that he would. But Logan was flesh and blood. He couldn't stop fire or bullets.

He could die, too.

Then what would happen?

I'd be without him again.

Her gaze lifted to his. There was arousal, need, so much lust in his eyes. But he wasn't pushing her, wasn't trying to kiss her, and his hand was falling away from her.

She'd told him no hours before. Told him to keep his distance. *We're done.*

He'd called her on the lie.

She still wanted him just as much as always.

He cleared his throat. "If we just knew where James had stashed the evidence…"

"I'd barely spoken to him in years." Because she'd seen what he'd become. Not the father she knew. He turned into someone cold, twisted. "He wasn't sharing any secrets with me."

Logan's head cocked to the right as he studied her. "Maybe not directly."

"Not *indirectly,* not in any way." She hadn't even seen

him last Christmas. She'd spent the holiday alone. "Wherever he hid the evidence—I don't know."

Logan squared his shoulders. "Okay, let's try this again. I'll come at you and you attack back, as hard as you can."

She pulled her bottom lip between her teeth, hesitated, then said, "Aren't you worried that I'll hurt you?"

He smiled. "I want you to."

Okay, then. If it was pain he wanted… Juliana turned her back to him. She'd give him as much as—

His arms closed around her, tight bands that stole her breath. His last attack hadn't been so hard and she hadn't expected him to come at her full force. Panic hit for an instant. Panic, then—

I won't be weak.

She hunched her shoulders, dropped low and slid out of his hold. She came up with her elbow, ready to hit him hard right in the groin, but Logan came at her. His body hit hers, and he pushed her back onto the rug, caging her body beneath his.

She lost her breath at the impact. He caught her hands, trapping them on either side of her head. "Use your feet, your legs," he gritted out. "Fight back with any part of your body that you can. Never give up."

No, she wouldn't. She twisted and her leg slid between his. Her breath panted out. Juliana yanked up her leg, driving her knee right toward his groin.

Logan twisted to the side, and her knee hit his thigh. "Nice," he said. "I knew you had a tough fighter inside."

His breath wasn't coming so easily, either. He still had her hands. Still had his body over hers.

She should tell him to move away. Should say…*enough.* But it suddenly wasn't about fighting. Her heart was still beating too fast, but the ache in her body, that wasn't from fear or adrenaline or anything but desire.

Need.

She'd had another relationship after Logan. It wasn't as if he'd been the only man she'd taken to her bed. Actually, she'd been with two other men over the years.

But the pleasure had never been the same.

And if she was honest with herself, when she'd closed her eyes... *I saw him.*

She hadn't been able to connect with the others, to let go. Not like she'd done with Logan.

"You shouldn't look at me like that." His voice was even deeper now, the sexy growl that she remembered. Lust could always make him growl.

"Like what?" But she knew.

"Like you want me to devour you."

She didn't move. The soft cotton of his sweatpants brushed over her leg. His hands were tight around her wrists but not hurting her. The man was always so conscious of his strength.

So strong, but she knew how to make him weak. Juliana had learned other lessons back in this cabin.

His hands released hers. "I think that's enough for now." He shifted his legs, pulling away from her.

Now it was her turn to grab him. Juliana's hands curled around his shoulders.

Logan froze. "Julie..."

"I did lie." They both knew it.

His pupils seemed to burn away the blue in his gaze.

"I still want you."

The muscles beneath her hands tensed. *Like steel.* "And I'm dying for a taste of you...." He moaned, then his mouth was on hers. Not easy. Not tender. Not like before.

So long ago.

This was different.

His tongue swept into her mouth. Took. Tasted.

He was different.

Her nails sank into his skin.

She was different.

The faint stubble on his jaw brushed against her. She liked the rough feel of it on her flesh, liked his taste even more. Her breasts were pushing against his chest, even as her hips arched against him.

The need inside, the need she'd wanted to hold in check, was breaking through, bursting like water out of a dam. She couldn't hold back, and right then, Juliana wasn't even sure why she *should* hold back. Pride?

Fear?

His mouth tore from hers. His lips pressed against her throat. He used the edge of his teeth. Her eyes fell closed, and she couldn't hold back her own moan.

"Missed...you..." His words were rough.

Her gaze flew open, but he was already sliding down her body. His fingers had eased under her T-shirt. Rough, calloused fingertips swept over her stomach, sliding over the flesh, shoving up the shirt and baring her to his hungry stare. Then he was touching her breast, stroking the hard tip and making her shudder.

Making her want him even more.

"Stop me," he told her as his left hand fisted her shirt. His right hand kept caressing her.

She didn't stop him. Instead, Juliana whispered, "I want your mouth...on me." In the midst of a nightmare, why couldn't she have her pleasure?

If death was stalking her, then she'd take the life that she could. The pleasure that was right before her.

Logan.

Then his mouth was on her breast. Not some tentative

kiss. His lips closed over her. He sucked, licked, and the hand that had been stroking her slid back down now, heading over her stomach, down to the waistband of her shorts.

Goose bumps rose on her flesh. Need electrified her blood. Every breath brought in his scent, filling her with him. She was touching him, learning the hard planes and angles of his muscled body once again. He was bigger now. Stronger.

She wanted to kiss that tattoo.

His fingers brushed against the waistband of her shorts. "Juliana…" he rumbled against her breast.

She arched her hips. There was no stopping. Not now. There was only need. Pleasure was so close, just out of reach.

She caught his hand. Pressed it against her. "I want you."

His gaze blasted her. "And I'd kill to have you."

She believed him. His words terrified a part of her, a part that wasn't wild with need and lust. This man—she knew how dangerous he was. To her and to others. But at that moment…

She didn't care. She wanted his strength. She wanted him.

So when his hand slid under the elastic waistband of her shorts, Juliana arched her hips up, giving him better access. She wasn't going to pretend she didn't want this—him. She needed his touch more than she needed breath right then.

Her whole body was tense. Too eager. Her muscles straining. Then he was pushing his long, broad fingers under the edge of her panties. Touching her in the most intimate of caresses. His name broke from her even as she squeezed her eyes tightly shut.

He didn't touch her with hesitation or uncertainty. He

touched her the way a man did when he knew his lover's body and knew how to give her the most pleasure.

His fingers slid over her flesh, found the center of her need. His touch grew more demanding. Her breath came faster, faster...

His mouth was on hers, kissing, thrusting his tongue past her lips. Her hands dug deeper into his shoulders. The pleasure was so close, driving her, making Juliana desperate for the release that would rip through her and take the pain away.

A shrill alarm cut through the room. The ringing pierced her ears even as she choked out Logan's name. The pleasure hit, fast, brutal, but he stiffened against her.

The alarm's shriek continued and Logan swore.

Juliana's body shook when Logan pulled her to her feet.

"Someone's coming," he snapped.

Her heartbeat was still racing. She swallowed as she tried to ease the dryness in her throat. Her hands fumbled and she attempted to fix her clothes.

"You're safe in here," he told her even as he stepped away and opened a nearby drawer. When his hand rose again, she saw that he was holding a gun.

Someone's coming.

Logan caught her hand and pulled her with him into the small room to the right, a room filled with about five monitors. On those monitors, she just saw trees. Empty woods. He must have been using some kind of night-vision cameras so that they could get the view, but she didn't see anyone approaching the cabin.

"Someone triggered the alarm." He yanked on a thick shirt, shoved into shoes.

Juliana shook her head. "They couldn't have found us already." It had just been hours. *Hours.*

Her thighs pressed together. The pleasure had left her

emotions raw, and this—*now?* "They can't be here," she whispered.

But as she stared at those monitors, she saw the men creep from the shadows and close in. Men dressed in black with hoods covering their faces and big guns cradled in their hands.

The images were grainy on the screens. She leaned closer, narrowing her eyes.

And the gunfire erupted. No sound came with the shots, but she saw the men begin to fall. Two staggered back, clutching their chests. The others lifted their weapons. Fired at enemies she couldn't see...even as they raced forward, their images flickering on the monitors.

"Give me a weapon," Juliana said, surprised that her words were so steady.

Logan glanced at her and studied her face with narrowed eyes.

"Give it to me."

Logan's team was out in those woods. She got that. They were firing at the men. But if they didn't take them all out, if someone got to the house...

Logan opened a thick safe on the left, nestled behind the screens. More guns were inside. Knives, too. What looked like a giant stockade of weapons.

He handed her a gun. "Here's the safety. Make sure it's off when you fire."

The weapon didn't feel heavy in her hands. She'd expected more.

It was cold. Hard.

The alarm was still beeping. She could hear the shots now, coming from outside. The battle was nearly at her door.

"Stay behind me," Logan ordered.

She nodded.

His fingers curved under her chin. He tilted her head up and flashed a smile at her.

"Try not to shoot me," he said, then he kissed her. A fast brush of his lips against hers.

His words surprised her enough that a rough laugh slipped from her. Laughing, now? Maybe she was as crazy as he was.

But then the shots came again, and the laughter was gone and only fear remained when she heard the voices shouting outside.

Logan had his own weapon up, ready, and—

Glass shattered. A window. Someone was coming in the window.

"Stand down!" Logan yelled.

Gunshots. They weren't standing down.

Wood cracked. The front door? Being broken down?

Logan pushed her back against the wall on the left. The door to their room was open a few precious inches. He put his gun barrel through that opening. Aimed—

The blast of his gun had her ears aching. Someone groaned, then there was a heavy thud of sound.

Silence, a long beat. Long enough to make her think that the battle was over. Safety was close and—

Gunfire erupted as all hell seemed to break loose in the small cabin.

Chapter Six

The hunters had arrived too soon. No way should have they already been at the cabin.

The Shadow Agents hadn't even had a chance to leave their trail of bread crumbs for Guerrero yet. They weren't ready for his attack.

They shouldn't have underestimated the man's resources.

A bullet tore right through the door next to Logan. He barely heard the thunder of the weapons, and he wouldn't let himself look back at Juliana. He didn't want to see the fear in her gaze.

He had to focus to get the job done. *To protect her.*

Kill or be killed.

Logan wasn't in the mood to die.

Not wasting any bullets, Logan took aim only when he had a target. When he had a target, his bullet slammed home, taking down another one of the attackers.

Logan panned for another mark.

Another one hit the floor.

They should have stood the hell down when he told them to. Logan's breath rasped in his lungs. Adrenaline had tightened his body, pumped through his blood and amped him up for the battle.

He'd always enjoyed the battles, but this time, with

Juliana's life on the line, the tension edging through him cut sharper than a knife.

From his vantage point, he saw when the next man rushed through the cabin's front door, but Logan didn't squeeze the trigger this time.

Gunner was the man in his sights.

Gunner's gaze swept around the room and he gave a low whistle. "Three down...all in the heart."

Kill or be killed.

Logan didn't open the door. "Clear?"

"Yeah, yeah, we're clear, Alpha One."

He finally glanced back at Juliana, but instead of the fear he'd expected to see burning in her eyes, the woman just looked mad.

Her fingers tightly clutched her gun, and he wondered...would she have used it, if she'd had to do the job?

As far as he knew, Juliana had never hurt another soul in her life. And shooting at another human, being ready to take a life, that was a line many couldn't cross.

Logan opened the door. *I never saw that damn line.* The kills had come too easily for him.

Monster.

He knew what he was, even if Juliana didn't.

A weapon. A killer. An assassin. Senator James had been right about him after all.

Now Juliana had just seen up close and personal how dangerous he could be. Her left hand reached up and curled around his arm. "Are we safe?"

He glanced back to the outer room. Gunner was checking the men. No point in that. They sure weren't moving.

His nod was grim.

Then Logan opened the door, making sure to keep his body in front of Juliana's, just in case. "What the hell," he began, voice lethal, "just happened?"

No way should those guards have gotten this close. Guerrero's men weren't even supposed to know about the location, not until they'd set up a more secure perimeter, but...

"We got slammed," Gunner said, staring at him with narrowed eyes. "Explosives, artillery...they came prepared, but we still managed to take them all out."

So they had. His feet crunched over the broken glass. The cabin was shredded, windows busted. The front door was ripped from its hinges and bullet holes lined the walls.

He'd loved this place once. It had been a sanctuary, courtesy of his stepfather. A place to lick his wounds.

A place to share with Juliana.

Not any longer.

Logan bent next to one of the fallen men. With Juliana so close, he hadn't been able to take any chances. *Kill shots.* If the men had survived, they would have just kept shooting at him.

"Tell me you have someone alive outside," Logan said, not glancing up. If they had one of Guerrero's men in custody, they could try to make him talk. The problem in Mexico was that too many there were too afraid to talk to authorities—really, to those who hadn't already been paid off by Guerrero. The guy wasn't called El Diablo for nothing. People feared him because he could bring hell to their lives.

"The ones still breathing turned tail and ran."

Figured.

Logan's hold tightened on his gun. This was just—

He heard the whisper of cloth almost too late. A rustle of sound that shouldn't have been there. He glanced up at the broken window and saw the barrel of the gun pointing toward him.

Logan started to lunge to the side even as he brought

up his own weapon, but then something—someone—slammed into him, knocking Logan to the floor.

His bullet blasted out, still heading for its target. A man screamed even as Logan grabbed for...

Juliana?

She'd been the one to knock into him. He twisted her, shoving her body behind his.

Gunner had already made his way to the window. He flew out with his hands, breaking the gunman's wrist and sending the weapon tumbling through the ground.

Logan's gaze swept over Juliana. *Okay. She's okay.*

He pushed her back and rushed to his feet. In the next instant, Logan was at Gunner's side. Logan grabbed the now-moaning man and dragged his sorry hide through the window.

Gunner kicked the man's discarded weapon a good five feet away.

Juliana had risen to her feet now. She still had her gun out—and aimed right at the moaning man.

Blood streaked down his face. He glanced up at her, and his lips twisted in a sneer. "You're...the one..."

Logan put his own weapon under the man's chin. "Where is he?"

The man's gaze, a dark brown, turned back to Logan. His sneer stretched. "The lover...think you're keeping her safe?" A shake of his head. "You're the one killing her... leading us...right to...*her.*" The man's voice was raspy. As Logan stared at him, he could see the jagged scars from an old injury that crossed the man's neck.

"No one's killing her," Logan growled. "You can be sure of that." He shoved the man back. He had to. The temptation to attack was much too strong.

Logan positioned his body near Juliana. He didn't want her to see what was coming, but he couldn't let her leave.

Not with the chaos outside. What if Gunner was wrong? What if there were more men? Gunner hadn't known about this one....

Gunner had shoved the man down to the floor, got him on his knees, and Gunner's weapon rested at the back of the man's head. "Who sent you?" They already knew, yet the question still had to be asked. They needed the man to confess.

But the bleeding man just laughed.

"Tell us," Logan snarled.

The man's laughter slowly faded. He tried to tilt his head to see Juliana, ignoring the gun pressed so close to him as if it truly weren't there. "Ah…little señorita…he'll keep coming for you."

Logan felt Juliana's hand tighten on his arm. "Your voice… *I remember you.*"

Then she lunged forward, trying to get to the man. Logan caught her around the waist and hauled her back.

"You were there!" Juliana yelled at the kneeling man. "That first night in Mexico, you were the one who took me…. You kept saying…little señorita! I didn't see your face, but your voice—I'll never forget it!"

He didn't move. Juliana sure did. She twisted and fought like a wildcat in Logan's arms. He snatched the gun from her hand and held her as tightly as he could.

If Juliana really could tie this man to her kidnapping, and they could link him to Guerrero, make him talk…

"I know your voice…." she snarled.

The voice was distinctive.

"I know *you*," Juliana said. She had stopped fighting, for the moment. Logan wasn't about to make the mistake of letting her go. The woman could just be trying to trick him.

Their captive's head had lowered. His shoulders sagged inward a bit.

"You work for Diego Guerrero," Gunner charged. He'd never once relaxed his stance. "And you're going to tell us everything we want to know about your boss, unless you want to wind up like your friends."

"Who are you?" Logan wanted to know. They'd start with a name and tear the guy's life apart, link him to Guerrero. Find the man and then—

Their captive's head tilted. He actually lifted his chin and shoved the back of his head against Gunner's gun, as if daring the other man to shoot. *"Mi nombre es Luis Sanches."*

Logan nodded. Okay, now they were—

"Muerte no me asusta."

Logan's body tensed. *Death doesn't scare me.*

The man's head shoved against Gunner's weapon again. "Do it! Kill me!"

Gunner's eyes narrowed to faint slits.

"El Diablo…he can do so much worse than *muerte* for me." His shoulders shook. "Much worse."

Logan released Juliana. "Don't move." He breathed the words into her ear.

Luis's gaze flickered toward them. "That's why he'll have her… He knows you… Always understands his enemy—"

"We can offer you protection," Logan said. He knew the drill. If you rolled on someone like Guerrero…yeah, you could expect one real short life. "Give you a new name, a new—"

But Luis was shaking his head. "I won't betray him."

Gunner hauled the guy to his feet. "When he finds out that we have you in custody, do you think that's gonna matter? Guerrero will just assume that you sold him out. You'll be finished either way."

Juliana wasn't speaking, just staring at Luis, and Logan realized—Luis was staring back.

"Little señorita, wish…I'd never seen you in Mexico," Luis said. His hands were by his sides. He looked beaten, hopeless.

"I wish you hadn't, either," Juliana said. Her voice was angry, snapping. "I wish none of this had ever happened."

"Sí…"

Logan glared at him. "You *will* help us to catch Guerrero." Every instinct that Logan had screamed that this guy wasn't an average flunky. He was older, with shades of gray spiking the edges of his dark hair. His eyes knew too much, had *seen* too much.

"No, I won't help you." Luis's voice held no emotion.

Logan turned away from him, marched over and grabbed his cell. Sydney answered instantly. "What do you see?" he asked her.

A faint hum of sound, then "All enemy bodies are down. Perimeter is secure." Her voice, calm, easy, belied the bloody nightmare that had to be waiting beyond the cabin.

"We need transport," he told her, glancing over at Luis Sanchez. "We've got a live one in here."

But Luis shook his head. "No, you don't."

Then he lunged forward, surging away from Gunner. Luis lifted his hand, and too late, Logan realized that when that man had been kneeling on the floor, when his hands had been at his boots…

He went for a backup weapon.

A glinting knife blade was grasped in Luis's hands. Logan brought up his gun in an instant. "Drop it."

Luis wasn't charging with the weapon. Not coming to attack. But—"My daughter...I will miss her...."

Then, even as Gunner lunged for the guy, Luis shoved the knife into his own chest.

"No!" Juliana screamed.

Too late.

Blood bloomed on Luis's shirt. His eyes widened. Not with fear or agony.

Relief.

Gunner grabbed Luis from the back. Luis's fingers were still clenched on the hilt of the knife. His legs gave way, and blood sprayed around him.

"What's happening?" Sydney screamed in Logan's ear. And he realized that he had the gun in his right hand, and he was still clutching the phone in his left.

He stared down at Luis's body. The man was a killer; he'd known exactly where to deliver the death blow.

"We won't need the prisoner transport any longer."

Luis was still alive, barely, but Logan knew he wouldn't be for much longer. Logan shoved the phone into his pocket as he stalked toward the dying man.

Gunner had lowered him to the floor. He hadn't tried to remove the knife. If he did...well, Logan knew Luis wouldn't even have a few moments left to live then.

They had to get the man to talk, while he still could.

"Where is Guerrero?" Logan demanded.

"My daughter..." Luis said with a smile. "She's... lovely..."

"Where is Guerrero?"

"He...won't touch her...now..."

Because Luis had chosen to die instead of rolling over on his boss? Rage burned inside of Logan.

"So beautiful...my sweet..." Luis's eyes flickered. "Marie..."

The man wouldn't be telling him anything more.

Logan glanced at the other bodies. Then his gaze found Juliana's. She was standing just a few feet away, her face too pale.

They found her already. How the hell did they do that?

Then he remembered the words that had tumbled from Luis right after he'd dragged the guy through the window.

The lover...think you're keeping her safe?

How had Luis known that he'd been Juliana's lover? He watched as Juliana's eyes dipped to the dead men and she swallowed. Her shoulders rolled back as she tried to straighten her spine.

You're the one killing her...leading us...right to...her.

He hurried forward and grabbed her arm. "Let's go." Syd would already have a cleanup crew en route, but this location was compromised. No longer the perfect trap, with the bait to lure Geurrero...

He's the one setting a trap for us.

And Logan wasn't going to just sit around while that man closed in for the kill.

But Juliana wasn't moving. "Where? Where do we go? He's going to find me. He found me here, after just a few hours and—"

He pulled her close. "Do you trust me?"

Her lips parted.

"Do you?"

Juliana nodded.

The relief he felt had his tense muscles aching. "Then let me get you out of here." He couldn't tell her his plans right then. More lies.

Would they ever stop?

He'd been lying to her since the first day they met, and those lies had torn a hole right through any dreams that he might have ever had.

The day Juliana found out the truth about him, about why he'd first walked into that diner to meet her...

It would be the last day she ever trusted him.

But he led her outside. Jasper already had an SUV idling near the porch steps. They jumped into the back, rushed away. The windows would be bulletproof, the vehicle's body reinforced.

The SUV drove fast, hurtling down that narrow road.

"We've got backup on site," Jasper said, his drawl barely evident. "Syd called in reinforcements. The road will be clear."

It might be clear, but that didn't mean Guerrero didn't have someone out there, watching them, following them.

Guerrero had definitely taken the bait. He wanted Juliana, wanted her alive, because not one single shot had ever been taken at her.

And when a man like Guerrero wanted something... he didn't stop.

Come for her yourself. Come and face me.

Because Logan wasn't the type of man to ever stop, either.

SHE DIDN'T KNOW how long they drove. She didn't really care. Juliana sat hunched in the car and saw the image of a man taking his own life flash before her eyes.

That man—Luis—had been so afraid of Guerrero that he'd killed himself instead of betraying his boss.

Logan hadn't so much as flinched.

During the ride, he'd been on the phone beside her, talking to the mysterious Mercer and demanding explanations. He wanted to know who'd leaked their location.

But every now and then, she could feel Logan's eyes on her. And she could have sworn there was suspicion in his gaze.

Why?

The vehicle slowed. Juliana blinked and glanced around even as the engine died away. "Another safe house?" she whispered, and yes, she'd put too much emphasis on *safe*. At this point, she didn't think anyplace was safe. Guerrero was going to keep coming.

The man could track like no one she'd ever seen before.

"Not exactly," Logan said. His voice was guarded, carefully emotionless. In the closed interior of the vehicle, she was too conscious of his body pressing next to hers.

Had she really been moaning in his arms just an hour or two before? That memory seemed surreal. The death, the violence—that had been reality for her.

Then Logan opened his door. She turned away and shoved open the door on her side and rushed out into what looked like a parking garage. A deserted one.

Jasper was by her side, waiting. "You all right, ma'am?" he asked.

He actually seemed worried. More worried than Logan. Juliana nodded.

"It's for your safety," Jasper said. "It might hurt, but..."

Wow. Hold up. She lifted a hand. "What's going to hurt?"

Jasper pointed to the left. Juliana turned and saw a redheaded woman in a white lab coat heading her way. Her gut knotted and she asked, "What's going on?"

"Just a small procedure," Jasper told her. He even put his hand on her shoulder and gave her a little stroke. As if that was supposed to be reassuring. "To make certain that you stay safe."

"So far, I sure haven't felt safe." Her own words snapped out.

Jasper winced. "This isn't the way things were planned.

No one should have found out about your location, not so fast, anyway. We were going to wait until—"

"Jasper." Logan's snarl shut up the other EOD agent. Jasper rocked back on his heels.

But it was too late. He'd said too much. Suspicion rolled within Juliana. "Tell me that he's wrong." He wasn't wrong. She knew it, but denial could be a fierce beast.

We were going to wait.

Wait and then leak her location to Guerrero? Wait and set a trap for the arms dealer, using her as the unknowing bait?

But Logan didn't speak; the doctor did. "I'm ready for her in the operating room. The implant can be placed immediately."

Implant? Juliana shook her head and backed up fast. Unfortunately, there wasn't anyplace for her to go, and her elbows rammed into the side of the SUV. "I'm not ready for you, lady." The doctor could just back off.

The redhead's lips thinned. "Do we need sedation for the patient?"

"What?" Juliana wasn't sure her voice could get higher than that startled yelp. "I'm not your patient! Stay away from me." Her gaze found Logan's. "You asked if I trusted you." First at that run-down hotel, then back at the cabin, in the middle of all that death. "I said that I did, but Logan, you've got to give me something here. Tell me—tell me that you weren't using me."

He still didn't speak. Maybe because he'd finally stopped lying.

It was Jasper who reached for her. "Come inside with us, Juliana, and I'll explain what's going to happen."

"It's a simple enough procedure," the doctor said.

Juliana felt her face flush. "Lady, I just came from a bloodbath, okay?"

Now it was the doctor who backed up a step.

Good for her.

Juliana ignored Jasper's outstretched hand. Her gaze locked on Logan. "Did you set me up as bait?" Her breath caught in her throat as she waited for his response.

"Yes."

That breath froze in her lungs.

"No," Jasper said in almost the same instant. "He didn't."

Her gaze darted to him, saw his lips tighten as he told her, "*We* did. Our EOD team had its orders. Logan didn't have a choice, still doesn't."

That was a fat line of bull. "There's always a choice." She rubbed her arms, chilled. She was standing there barefoot, wearing shorts and a T-shirt. She smelled like death and Logan's touch seemed to have branded her skin.

How wrong was that?

"Not always," Logan said. She became aware of the others then, men who'd been hanging back in the shadows. Armed. Wasn't everyone in the EOD always carrying a weapon? "My goal is to bring in Guerrero."

Her laugh was bitter. "I thought the goal was to keep me alive." So much for thinking she ranked high on his priorities.

And damn it, she caught a flash of pity in Jasper's eyes. Not what she needed to see right then. Her chin shot up.

"It is," Logan growled. Then he looked around at their audience and swore. In the next instant, he was pulling her toward the double doors on the right. Juliana was marching on his heels, more than ready to clear the air between them.

His palm slammed into the door and then they were inside a small hallway. More guards were assembled. Logan turned to the left and pushed open the door that led into what looked like a small waiting room.

Or an interrogation room. Her gaze darted to the wall on the right. A wall that looked as if it was just a mirror, only, she'd seen walls like that on television shows. Two-way mirrors. "Where are we?"

"Government facility. Off-the-books."

Wasn't just about everything off-the-books these days?

"I'm not... Hell, it's not about using you."

At his outburst, she spun around. "You were going to lure Guerrero to that house! Dangle me in front of him as bait!" She was so angry her words came out rapid-fire.

"I was—*am*—going to keep you under guard. We have to take out Guerrero. You're not going to be safe until he's in custody or until he's dead."

Her breath panted out. "You should have told me the truth." She felt as if Sydney was the only one giving her real insight into what was happening. Yes, they all wanted Guerrero stopped, she understood that. But did they have to lead her around like a lamb to a slaughter?

He shook his head. "There are some truths you don't want to hear."

That did it. Juliana shot across the room and jammed her finger into his chest. *"Don't."*

His brows rose.

"I'm not a child, Logan. I've handled death, disillusionment and betrayal just fine for years." Handled it and kept going. She wasn't going to break, not now and not ever. "So don't make decisions for me. Don't hide the truth from me." Her father had done that for the past ten years. "Just...tell me."

His gaze searched hers, then he gave a slow nod. "You're right. I'm sorry."

Damn straight he should be. And sorry wasn't going

to cut it for her. "Sydney told me about Gunner's brother. About how Guerrero was responsible for the attack that killed him." Her breath heaved out. "I *get* that your team has a personal stake in this, all right? I get it. But we're not just talking about your team. We're talking about my life."

His eyes blazed.

"Talk to me." Now she was the one giving orders. "Tell me what's going on."

His nod was brief. Then "You're in a government medical facility, one that was set up to assist agents in tracking their witnesses."

She realized her finger was still stabbing into his chest. Juliana dropped her hand. "Tracking them how?"

"A small chip is implanted just under the skin. With that chip, we're able to track a person anyplace that he or she goes."

Anyplace. "You mean in case Guerrero gets to me—"

"He won't—"

She waved that away. "If he gets to me, this chip is going to help you follow me."

His jaw clenched. "Yes."

Suspicion made her push because the trust she'd had… it was brittle. "Are you going to let his men take me… act like I'm protected but really ease back so they can grab me?"

His eyes chilled.

But she kept going. "Then you can just follow my tracking signal—what, some kind of GPS?—all the way back to Guerrero. You can get him. Get what you want, and hell, maybe all I'll have to do is get tortured or killed so you can bring him down."

His hands wrapped around her arms and Logan pulled her against him. "That's not going to happen."

"Promises, promises?" The taunt snapped out. "Because I don't think I can *trust* you on this, Logan." The pain from the past struck out at her. "I trusted you before, remember? We were going away together. I was there that night. Ready to leave everything I knew behind. I was there for hours." She couldn't hold back any longer. "Where the hell were you?"

Chapter Seven

His fingers were too tight on her arms. Logan knew it. Taking a deep breath, he forced himself to step back. There was so much anger, no, rage in Juliana's eyes. He hated that.

Even as he knew he could do nothing to change the past. "We were just kids, Julie. Two confused kids."

"I was twenty. You were twenty-two. It's not like we were playing in the sandbox back then."

She wouldn't make him flinch. Terrorists, killers— he'd faced plenty in his time. He'd taken bullets and been sliced by knives. He hadn't flinched then.

I hate the way she's looking at me. "We were too young. It wasn't love. Wasn't meant to be forever."

She just kept staring at him, as if she could see through his lies. "No, it wasn't." Her breath rushed out. "I counted the minutes on that stupid clock in the bus station. That stupid, huge clock that hangs over the counter. I counted until midnight, when I had to give up." Her stare was burning him alive. "At midnight, I promised myself I'd never let you betray me again. But…I guess I was wrong about that, too."

The woman was carving his heart out of his chest with every word she uttered.

"Forget it." Then she shoved away from him with more

force than he'd expected. "So I get an implant, huh? That's the next big deal? Someone to slice me open, whether I want it or not."

He wanted the tracker on her, just as a precaution. After the way things had gone down at the cabin, he wanted to make sure he'd have a way of finding her. "Hostages, witnesses—they've been taken before. They're stripped, their bags are tossed. We realized a few years ago that we needed technology that wouldn't be ditched so easily." The tracker was tiny, barely noticeable at all, and easily inserted under the skin. A little piece of tech that Uncle Sam hadn't shared with many others.

"A few hours after the insertion, you'll barely even notice it's there."

She finally glanced away from him. "I'll notice." Her words were clipped. So unlike her usual voice. "But I'll do it anyway because if Guerrero does get to me, the EOD had better haul butt to save my life."

He would.

Juliana had already turned from him and headed for the door. He should let her go but he had to speak. "I really am...sorry." The apology came out sounding rusty and broken.

She pulled open the door. "For what?" Juliana didn't bother looking back at him. "Leaving me before...or setting me up now?"

Both. "I wanted you to be happy. You wouldn't—you wouldn't have been happy with me." The line he'd told himself for years. She deserved better. She'd have better. It was only a matter of time until some Prince Charming took her away.

His hands were clenched so tightly that his knuckles ached.

"Don't tell me what I'd be," she said, her spine stiff

and too straight. "I'm the only one who understands how I feel *and* what I want."

Then she walked through the door, calm and poised. So what if she was barefoot and her cute little toenails were flashing bright red? The woman had held court too long in her life not to walk with that easy grace.

"Come on, Doctor," she called out and he knew that Liz Donaldson had to be close by. "Let's get this over with."

Logan exhaled slowly. He looked up and stared straight into the mirror that was less than five feet from him. His reflection stared back. His jaw was lined with stubble, eyes and face worn.

She wouldn't have been happy. The words were stubborn, but they weren't his, not really. Her father had been the one to first speak them.

You can't make her happy. When she finds out what you did, how do you think she'll ever be able to look at you again?

His teeth ground together, but he managed to say, "Come on out, Jasper. I know you're in there."

After a moment, he heard the slow approach of Jasper's booted feet. Then the Ranger was there, filling the doorway, shaking his head even as he crossed his arms over his chest. "You are one dumb SOB," Jasper said.

"Don't push me now," Logan ordered. Jasper was always pushing. In the field, in the office—everywhere. *Death wish?* Yeah, he had one.

Jasper's mouth lifted in his usual sardonic smile. "Left her there all alone, huh? Didn't even go to see the pretty girl at the bus station. That's cold."

He stared at Jasper but didn't see him. "A blue dress that fell to her knees. A ponytail pulled to the side. A small black bag at her feet." He forced his hands to unclench. "She was sitting five feet from the front desk, turned so that she could see the entrance."

But he'd been there long before she'd arrived, hidden in the shadows, watching what he couldn't have.

A furrow pulled up Jasper's brows. "You were there, but you didn't say anything? Man, what are you—crazy? Why'd you let a woman like that walk?"

"You know what I am." Jasper had seen him at his worst, covered in blood, fighting for his life. More animal than man. He'd seen Logan when his control broke and the beast inside broke free.

Born to kill.

He'd been told that for so long.

"No, man, I know what you *think* you are," Jasper said with a sigh. "But I tell you this…if a woman like her ever gave me the look—the kind of look I saw her give you— I'd do anything for her."

He had done anything. He'd given her up. That had been everything. "Don't push me on this," Logan warned. He'd hate to have to kick his friend's butt again.

But Jasper just blinked slowly and kept his smile. "Maybe I should be talking to her, comforting *her.*"

"You stay away from her."

"Like that, huh?" Before he could answer, Jasper gave him a long, considering look and said, "At twenty-two, I can still see you being a dumb kid who could manage to give her up. But now, after everything you've been through, after all we've done, I'm betting that sweet slice of paradise is pretty tempting, isn't it?"

She'd tempted him from day one and was still tempting him. When he'd had her beneath him at that cabin. When he'd been touching her skin, feeling her soft flesh beneath his…

"You really think you can let her go again?"

Logan didn't speak.

Jasper nodded. "Thought so." Whistling, he stalked away.

This time, Logan didn't look at his reflection. He didn't want to see the man who stared back at him. The man who just might be desperate enough to try to force Juliana to stay with him.

Even when he knew she deserved more.

JULIANA SAT ON THE small bed in the lab room, her head down, staring at the tiled floor. Logan stood in the doorway for a moment, watching her.

But then her head tilted back, and her gaze found his.

Silence, the kind that said too much.

He hesitated, then said, "I've got clothes for you. Shoes." Logan strode forward and put the bag down beside her. Then, because he couldn't help himself, his hands rose toward her.

She tensed.

"Easy," he whispered. "I just want to check…" He brushed back her hair, knowing exactly where Liz would have placed the implant. His finger slid up her neck, then slipped around beneath the heavy weight of her hair. The bandage was small, barely an inch long, and flat.

"I'm fine," Juliana said. He stood close to her, intimately close. And Logan didn't remove his hands.

He didn't want to. "Are you sure? Any pain, any—"

She shook her head.

Step back. He pulled in a breath and dropped his hands. "Once you've changed, we'll head out."

Her hand grabbed his arm. He was the one who tensed then. "Where are we going this time? Another cabin in the woods? Another safe house?"

"No."

Confusion filled the darkness of her gaze.

"No more hiding." The order had come from above. From the man who'd formed the EOD. Syd had picked up rumors online that Guerrero was on American soil. Rumors they suspected were fact. He was close…they just had to make him come in even closer.

And Logan's boss wanted them on the offensive.

"We need to make Guerrero afraid. We want him to worry that he's been compromised." Mercer's words. He'd talked to Logan on the phone less than five minutes ago. *"When the woman is hiding, he knows he has the power. Get her out. Put her in public. Make Guerrero think we've got the evidence on him. He needs to be the one running."*

Easy for Mercer to say. He didn't know Juliana. She was just a witness to him. An important one, no doubt, but the idea of putting her in danger wouldn't rip his guts out.

"Where are we going?" Juliana asked again, then her eyes widened. "Unless…maybe there's no 'we' now, maybe the EOD—"

"We're staying with you." As if anyone could pry him away when she was in danger.

She nodded, exhaling.

"But we're not hiding. Guerrero's power is fear. He wants you afraid. Pulling you away from everything you know. He wants to isolate you. That's key for him." The man knew how to intimidate and control his enemies.

And his friends. Luis Sanchez…hell, he still couldn't believe the guy had chosen to shove a knife into his heart instead of talking.

"Marie…"

He pushed the memory away, just like he did all the bloodstained memories that wanted to haunt him.

As far as the EOD was concerned, it was time for a new tactic with Juliana. "My boss—Mercer—he wants you seen in public. We want to make Guerrero become the one who's afraid. We want him to think that we've found the evidence. That we're secure. The idea is that he'll get desperate when he thinks we're closing in, and desperate men make mistakes." He'd seen it happen over and over again.

"Do I have a choice in this?"

Her words stopped him cold, and in that instant…

Logan realized that some things were more important than following orders.

"Yes." He kept his voice calm with an effort. "You do. If you want me to take you out of Mississippi, to get you as far from Guerrero and his goons as I can, you say the word."

Her lips parted.

"If you want to stay here, to stand off against him and make him become the hunted, then we'll do that. It's your life. *You* make the choice." He'd back her up, even if he had to go alone, without the other EOD agents riding shotgun.

So Logan waited.

Her hand rose. Touched the small bandage on the back of her neck. "I don't want to spend the rest of my life running."

Logan knew people who had spent years running. That life—it stunk. Always looking over your shoulder, never letting your guard down.

But there was something else she needed to understand before she made her choice. "Mercer's worried we have a leak at the EOD. That if we tried to take you to another secret location…" *It wouldn't be secret.* "Guerrero shouldn't have found us so quickly. Shouldn't have known the things he did."

So Mercer was saying that hiding wasn't an option. No, that hiding *with* the EOD wasn't an option.

Logan was pretty sure he could make Juliana disappear just fine on his own.

He could see the struggle on Juliana's face. Safety… where did it lie?

With me. If she'd just trust him again.

"No hiding." Juliana gave a slow nod. "That's not… that's not the way I want to live. I don't want to be afraid, every day, that he's coming after me."

Did she even realize how strong she truly was?

"I want to go after him. I want Guerrero to fear. He took away so much." She swallowed and exhaled slowly. "It's time for me to take away from him."

Damn straight.

"Let him think I have the evidence. Let him think we're tearing his life apart." Her words came stronger now. "And then let's destroy him."

"We will." A vow.

Diego stared at the man before him. A man who sat, bound, with his arms and legs tied to a chair. A black bag covered his head and the fool was screaming at the top of his lungs.

Did he actually think help would come?

Diego sighed. "Why were you getting ready to leave town, Mr. McLintock?" Because he had been. Diego had sent a man to follow McLintock months ago. Back when he'd first realized that the senator was holding back.

The senator had to trust someone. Someone had been there to help with all the deals.

The someone who'd just stopped screaming.

"I—I was just going to visit my mother. She—she lives in Florida."

It was the wrong response. Ben McLintock should have been asking why he was being held. Demanding to know who'd taken him.

Not rushing to answer with a pat response.

"After all that happened with the senator, I—I needed to get away."

Still wrong.

Diego nodded to his men. The bag wasn't needed any longer.

One man stepped forward and yanked it from McLintock's head. McLintock's gaze flew around the small room, then locked on Diego.

"You know who I am," Diego said as he stared right back at the other man.

McLintock gave a small nod.

"That will make things easier." Diego lifted his hand and gave a little two-fingered wave. His man, Mario, knew what that signal meant.

A knife was immediately shoved into McLintock's shoulder.

The senator's aide screamed.

Diego dropped his hand. "You were working for the senator." The authorities had to know that, too. So he'd had to be so careful when he made his move on this man. But lucky for him, McLintock had been the one to escape from the guards that the government had put on him.

His man had been driving the taxi that picked up McLintock.

"I—I don't know what—"

Sighing, Diego lifted two fingers.

"No!" McLintock said. Mario paused and Diego cocked a brow. "I—I was… I just delivered packages for him, okay? I didn't even know what was in them, not until the feds came in and started asking all their questions."

Blood soaked his fancy shirt. "Then Aaron offered me money to keep quiet."

Sure, as if Diego believed that was the way things had gone down. This man had known about the deals. Probably from day one. He'd been taking money, stashing it away just like James had.

But James hadn't escaped. Neither would McLintock.

"Where's the evidence?"

"I don't know. I swear!"

Diego gave his two-fingered wave. The knife sank into McLintock's left shoulder this time. More screams. More blood.

"I'll ask again."

"I don't know!"

The knife sank into his left thigh.

"I need that evidence…"

"J-James said he was giving it…to his daughter… s-safekeeping…"

The knife sank into his right thigh.

"I don't know anything else!"

He could almost believe him.

"*Please*…let me go…"

Was the many crying now? How pitiful. "I will," Diego promised him. What would be the point in keeping him? A few more moments, and he'd know if McLintock had any more secrets to tell. After that…

He could go free.

"Tell me, what do you know about the bomb in the cemetery?"

McLintock flinched. "Nothing!"

"Lies just make the pain last longer." He knew exactly how to get to this one. Pain. McLintock howled when Mario went to work on him again.

"I didn't set it! I didn't!" McLintock was definitely crying now.

He also sounded honest. Pity. McLintock had been one of the few with open access to the senator's house and to his car. But if it hadn't been McLintock, then that did narrow down his pool of suspects.

Diego nodded to Mario. "You know what to do."

A muscle flexed in Mario's jaw.

"Y-you're gonna let me go, right?" McLintock was soaked in blood and straining against his bonds. "You'll let me go?"

"Of course." Diego turned away. "Once I'm sure you don't have any other secrets to tell…"

Fear tightened McLintock's face.

"So perhaps you'd better keep talking," Diego advised, "or else Mario will keep cutting."

THE MANSION THAT SAT high up on the hill, its stone walls stark and cold, had never seemed like home to Juliana.

The building had felt more like a tomb.

It sure looked like one from a distance.

"We've got a press conference scheduled for eight o'clock," Gunner said from his seat up front. "You're gonna focus on Guerrero during that talk. Time to start rattling the SOB."

Right. She nodded. She'd say or do whatever was necessary. *No more fear.* She wasn't going to stand in the middle of any more bloodbaths. As it was, Juliana had more than enough gore floating around in her mind to give her plenty of nightmares, thank you so much.

The SUV pulled to a stop. A cop car was behind them, another in front. Their escorts. Juliana knew that a large guard force would stay at the mansion. Added cover, sure, but the bodies were also designed to attract extra attention for them.

Here I am. Come and get me.

So they could get Guerrero.

Gunner exited the SUV and headed for the main entrance. Juliana knew the heavy iron security gates would have already closed behind them, locking the vehicles inside.

She glanced over at the house. This had been her father's place, not hers.

"Why did you always hate it here?" Logan's quiet question surprised her.

Shrugging a little, she said, "Because it's cold inside. It's just a big fancy tomb." Her palms flattened against her jeans. "My mother died one week after we moved into this house. She was coming home and a drunk driver slammed into her."

Juliana had been twelve. Her mother's death had torn her whole life apart.

And her father—he'd become someone completely different. He'd stopped caring about people. Only focused on *things*. More wealth. More houses.

"It was never home," she said, staring at all the windows. "And it always smelled like a funeral." Because of the flowers. So many had come after her mother's death. For weeks the house had been overflowing.

Then the flowers had started to wither and die.

She glanced back at Logan and was surprised by the pain she saw flash across his face. "Logan?"

"I'm sorry about your mother. I heard…she was a great lady."

This part she could remember so well. "She was." Her mother had been the good that balanced out her father.

She'd always made him be *better.* Without her, he'd fallen apart.

Juliana reached for her door. Her shoes made no sound as she headed up the elaborate walk. Logan was at her side and—

"You're alive!"

The woman's high cry had Juliana's head jerking up. Then she saw Susan Walker, her father's assistant, rushing toward her.

Susan caught her in a big, tight hug, a hug that smelled of expensive body lotion and red wine. "I thought you'd died! You disappeared after the explosion and no one would tell me anything...." She pulled back, gazing up at Juliana with wide, worried eyes. "I mean, on the news, they said that you'd survived. But I never *saw* you!" Susan's words tumbled out too fast. "And I was so worried!"

Susan's perfectly smooth face gave no hint to her age. She could have been thirty; she could have been forty-five. The woman had been a fixture in her father's life for the past eleven years.

His closest confidant. The person who organized his life.

And...

Juliana was pretty sure, her father's lover.

"We need to go inside," Gunner said in a quiet voice.

Susan jumped, as if she hadn't even noticed the men surrounding them. Then, after a frantic look around, she said, "Yes, yes, of course..." She ushered them inside the house. She was in a robe. A white silk robe that skirted around her ankles.

When Juliana entered the house, she heard the faint strains of music playing in the background.

They entered the den, and Juliana saw the wineglass on the table.

"I, um...I was just trying to relax a bit." Susan's lips pressed together for a moment. "You knew I moved in last spring, right?" She asked as her fingers nervously toyed with the robe's belt. "I mean, it just... The move gave me better access to your father. There was so much work to do and I—"

"You were sleeping with him." The words just came out. She wasn't in the mood for more lies or sugarcoating. Her mother was gone. She'd known her father had lovers, and Susan—well, the woman had always been kind to her.

Susan paled. "I was his assistant! I was—"

"His lover." Juliana rolled tired shoulders. "It's all right. You don't have to pretend with me."

Logan and Gunner were silent, assessing. She knew they'd run a check on Susan, on all the employees who worked so closely with her father.

All of the employees had turned up clean, no connection to Guerrero. But Logan was still suspicious, and she knew the EOD was still digging deep for dirt.

"Who are these men?" Susan glanced first at Gunner. Then Logan.

"Her protection," Logan said with a smile. "In light of all that's happened, I'm sure you understand why we'll be staying here with Juliana."

"Here?" Susan parroted as her eyes widened.

Right. Well, with her father dead, the house was technically Juliana's. Even if he had been sleeping with Susan. Talk about awkward. She didn't want to make Susan feel uncomfortable, but this was where they needed to be, at least for the next few days. *Just tell her.* "We're going to be moving in for a while." Hopefully, it wouldn't be for long. But in case it was longer, Juliana desperately needed a base to use so that she could get back to her life. She wanted to paint. Painting was her livelihood and she had work to deliver, but more, painting gave her a release. It could help take her mind off all the death.

Logan had told her that supplies would be brought in to her. When he'd said that, she'd almost kissed him. She'd caught herself, though, because she knew just where a kiss would have lead them.

To us both being naked. The awareness simmered between them.

"You can't stay here." Susan's rushed denial had Juliana blinking. "This isn't… You've *never* stayed here, Juliana."

It was late. Juliana was exhausted. She wanted to hit the bed and fall into oblivion. "I'm going to be staying here now. So are they." Simple.

Susan just shook her head.

"Which rooms are free?" Juliana asked her. "There should be more than enough for us to use." She was already getting a chill from being inside the house. The place was always so cold. Her father had restored every inch of the old antebellum. Or rather, he'd paid folks to restore the house. Maybe it was cold because the place was so big and drafty.

Maybe.

She knew her father kept a small staff in the house. A driver. A housekeeper. A cook. And—

"Take any room you want," Susan said softly as her shoulders sagged. "Take everything… It's yours, anyway." Then she brushed by Juliana. "I'm in your father's room."

Juliana felt badly about upsetting Susan. She knew the woman was hurting, too. She was pushing into this place—*where I don't belong*—and ripping into Susan's life. Bringing her hell right down on the hapless woman. "Susan…" She wanted her to be safe. Juliana took a breath and though she hated to say it, she forced the words out. "Maybe you should leave for a few days, until…" *Until it's safe. Until I'm not afraid you'll get caught in the cross fire when Guerrero attacks.*

Susan truly had always been kind to her, and when this nightmare was over, Juliana would give her the house. She could take it and be happy.

Juliana sure didn't want the place. She much preferred her small house on the beach. It never seemed cold there.

Susan's pretty face tightened. "You're kicking me out?"

And she'd screwed up. Juliana tried to back up. "No, no, that's not—"

"For your protection," Logan inserted smoothly. "The government will be happy to provide you with temporary lodging for a few days, until the situation becomes more stable."

Susan just shook her head. Her gaze seemed to swim with tears. "I'm not in any danger. No one would want to hurt me!"

"I'm sure that's what Charles thought, too," Juliana said quietly. She'd arranged to send flowers to his family, but she'd do more for them, too. When her father's estate was settled—after the government had their turn to go through everything, she'd see that they were taken care of.

"Wrong place," Gunner added darkly. "Wrong damn time."

Susan flinched. Then her eyes focused on Juliana. "Why? Why is this even happening?"

"Because my father was involved with some very dangerous people." Susan would have been the prime person to realize that truth, only, she seemed clueless. "Now they want me dead."

"We'll be escorting you out tonight, Ms. Walker," Gunner said. "Just show us to your room, and I can help you pack up."

Susan was still staring at Juliana. "I told you. I shared a room with the senator." Then she turned away, moving toward the circular staircase with her head up. But at the stairs, she paused with her hand on the banister. "He was going to marry me."

Juliana barely heard the quiet words.

"We'd planned… He was going to give up his office. Retire. Stay with me." Her head tilted and Juliana saw her scan the house. What did Susan see when she looked around?

Not death and ice, like Juliana saw.

Antiques, wealth, good memories?

"It's all gone," Susan whispered and she climbed up the steps.

Juliana's gaze darted to the closed study door. Her father had died in that room. He'd put one of his prized guns to his head and squeezed the trigger.

Susan had found his body. So that meant she must have found the suicide note, too. She knew that the senator had fallen far from grace.

It's all gone.

Yes, it was.

The little bitch was back.

Susan closed the bedroom door behind herself. Flipped the lock—then slapped her palm against the wood.

The pain was fresh, staggering, and it helped her to push back the fury that had her whole body shaking.

Juliana had just marched in…and kicked her out.

After all of these years. After all the work she'd done.

Juliana hadn't stayed around to look after Aaron. She hadn't been there, day in and day out, working to keep the man on a leash. Working to make him look sane when the man hadn't cared about anything.

Or anyone.

Susan glanced at the ornate bed.

I was here.

And everything—it was supposed to be hers now. Aaron had promised to take care of her. Only, he hadn't.

He'd been weak until the end. Weak and desperate, and he'd taken the easy way out.

A bullet to the brain. She would have made him suffer more. He'd dangled his promises in front of her for so long.

It should all be mine. The money. The houses. The cars. Every. Single. Thing.

She was so tired of pretending. She'd pretended for years. Yanked herself out of the gutter. Pushed her way into Aaron's life.

His weakness had been an advantage for her, at first. But now...

Her gaze roamed around the room. Right past the paintings that he'd ordered hung on the wall. Juliana's paintings. Her precious work.

Did the girl even realize her father had bought them? That he'd ordered the pieces, paying far too much, and had them delivered back here?

Susan hated them. Storms, dark skies and threatening clouds.

Susan had been so tempted to slice the paintings in the past few days. To just rip them apart.

Payback.

But she'd kept up her image, for all the good it had done her. Kept it up even when she'd shattered on the inside.

"Ms. Walker." A rap sounded at her door. "We'll be leaving soon." An order.

She recognized the voice, of course; it belonged to the first man who'd come into her home. The dark man with the darker eyes.

His stare didn't scare her. She'd seen plenty of darkness as a kid.

"Just a minute," she called, trying to keep her voice level. Now wasn't the time to lose her control. Now was the time to keep planning. To keep her focus.

She headed for the nightstand and the small safe that she knew waited inside.

There were files in that safe. A small handgun. Sure, the police and the FBI and who the hell knew who else had been in the house, and they'd searched everywhere, but...

But they didn't see the papers inside the safe.

She'd made sure of it. She'd taken those papers, hidden them, then brought them back when the agents backed off.

I knew I could use them.

Another rap. "You need to hurry, Ms. Walker. A car's waiting downstairs for you."

Her jaw ached, and she forced her teeth to unclench. She'd recognized the other man downstairs. He'd changed over the years, yes, but she'd still remembered him.

His eyes were the same.

She pulled out the papers from the safe. Flipped open the file.

Logan Quinn's eyes stared back at her.

Once upon a time, Senator Aaron James had wanted Logan Quinn eliminated from his daughter's life.

Susan had taken the necessary steps for that elimination. She'd been the one to do the research. To destroy the budding romance.

She knew all about Logan's secrets. It was time for Juliana to learn about them, too.

You think you're safe, don't you? Her gaze darted back

to the paintings. *You think he'll keep you safe. But what happens when you learn about all of his lies?*

Susan left the safe open just a few inches, and she left the manila file pushing out.

Juliana would find it soon enough.

Then she'd be vulnerable.

And Juliana wouldn't survive the next attack on her life.

Susan exhaled slowly and made her way back to the door. She flipped the lock and opened it carefully. "I'm sorry…" A quaver entered her voice. "It's been a…rough few days."

He nodded. "I understand, and the move—it's just for your safety."

She looked at him from beneath her lashes. Not her usual type. Too rough. She'd felt the calluses on the man's fingertips, but…

Sometimes it wasn't about what you liked.

It was about what you could use.

Susan rested her fingers on his chest. "I'll be able to come home again soon, right?"

He glanced at her hand, then back up to her face. The guy's expression hadn't thawed any. "When it's clear."

It would be clear, just as soon as Juliana was rotting in the ground.

JULIANA WAS STANDING at the foot of the stairs when Susan came down. Gunner was just a few steps behind, carrying her suitcase in his hand.

It looked as if Susan had been crying.

Great. Juliana shifted her body and blocked the bottom of the stairs. "It's just temporary, Susan."

Susan's eyes were red. She *had* been crying. "It's not going to be my home. You and I both know…in the will, he left everything to you." Anger thinned her lips. "You couldn't be bothered to see him, but it all still goes to you."

"I don't…" *Want it.* "This isn't my home any longer. As soon as Logan and his team stop the man who's hunting me…"

Susan's gaze flickered to Logan. "I remember you."

He was by the door. Arms crossed over his chest. At her words, his head cocked toward Susan.

Susan stared right back at him. "Aaron always told me that you were dangerous."

Juliana eased to the side, blocking her view. This wasn't about Logan. "Susan, when this mess is over, I'll call you. We'll sort everything out. The house, the will—everything."

Susan's lips twisted in a sad smile as her gaze focused on Juliana. "He loved you. Probably more than you'll ever realize. It's too bad you didn't know anything about him." She brushed by Juliana. "Maybe you should take a look at what's on the walls of his room. It might surprise you."

Then she was gone. Gunner followed behind her, shaking his head.

But Juliana saw Logan grab Gunner's arm before he could walk through the doorway. "Find out what she knows."

Gunner gave an almost imperceptible nod.

The door closed behind him with a click.

Juliana rubbed at the bandage on her neck. She'd almost forgotten about her injuries. Her head had finally stopped throbbing. She just—

"Don't."

Logan stalked toward her. He caught her fingers, pulled them away from the small bandage. "Don't do anything to draw attention to it."

"No one's here to see." His team had cleared out the

house. They were alone—all of the guards were stalking along the exterior of the place.

Alone with Logan. When he was this close, the awareness between them burned. But she turned away. "I'm… I'm going to shower." She didn't want to see what waited in her father's room. Not then.

She wanted to wash away the memories of blood.

Logan's fingers curled around her wrist. "Are we going to talk about it?"

Her throat went desert dry. "It?"

"You…almost coming…"

There'd been no almost about it. She glanced back, and from the look in his eyes, Juliana knew he realized that truth.

"Or are we just going to pretend that it didn't happen?"

Juliana gave a slow shake of her head. "I'm not that good at pretending."

His gaze searched hers. "You're mad because of the setup. I get that."

Good for him.

"But I swear, I wouldn't risk your life for anything. You're my priority."

She believed that. After all, wasn't keeping her safe his job?

His fingers tightened around her wrist. "You're just going to walk away, aren't you?"

It was what he expected. She knew that. But there was more at stake right then.

Juliana had realized just how vulnerable she still was to Logan. He'd gotten into her heart once, and no matter how hard she tried, she'd never been able to shove him out.

She still cared for him, probably always would.

But she couldn't let herself love him again. It was too dangerous. Too painful.

Take the pleasure he can give you. A tempting whisper from inside. *Then you be the one to walk away.*

Only, there was a problem with that plan. If she took him back to her bed, Juliana was afraid she might not want to walk away.

So she pulled her arm free, and before she gave in to that temptation, she headed up the stairs.

I can walk away now.

Juliana just wasn't sure that walking away was what she really wanted.

DIEGO SHOOK HIS HEAD as he stared at the man seated in front of him. McLintock couldn't even keep his head up anymore. Blood and sweat coated his body.

"I didn't have anything to do with that explosion at the cemetery. I promise!" Ben McLintock mumbled, voice rasping. He'd already said this over and over, and Diego actually believed him.

Why keep lying at this point? McLintock had no one to protect. No family. No lover. The guy had always just been out for himself.

But if it hadn't been McLintock... Diego's eyes narrowed.

He waved the guard back and strolled toward McLintock. He put his hands on the other man's shoulders and shoved him back. McLintock blinked blearily as Diego leaned in close. "This can all be over," Diego promised him. "I just want to know who's after Juliana James. I want to know who set that bomb in her car." Who'd almost screwed his plans to hell.

I need that evidence. Another loose end. There were too many.

"I...don't know! I swear—I don't..."

His hands tightened around McLintock's thin shoulders. "Did you know that Mario over there—" he tilted his head toward the guard "—has one thing that he's particularly good at? Death. He can kill in a hundred different ways. He *likes* killing."

McLintock was crying. Had been for a while now.

Did he realize that no matter what happened, he wouldn't get out alive? Probably not. People always clung to hope so desperately. Even when they had no reason for that hope.

"Did you see anything…anyone suspicious at the cemetery?" Diego pressed. "You rode over in that limo. Who was there when you got in it?"

"Just…the driver, Charles…"

The man wouldn't have killed himself.

"Cops were…there." McLintock licked his lips. Tried to hold up his sagging head. "Federal…agents. I thought—I thought everything was…safe."

No place was safe.

With the cops swarming around, though, the person who'd planted that bomb would have needed good access—an "in" at the mansion.

"I rode…in the car, just…me, Juliana and…Susan…"

Susan. Diego paused, remembering a woman with sleek blond hair and too-sharp eyes. He'd seen her before, with the senator.

He'd seen Susan, but she'd never seen him.

Aaron's lover. Would a lover kill a daughter?

Yes.

"When it was time to leave the cemetery, why weren't you in the limo?" This was the important question. From what he'd learned, Juliana had been about to climb into the limo. What about the other passengers?

"Susan…Susan said she wasn't…feeling well." The words were soft. Weak. The blood loss was definitely taking its toll on the man. "She…asked me…stay with…her. Wanted to get…some air. Said we could get…ride back… with someone else.…"

Diego smiled. "Was that so hard?"

Looking confused, McLintock actually tried to smile back even as his eyes flickered closed.

Diego fired a hard glance at Mario. "Find the woman—this Susan. Bring her in to me."

McLintock drunkenly shook his head. "No. Susan… didn't do this… She doesn't know anything about—"

"A man's lover always knows him better than anyone else." That was why Diego made a habit of not leaving his lovers alive. They'd just betray him if they lived.

There was too much betrayal in the world.

His father had taught him that lesson early on. In Mexico, his father had amassed a fortune by dealing in the darkness. The law hadn't applied to him. But…he'd always been so good to Diego. Given him a good life, nice clothes, toys. A home.

Diego had known his father was a dangerous man, but he'd trusted him. A boy trusted his father.

Until that night… He'd heard screams. He'd followed the cries. Found his mother dying, and his father—covered in her blood.

"She was selling me out!" His father had wiped the bloody blade of his knife on his pants. *"Trying to make a deal with those Americans… She was going to take you away from me!"*

His mother had looked like a beautiful angel. Lying on the ground, her white nightgown stained red.

"No one will take you from me!" his father had snarled. *"They think they can use you against me, make me weak!"*

His father had been so good to him before.

But Diego had seen the real man that night.

No one is good.

His father had stalked toward him with his knife. The knife he'd used to kill Diego's mother. *"No one can use you against me."*

And he'd known that his father had snapped. He'd cried as he looked at his mother and he'd realized— *He's going to kill me, too.*

Only, Diego hadn't been ready to die.

They'd fought. The knife had cut into Diego's flesh. He still had the long scar on his stomach, a permanent reminder.

Trust no one. Especially not those close to you.

But Diego hadn't died. At twelve, Diego had killed his father. Then when he'd walked out of that house, covered in blood, with the bodies of his mother and father behind him…

El Diablo.

His father's men had given him a new name—and they'd feared him. Everyone had.

Diego realized that he was staring down at McLintock. The man was barely breathing, and the hope was almost painful to see in his bleary eyes.

Giving a slow nod, Diego stepped back. "You've given me the information that I needed." And he was sure that Susan would be coming to join him very soon.

"You'll let me go? Please?" The man's voice was thready, so weak. No man should talk like that. Diego barely held his disgust in check. No man should beg. His father hadn't begged.

"The knife," Diego said as he opened his hand. Without any hesitation, Mario gave him the blade.

McLintock sighed raggedly. Did he think Diego was going to cut his bonds and let him go?

"You're free," Diego told him and drove the knife right into McLintock's heart.

When he turned away from the body, he saw the fear... the respect...in Mario's eyes.

El Diablo.

As long as there was fear, he didn't need trust or loyalty.

Chapter Eight

The bathroom door opened, sending tendrils of steam drifting into the bedroom. Juliana walked out wrapped in a towel, with her wet hair sliding over her shoulders.

The woman was every fantasy he'd ever had. Just seeing her—arousal flooded through Logan, hardening his flesh for her.

She was looking down when she entered the bedroom, but after just an instant, she seemed to sense him. Juliana glanced up and froze.

Maybe he should be a gentleman and turn away while she dressed. Juliana was probably used to gentlemen. The guys who spoke to her so softly, held her hand and greeted her with flowers.

And didn't constantly think about ripping her clothes away—or her towel—and taking her in a wild rush of lust and greedy need.

The gentleman role wasn't for him.

So Logan kept watching and enjoying that world-class view.

Juliana's eyes narrowed to dark slits, and even that seemed sexy. "Do you mind?"

"Not at all." In fact, this was going on his highlight reel for later.

Her lips tightened. He liked her lips soft. Wet. Open. On his.

"Why are you in here, Logan?"

Because I want you. He'd had a taste before, and it had just left him craving more. Their time was limited. He knew that. As soon as the nightmare ended, Juliana would walk away and not look back.

Why couldn't he have her just once more? Before the real world ripped them apart. He needed more memories to get him through the dark and bloody nights that would come.

When he was in hell, her memory got him through the fire.

But he pushed back the flames and said, "I thought you needed to know...Ben McLintock is missing." Syd had called with the news just a few minutes before.

"Missing?"

"Uniforms were on him, stationed at his house." Because anyone who'd worked so closely with the senator was getting extra attention from the government and the cops. "But it looks like he slipped away." Or rather, deliberately ditched the eyes on him and vanished.

She shook her head. "Ben? Ben ran away?"

Innocent men don't run. Logan bit the words back and tried to keep his gaze on her face. He shouldn't have to say the words, anyway. Juliana would know the truth.

And sure enough, he saw the painful truth sink in for her. "The car bomb. You said...someone would have needed access to this house. The limo was here."

Ben had been there. The guy had been given 24/7 access to everything the senator had.

Juliana's hands lifted and she clutched the towel closer to her body. "You think...you think he set the car bomb." Not a question.

"It's a possibility." One that Sydney was following up on with the authorities.

"He always seemed so nice." Her words were dazed.

"Nice men can make perfect killers." Because the nice veneer was so convincing. A way to fool others so you could get close.

He realized he was staring at the tops of her breasts. Logan cleared his throat. "We'll find him." The guy had either run on his own…or Guerrero had him. But either way, Logan's team was tracking him now. Ben McLintock wasn't going to just vanish. They wouldn't let him.

He pulled in a breath and caught the scent of vanilla. The scent drifted from the open bathroom door. From Juliana. A sweet but sensual scent.

Logan spun around and headed for the door. "Get some sleep." He sure as hell wouldn't. He'd be thinking about her—what *should* have been.

"Logan." Her voice stopped him at the door. His hand had lifted, and he fisted his fingers before slowly turning back to face her.

Juliana hadn't moved from her spot just outside the bathroom. More steam drifted around her. Her skin gleamed, so smooth, so soft.

"You still look at me—" her chin lifted "—like you want—"

"To eat you alive." Yeah, he knew how he looked. Starving. But Juliana had always made him that way. Desperate for what he wanted, for what he'd taken before.

Her hands were still at the top of the towel. "In Mexico, you told me that if I offered myself to you again…"

He couldn't think about that night right then. Being close to her after all those years—he'd gone more than a little crazy.

"You said you'd take me," she finished.

Logan didn't speak.

"But I've changed my mind."

His whole body had turned to stone.

"I've thought about what I want. What I don't want."

He couldn't hear this.

"I know we don't have forever. I know you'll go back to—to wherever the next battle is, and I'll go back to Biloxi when this is all over."

Biloxi. Her home on the beach. He'd seen it before. After a battle that had taken two of his best friends. When he'd been broken and weak, he'd had to find her.

So he'd gone to her beach. He'd watched her from a distance, gotten stronger just from seeing her.

But he'd stayed in the shadows. After all, that was where he belonged.

"We don't have forever," Juliana said again, the words husky, "but we do have now."

He took a step toward her and shook his head. No way had he just heard her say—

"But I'm not offering."

Son of a—

"This time, *I'm* taking." She dropped the towel. His mouth dried up. "I want you, and right now, I don't care about the past or the future. Now—now is all that matters to me."

She was all that mattered to him. Logan was already across the room. His hands were on her, greedy for the feel of her flesh. He pulled her against him, pressed his mouth to hers, thrust his tongue past her lips and tasted the paradise that waited.

The bed was steps away—steps that he didn't remember taking. But they were falling, tumbling back, and he had her beneath him on the mattress.

He'd woken from hot, desperate dreams of her for years, and part of him wondered... *just a dream?*

Then her nails bit into his back. Her legs slid over his hips and she pulled him closer.

No dream ever felt this good.

His mouth was still on hers because he had to keep tasting her. His hands were stroking her body because he needed to feel her silken flesh.

But she wasn't just lying passive beneath him. Her body arched against him, and Juliana caught the hem of his shirt—and then she yanked the shirt off him.

Their lips broke apart and the shirt went flying. A wild smile pulled at his lips. Only Juliana. She was always—

His.

He caressed the pert curve of her breast. The nipple was tight, flushed pink, and when he put his lips on her, she whispered his name.

And scored her nails down his back.

He should go slowly. Learn her body again, remember every inch.

But her scent was driving him out of his mind. She was pulling him closer. She was all he could feel. All he could breathe.

Everything.

He yanked down the zipper of his jeans. Found protection for them, then he positioned his aroused length at the delicate entrance of her sex.

Logan caught her hands and pushed them back against the mattress. Their fingers threaded together, their gazes locked.

The years fell away.

The only girl I ever loved.

"Logan..." She whispered his name. "I've missed you," she confessed.

Then there was nothing else but her.

Logan pushed into her moist, hot core, driving deep and steady, fighting to hold on to his control when he just wanted to take and take and take. But he had to show her pleasure. He had to make sure she went as wild as he did.

Her legs wrapped around him. No hesitation. No fear. She smiled up at him.

His hips pulled back, then he thrust deep. Her breath caught and the smile faded from her lips. The passion built between them, the desire deepening. The thrusts came faster, harder, and the control he'd held so tight began to shred.

The pleasure filled her eyes, making them seem to go blind. He'd never seen anything more beautiful than her. Nothing…no one…

Her climax trembled around him and she cried out in release. Her breaths came in quick gasps as her legs tightened around him.

The release hit Logan, not a wave or a rush but an avalanche that swept over him with a climax so powerful his body shuddered—and he held on to Juliana as tightly as he could.

And when his heartbeat eased its too-frantic pounding, he stared back into her eyes and realized just how dangerous she still was…to him.

THE SCENT OF BOOZE HUNG heavily in the air. Beer. Whiskey. *But even more than that…he could smell the blood.*

"Dad?" Logan called out for him even as he pushed against the dashboard. It had fallen in on him, and he had to twist and heave his body in order to slide out from under the dash. He yanked at the seat belt, his hands wet with blood, and finally, finally, he was free.

His dad wasn't.

Logan stared at the wreckage of the pickup. Twisted metal. Broken glass. And his father pinned behind the wheel, head craned at an unnatural angle.

His fingers trembled when he put them to his father's throat. No pulse. No life. Nothing.

"Help..."

The barest of cries. So soft. A whisper. But he stiffened and whirled around.

That was when he saw the other car. A fancy ride, with a BMW decal on the front—and the entire driver's side smashed inward.

"Help..." The cry came again, from inside that shattered wreck. A woman's voice.

And Logan remembered...

The scream of tires. The roar of crunching metal.

The sound of death.

He tried to get to the woman. Cuts covered her pretty face. She was so pale. So small.

"It's going to be all right," he told her, reaching for her hand. "I'll get you help."

She looked at him, opening dazed eyes. "Ju...Juliana?"

Then her breath heaved.

She didn't say anything else ever again.

LOGAN STOOD AT THE TOP of the stairs as the memories rolled over him. He'd fought to keep that dark night buried for so long, but here, in this place, with Juliana once more...the past had gotten to him.

Some nights could never be forgotten, some mistakes never erased.

The life he'd known had ended that night. Two people had died. He'd...

"What are you doing?" Juliana's soft voice came from the darkness behind him.

Logan stiffened. "Just doing a sweep." Total BS. But he couldn't face her yet. Not after what he'd done.

Back then and…now.

Juliana had fallen asleep in his arms. Sleep wouldn't come so easily for him. Never had.

He'd searched the house. The agents and cops had already done plenty of sweeps. *He'd* done his share of searching before, too, but he'd had to look again.

Because there'd been something in Susan's eyes…

The woman had wanted Juliana to go into Aaron's room. Now Logan knew why.

He'd found the safe, conveniently left open. He'd seen the documents inside.

That safe had been empty just days before—well, empty except for the small gun. The senator had always seemed to be keeping guns close.

Too close.

Juliana hadn't seen her father's body after the suicide, but Logan had. He'd never forget the image.

But those files hadn't been in the safe days before. He knew because he'd cracked it himself and made sure the senator hadn't hidden any evidence inside. Since the safe had been empty then, it meant that someone else— *Susan*—had deliberately placed the files and the car-crash photos he'd discovered in that safe.

Susan knew what he'd done, what the senator had done. And she'd wanted Juliana to find out, too.

Why? So she'd turn against me?

He couldn't afford to have Juliana turn away from him, not now. It would be too dangerous for her.

"Dawn's close," she said, her voice husky. Sexy.

Dawn was coming. He could see the sky lightening behind the big picture windows. Faint hues of red were streaking through the darkness.

They'd have to get ready for her press conference soon. More plans. More traps.

Her fingers were on his back, tracing lightly over the scar that slid down near his spine. "What happened here?" she asked him softly.

Her touch was light, easy.

Logan swallowed and tried to keep his body from tensing. "A mission in the Middle East. Hostage rescue. It didn't go…quite as planned." He'd had to take the hit in order to protect the hostage. At the time, he'd barely felt the pain. And he'd killed in response to the attack—instantly. No second thought, no hesitation. In the field, there wasn't ever time for hesitation.

Kill or be killed.

Her fingers slid around his side. So delicate on his flesh. Logan turned to face her.

"And here?" Juliana asked. She was tracing the jagged wound that was too close to his heart. As she leaned forward to study the scar, her hair slid over his arm.

Logan took a breath and pulled her scent deep into his lungs. "A bullet wound in Panama." A drug lord hadn't liked having his operation shut down. Too bad for him. And that shot had almost been too close for Logan.

Her head tilted back as she studied him and let her fingers rise to slip under his chin. "And here? What about this one?"

His smallest scar. He stared into her eyes. "That one came from a bar fight…in Jackson, Mississippi."

A furrow appeared between her eyes.

Why not tell her? "One day, I lost my girl, so I got drunk in the nearest bar I could find." The only time he'd gotten drunk. *Won't be like him. Can't.* "There was a fight." His fingers lifted, caught hers, moved them away from the scar. "A broken whiskey bottle caught me in the chin."

Her gaze searched his. "You didn't lose me."

"Didn't I?"

She pulled her hand away. Logan saw that she was wearing a robe, long and silky. He wanted to pull her back into his arms but—

The phone in his back pocket began to vibrate. Logan pulled it out, keeping his eyes on hers. "Quinn."

"We just found McLintock," Jasper said, his voice rough.

"Where?"

"Cemetery. They dumped his body on the senator's grave."

Hell, that was a pretty clear message.

"He was carved up. Someone sure took their time with him."

Because Guerrero had wanted McLintock to talk, and Logan was betting that the guy had talked plenty, before his attackers killed him.

Guerrero and his men liked to get up close and personal with their targets. From the cases that he'd worked before, Logan knew that Guerrero's weapon of choice was a knife. He liked the intimacy of the blade. The control it gave him as he slowly tortured his prey.

That was why the cemetery bombing had never fit for him. Not up close and personal enough. The guy enjoyed watching the pain on his victims' faces.

"I'm going with the ME now," Jasper said, and there was the rumble of another voice in the background, "but I'll meet you at the press conference."

The press conference. Right. They still had their show to do. Logan ended the call. His eyes never left Juliana's. "You heard." She'd been too close to miss Jasper's words.

A faint nod. Her pupils had widened with worry.

"And you still want to go out there?" He pushed her because his instincts were to grab her and run. To hide her. To keep her safe and protected. *Not* to put her on display for the killer. "You still want to challenge Guerrero?"

"He killed Ben…."

"No, he tortured Ben, probably for hours, *then* he killed him." Brutal, but that was what they were dealing with, and they all had to face that truth. "You're going to bait Ben's killer on television. Taunt him. You ready for that?"

Maybe he expected her to back down. Maybe he *wanted* her to. Because then it would be fine when he kidnapped her and they vanished.

"How many others has he killed?"

He didn't even know. No one was sure. Hundreds. With the weapons that Guerrero had sold? Thousands.

"That's what I thought," Juliana said. Her chin lifted a little. Her shoulders seemed to straighten beneath the silk robe. "I'm ready for this. I'll do what I have to do, and we'll stop him."

And he knew there would be no running away. It was Juliana's choice, and he'd never take her choice away. He'd stand by her. Keep her safe. *No other option.*

He stared at her and realized…he'd *hoped* that she would want to run, but deep down, he'd actually expected her to do exactly what she was doing. Because he knew Juliana—the woman had a fierce core of steel.

She turned away from him, and he knew…things were only going to get more dangerous for them.

So he'd damn well stay by her side.

But she'd only taken a few steps when she stopped and pulled in a sharp breath, as if she were bracing herself. Then Juliana turned back to face him, her pretty face set with lines of determination. "There's something I have to tell you."

He raised a brow. Waited.

Her tongue swiped over her lower lip. "It was my fault."

Logan had no idea what she was talking about. "Juliana?"

"All of those men who died at your cabin, everything that happened there…it was *all because of me.*"

He stepped toward her. "No, baby, it's not you. It's Guerrero. He's crazy. He'll torture, kill—do anything that he has to do in order to get what he wants."

Logan tried to take her into his arms, but she moved back.

"There was… I didn't tell you everything." She wrapped her arms around her stomach and rocked back on her heels. Pain glinted in her dark stare. "When I was in Mexico, when I was with John—"

Not John. Guerrero.

"We talked for so long. About everything. Nothing. Things that I didn't think mattered to anyone but…me."

A knot formed in his gut. "What did you tell him?" They'd gone over this before, on the plane ride back from Mexico, but they'd just focused on any revelations she might have made about her father. And now that he thought about it, Juliana had never quite met his gaze during that interrogation. She'd kept glancing away, shifting nervously. All the telltale signs of deception had been there, but he'd just thought—

Not her.

Juliana wouldn't lie. He was the one who lied. She'd just been nervous, in shock from everything that happened.

"I never realized what I said would matter." She was meeting his stare now. With guilt and stoic determination battling the pain in her gaze. "I should have told you sooner."

"Told me what?"

"Guerrero knows about you. About us." She looked down. "I told you…he wasn't asking about my father's work. He was just asking about me, my life."

And she'd mentioned him? "Why?"

After a moment, her gaze came back to him. "I thought that I was going to die. I didn't expect a rescue."

As if he'd ever leave her to that hell. He'd been ready to bring that whole place down, brick by brick, in order to get her out.

"John…asked me if I'd ever been in love." Her laugh was brittle. "That's one of the things you think about before death, right? Did you love? Are you dying without that regret?"

That knot was getting bigger every moment. "You told him that you loved me."

"I even gave him your name," Juliana admitted in a sad rush. "With his connections, it would have been so easy for him to do a check on you and to—"

"Find the cabin under my name." Hell. The pieces fit. And that sure explained how Guerrero's men had tracked her so quickly.

"When you got me out, I didn't think what I'd said mattered." Sadness trembled in her tone. "I mean, I'd told him how you felt so I never expected—"

Logan caught her hands, pulling them away from her body. The tumble of her words froze and she stared up at him with parted lips. "How did I feel?" It scraped him raw on the inside to think that she'd been talking with Guerrero, laying her beautiful soul bare.

Juliana swallowed. "I told him that you didn't love me back."

His focus centered only on her. On the rasp of her breathing. The scent of vanilla. The ghost of pain in her eyes.

"So I thought he'd know there was nothing between us. I never thought he'd go into your life or that he'd—"

Logan put his mouth on hers. His tongue slipped past her lips. The kiss was probably too hard, too rough, but so was he right then.

I told him that you didn't love me back.

Her hands rose to his shoulders. Her mouth moved against his, gentling him.

After a few moments, Logan forced his head to lift. He stared down at her. "You didn't...you didn't do anything wrong." His voice came out as a growl.

She gave him a faint smile. "Yes, I did. But I won't make any more mistakes again. I promise." Then she turned, pulling away. With slow steps, Juliana headed back to the bedroom.

But she had it wrong. The fault wasn't hers. He was the one who'd screwed up. The one who'd never told her the truth.

"Logan...come back to bed with me."

His head jerked up. He'd been staring at the floor. At nothing.

Now he saw that she'd looked back over her shoulder at him. Her hand was up, reaching for him.

He should tell her the truth. She wasn't a kid any longer. Neither was he. He *would* tell her. Because of Susan, he'd have no choice.

If he didn't tell Juliana about that dark night, Susan would.

Guerrero will. The guy would be digging into his past, learning every secret that he could. And he'd try to use those secrets against her.

Maybe Juliana thought that Logan didn't care, but Guerrero...

"Logan?"

Guerrero would figure out the truth.

He rushed to her. Took her hand. Kissed her.

I loved you back.

Juliana might have gotten over him. She might just be looking for pleasure in a world gone to hell, but she mattered to him.

Always had.

He lifted her into his arms.

She always would.

Susan Walker watched as the poor little rich girl stepped toward the microphone. Looking dutifully mournful but determined. *Cry me a river.*

"The allegations that you've all heard about my father are true." Juliana's voice was clear and pitched perfectly to carry to all the microphones that surrounded her. "Senator Aaron James was using his position to perpetrate criminal acts. He was working with an arms dealer, a man that the government has identified as Diego Guerrero, and selling weapons off to the highest bidder."

There was an eruption of questions as the reporters attacked like sharks.

Juliana held up her hand. "My father took his life because he couldn't face what he'd done, but he left evidence behind." She glanced toward the men in black suits beside her. Men who screamed FBI or CIA. "That evidence has been recovered and is being turned over to the authorities."

Susan fought to keep her expression cool as Juliana continued talking. The reporters were eating up her every word. The woman looked like a perfect victim, sad-little-me, having to be so brave and struggle on after daddy's treachery.

The mob around Juliana would probably make her into a celebrity. Hell, there was no *probably* about it.

And there stood Logan. Just a few feet away from Juliana. The reporters hadn't noticed him. They'd followed Juliana's gaze to the other agents, not ever seeing the real threat right under their noses. Blind fools.

"The authorities have told me that Diego Guerrero is in the country, possibly operating under one of his aliases…" Now Juliana was staring straight into the cameras. "John Gonzales is a name he's used before."

One of the suits rushed forward. He held up a picture.

"This is a sketch of Diego as his Gonzales persona," Juliana continued. "We'll make sure you all get a…"

Susan spun away, took two furious steps forward and slammed into the man she now knew was called Gunner.

Gunner just stared down at her with a raised brow. "Going somewhere?"

She forced a smile. "I just… It's too much, you know?" She waved her hand back to the crowd. "I don't know why you insisted on escorting me here today. I told you already—you and the other agents—I had no idea what—"

"Ben McLintock said he had no idea, too." Gunner's dark stare seemed to measure her, looking for secrets.

You won't find them.

"But we still found his body this morning. Dumped on the senator's grave."

Susan staggered back. She hadn't expected…

"I guess Guerrero thought he was holding back." Gunner lifted one shoulder in a faint shrug. "By the looks of things, I'm thinking McLintock talked to Guerrero, told him everything he knew. Guerrero *made* him talk."

Her heart beat faster. Her palms started to sweat. Damn Mississippi heat. Even in the spring, she was melting.

"So maybe you should be rethinking that offer of protection," Gunner murmured with an assessing glance.

Rethinking it? Why? So they could get close and find out exactly what she'd done and lock her away? No dice. She'd gone that prison route before.

She'd lost two years of her life to a juvie jail. She wouldn't ever be going behind bars again.

It had taken Susan too long to build her life again. Or rather, to steal the life that she had. Before she got in trouble, she'd been Becky Sue Morris. After juvie…

Hello, new me.

"I don't know anything," Susan said. Juliana was still talking, feeding her lines to the reporters. Why? "Guerrero wouldn't learn anything from me."

"No, but he'd still kill you. Slice you open just like he did your friend McLintock."

Ben hadn't been her friend. He'd just been an annoying lackey who stood in her way. He'd been working for Aaron before she'd arrived on the scene, and while she might have gotten access to Aaron's bed, Ben had been the one to know his secrets. Yes, she bet that Ben had known all about the deals with Guerrero. The twit had probably been in on everything.

How much money had they made? And she hadn't seen so much as a dime.

Now Juliana was walking away from the microphones. The big show was over. No, Juliana's show was over.

Susan's show was just beginning.

Her gaze moved back to Juliana. Logan was being her shadow. Her guard dog. What else was new? Juliana must not have found the file she'd left for her.

Logan glanced up then and his gaze cut right to her.

He found it.

Susan kept her breathing easy and smooth. That gaze of his seemed to burn her flesh.

"Is there a problem?" Gunner asked quietly.

She put her hand on his arm, stumbled a bit. "It's...so much. Ben. Aaron. I need a few minutes." She glanced up, offering him a tired smile. "Give me a little time, okay?" Her voice was weak. Lost. She thought it sounded pretty perfect.

Gunner nodded. Right. What else was a gentleman supposed to do?

After taking a deep breath, she made her way to the nearest ladies' room. Susan checked, making sure that no one else was around. Then her glance darted around the small room...and landed on the window to the right.

Time to vanish.

"Where's Susan?" Logan demanded as he headed toward Gunner.

The agent jerked his thumb toward the restroom.

Eyes narrowed, Logan immediately headed toward the ladies' room door.

"What are you doing?" Juliana grabbed his arm. "You can't go in there!"

Watch me. He knew that Susan was trying to drive a wedge between him and Juliana, and he also knew...

I don't trust her.

So he knocked on the door, a hard, fast rap. "Susan! Come out! We need to talk." Just not in front of Juliana. He glanced over his shoulder at Gunner. "Take Juliana to the car. I'll be right behind you."

Juliana was looking at him as if he was crazy.

And he heard no sound from inside the bathroom.

Hell. "Susan?" Another hard knock at the door.

No response. Not so much as a whisper of sound.

His instincts were screaming now. Logan shoved open the door. Scanned under the stalls.

Gone. And only an open window waited to the right.

He spun back around to face Gunner. "What did she say to you?"

Gunner was shaking his head. "Out the window. Who would have—"

"What did she say?" Logan demanded again. Juliana stood behind Gunner in the doorway. Her gaze was watchful. Wary.

"We talked about McLintock. I told her what happened—"

"She got scared," Juliana broke in. "She must have run because she was afraid she'd be targeted, too."

Maybe.

But he doubted it. There were plenty of reasons for people to run.

He yanked out his phone and had Syd on the line in an instant. "Susan Walker is gone," he said. "We need to start searching the area for her, now." The bright sunlight hit him when he stepped outside and began to sweep the lot.

"Her car's gone," Gunner said from beside him. The man's voice was tight with anger.

The vehicle sure as hell was gone. Gunner had driven Susan's vehicle to the press conference, but it looked like the lady had reclaimed her ride. "Get the cops to put out an APB on her," Logan said. He wanted to talk to Susan, *yesterday.*

He glanced to the left and saw Juliana staring at him with her brows up. "It's for her protection," he said, the words half-true.

Half lie.

Susan was a dangerous woman—she knew the truth

about him, and he was willing to bet she knew plenty of secrets about the senator.

If Guerrero got ahold of her, the man would make her spill those secrets, just like he'd done with McLintock.

SUSAN NEVER EVEN saw the man approaching. She was fumbling with her keys, trying to rush back inside her old apartment—*good thing I kept the lease*—when hard arms wrapped around her.

"Someone wants to see you." She felt the blade bite into her waist.

A whimper rose in her throat. No, this couldn't be happening. She had planned too well.

But then the guy yanked her away from the apartment. There were no neighbors to see her.

He shoved her into the trunk of a black car. She tried to scream for help, but there was no help. The car sped away quickly, knocking her around in the trunk, sending her rolling back and forth.

Susan shoved and kicked at the trunk. Her breath rasped out. It was so dark. Only one faint beam of light trickled into the trunk. Without that light, it would be as if she was in a tomb.

Buried alive.

Susan screamed as loud as she could. The car kept going.

"Help me! Help me! Somebody, please!" She'd hated the dark for years. Ever since her mother had gone away.

Susan had been six. Her mother had just…put her in the closet. "Be a good girl. Mommy has to leave for a while. And you…you have to be quiet until I get back."

She'd put her in the closet, then never come back. Just…*put me in the closet*.

"Help!"

Her mother had been an addict. A whore. Social services had finally come to find Susan...because her mother had overdosed. They'd taken her out of that closet.

"Get me out!" Susan screamed as she kicked toward the back of the car.

She'd promised herself never to go back into the dark again. She'd fought for a better life. Clawed her way to that promise of wealth and privilege.

She couldn't go out like this. Not in a trunk. Not cut up with a knife, like McLintock.

She should have more.

The car stopped. She rolled, banging her knees, still screaming for help.

Then she heard the voices. Footsteps coming toward her.

The trunk opened. Light spilled onto her. Susan stopped screaming.

And she started plotting.

I'm not dead yet. Her heart thundered in her ears.

Survive. That was all she had to do. Stay alive. Escape.

She just had to play the game right....

Chapter Nine

Juliana didn't know why she went into her father's room. Despite what Susan had said, Juliana didn't expect any big revelations. She and her father—they hadn't been close.

Not in years.

She stood in the doorway, feeling like an intruder as her gaze swept over the heavy furniture. The room was cold but opulent. Her father had always insisted on the best for himself.

He just hadn't cared about giving that best to others.

Such a waste. Because when she tried hard enough, Juliana could almost remember a different man. One who'd smiled and held her hand as they walked past blooming azalea bushes.

She turned away, but from the corner of her eye, she saw...

My paintings.

Goose bumps rose on her arms, and she found herself fully entering his room. Crossing to the right wall, she stared at those images.

Storm Surge. The painting she'd done after the horror of the last storm had finally ended. On the canvas, the fury of the storm swept over the beach, bearing down like an angry god.

Eye of the Storm. The clouds were parted, showing a

flicker of light, hope. The fake hope that came, because the storm wasn't really over. Often, the worst part was just coming.

Her hand lifted and she traced the outline of her initials on the bottom left of the canvas. Her father...he'd told her that her art was a waste of time. He'd wanted her in law school, business school.

But he'd bought her art, framed it and hung it on his wall.

So he'd see it each day when he woke?

And right before he went to sleep each night?

"Who were you?" she whispered to the ghost that she could all but feel around her in that room. "And why the hell did you have to leave me?" There had been other ways. He shouldn't have—

A woman was crying. Juliana's head whipped to the left when she heard the sobs, echoing up from downstairs.

She rushed from the room, leaving the pictures and memories behind. Her feet thudded down the stairs. She ran faster, faster...

Susan stood in the foyer, her face splotched with color, and streaks of blood were on her arms and chest.

Gunner waited behind her. His face was locked in tense lines of anger.

"What the hell is going on?" Logan demanded as he rushed in from the study.

"Some of the guards near the gate found her...." Gunner picked Susan up and carried her to the couch. "She was walking on the road outside of the house."

Susan was still crying. Her eyes—they didn't seem to be focusing on anyone or anything.

"We need an ambulance!" Juliana said, grabbing for the nearest phone. There was so much blood... She could see the slashes on Susan's arms.

Juliana glanced up and met Logan's hard stare.

"The bastard just dumped her in the middle of the road, like garbage," Gunner growled, but though fury thickened his voice, the hands that ran over Susan's body were gentle.

Juliana started to rattle off her address to the emergency dispatcher.

"No!" Susan jerked away from Gunner and her gaze locked on Juliana. "Don't let them take me! I don't want to go! I want—I want to be home!" Tears streaked down her cheeks. "Let me st-stay, *please*."

Gunner grabbed her hands and began to inspect the slices on her body.

Juliana hesitated with the phone near her ear. The operator was asking about her emergency.

"Does she need stitches?" Logan leaned in close.

Gunner's tanned fingers slid over Susan's pale flesh. He caught her chin in his hand, forcing her to look at him. "Are there any other wounds?"

She just stared at him, eyes wide.

"Susan, tell me…*are there any other wounds?*" When she still didn't answer, his hands moved to the buttons on her shirt.

She jerked, trembled. "No! No, there aren't any more…" Her gaze darted back to Juliana. "I want to be home." She sounded like a lost child. "Please, I told them that I just wanted to go home."

Logan gave a small nod. Juliana's fingers tightened on the phone. "Never mind. It's my mistake. We don't need any assistance." She put the phone away and hovered near the couch. She could see bruises already forming near Susan's wrists. And those cuts… Someone had definitely used a knife on her.

Susan's breath choked out. "Thank you."

"Don't thank us." Gunner's voice still shook with fury. "We're gonna have to take you in."

Her face crumpled. "Why?" Desperate.

"Because there's evidence on you," Logan told her, his own face grim. "The techs can check you. Whoever attacked you—there'll be evidence left behind."

Susan's laugh was brittle and stained with tears. "We both know who attacked me. Guerrero—or rather, his men." Her lip quivered but she pulled in a deep breath. "He took me from my apartment, threw me in a trunk."

"He? You *saw* Guerrero?" Juliana asked, stunned. If Susan had seen Guerrero and gotten away...

Susan gave a slow shake of her head. "I never saw anyone. The man—at my apartment—came at me from behind. Took me someplace, but when he opened the trunk, he had on a ski mask." Her gaze found Gunner's again. She kept turning back to him. "I can't tell you anything about him. I don't have any evidence or DNA on me. I didn't touch him, didn't claw him, didn't fight." She swiped her hand over her cheek. "I was too scared."

"How did you get away?" Juliana asked. She hated seeing Susan like this. She'd wanted to protect her, but...

It seemed she couldn't save anyone.

"I didn't know anything." Another swipe of Susan's hand across her face. "I *didn't!* I kept telling him that, over and over..."

Juliana fired a fast glance over at the grandfather clock. It had been five hours since the press conference.

Five hours of torture for Susan.

"It felt like I was there forever," Susan whispered. "Then...then he said I could go if I delivered a message."

Logan's gaze locked on Susan. "What message?"

"Guerrero...said to tell you...there is *no* evidence.

There's no escape." She looked at Juliana. "And you're going to die." A sob burst from her. "I'm so sorry!"

Susan was apologizing to her?

"He's coming...he'll kill you, and he said he'd kill your lover." A fast glance toward Logan. "He knows what Logan did. I told him, I had to tell him! He was cutting me and I wanted him to stop. I didn't have any information on Aaron, and it was the only thing I could say—"

Juliana shook her head, lost. "What did Logan do?"

Silence. Then the grandfather clock began to chime.

Susan's jaw dropped. "I don't..." She fired a wild glance at Logan. Then Gunner. Then Juliana.

Juliana gripped the back of the leather sofa. "What did Logan do?" Something was off. Wrong. She could see the fear in Susan's eyes, and Logan...

Why had the lines near his mouth deepened? Even as his gaze had hardened.

"We should talk," Logan told her softly.

Susan was still crying. "He knows..." she whispered. "I told him what Aaron...how he kept you away from her..."

Her father had kept Logan away? Since when? Logan had *walked* away. Hadn't he?

"The man who took me, he said—" Susan was talking so quickly that all her words rolled together "—he would kill Juliana...make you watch..."

Logan's gaze seemed to burn Juliana. "No, he's not." He jerked his head toward Gunner. "Take Susan upstairs, then call Syd. I want techs out here to check her out."

But Susan tried to push against Gunner. "No, I don't want anyone else to see what he did! No!"

Gunner lifted her into his arms once more. "Shh. I've got you."

She'd never expected him to be so gentle. So…easy.

Susan's cries quieted as she stared up at him with hope in her eyes. "He won't come back?"

"No."

Juliana didn't speak while they climbed the stairs. Her palms were slick on the leather sofa. Logan's face had never looked so hard, so dark before.

He knows what Logan did.

She pushed away from the couch and marched to him. "What's going on?"

"The sins of the past…Guerrero thinks he can use them against me." His smile was twisted. "And he can." His hands came up to rest on her shoulders. "When I tell you… you can't leave. You're going to want to leave. To get as far from me as you can. That's what Guerrero will want."

He was scaring her. What could he possibly have to say that would be so bad?

"I can't let you leave me. Guerrero will be out there, just waiting for the chance to get you. He's trying to drive us apart, and I won't let him."

"Tell me."

He braced himself as if—what? He were about to absorb a blow? Did he actually think she'd take a swing at him? If she hadn't done it before, it wasn't as if she was going to start now.

"It wasn't just chance that led me to that diner all those years ago." His voice was flat, so emotionless. "I was there because I'd been looking for you. I wanted to talk to you. I *needed* to."

She remembered the first time she'd met Logan. She'd been at Dave's Diner, a dive that high-school kids would flock to right after the bell. She'd been home from college on summer break, hanging out with some girlfriends. Juliana had been leaving the diner and she'd run into him, literally. His hands had wrapped around her arms to steady her, and she'd looked up into his eyes.

She'd always been a sucker for his sexy eyes.

Juliana held her body still. Inside, a voice was yelling, telling her that she didn't want to hear this. Susan had been too upset. This wasn't good. But she ignored that voice. Hiding from the truth never did any good. "Why?"

"I came to find you...because I wanted to apologize."

That just made her feel even more lost. "You didn't know me. There was nothing you'd need to apologize for."

His gaze darted over her shoulder. To the picture that still hung over the mantle. The picture of her mother. "I didn't know you, but I knew her."

Her breath stalled in her lungs.

"I told you about my father."

He had. Ex-military, dishonorably discharged. A man with a taste for violence who'd fallen into a bottle and never crawled out. Logan had told her so many times, *I won't ever be like him.* As if saying the words enough would make them true.

"The military was his life, and when they kicked him out, he lost everything."

She waited, biting back all the questions that wanted to burst free. Her mother? She wouldn't look at that picture, couldn't.

"I tried to help him. Tried to stop him, but he didn't want to be stopped. He was on a crash course with hell, and he didn't care who he took with him to burn."

She *wouldn't* look at her mother's picture.

"I tried to stop him," Logan said again, voice echoing with the memory, "I tried..."

THE BEDROOM DOOR shut softly behind them. Susan could feel Gunner at her back; his gaze was like a touch as it swept over her.

He saw too much. She didn't like the way he looked at her. As if he could see right through her.

She swiped her hands over her cheeks once more. No matter how hard she wiped, Susan could still feel the tears. "I need to shower. I have to wash away the blood."

But he shook his head. "You'll just wash evidence away. We told you—"

"I'm not a crime scene!" The words burst from her. "I'm a person! I don't want to be poked and prodded by your team. I just want to forget it all."

His dark gaze drifted over her bloody shirt. "Is that really going to happen?"

No.

She glanced around the room, her gaze sweeping wildly over every piece of furniture. Every picture on the wall. *Every. Picture.* Her heart kicked into her chest.

"I know what it feels like," he told her, and the gravelly words pulled her gaze back to him.

"I was taken hostage by a group in South America." He lifted his shirt and she gasped when she saw the scars that crossed his chest. Not light slices like the ones she'd carry on her flesh. Deep, twisting wounds. Ugly. Terrifying. "They took their time with me," he said. "Five days... five long days of just wishing that pain would stop."

She'd had five hours. Susan never, ever wanted to imagine having to go through days of that torment. It wouldn't happen. She wouldn't let it happen.

Her gaze swung back to the wall. Juliana's canvases. Those storms. Surging.

A storm was at the door. A hurricane that was going to sweep them all away.

Not her. She wouldn't let it hurt her.

"What did you do?" she asked, taking a small step toward him, unable to help herself. "What did you do to get away?"

That stare was like black ice. "I killed them. Every single one of them."

Susan shivered. She hadn't been strong enough to kill the man who came after her. He'd been too big. That knife…

"I just cried," she said, voice miserable. "I cried, and I told him everything he wanted to know." Because she'd just wanted the pain to end.

She'd always thought she was so tough, but in the end, she'd broken too easily.

"You'll get past this," Gunner promised her as he lowered his shirt, hiding all of those terrible, twisting scars. "I did."

But she wouldn't.

"I WAS ALWAYS dragging my father out of bars. Or finding him in alleys passed out. But even when he was sober—days that were far too few—my father…had a darkness in him."

It seemed as if every word came slowly. The grandfather clock's pendulum ticked off the time behind him, with swinging clicks that seemed too loud.

"My father was a good killer. An assassin who could always take out his targets." Logan's breath expelled in a rush. "He told me, again and again, that I was like him. Born to kill."

And Logan had told her—again and again—*I won't be like him.*

"Why—why was he discharged?" Juliana asked.

"Because on his last mission, he had what some doctors called a psychotic break. He had to be taken down by his own team. He wasn't following orders. He was just *hunting*."

And that broken man had come home to Logan? "Where was your mother?"

"She left him."

And you? She forced the words out. "And what about *my* mother?"

He lifted his hand as if he'd reach for her, but his fingers clenched into a fist before he touched her. "That night, I found him at another bar. He jumped in his truck and wouldn't give me the keys." He lifted that clenched hand to his jaw and rubbed his skin as if remembering. "He punched me. Hit me over and over then got in that beat-up truck. I couldn't…I couldn't just let him leave like that. I climbed in. I thought I could get him to stop."

She didn't hear the grandfather clock any longer. She just heard the drumming sound of her heartbeat filling her ears.

"He was going too fast, weaving all over the road. I was trying to get him to stop…." A muscle flexed along the hard length of his jaw. "I saw the other car coming. I yelled for him to stop, but it was too late."

Too late.

"I guess I got knocked out for a few minutes, and when I opened my eyes again, he was dead."

She blinked away the tears that she wouldn't let fall. "And my mother?"

His gaze held hers. "She was…still alive then."

Her knees wanted to buckle. Juliana forced herself to stand straighter.

"I rushed to her. I tried to help." He drew in a rough breath. "She said your name."

Her heart was splintering.

"It was…the last thing she said."

She stumbled back. But he was there, rushing toward her, grabbing her arms, holding tight and pulling her close.

She didn't want to be close then. She didn't want to be anything.

"She loved you," he said, voice and eyes intense. "You were the last thought she had. I came to find you… I was in that diner because you should have known how much she loved you. I wanted to tell you, I *needed* to. But then you looked up at me." He broke off, shaking his head. "You looked at me like I was something—*somebody*— great, and no one had ever looked at me like that before."

She couldn't breathe. Her chest hurt too much.

"You loved me," he said. His eyes blazed. "With you, then, everything was so easy. I knew if I told you that I was there that night, that my father was the one driving when your mother died…you'd hate me."

Her whole body just felt numb. "I read…the reports. Talked to the cops. The man driving the car, his name was Michael Smith." She'd dug through the evidence when the memories and pain got to be too much for her.

Her father had never talked about the crash. She'd been seventeen when she went searching for the truth herself.

"After he died, I took my stepfather's name." His fingers were still tight around her. "My mom had remarried another man. Greg Quinn. Greg…was good. He tried to help us."

Her heartbeat wouldn't slow down. "The reports… The police said a minor was in the car." They'd told her…the teenager had been the one to call for help. When they'd arrived on scene, he'd been fighting to free her mother.

Logan?

He would have been what then, fourteen?

"I went by Paul back then," he said. "Logan's my middle name."

All these years...he'd kept this secret?

"I was arguing with him," Logan told her, his voice slipping back into that emotionless tone that she hated. "He wasn't paying attention. I was arguing, he was drunk..."

"And my mother died."

A slow nod. He released her and stepped back. "If I'd been stronger, I never would have let him in that truck. If I hadn't been yelling at him, maybe he would have seen her car coming.... *I could have saved her, but I didn't.*"

Her face felt too hot. Her hands too cold. "My father knew."

"Yes."

Another secret. More lies.

Juliana held his gaze. "You asked me to run away with you. You said you wanted us to start a life together." Kids. A house. "And all that time..."

"I wanted to be with you more than I ever wanted anything else in my life." Now emotion cracked through his words. "Your father investigated me, found out who I was. The son of a killer."

He was more than that.

"He was going to tell you. He told me to leave, or he'd—"

"And that made you just walk away? His threat?" She wasn't buying that line. Time to try another one.

But he gave a hard shake of his head. "No, I left because he was right. You deserved more than me. My father was right, too, you know... In a lot of ways, I am just like him." He lifted his hands, stared at his fingers. "I was made to kill."

"Maybe you were made to protect." She was tired of

this bull. "You don't have to be like him. Be your own person! You didn't have to leave me alone—"

"You looked at me like I was a hero. I never wanted you to look at me…the way you are right now."

She stepped back. "You should have told me from the beginning." Everything could have been different between them. No secrets. No lies. "You just left me!"

Juliana took another fast step away from him.

"I came back."

Her eyes narrowed.

"Six months," he said, jerking a rough hand through his hair. "I'd joined the navy. Tried to forget you. *I couldn't.*"

"You didn't come back for me." The lies were too much. Why couldn't he ever tell her the truth?

"You weren't alone."

Juliana blinked.

"You called him Thomas. He was blond, rich, driving a Porsche and holding you too close."

"How do you know about him?" Thomas had been her friend; then after Logan left, he'd been more. She'd just wanted to forget for a while. To feel wanted, loved by someone else.

"You were sleeping with him."

There was anger, jealousy—rage—vibrating in his voice now. She almost wished for that emotionless mask.

"I couldn't breathe without thinking of you, but you'd moved on. Gotten someone better."

She and Thomas had broken up after a few months. He'd been a good guy, solid, dependable, but he hadn't been…

Logan.

"You had what you needed. I had no right to come back in and screw up your life."

He'd come back.

"So I stayed away." His hand rose to his chest. Pressed over the scar that was a reminder of the battles he'd faced. "I did my job."

Susan stared up into Gunner's face. Not a handsome face. Too hard. Too rough. This wasn't an easy man before her.

She let her head fall forward, so weary she could hardly stand it. "I never wanted things to be like this."

His hands came up to her shoulders. "You're safe."

She wasn't. "I grew up with nothing." Nothing but the looks of pity others gave her. "I swore that one day I'd have everything." But Aaron was dead. His daughter was still alive. The will gave Susan *nothing*.

Just what I've always had.

Unless Juliana died, Susan would just get scraps.

Now she had Guerrero out there, waiting in the shadows.

Her shoulders hunched as she leaned toward him. "This isn't the way I wanted my story to end."

"It's not over," he told her as his hands tightened around her shoulders. "You think I didn't want to give in when they had me in that pit? Giving up is easy. Fighting to live is the hard part."

Yes, it was, but… "I'm a fighter." Always had been.

"Good, you should—" His words broke off, ending in a choked gurgle.

Susan didn't look up at his face. Her eyes were on her hands—on the knife she'd just shoved into his stomach.

You should have searched me. Guerrero had been right. An injured woman could get past nearly any guard. Some men just had blind spots. *I slipped right past yours, Gunner.*

She twisted the knife. "I'm not going back to nothing."

Another choked growl.

Susan looked up into his eyes. His hands had fallen from her. "Sorry, but this time, you need to give up. There's no point in fighting."

Because he wasn't going to keep living.

He slumped over and hit the floor with a thud.

A FAINT THUD REACHED Juliana's ears. She frowned and glanced back up the stairs.

"We can't change the past. If I could, hell, yes, I would," Logan said, "but we—"

Glass shattered. Logan jerked—and red bloomed on his shoulder.

Then he was leaping toward her. He threw his body against Juliana's, and they fell to the floor, slamming down behind the couch.

She heard shouts. Screams. More gunshots.

It sounded as if an army was attacking.

With Guerrero, that might be exactly what was happening. They had guards outside, local cops who'd been assigned to protect the house and her. Surveillance was watching, and backup would come, but...

More gunfire.

She grabbed Logan's arm. Felt the wet warmth of his blood. "Logan?"

He raised his head. Stared at her with an unreadable gaze.

"Guess he took the bait," he said.

The words were cold.

"Stay here, and keep your head down."

What? He was leaving?

She held him tighter. Logan winced, and her hand dropped. "You can't go out there!"

"I'm a SEAL. That's exactly where I need to go."

Into the fight.

"You won't be afraid anymore. We'll get his men. I'll make sure one stays alive, and we *will* track Guerrero." Then he kissed her. A hard, fast press of his lips. "Stay down."

And he was gone. Rushing away and his blood was on her hands.

Juliana crouched behind the thick couch, breath heaving in her chest. Then she heard the scream. Wild, desperate and coming from upstairs.

Susan.

The guards outside were already under attack. Susan couldn't get caught in the crossfire. The woman had suffered enough.

Because of my father. Because she was close to us.

Juliana knew she had to help her. Keeping low, she rushed across the room and used the furniture for cover as best she could.

Her hand was on the banister when another round of gunfire erupted in the room.

Chapter Ten

They were outgunned.

Logan grabbed the injured cop who'd been slumped near the porch and pulled the guy back, giving him cover. He let out two fast shots as he fired back at the attackers, who just weren't stopping.

A quick sweep counted ten men. Twelve.

The cops at the front door were both down. Gunner was in the house. *He'll be out soon.* Gunner never could stay away from a gunfight.

Jasper was firing, attacking from the distant right side, back near the heavy gate—a gate that was currently busted open.

Blasted your way in.

Syd would be coming. The woman was always their eyes and ears. She'd be watching the video surveillance, sending backup and joining the fight herself.

The woman could be lethal.

Logan grabbed the cop's hand and shoved it against the guy's wound. "Keep pressure on it." The uniform was as pale as death, shaking, but he'd be okay. Provided he didn't take another bullet.

Logan ignored his own injury, barely feeling the pain. He didn't have time for it then. These men—they weren't getting into the house. They wouldn't get to Juliana.

He eased away from the cop and began to stalk his prey. He'd been trained for up-close-and-personal kills. He could get close and the prey wouldn't know it. Not until it was too late.

Jasper kept firing and distracting the attackers so that Logan would have time to sneak up on them.

Leave some alive. He wanted to take them down but would kill only if necessary. These men had to be brought in alive—*we'll make you turn.*

No one would be pulling knives and taking the easy way out of this mess.

Logan wasn't going to allow for easy.

He snuck up on one of the gunmen, grabbed his hand and broke the wrist. The man's weapon flew to the ground but he tried to kick out at Logan.

Logan punched him in the throat. The man never even had time to scream. In seconds, he was on the ground, and he wasn't going to be getting up anytime soon.

One down.

CHIPS OF WOOD FLEW from the banister as Juliana rushed up the stairs. That last bullet had come too close for any kind of comfort.

She jumped off the stairs and hurried down the hallway. Just a few more feet…

Juliana shoved open her father's bedroom door. "Susan!"

Susan spun toward her, a knife in her hands.

Juliana shook her head, stunned. "What—"

Her paintings were behind Susan. They'd been slashed. "Run…"

A whisper. So faint she almost didn't hear it, but Juliana's gaze jerked toward that hoarse sound.

Gunner. On the floor. Covered in blood.

But then Susan leaped toward her and grabbed her hand. "You're not running anywhere." That knife flashed toward Juliana.

When you attack, use the strongest part of your body.

Juliana grabbed for the knife with her right hand even as she slammed her left elbow into Susan's stomach. Susan stumbled back and grunted in pain.

The knife skittered across the floor.

"What the hell are you doing?" Juliana screamed because she didn't want to believe what she was seeing. Susan couldn't be in on this mess.

But then Susan yelled and launched herself at Juliana. The two women hit the floor, rolling in a tangle of limbs. Susan was the same size as Juliana, and the woman was fighting with a wild, furious desperation.

But she wasn't the only one desperate to win this battle. Juliana felt more than a little desperate, too.

"Should have...died at the...cemetery..." Susan snarled as she slammed Juliana's head into the floor. "Should have..."

Juliana shoved her fingers toward the other woman's eyes. Susan shrieked and leaped back.

"*You* set the car bomb?" Juliana lurched to her feet as she tried to prepare for another attack.

Only, Susan wasn't advancing on her. Instead, she'd run toward her father's open safe. As far as Juliana knew, the only thing her father had ever kept in that bedside safe was a gun.

Juliana dived for the knife. It was close. She could get it and attack—

"Don't move." Too late. Susan had the gun. She had it aimed at Juliana. And the woman was...smiling.

Gunfire echoed from outside and Juliana tensed, but Susan just kept staring at her. "I went to so much trouble...

had everything timed perfectly. But you wouldn't get in the car."

Juliana licked her lips. Susan's back was to the large picture window in her father's room. Gunner was to the right, lying in a growing pool of blood. The knife was a light weight in Juliana's hand, but what good would it do against a gun?

Not much.

"Why?" Juliana asked with a shake of her head. "Why are you doing this?"

More gunfire erupted from below. A man's pain-filled cry was abruptly cut off.

"Is Guerrero forcing you to help him?" Juliana pressed. She lowered the knife to her side, wanting Susan's attention to shift away from the weapon.

But Susan just laughed. "The bomb was *me.* You think you know me? You don't know anything about me or where I come from. Aaron didn't know, either. He thought I was just another one of the brainless whores who'd be happy jumping at his beck and call."

From the corner of her eye, Juliana thought she saw Gunner shift just a bit.

"I've seen things…done things…" Now Susan's laugh held a desperate edge, but the gun in her hand never wavered. "I'm not going back to nothing because of you!"

"Susan, I haven't done anything—"

"*It all goes to you!* The money. The house. Everything. He promised, but I saw the will—*it's all yours.*"

Was this what it was about? Money? "Charles died in that bomb blast."

"Am I supposed to care?" Susan lifted the gun. "I have to look out for myself. If I don't…who will?"

There was no more gunfire from below. Was that good?

Or bad? *Logan, be safe.* "I don't care about the money. Take it."

"I will." Susan's smile was grim. "When you're dead. When everyone thinks that Guerrero took you out, I'll take the money." Now Susan did glance back over her shoulder toward that big window.

Susan had led Guerrero's men to the house. The woman might have even given them security codes to get past the gate and inside the house. She had access to everything there, so getting those codes would have been easy for her.

"Guerrero wanted the evidence…." Susan's gaze flickered back to the slashed paintings and hardened. "I thought I could give it to him."

Juliana was guessing she'd thought wrong.

"Doesn't matter," Susan muttered. "He can still take you. Take you, kill you, and this mess will be over!"

Juliana inched forward. Slowly. Carefully. "You think he's going to just let you walk away? That's not how he works. No one walks away from him and survives."

Susan's smile twisted her lips. "That's okay. Susan Walker was never meant to live forever."

The woman was insane. How had she hidden this craziness for so long?

"Susan never existed, but Becky Sue Morris…Becky Sue existed—and she'll keep existing. Becky Sue is going to wire the money to her accounts. She's going to take all the jewelry. Take everything she can." She swiped her tongue over her bottom lip and glanced back at the window. "Becky Sue…knows how to survive. How to wire a bomb. How to put a price on someone's head so they get taken out." Her breath heaved. "She learned early how to do all of those things."

And she learned how to blend in and become someone else. Juliana stared at the gun and realized she didn't have a choice. Susan or Becky Sue or whoever the hell the woman really was—she wasn't going to let her escape.

Death wasn't an option. Juliana wasn't ready to die. She had too much to live for.

She took another step forward. Susan didn't even seem to notice that only a few precious feet separated them now.

Can I move fast enough?

She'd have to because there wasn't another option.

But first, Juliana knew she had to distract the other woman. "He's going to torture you before he kills you. Just like he did with Ben."

Susan was sweating. "Shut up."

"That's what he does. Sure, he'll kill me. That's a given, but he'll kill you, too. You won't get the money or the house or anything because you'll be rotting in the ground with me."

Another step.

Susan's eyes were wild. "Shut...*up!*"

"Why? I'm already dead, right? What more are you going to do to me?"

"I'll kill your Logan."

No, you won't.

"Some men just don't see the attack coming. They think we're weak, helpless...all because of some tears and a little blood."

A little blood? Susan's shirt had been soaked with her blood.

"Their mistake," Susan whispered.

"You're not going to hurt Logan." Juliana's fingers had clenched around the knife so hard that her hand ached.

Susan's head jerked. "You still care about him." Now she sounded shocked. "You know what he did. I mean, I had to spell it out for you! The guy killed your mother, used you—then walked away."

Another step, close enough to strike.

"And you still love him."

Rat-a-tat. The sudden burst of automatic gunfire had Susan's head whipping toward the window.

"Yes," Juliana growled. "I still do." Then she lifted her knife and lunged for Susan. Susan sensed the attack a few seconds too late. She screamed as her head swung back toward Juliana.

The knife shoved into Susan's left shoulder, and Juliana twisted her body, bending low for another attack.

Susan's fingers tightened around the gun and—

Gunfire erupted. Not down below, not outside. But from *in* the room. Gunner had crawled forward, and Juliana saw that he'd reached into his ankle holster and pulled out his backup weapon.

"Don't think—" his voice was a rough rasp "—you're… helpless…"

Susan staggered back. A balloon of red appeared on her chest. Her eyes were wide, her mouth hanging open in shock. She took another step back, another, her feet stumbling.

Then her eyes closed. Her head fell backward—her whole body fell—and she tumbled straight through that glass window.

LOGAN WHIRLED AT THE sound of shattering glass, and when he saw a woman's delicate form plummeting from the window, his heart stopped.

He lurched forward, all of his instincts forgotten. It was too dark. All he could see was the tangle of hair on the ground. A broken body. Blood.

No!

A knife shoved into his back.

"Don't worry," a voice whispered in his ear, "I'll make sure the pretty lady joins you in hell."

Not Juliana.

Through the moonlight, he could just see the woman's face. Not Juliana. Susan.

He spun around and grabbed the man behind him by the throat. "You're not...touching her."

This time, the man drove a knife into Logan's chest.

Logan attacked. He shattered the man's wrist, pounded with his fists, went for the man's throat. His prey was near death when...

Another man appeared and drove a needle into Logan's neck. Logan roared and tossed him back. The second attacker fell, his body crumpling into a heap.

But it was too late.

Logan's body began to shake. His vision blurred. He tried to swing out at the man charging him, but Logan's body slumped to the ground. He wanted to shout a warning, to Jasper, to Gunner, to *Juliana,* but he couldn't speak.

Shadows closed in on him, faces he couldn't see. Then a blade pressed over his throat.

"You're going to be all right," Juliana said as she pressed towels against Gunner's wounds. "I'm getting you help, okay?" She'd tried to call an ambulance, but the telephone upstairs had been dead. With the firefight going on out there...where was the backup?

More cops had to be coming. Cops and EMTs. They'd fix Gunner. They had to.

He caught her hand. His fingers were bloody, and they slipped over her skin. "Hide."

She shook her head. "I'm not leaving you."

"No more…gunfire."

He was right. But there'd been a lull in the gunfire before. She wasn't about to think it was safe just to have bullets start blasting again.

"Stay…down."

Now he sounded just like Logan. She tried to smile for him. Hard, when she was sure the man was bleeding out right in front of her eyes.

"I'm going to my room and getting my cell phone." She'd call for help. She wasn't letting him die while she did nothing. So those attacking might have cut the lines that connected the house phones, but they wouldn't be able to stop her from using her cell. "Everything's going to be okay." Juliana hoped she sounded more reassuring than she felt.

Gunner's dark, tired gaze called the words a lie, but he didn't speak. Maybe he couldn't speak any longer.

Juliana lurched to her feet. She took a staggering step forward and—saw a faint glint from the corner of her eye.

She spun back around, her gaze flying to the painting. Susan had slashed it over and over, and there, hanging out from the bottom of the canvas, Juliana could just see the faint edge of…

A flash drive.

He said he gave you the evidence.

She grabbed the drive with her bloodstained fingers. People were dying outside because of this tiny thing. She shoved the drive into her pocket and rushed for the door.

Get. Help.

She was almost to her room when she heard the creak of the stairs. Juliana tensed. It could be Logan, but if it were him, then wouldn't he have called out to her?

Her fingers reached for the doorknob. Then she heard another creak. Another. The soft pad of footsteps heading toward her father's room.

Gunner.

Juliana spun around. She had taken Gunner's gun, and the weapon felt slippery in her palms. "Stay away from him!" She rushed forward.

And nearly ran into the man who haunted her nightmares.

Juliana skidded to a halt. She'd expected to face his flunkies. The hired killers. Not…

John.

He smiled at her. The same tired, slightly crooked smile he'd given her when they were trapped in that hell. "Hello, Juliana."

Ice chilled her. Logan would never have let the arms dealer get inside the house. The only way this man could have gotten past him…

No, Logan's not dead.

John's stare—no, *Guerrero's stare*—dropped to the gun. "Give that to me."

No way. "I'll give you a bullet to the heart!"

His smile stretched. "I don't think so."

"You need to think again." She wasn't backing down. This man had destroyed her world. She wasn't about to just stand there and be a lamb for his slaughter. She had the gun. She had the perfect chance to shoot.

Then Guerrero lifted his hand, and within his grip, a bloody knife blade glinted. "This is your lover's blood."

No. "Is he dead?" Her heart already felt as if it was freezing.

"My men will make sure that he is if you don't come with me now." Guerrero dropped the knife on the floor and opened his hand to her. "I'll let him keep breathing, but you give me the gun and we leave."

"He's already dead." The man thought she was a fool. "And so are you." *Logan.* The scream was in her head, desperate to break out, but she saw herself calmly aiming the gun right at his chest. One shot would be all that it took. Of course, she couldn't aim with her trembling fingers, so maybe she'd just empty the gun into his chest.

That would work.

His smile vanished. "*You're* killing him. Every moment you waste, every second. My men are so eager to pull the trigger..."

Only, there wasn't any thunder from gunfire outside. Just silence.

"Jasper...he's there." Jasper would still be fighting. And there were other guards. Other cops.

"The one at the gatehouse? The sniper? It took some doing, but we took him out, too." His hands were up in front of him. "There's no one out there to help. Backup might be coming, but they'll get here too late." No Spanish accent coated his words. "By the time they arrive, Logan will be dead."

"*He's already dead.*" And Guerrero was just jerking her around.

"Come with me," he said, his voice low, emotionless. "I'll prove that he's alive."

She wanted to believe him.

"Or stay here," Guerrero said as his dark eyes glittered, "and you will be responsible for killing him."

"Move," Juliana ordered. "Head down those stairs and keep your hands up!"

He laughed, but he moved, taking slow, measured steps

as he headed down the stairs. She expected him to try for the gun, to attack her, but he didn't.

He didn't even glance back at her as he walked.

The front door hung open. He was just about to head out that door now.

"Wait!" She hated to get close to him, but there wasn't a choice. Juliana rushed forward and shoved the gun into his side. She didn't know what might be waiting out there, and she wanted a shield.

He grunted when the barrel of the gun dug into his body. "So different...than the girl in Mexico."

"Maybe you didn't know that girl so well."

His eyes flashed at her.

"Anyone comes at me, I'll kill you." Just so they were clear.

His head inclined toward her. "I think you mean it."

"I do."

"Pity..." Then he started walking, nice and slow. "Don't you wonder why more cops aren't here? Why it was just your lover and the skeleton staff of guards?"

Yes, she did. Where the hell was the backup?

When she went outside, all she saw was carnage. Bodies on the ground. Men moaning, twisting. Shattered glass. Susan—

Juliana jerked her gaze away.

"Money can buy anything in America. A slow response time from cops. The right intel from a disgruntled detective who feels like everyone is going over his head on yet another case."

Two men had risen from the ground. They were bloody, bruised, but coming right toward them.

"Tell them not to come any closer," Juliana whispered.

"Don't come any closer," he called out easily enough.

"Such a shame that things had to be this way between us. You know, I became quite fond of you in Mexico."

The man was the best liar she'd ever met. "Where's Logan?"

She didn't see him. Hope had her heart racing too fast in her chest. Guerrero was a liar, but maybe, maybe Logan wasn't dead.

Don't be dead.

Guerrero pointed to a black van that was idling on the right. "In there."

She kept her gun to his side. They walked slowly toward that van. It seemed to take them forever to reach that spot.

Where is Jasper? He should be out there but she sure couldn't see any sign of him.

"Open the door," Juliana ordered when they drew close to the van.

Guerrero moved forward. He grabbed the side door on the van and yanked it open. It was dark in the van, but Juliana could just see the crumpled form of…a man inside. She couldn't tell if the body was Logan's. It could have been anyone. Any—

Gunfire.

Blasting right near her body. No, near Guerrero. Her head whipped up. Gunner was leaning out of the broken second-story window, firing down on them.

Then Juliana was hit from behind, rammed so hard that she stumbled forward and fell into the back of the van.

More gunfire.

Coming from behind her now. Jasper? Finally?

But the van door had closed behind her. The gun had fallen and she'd slammed face-first onto the van's floor. Her forehead hit hard and pain splintered through her skull.

And she hit—someone. The man in the van. The man who wasn't moving. She shoved her hands against the van's metal floorboard even as the vehicle lurched forward. She was tossed back a bit and tires squealed. More gunfire.

The van kept going—racing away.

She lifted her hands, afraid, and touched warm skin. Her hands slid over the man's body nervously. Wide shoulders. Strong muscles. She touched his neck and felt the thready beat of his pulse.

Her finger smoothed higher. Felt his chin...and the faint scar that raised the skin there.

Logan.

She wrapped her arms around him and pulled him close and—felt the wetness of his blood on her. "Logan?"

"Isn't that sweet?" Guerrero's voice. Her head jerked up. In the darkness, she could make out two men in the front of the van. The driver—and the shadowy form of the man who held a gun on her.

"Told you he was alive," Guerrero said as the gun's barrel swung between her and Logan. "And if you want him to stay that way, you hold him tight, and you don't so much as *move* until I tell you to do so."

They were leaving the senator's mansion, heading down the twisting roads of the swamp. Roads that could take them to a dozen secluded locations.

"This time," Guerrero promised, "we won't be interrupted, and if you don't tell me everything I want to know, then you'll watch while I slice your lover apart."

He'd already started slicing.

"He'll be the one who screams soon, Juliana. You could hardly bear it when you heard the sound of a stranger

screaming. Tell me, what will you do when those cries
come from someone you love?"

Anything.

And Guerrero, damn him, knew it.

Chapter Eleven

Logan opened his eyes, aware of the pain that throbbed through his body in relentless waves. It was the pain that had forced him to consciousness.

The darkness hit him first. Wherever he was, there were no windows, no fresh air. He was sitting, bound with his arms pulled behind him and tied to the wooden slats in the back of his chair.

He also wasn't alone. He heard the soft rasps of breath coming too fast. So close to him.

There was a faint beam of light on the floor to the right, just a sliver that came from beneath what Logan suspected to be a door.

He tried to shift in his chair but the pain doubled, knifing through him.

Hell, yeah, he'd been knifed all right—

"Logan?"

He stilled. That was Juliana's voice, and when he took a breath, he smelled vanilla. Beyond the blood and dust and decay in the room, he smelled her.

No. Gunner should have been keeping her safe. He'd made a dumb move; Logan knew it. He'd seen the body falling and fear had made him reckless for a moment, but Juliana—

"Please, Logan, talk to me. Tell me you're okay."

"I'm…" He cleared his throat because his voice was no more than a growl. "I'm okay, baby." A lie, but he would have told her anything right then. He didn't know how much blood he'd lost; Logan just knew he was too weak.

The cops have been working for Guerrero. He'd figured that little fact out too late. From the sounds of the battle that had echoed in his ears, he knew Jasper had reached that same conclusion.

Too late.

You couldn't even trust the good guys these days. But then, maybe there weren't any good guys.

"I was afraid… I thought you were dead."

"Not yet."

Her laughter was choked. Desperate. "That's what Guerrero said."

And Logan knew how the guy had gotten her out of the house. *This time, I was the bait.* "G-Gunner?"

Silence from her, the kind that told him something had gone very wrong.

Of course something went wrong. We're both being held in this hole, and Guerrero is about to come in and start his sick games.

Games that Logan couldn't let the man play with Juliana.

"Susan stabbed him. When we left…he was alive. He was shooting at Guerrero."

If Gunner was still breathing, then they had hope. He'd get Sydney. They'd track Juliana through the implant.

All his team needed was a little bit of time.

Logan could give them that time. He could take torture, as much as necessary. *As long as Juliana makes it out.*

He'd suffered plenty over the years. It wasn't the first time he'd been taken hostage. He'd gotten out before. He would now.

"I'm sorry." He had to tell her that. He couldn't stand to be there, to all but feel her next to him, and not say the words. When he'd last seen her eyes, she'd looked as if she hated him.

If they weren't in the darkness, would that same hate glitter in her stare?

"I didn't want to hurt you." Truth. "I didn't want—"

"Logan, we can talk about that later." Something thudded—her chair. Her leg brushed his. *So close.* He wanted to reach out and touch her, but the rough rope just dug into his wrists and arms.

"You will get out of here."

"*We're* getting out." Her voice vibrated with intensity. "I've been in this dark, you weren't talking, I was afraid— I *never* want to think that you're dead again, got it? You were so close, and I thought you had died."

His hands fisted. "I won't die." But he had to warn her. He wasn't going to lie to Juliana, not ever again. "But it's going to be bad, baby. What comes…" He swallowed and said what she had to hear. "I can take it, understand? You stay strong and just know that I'll be all right."

Guerrero and his torture games. Logan had seen the bodies left behind after Guerrero's playtime was over.

"I'm not going to let him slice into you!" Her voice was fierce. "I'll give him what he needs. I don't care."

But they didn't have anything to give him. Even if they did… "The minute you talk, we're dead." She was only alive because Guerrero couldn't stand the idea that evidence was out there floating around. Evidence that could lead a path back to him.

"He's not letting us escape," Juliana whispered, her voice so soft in the darkness.

Logan kept pulling at those ropes. She was right. Guerrero wasn't going to let them slip away.

"What happened?" Juliana asked. "What went wrong?"

They'd trusted the wrong local cops.

The silence must have stretched too long because she said, "Logan?", her voice sharp.

He exhaled slowly. "The cops were working for him. When I went out, they turned on me instead of fighting off his men." Those who'd been left alive, anyway. The cops on their side had been taken out or injured instantly. Money could talk, and Guerrero sure had a lot of dough. "Guerrero probably had a contact at the P.D., one who knew just which cops would turn for the cash." Enough cash could make even the strongest men weak. "Hell, some of 'em might not have even been cops, just plants who were sent in."

But he'd been fighting them back. He and Jasper had been holding their own against them all.

Until he'd lost his control. He'd seen the body and… "I thought it was you." He'd never forget the fear. How could he? Echoes of it still burned in his bleeding gut.

"What was me?"

"When the body fell, for an instant…" He wished he could see her through the darkness. His eyes had adjusted, and he could make out the outline of her body, but that wasn't good enough. He wanted to look into her eyes. To *see* her while he had the chance.

Time was all they needed. *Hurry up, Syd.*

His breath expelled in a rush. "I thought it was you, and I've never been so scared in my life." Not even that horrible night when his father had destroyed three lives.

The night that was between them. Always would be.

His fear, that crack in his control, had cost them both. Guerrero never would have gotten the drop on him if he'd stayed focused.

But with Juliana, focus had never been his strength.

"Logan, I need to tell you…" Juliana began, her voice soft.

He wasn't sure he could stand to hear what she had to tell him. He heard footsteps coming in the hallway, heading toward them.

"Lean toward me," he told her.

He heard the rustle of her clothes. The creak of her chair. She was bound just like he was, but when they leaned forward, they were just close enough—

To kiss.

Logan's mouth took hers. He kissed her with all the passion he felt. The need. The hunger. But he kept his control. He just wanted her taste on his lips. Wanted the memory to hold tight and to get him through the pain that would come.

His lips slipped from hers. "I always loved you." He hadn't meant for the confession to come out, but as soon as the words rumbled from him, Logan didn't regret them. It was the truth, one he'd hidden, one he'd carried, and in case Syd didn't get there fast enough, he wanted Juliana to know.

"What?"

"You deserved better than to be with a killer's son." No, he'd tell her everything. *No more lies.* "You deserved better than to be with a killer. That's what I am. What I've always been, inside. My father, he knew. He saw it in me. Told me I'd be just like him, and when I got in the military…" It had all been too easy for him.

He pulled in a breath. Still tasted her. "You're the one good thing that I've known in my life. I walked away from you because…hell, Julie, how could you not hate me knowing what happened? But I carried you with me every place I went. *You were there.*" She'd gotten him out of more hells than he could count.

Silence. Then "Logan…"

The footsteps were closer. Their time was up. "Just remember that, okay?" He wanted to touch her, so he kissed her again. "Remember." No matter what came.

The door creaked open. Light poured onto them. He saw Juliana's face then, pale, beautiful, but marked by dark bruises near her forehead and on the curve of her left cheek.

"You son of a bitch," he snarled and turned his head. His gaze locked on the man advancing in that bright light. A man with dark hair, dark eyes and a grin the devil could wear.

"Hello, Mr. Quinn," Diego Guerrero said, his voice calm and flat. "I was wondering how much longer you'd be out."

Because he'd been drugged. Yeah, Logan had figured that out fast enough. He remembered the slice of knives, but he also remembered the prick of a needle that had taken him down during the battle. Guerrero had wanted a live hostage. *So you could use me against Juliana.*

Guerrero was a man who knew how to plan well. Just not well enough.

Logan smiled at him. "Tonight, your empire's going down. You're about to lose everything."

Guerrero laughed at that. Two men followed him into the room. Men who already had knives in their hands.

"No, Mr. Quinn…or shall I just call you Logan? Logan, tonight, you're the one who's going to lose…" Guerrero walked over and stood behind Juliana. His hands wrapped around her throat. "You're going to sit there and watch while you lose everything that matters to you."

SHE HADN'T EXPECTED a bloodbath. Sydney Sloan raced through the senator's mansion, her gun in her hand. Jasper hadn't been outside. He should have been out there, waiting for her.

Instead, she'd just found the ground littered with bodies. Some still alive, some way past dead. Cops. Men in ski masks. Men with pain contorting their faces.

But she hadn't seen the two men that she needed most. *Gunner and Jasper.* Where the hell were they?

She'd called her boss, Bruce Mercer. Federal agents were minutes behind her. Whatever screwup had happened with the local law enforcement, it wouldn't be happening again. The agents would take care of the cops and men who still lived. She just needed—

A ragged groan came from the right. Sydney tensed as adrenaline spiked through her body. She flattened her body against the wall, sucked in a deep breath.

Then she rushed into the room with her gun ready to fire.

"Freeze!" she yelled.

But the men before her didn't freeze. Jasper was crouched over Gunner, and they were both covered in blood. Gunner wasn't moving. He barely seemed to breathe.

She grabbed for her phone. "Where's the ambulance?" Sydney demanded. This scene—it was too similar to one she'd seen before. Only, that time, she'd lost her fiancé.

She wasn't losing her best friend.

Sirens wailed outside, answering her question before the other agent on the line could.

"Get those EMTs into the house," Sydney ordered. "Second floor. First room on the right. We've got an agent down, and he's priority one."

The only priority for her then.

Sydney dropped to her knees. Jasper had his hands over Gunner's wounds, trying to keep the pressure in place. She added her hands, not caring that the blood soaked through her fingers. "What happened?"

Jasper grunted. "Susan—she was working with Guerrero. She got too close to Gunner."

Because Gunner always had a weakness for the helpless damsels. She shook her head and blinked eyes that had gone blurry. When would he learn?

"Guerrero took Logan and Juliana." Jasper's voice vibrated with his rage. "I tried to stop them, but…"

Then she realized that all of the blood wasn't Gunner's. Her eyes widened.

"I knew if I didn't stay with him he'd die." Jasper didn't even glance at his own wound. He came across as a tough SOB.

And he was.

But he also cared about his team.

"We'll get them back," she promised. There wasn't an alternative for her. She'd lost others she cared about over the years. She wasn't losing any of her team.

Shouts came from downstairs and drifted up through the broken window. Sirens yelled. The ambulances had arrived. Backup.

"Hurry!" she screamed.

Soon there was the thunder of footsteps on the stairs. The EMTs pushed her back, but…but Gunner grabbed her hand.

His eyes, weak, hazy, opened and found her. "Syd…"

She swallowed and tried to pull back. "It's all right, Gunner. You're going to be fine." He'd have to be.

He tried to smile at her, that disarming half grin that had gotten to her so many times, but his lashes fell closed and his hand slipped from her wrist.

Her heart slammed into her chest but the EMTs were working on him. They got Gunner out of that room, into the ambulance. The lights were swirling. Agents were racing around the scene.

She wanted in that ambulance, too. She wanted to be with Gunner, holding his hand.

But she stood back and watched the lights vanish.

Jasper was behind her. He had barely let anyone see his injured shoulder. He'd just growled, "Back the hell off."

That was Jasper.

She swallowed and hoped the mask she usually wore was back in place. "You ready to hunt?" she asked him. Not waiting for his answer—she already knew what it would be—Sydney yanked out her phone, punched in the code.

The GPS screen lit up instantly.

Got you.

Because Guerrero might have taken Logan and Juliana, but they were going after them. They would get them back.

And Guerrero would get exactly what he deserved.

GUERRERO BROUGHT HIS blade against Juliana's throat. "You have proven to be so much trouble…"

"Then maybe you should have just killed me in Mexico."

Logan blinked, surprised by the rough words that had tumbled from Juliana's lips. No, no, she didn't need to be antagonizing a killer. Logan wanted Guerrero's anger directed at him.

Not her.

The blade bit into her flesh. A rivulet of blood slid down her pale throat. The lights were on now, too bright, too stark. "Maybe I should have," Guerrero agreed.

"But then, you knew you'd never get your hands on that evidence!" Logan snarled at him. "And your house of cards would fall on you."

Guerrero looked up at him. "I'm beginning to think that evidence doesn't exist." But he lifted the blade from Juliana's throat.

Logan's heart started to beat again.

But then the goon on his right shoved his blade into the wound on Logan's side. Logan clenched his teeth, refusing to cry out as the blade twisted.

"I mean, if Juliana had the evidence, if she knew anything about it…she'd say something…*now,* wouldn't she?" Guerrero asked, glancing down at the blood on his blade.

"Stop!" Juliana screamed. "Stop hurting him!"

"Oh, but we're just getting started." Guerrero nodded to his henchman, and he shoved that blade in even deeper.

Logan's hands fisted and he yanked against the ropes. "Have your…fun…" he rasped. "When I'm free…I'm… killing you."

"Promises, promises," Guerrero muttered.

"Yeah, it's a…promise." One he intended to keep. Guerrero and his torture-happy guards weren't getting away.

The knife slid from his flesh. Logan sucked in breath, but he hadn't even brought it fully into his lungs when Guerrero waved his hands and said, "Cut off his fingers."

"No!" Juliana lurched forward in her chair, yanking against the binds that held her. "Don't!"

Logan braced himself. The guard came around him and—

Logan kicked out with his feet. Idiots. They should have secured his legs. One kick broke the hand of the guy with the bloody knife. The weapon flew away. He caught the other guard in the knee and there was a solid crack that made Logan grin.

He stopped grinning when Guerrero put his knife to Juliana's throat once more.

Guerrero glared at him and said, "Always the hero…"

The guards scrambled back to their feet. They lurched forward as they came for Logan again, only this time, they stayed away from his legs. One slugged him in the jaw. The other grabbed his fallen knife and charged at Logan.

That's right. Focus on me. Leave her alone.

"Stop!" Guerrero's order froze the men.

And Logan realized…Guerrero was still focusing on Juliana. He'd grabbed her hair and tangled it around his fist. That knife was pressed against her throat, and Juliana's eyes were on Logan.

There was fear in her stare. But more, trust. Faith. She thought he'd save her.

I will.

There was more emotion burning in her eyes. But he didn't want to let himself believe what he saw. Not then.

Guerrero yanked back hard on Juliana's hair. "You both have information that I want. She has my evidence."

"I…don't," Juliana gritted. A tear leaked from the corner of her eye.

"And you…" Guerrero's eyes narrowed on Logan. "You're EOD."

Logan shook his head. "What the hell is that?"

The blade dug into Juliana's skin. "Don't lie, agent," Guerrero snapped. "I can see right through lies."

Oh, right, because he was clairvoyant? No, just your standard sociopath.

"My men have been digging into your life. Ever since Juliana here was so helpful in sharing her lover's name.

A SEAL, but you're not working in the field any longer. At least, you're not supposed to be."

Because he was with a new team now and had been for the past three years.

"The pieces fit for you. The more I dig, the more I know."

Guerrero's eyes reminded him of a cobra's watching his prey, waiting for a moment of weakness so he could strike.

Come on. Strike at me. Leave her alone.

"The EOD has dozens of teams in operation."

Guerrero's intel was good.

"I want to know about them all. Those agents…their names…their lives. I can sell them all to the highest bidder."

And there would be plenty of folks willing to pay.

"Don't know about them." He tried for a shrug, but the ropes pulled on his arms. "I'm just an ex-SEAL who did a favor for a senator."

Guerrero's laugh called him on the lie. "And after the senator died, you stuck around because…?"

"Because I asked him to!" Juliana tossed out before Logan could speak. "I was scared. After the explosion at the cemetery, I asked him to stay with me."

She was protecting him.

But Guerrero wasn't buying it. "He took out my men at the cabin. Eliminated them in an instant."

"What can I say? Once a SEAL…"

Guerrero lifted the knife from Juliana's throat. His eyes were on Logan's arm. On the blood that dripped to the floor. Logan wasn't moving, not making a sound.

"Trained to withstand anything, were you?" Guerrero asked.

Just about.

"She wasn't." Then he put his blade just under Juliana's

shoulder, in the exact spot the guard had sliced Logan's arm. "So when I start cutting her, I bet she'll scream."

He sliced into Juliana's arm.

"Stop!" Logan roared.

Juliana gasped but made no other sound.

Guerrero frowned. "Interesting…"

"No, it's not." Rage was choking Logan. "Get. Away. From. Her."

Guerrero lifted his knife. "Juliana, I believe you were wrong about him. I believe your lover does care…and he's about to show you just how much."

Juliana's eyes met Logan's.

"Two things can happen here," Guerrero said, and there was satisfaction in his voice. "One…I start cutting her, and she breaks. She can't handle the pain—no one ever can—and she tells me where I can find my evidence. I mean, she has it, right? That's what she told the reporters."

Juliana was still staring at Logan. *Keep looking at me, baby. Don't look away. Everything's okay.*

"Or we have option two…" Guerrero walked behind Juliana and the blade moved to her right shoulder. "I start hurting her, and *you* talk, Logan. You talk…and I make her pain stop."

Logan's teeth ground together.

Guerrero sighed. "You think I don't know about the EOD? Those agents have caused plenty of trouble for me and my…associates over the years. I know I'd enjoy some payback time."

Too many would.

"You talk, you tell me about the agents, where I can find them, any aliases they have, and I'll make Juliana's pain stop."

The ropes were cutting into Logan's flesh. Thick, twisted, they held him so tight.

"Tell me, and I'll make her pain stop." The blade dug into Juliana's arm. Her teeth sank into her bottom lip, and Logan knew she was trying to hold back her cries.

He'd never loved her more. *"Let her go."*

Guerrero bent near her ear. His lips brushed over the delicate shell when he asked, "Where's the evidence, Juliana? What did you do with it?"

"We…lied to the reporters," she whispered.

"Where is it?" he pressed.

Juliana shook her head.

Logan marked Guerrero for death. He stared at him, knowing this was one target that wouldn't be brought in alive. "You made a mistake," Logan told him.

Guerrero yanked that bloody blade from her flesh. Juliana's shoulders sagged.

"You should never have brought me in alive." Guerrero had let him get close, and Logan definitely intended to kill El Diablo.

"So tough." He lifted the blade again, and drops of blood fell to hit the floor as he turned back to Juliana. "Now, where were we?"

"Mexico," she said, voice trembling.

The guards weren't looking at Logan. They were focused on Guerrero. On Juliana. There was eagerness on their faces.

They liked the torture.

Guerrero was still crouched near Juliana's side, his mouth too close to her ear. "What about Mexico?"

"Why didn't you just…torture me then?"

"Because getting under your skin was half the fun." His fingers slid down her arm, sliding over the blood. "You've got such lovely skin."

"Guerrero," Logan snarled.

"She does, doesn't she?" Guerrero murmured. "A beautiful woman." Now the knife rose to her face. "But you won't be that way for long."

Logan's vision bled red. He heaved in his chair.

"I don't think you wanted to hurt...me." Juliana's fast words froze Guerrero—and his knife. "We talked in Mexico for so long. Had you done that before? Ever gotten close with...someone like me?"

"I've lied to more men and women than I can count." He glanced at his knife. "Pain tells me what I want to know. But sometimes, lies are easier."

"And less bloody," Juliana whispered, swallowing. "Because I don't think...I don't think you wanted blood. I don't think...you wanted this life."

"This is the only life I want."

Juliana shook her head. Her eyes weren't on Logan any longer. They were on Guerrero. "You told me... You said you weren't perfect.... You said I didn't deserve what was happening to me.... You meant that, didn't you?"

A muscle flexed in Guerrero's jaw. Juliana kept talking, pressing her point as she said, "You didn't want to kill me then. That's why you kept me in that room...why you talked to me for so long."

"I was using you, getting intel from you. Keeping you alive long enough to make the senator squirm."

"Was John all a lie? Or was he...was he the man you could have been? What happened..." she asked him, speaking quickly, keeping the man's focus on her and keeping that knife off her body, "to change you? Why did John die...and El Diablo take over?"

"Because only the strong survive." A flash of pain raced over Guerrero's face. "I learned that lesson when I walked in my mother's blood."

Juliana flinched at that revelation.

Then Guerrero straightened, moving back a bit from

her. "It's a lesson you're going to learn now, too, Juliana."
He frowned down at her, seemed almost lost an instant,
then he said, "I'm sorry…" and lifted the knife to her face.

Chapter Twelve

Juliana braced herself, knowing that there was nothing she could do to stop that knife from cutting her face. She wouldn't scream. She'd hold back the cries no matter what.

The knife pricked her skin. The pain was light, the faintest press, but she closed her eyes, knowing what was to come.

But then she heard a choked cry, the thud of flesh on flesh, and her eyelids flew open even as the knife was ripped away from her skin.

Logan had leaped from his chair. The ropes were behind him, some still dangling from his wrists. He had Guerrero on the ground and he was punching him again and again and again.

Guerrero's men seemed to shake from their stupor, and they lunged for him.

"Logan!"

His head whipped up. His eyes were wild. She'd never seen him look that way before. *His control is gone.* "Behind you!" But her shout was too late. One of the guards, a big guy with thick, curling hair, plunged his fist into Logan's back even as the other raced forward with his knife.

Juliana shoved out her feet, tripping the man with the knife. The weight of his body sent her crashing to the floor. Her chair shattered, and it felt as if her wrist broke, but Juliana twisted like a snake, moving quickly, and thanks to that broken chair, she was able to get out of the ropes.

She rushed to her feet. The guards were both attacking Logan now. One had a knife, but before he could attack, Logan just ripped that knife out of his hands. Then Logan knocked that guy out with a flash of his fists.

The other guard froze, glanced down at his buddy. She could feel the man's fear. But…Logan was bleeding. His body shuddered. The fool must have thought that was a sign of weakness.

He went in for the kill.

Logan stepped back, half turned and caught the man in a fierce grip.

"Wrong move." The whisper came from right beside Juliana. She jerked, but Guerrero already had her. He grabbed her, his arms wrapping around her from behind.

"Juliana!"

She didn't waste time looking at Logan. She hunched her shoulders and dropped instantly from Guerrero's grasp, just like Logan had taught her. Then she drove her elbow back into Guerrero's groin. He groaned and stumbled back.

Not such easy prey, am I? Not this time, she wasn't.

Logan rushed past her and crashed into Guerrero. They both hit the ground, rolling in a ball of fists and fury.

The second guard…he was still moving, trying to crawl for the discarded knife.

Thunder echoed outside.

Juliana grabbed the chair that Logan had been tied to. She lifted it as high as she could and slammed it down onto the guard's back.

He stopped moving then.

Juliana spun back around. Guerrero had a blade in his hand. A blade he was driving right at Logan's throat.

Juliana screamed and ran forward.

Logan grabbed Guerrero's hand, twisted it back and shoved the blade of the knife into Guerrero's throat.

A choked gurgle broke from Guerrero's lips.

"Told you," Logan growled, "you never should have brought me in alive."

Guerrero's body shuddered. He tried to speak, couldn't.

And as she watched, as Logan rose to his feet, El Diablo died. He was crying when he died. The tears leaked down his face even as the blood poured from his neck.

Her breath heaved out of her lungs. Juliana looked down and realized that she was dripping blood. She'd forgotten her wounds. She'd been too worried about Logan. But now...

Now she *hurt*.

He turned toward her. "Julie..."

Footsteps raced outside the room. Logan swore. He grabbed the knife and yanked it from Guerrero's throat. Then he pushed Juliana against the wall, sheltering her beside his body as he waited for the next wave of guards to come into the room.

A man raced in, a gun in his hands.

Logan kicked the gun away and put his knife at the man's throat in a lightning-fast move.

"Don't!"

Not Juliana's cry. Sydney's. Juliana saw the woman rush through the door. Her eyes were wide and worried and locked on Logan—Logan and Jasper.

"Here to...save you..." Jasper wheezed.

Logan lowered his arm. "Little late, buddy. Little late..."

Sydney and Jasper glanced at the bodies on the floor. "Yes, it looks that way."

Logan used the knife to cut away the last of the ropes that dangled from his wrists. She'd barely even noticed them during the fury of the fight. "Are we clear outside?" Logan demanded.

Sydney nodded. "I don't think Guerrero was expecting us to come so soon." Sydney edged closer to the body. "Only a handful of men waited outside."

Juliana didn't want to look at the body. Her hand lifted, and she touched the raised skin on the back of her neck. The tracker had come in handy, just like Logan had said it would. "It's over," she whispered, almost afraid to believe the words were true.

Logan's head whipped toward her. His eyes—the wildness was still there. A beast running free. And there was fury in his blue stare.

Fury...and fear?

Juliana dropped her hand. He'd told her that he loved her. Sure, they'd both been about to die, but she wasn't about to let him take those words back.

Sydney was talking into her phone, asking for more men. A cleanup crew. Boots on the ground.

Jasper had bent over the guards. He gave a low whistle. "Someone plays rough." He looked back up at Logan.

Logan shook his head and jerked his thumb toward Juliana. "That one was hers."

Jasper blinked and stared at her with admiration. "I think I'm in love."

"Get in line," Logan muttered.

Juliana wrapped her arms around her stomach. Maybe they were used to this kind of scene, but she wasn't. The smell of blood and death was about to gag her, and her wounds ached and throbbed and—

Logan was there. "She needs medical attention."

A choked laugh slipped from her, and she didn't know where that had come from. Wait, she did. *Shock.* "You're the one who was gutted."

"Barely a scratch," he dismissed as he lifted her arms to study the wounds, but his face was pale, and the faint lines near his eyes and mouth had deepened.

When he stumbled, it was her turn to grab him. "Jasper!"

The other Shadow Agent was there instantly. "Damn, man, you should have said…"

Logan gave a quick shake of his head and cut his eyes toward Juliana.

The flash of fear instantly vanished from Jasper's face, but it was too late.

It's bad.

"Let's get out of here," Logan muttered. "I want… Juliana safe."

"I am safe," she said quietly. "Whenever I'm with you, I know I'm safe." A man who'd kill to protect her. How much more safety could a girl ask for?

His gaze held hers. *I always loved you.* The words were there, between them. Had he confessed out of desperation? Because he'd thought they were going to die?

And did the reason why even matter? *No.*

I always loved you.

They made their way outside. Juliana stayed close to Logan and she tried not to notice the trail of blood he left in his wake.

They were at the edge of the swamp. Insects chirped all around them. Armed federal agents were swarming the scene, and an ambulance was racing toward them along that broken dirt road.

"Maybe we'll find evidence inside," Sydney said as she

rubbed the back of her neck and watched an EMT work on Logan. "Maybe we'll be able to connect his network and shut down some of the—"

"Here." Juliana reached into her pocket and pulled out the flash drive. Guerrero hadn't bothered to search her. His mistake. He'd just tied her up. Started his torture. When all along, the one thing he needed was right in front of him.

Silence. Even the insects seemed to quiet down.

She glanced up. Logan had been put on a stretcher, but he was struggling to sit up and get to her. "What the hell?"

Jasper shook his head. "The evidence. You had it all along?"

"No. I found it when I was fighting with Susan." A shiver slid over her as she remembered Susan's scream when the woman had been shot. Juliana could still hear the shatter of the breaking glass as Susan had fallen. "My father…he hid the flash drive in one of my paintings, one that he kept in his bedroom."

Syd took the drive. A grim smile curved her lips. "You just made my job a whole lot easier."

Juliana glanced at the blood on Logan's body. At the injured men on the ground. "If I'd found it sooner, it would have been easier for everyone."

The EMTs were loading Logan into the back of the ambulance. Someone else—another EMT, a woman this time—was reaching for Juliana.

Pulling them apart.

She didn't want to be apart from him any longer. They'd already wasted so many years. Too many.

She stepped toward the ambulance. "I was going to give it to him." Logan should know this.

He stared at her with glittering eyes.

"I wasn't going to sit there and let him kill you. I was going to trade the drive for your life."

"Ma'am, you're going to need stitches," the EMT next to her said. "We have to get you checked out."

She didn't want to be checked out. "Logan..."

He was yanking at the tubes the EMTs had already attached to him. Trying to get out of the ambulance, even as the two uniformed men beside him attempted to force him back down.

Juliana rushed forward and leaped into the ambulance. "Don't! You'll hurt yourself!"

He caught her hand in his and immediately stilled. His fingers brushed over her knuckles.

"Let's get the hell out of here," one of the EMTs muttered, a young man with close-cropped red hair, "before the guy tries to break loose again."

The ambulance lurched forward.

Logan wasn't fighting any longer. He let the men tend to his wounds. Juliana let them examine the deep cuts on her arms.

Logan kept holding her hand.

She kept staring at him.

There was so much to say, and she wasn't sure where to start. They'd been through hell. Death. Life.

Could they go back to the beginning and just be two people again? Two people who wanted a chance at love?

He brought her hand to his lips and pressed a kiss to her knuckles. "Don't leave me."

Her chest ached. "I won't."

The sirens screamed on, and they left the blood and death behind them.

WHEN LOGAN OPENED his eyes, the first thing he saw was Juliana. She was in the chair next to his bed, her head tilted back against the old cushion. Heavy bandages covered the tops of her arms. She was holding his hand.

He stared at her a moment and watched her sleep. She'd always been so beautiful to him. So beautiful that his chest burned just looking at her.

When Guerrero had threatened to use his knife on Juliana's face, when she'd braced herself, drawing in that deep breath and trying to be strong, something had broken inside of Logan.

He'd killed before. Killing was part of his job, part of surviving.

But this time, it had been pure animal instinct. Savagery. The primal urge to protect what was his.

Juliana was his. That was the way he'd thought of her for years.

But there weren't any secrets between them now, and he didn't know… *What does she think of me?*

His fingers tightened around hers, and almost instantly, she stirred in her chair. Her lashes lifted and her gaze locked on him. Then she stared at him. A slow smile curved her lips and her eyes—

She still looks at me like I'm some kind of hero.

When she, more than any other, knew he wasn't.

"Took you long enough," she said as she leaned toward him. Her voice was a husky caress that seemed to roll right over his body. "I was starting to wonder when I'd get you awake again."

"How long…" He paused and cleared his throat so he'd sound less like a growling bear. "How long was I out?"

Shadows darkened her eyes as her smile dimmed. "They had to operate on you, stitch you back up from the inside out."

Yeah, he could feel the pull of the stitches. He ignored the pain.

"And you've been sleeping for a couple of hours since then."

"You were…here, with me?"

She nodded. "You told me not to leave." One shoulder lifted, stretching the bandage on her arm. "I got stitched up while you were in surgery, and they let me come back once you were stable."

She rose from the chair and his fingers tightened around hers automatically, a reflex because he didn't want to let her go.

She glanced down. A frown pulled her brows low, and he forced himself to release her.

"Gunner's going to be all right, too," she said, and her words came a little fast, as if she were nervous. "Sydney's with him. She's been in his room…well, almost as long as I've been in here."

He knew why Sydney would stay with Gunner. Those two…there had always been something there. Something neither would talk about.

While he'd spent his years thinking about Juliana, Gunner had spent his time watching Syd—when he thought she wasn't looking.

"So I guess everything is over now," Juliana continued, easing away from the bed a bit. "The bad guy is dead. The EOD has the evidence and I can get my life back."

"Yes." The word was even more of a growl than before. Logan couldn't help it. Fear and fury were beating at him. *Don't want to lose her.*

"Thank you." Her gaze was solemn. "You risked your life for me. I won't ever forget that."

She turned on her heel, began to head for the door.

No damn way. "I wouldn't have much of a life without you."

Juliana stilled.

"I lost you once, and if you walk away…" Like she was doing. *Hell, no.* "Don't, okay? Don't walk away. Give me a chance. Give us a chance." And he was getting out of that bed. Yanking at the IV line attached to his arm. Swearing at the bandages and stitches that pulled his flesh.

Juliana turned back around. Her eyes widened when she saw him and she rushed back to his side. "Why do you keep doing this?" She pushed him onto bed. "I was just going to tell Jasper that you were awake. I wasn't leaving you."

So he'd panicked. A guy could do that when the woman he loved had almost died. And he did still love her. He'd tried to deny it, tried to move on.

Hadn't happened.

"I meant it," he told her, and yeah, he was holding tight to her hand again. He just felt as if she was about to disappear. Slip away.

"Logan?"

"When I said I loved you, it was true. I wanted you to know in case…" In case Guerrero had carried through on his threats. Logan shook his head. "I know you hate me—"

"No, I don't."

He wouldn't let the hope come, not yet. Not hating someone was a long way from loving the person. "I should have told you the truth about your mother the first day I met you. I was scared," he admitted as he stared her straight in the eye. "Scared you'd walk away. Scared that I'd see disgust in your gaze."

"Is that what you see now?"

"No." But he wasn't sure…

"I read the reports about my mom's accident. Her death wasn't your fault. I know you tried to save her."

It hadn't been enough. It would never be enough.

"You aren't your father. You aren't like him." Her lips pulled down. "And I'm not like mine." Her breath whispered out in a sad sigh. "Maybe things could have been different for them, too, but now it's too late."

Too late for their fathers. But… "What about us?"

Her lashes lowered. "What do you want from me, Logan?"

Everything. "A chance. Just give me a chance, Juliana, to show you what I can be."

"I already know what you are."

The pain in his chest burned worse than the stitches. "No, you—"

"You're the man that I love." Her lashes swept up. "I've known that since the first time you kissed me."

Hope could be a vicious beast. It bit and tore inside of him, ripping past the fear and driving him to pull her ever closer.

Her legs bumped against the bed. Her lips were just inches from his. "Juliana, don't say it unless…"

"Unless I mean it? But I do mean it." Her left hand lifted and pressed lightly against the line of his jaw. "Logan, I love you."

He kissed her. His mouth took hers, rough, hungry, because he couldn't hold back. He needed her too much. Always had.

The pain of his wounds didn't matter. The pain of the past years—being without her—didn't matter. She was with him now. In his arms.

He pulled her even closer. She stumbled against the bed and laughed against his mouth. That laugh was the sweetest sound he'd ever heard.

He wanted to spend the rest of his life making her happy, hearing her laugh and seeing the light in her dark eyes.

He wanted forever with her.

His tongue slid past her lips and tasted that laughter. So sweet. Just like her.

"Logan…" she whispered as she pulled her lips from his. "We can't. You'll get hurt…"

"The only thing that can hurt me is being away from you." That had gutted him before. Hell, this wasn't the time. Not the place. But… "Marry me."

Her eyes widened. She tried to pull away. He wouldn't let her.

"Logan, you just asked for a chance, and now you want forever?"

He smiled, and for the first time in longer than he could remember, it was a real smile. His chest didn't burn anymore. He didn't feel as if he'd lost a part of himself.

She's right here.

"I'm a greedy bastard," he confessed.

An answering smile, slow and sexy, tilted her lips.

"Besides, I've had your ring since you were twenty years old." He'd kept it, not able to let it go. "And I'd like to start making up for lost time."

"You had a ring…all this time?"

Because maybe he hadn't ever given up hope. Maybe he'd thought…one day.

That day was today.

"Let me make you happy." He had to make up for all the pain. The grief. The anger. He could do it. "I *will* make you happy. I swear."

This time she kissed him. Her head dipped toward him. Her mouth, wet, hot, open, found his. She kissed him with a passion that had his body tensing and wondering just how much privacy they'd be able to get. Because he was tempted…so tempted.

By her.

"You do make me happy," she told him. Her eyes searched his. "And yes, I'll marry you. I just want to be with you."

That was what he wanted. To spend his nights with her. To wake up in the morning and see her beside him. Every day. Always.

"I love you." He had to say the words again.

The hospital door opened behind Juliana.

Jaw clenching—*not now*—Logan glanced at the door. Jasper stood there with his brows raised.

"Guess you're going to be all right," Jasper said, his lips twitching.

"I'm going to be better than all right…." Logan laughed. "Man, I'm going to be married!"

Jasper's jaw dropped.

Before his friend could say anything else, Logan turned back to Juliana. His Julie. The angel who'd been in his heart for so long.

The woman he'd love until he died.

"Thank you," he told her as his forehead pressed against hers.

"About time," Jasper said as his feet shuffled across the floor. "If I'd had to spend another day watching you moon over her…" The door swooshed as he left the room.

"What do you have to thank me for?" Juliana asked him.

"For loving me."

"It's not going to be easy, you know," she said. "We'll have to adjust, both of us. You have your job, I have mine. You're not perfect…"

He laughed at that. "No, but you are."

Her grin flashed. "And when the kids come…"

Yes. "I can't wait." For the dream he'd wanted. For the life that he'd thought was long gone.

He'd fight for that dream, every damn day. Just as he'd fight for her.

The woman he loved.

His mission. His job.

His life.

* * * * *

Keep reading for an excerpt of a new title
from the Intrigue series,
WETLANDS INVESTIGATION by Carla Cassidy

Chapter One

Private investigator Nick Cain drove slowly down the main street of the small town of Black Bayou, Louisiana. It was his first opportunity getting a look at the place where he'd be living and working for at least the next three months or longer if necessary.

His first impression was that the buildings all looked a bit old and tired. However, in the distance the swamp that nearly surrounded the town appeared to breathe with life and color. And it was in the swamp he believed he would do much of his investigation. At the very thought of going into the marshland, a wave of nervous energy tightened his stomach muscles.

He'd been hired by Chief of Police Thomas Gravois to assist in the investigation of four murdered woman. Apparently, a serial murderer was at play in the small town. He would work as an independent contractor and not as a member of the official law enforcement team.

Before he checked in with Chief Gravois, he needed to find the place he'd rented for his time here. It was Gravois who had turned him on to the room for rent in Irene Tompkin's home. Irene was a widow who rented out rooms in her house for extra money.

Once he turned on to Cypress Street, he looked for the correct address. He found it and pulled into the driveway. The widow Tompkin's home was a nice, large two-story painted beige with brown shutters and trim. An expansive wraparound porch held wicker furniture and a swing that invited a person to sit and enjoy. The neighborhood was nice with well-kept lawns and older homes.

He decided to introduce himself first before pulling out all his luggage so he got out of the car, walked up to the front door and knocked. The early September sun was hot on his back as he waited for somebody to answer.

A diminutive woman with a shock of white hair and bright blue eyes opened the door and her wrinkled face wreathed with a friendly smile. "Even though you're a very handsome young man, I'm sorry but I'm not buying anything today," she said.

"That's good because I'm not selling anything. My name is Nick…"

"Oh, Mr. Cain," she replied before he had even fully introduced himself. "I've been expecting you." She grabbed his hand and tugged him over the threshold. "I'm so glad you're here. It's such an honor for you to stay in my home and the town needs you desperately. Let me show you the room where you'll be staying." She continued to pull him toward the large staircase. "How was your trip here?"

"It was fine," he replied, and gently pulled his hand from hers as he followed her up to the second floor.

"Good…good. I baked some cookies earlier. I thought you might want a little snack before you get to your detective work." They reached the top of the stairs and walked down a short hall, and then she opened a door and gestured him to follow her inside.

The bedroom sported a king-size bed, a dresser and an en suite bathroom. The beige walls complemented the cool mint-green color scheme. There was also a small table with two chairs in front of the large window that looked out on the street and a door that led to an old iron fire escape staircase to the ground.

"Is this okay for your needs?" She turned

to look at him, her blue eyes filled with obvious apprehension.

He smiled at her. "This is absolutely perfect." It was actually far better than he'd expected. His main requirement was that the place be clean, and this space screamed and smelled of cleanliness.

"Oh good, I'm so glad. Well, I'll just leave you to get settled in and then we can have a little chat?"

"Of course," he replied.

She scurried out of the room and he followed after her. At the foot of the stairs, she beelined into another area of the house and he went outside to retrieve his luggage.

Within thirty minutes he was unpacked. He went back downstairs and stood in the entry. "Mrs. Tompkin," he hollered.

She appeared in one of the doorways and offered him another bright smile. "Come," she said. "I've got some cookies for you and we can have a little chitchat about house rules and such."

The kitchen was large and airy with windows across one wall and a wooden table that sat six. She ushered him into one of the chairs. In the center of the table was a platter of what appeared to be chocolate chip cookies.

"Would you like a cup of coffee?" she asked.

"That sounds nice," he replied.

"It's so easy now to make a cup of coffee with this newfangled coffee maker," she said as she popped a pod into the machine. She then reached on her tippy-toes and pulled a saucer from one of the cabinets and carried it over to the table.

"You have a very nice place here," Nick said.

She beamed at him as she placed three cookies on the saucer and then set it before him. "Thank you. Me and my husband, Henry, God rest his soul, were very happy here for a lot of years. He passed five years ago from colon cancer."

"I'm so sorry for your loss," he replied.

"It's okay now. I know he's up in heaven holding a spot for me. And that reminds me, there's no Mrs. Tompkin here. Everyone just calls me Nene."

"Then Nene it will be," he replied.

"I just thought we needed to chat about how things go around here. I have one other boarder. His name is Ralph Summerset. He's a nice man who mostly stays to himself. He's retired from the army and now works part-time at the post office. Cream or sugar?" she asked as she set the cup of coffee in front of him.

"Black is just fine," he replied.

She sat on the chair opposite him and smiled at him once again. Nick would guess her to be in her late seventies or early eighties, but she gave off much younger vibes and energy.

"Anyway, I provide breakfast anytime between six and eight in the mornings and then I cook a nice meal at around five thirty each evening. If you're here, you can eat, but if you aren't here, I don't provide around-the-clock services."

"Understandable," he replied. Even though he wasn't a bit hungry at the moment, he bit into one of the cookies.

"I usually require my guests to be home by ten or so, but I'm making an exception for you." She reached into the pocket of the blue housedress she wore and pulled out a key. "I know with your line of work, your hours are going to be crazy, so take this and then you can come and go as you please. Just make sure when you come in you lock up the door behind you."

"Thank you, I appreciate that." He took the key from her and then finished the cookie and took a sip of his coffee. He was eager to get to the police station and find out just what he was dealing with, but he also knew it was important to build relationships with the locals. And that started here with Nene.

He picked up the second cookie. "These are really delicious," he said, making her beam a smile at him once again.

"I enjoy baking, so I hope you like sweets," she said.

"I definitely have a sweet tooth," he replied. "And I'm sorry, but two cookies are enough for me right now." He took another drink of his coffee.

"I hope you're good at detecting things because these murders that are taking place are frightening and something needs to be done to get the Honey Island Swamp Monster murderer behind bars."

"Honey Island Swamp Monster?" He gazed at her curiously, having not heard the term before.

"That's what everyone is calling the murderer," she replied.

"And who or what is the Honey Island Swamp Monster?"

She leaned forward in her chair, her eyes sparkling like those of a mischievous child. "Legend has it that he was an abandoned child raised by alligators. He's supposed to be over seven feet tall and weighs about four hundred pounds. He has long dirty gray hair and golden eyes, and he stinks to high heaven."

Nick looked at her in disbelief. "Surely nobody really believes that's what killed those women."

Nene leaned back in her chair and released a titter of laughter. "Of course not." The merriment left her face as she frowned at him. "The sad part is now you got town people thinking somebody from the swamp is responsible and the swamp people think somebody from town is responsible and our chief of police seems to be clueless about all of it."

She reached across the table and grabbed one of Nick's hands. "All that really matters is that there's somebody out there killing these poor young women and the rumors are the killings are horribly savage. I really hope you can help us, Mr. Cain." She released his hand.

"Please, make it Nick," he replied as he tried to digest everything she'd just told him. He'd learned over the years not to discount any piece of information he got about a particular crime. Even rumors and gossip had a place in a criminal investigation.

She smiled at him again. "Then Nick it is," she said. "Anyway, Nick, I read a lot of romance books and you look like the handsome stranger who comes to town and not only saves the day but also finds his one true love. Do you have a one true love, Nick? Is there somebody waiting for you back home?"

"No, I'm pretty much married to my job."

"Well, that's a darned shame," she replied. "Now don't make me stop believing in my romances."

"I'm sorry, but I'm definitely no romance hero," he replied. His ex-wife would certainly agree with his assessment of himself. Three years ago, Amy had divorced him because he wasn't her hero. At that time, he'd permanently written love out of his life.

His work was what he could depend on and thinking of that, he rose to his feet and grabbed the house key from the table. "If we're finished here, I really need to get to the police station and get to work."

"Of course, I didn't mean to hold you up as long as I have." She got out of her chair and walked with him to the front door. "I hope to see you for dinner, but I'll understand if you can't make it. I know you have important work to do so I won't delay you any longer."

They said their goodbyes and Nick got back in his car to head to the police station. As he drove toward Main Street, he thought about Nene and the conversation he'd just had with her.

His impression of his landlady was that she was a sweet older woman who was more than a bit lonely. He had a feeling if he would have continued to sit at the table, she would have been perfectly satisfied talking to him for the rest of the afternoon.

With his living space sorted out he could now focus on the reason he was here. When he'd seen the ad in the paper looking for help in solving a series of murders, he had definitely been intrigued.

He'd spent years working as a homicide detective in the New Orleans Police Department. He'd won plenty of accolades and awards for his work and he'd labored hard on putting away as many murderers as possible. However, two years ago he'd decided to quit the department and open his own private investigation business, but that certainly hadn't meant he was done with killers.

When he'd reached out to Thomas Gravois, the man had told him about the four young women from the swamp who had been brutally murdered by the same killer, but he hadn't said anything about fighting between the swamp people and town people. In fact,

Nene had given him more information about the crimes than Gravois had.

Still, that didn't matter. Gravois had hired him over a phone call after seeing all of Nick's credentials. Nick was now more intrigued than ever to get a look at the murder books and see where the investigations had gone so far and what kind of "monster" he was dealing with.

He didn't know if his fresh eyes and skills could solve these murders, but he'd give his all to see that four murdered women got the justice they deserved.

SARAH BEAUREGARD SAT at the dispatch/reception desk in the police office lobby and drummed her fingernails on the top as nervous energy bubbled around in the pit of her tummy.

She'd been working for the police department since she was twenty-one years old and for the past twelve years Chief Gravois had kept her either on desk duty or parked just off Main Street to hand out speeding tickets.

Over those years she'd begged him to allow her to work on any of the cases that had come up, but he'd refused. She had just turned twenty-one when her parents had been killed in a head-on collision with a drunk driver.

She'd been reeling with grief and loss and Gravois, who had been close friends with her father, had taken her under his wing and hired her on as a police officer. However, his protectiveness toward her on the job had long ago begun to feel like shackles meant to hold her back from growing as an officer.

Until now…once again butterflies of excitement flew around inside her. She stared at the front door, waiting for her new partner to walk in.

She frowned as fellow officer Ryan Staub walked up and planted a hip on her desk. "So, the little lady is finally going to get to play at being a real cop," he said.

"First of all, I'm not a 'little lady' and second of all you're just jealous because I got the plum assignment of working with the new guy on the swamp murders."

His blue eyes darkened in hue. "I can't believe Gravois is letting you work on that case. He must have lost his ever-loving mind."

"He's finally allowing me to work up to my potential," she replied firmly. "Besides, you already worked the cases and nothing was solved. And get your butt off my desk."

Ryan chuckled and stood. "Why don't you go out with me for drinks on Friday night?"

She looked up at the tall, handsome blond

man. "How many times do I have to tell you I'm not going out with you? I've told you before, I find you impossibly arrogant and you're a womanizer and you just aren't my type."

He laughed again. "Oh, Sarah, I just love it when you sweet-talk me." He leaned down so he was eye level with her. "Do you want to know what I think? I think you have a secret crush on me and you're just playing hard to get."

Sarah swallowed against a groan of irritation. "Don't you have something better to do than bother me?"

He straightened up. "Yeah, I've got some things I need to get to."

"Feel free to go get to them," Sarah replied tersely. She released a sigh of relief as Ryan headed down the hallway toward the room where all the officers had their desks.

She and Ryan had known each other since they were kids, but it was just in the last month or so that he'd decided she should be his next conquest. And he'd already had plenty of conquests with the women in town.

At thirty-three years old, she had no interest in finding a special man. She'd thought she'd found him once and that romance had gone so wrong. Still, if she was looking,

Ryan would be the very last man on earth she would date.

At that moment the front door whooshed open and a tall, handsome hunk of a man walked in. She knew in an instant that it was *him*…the man Gravois had hired to come in and help investigate the four murders that had taken place.

She'd read his credentials and knew he had been a highly respected homicide detective with the New Orleans Police Department. His black hair was short and neat and his features were well-defined. A black shirt stretched across his broad shoulders and his black slacks hugged his long, lean legs. Definitely a hunk, and her new partner.

He approached her desk and offered a brief smile. Not only were his twilight-gray-colored eyes absolutely beautiful, but he also had thick, long dark lashes. "Hi, I'm Nick Cain, and I'm here to see Chief Gravois."

"Of course, I'll just go let him know you're here." She got up from the desk and headed down the hall to Chief Gravois's office.

It really made no difference to her that Nick Cain was a very handsome man. What she was most eager about was diving into the murder cases and perhaps learning something from the far more experienced detective turned private investigator.

She knocked on the chief's door and heard his reply. She opened the door and peeked inside. "He's here."

Gravois was a tall, fit man with salt-and-pepper hair and sharp blue eyes. "Get Shanks to sit on the desk and you bring him back here so I can talk to both of you at the same time."

Once again, an excited energy swirled around in the pit of her stomach. She opened the door behind which all the officers on duty sat. There were only three men in house at the moment, Ryan and Officers Colby Shanks and Ian Brubaker, who was the deputy police chief. "Colby, Gravois wants you on dispatch right now."

The young officer jumped out of his seat. He was a new hire and very eager to learn about everything. "Sure. Is the new guy here?" he asked as he followed just behind her.

"He is," she replied.

"Cool, I hope he's as good as he sounds."

"Let's hope so," she said.

They returned to the reception area where Nick Cain stood by the desk. "Sorry for the wait, if you'll just follow me, I'll take you to Chief Gravois."

"Thank you," he replied.

As she led him down the hall, she could feel an energy radiating from him. It was an attractive energy, one of confident male.

Suddenly Sarah wondered if her hair looked okay. Was the perfume she'd spritzed on that morning still holding up? She checked these thoughts, which had no place in her mind right now.

While she was working these cases with this man, she was a police officer, not a woman. Besides, one time around in the world of romance had been far more than enough for her.

She gave a quick knock on Gravois's door and then opened it. Nick followed her in and Gravois stood and offered his hand to him.

"Thomas Gravois," he said as they shook hands. "Please, both of you have a seat. It's good to have you here, Nick."

"Thank you, it's good to be here," Nick replied.

"Have you gotten all settled in at Irene's place yet?"

"I have," Nick replied.

"Okay then, first of all I want to introduce you to your new partner, Sarah Beauregard." Gravois pointed at her. "She will work side by side with you while you're here."

Nick nodded at her and Gravois continued. "Right now, you will be the only two working this investigation. If you need additional help then we can talk about that. I've set you two up in a small office that should have all you need. However, if there is something more that you want, please just let me know about it. In fact, I'll take you back there now and show you the setup."

The three of them stood and Gravois led the way down the hall to the office, which was really just an oversize storage area. A table had been set up in the center and a small filing cabinet hugged one of the corners. There was also a large whiteboard on one wall.

"I've put the murder books there in the center of the table, along with extra notepads for you to use. I'm sure you're eager to get started. I'm glad you're here, Nick. We need to get this guy off the streets as soon as possible."

"I hope I can help you with that," Nick replied.

"Later this afternoon I need to have a chat with you to finalize exactly how things are going to work," Gravois said. "I've also got some paperwork for you to sign."

"Whenever you're ready, sir," Nick replied.

"I'll just leave you to it and I'll check in

with you later," Gravois said. He left the room and closed the door behind him.

Instantly the room felt too small. She could now smell the scent of Nick, a spicy intoxicating fragrance that she found very appealing. He gestured her toward a chair at the table and then he sat opposite her.

"Officer Beauregard," he began.

"Please make it Sarah," she said.

"Sarah, how long have you been with the police department?" he asked.

"I've been with the department for the past twelve years," she replied.

"Perhaps you have some insight into the murders?" He looked at her expectantly.

"Uh...to be honest, I haven't been involved in any of the investigations into the murders up to this point," she confessed.

He looked at her for a long moment and then released a heavy sigh. "So, what investigations have you been involved in during the last couple of years? I'm just trying to figure out here what I'm working with."

"You're working with a police officer whose sole desire and interest is to solve these four murders. I'm hardworking and tenacious and I'll have your back like a good partner should," she replied fervently.